ALEMBIC

By the Same Author:

A Bibliography of the Works of Montague Summers (1964)

Love in Earnest: Some Notes on the Lives and Writings of English "Uranian" Poets from 1889 to 1930 (1970)

R. A. Caton and the Fortune Press: A Memoir and a Hand-list (1983)

The Books of the Beast: Essays on Aleister Crowley, Montague Summers and Others (1987)

Peepin' in a Seafood Store: Some Pleasures of Rock Music (1992)

TIMOTHY
d'ARCH SMITH

A·L·E·M·B·I·C

a novel

Dalkey Archive Press

Library of Congress Cataloging-in-Publication Data
D'Arch Smith, Timothy, 1936-
Alembic / Timothy d'Arch Smith.
I. Title.
PR6069.M559A79 1992 823'.914—dc20 92-12721
ISBN: 1-56478-009-0

First Edition

Partially funded by grants from the National Endowment for the Arts and the Illinois Arts Council.

Dalkey Archive Press
Fairchild Hall/ISU
Normal, IL 61761

Printed on permanent/durable acid-free paper and bound in the United States of America.

for
John Norton

1

A strong salt wind blew in from the sea. Rain spat from an isolated cloud, blue-black, slung low in the scudding sky. It was cold. Up at the railway-station end of the town, not at all to be accounted the 'better' part, signpost after signpost labeled *To the Front* recommended diversion in quick time away from a quarter construable as an embarrassment to civic authorities responsible for, perhaps washing their hands of, this drab outpost of commerce. Shops here bore maritime names—Seaspray Fashions, The Billows Bedding Company, Octopus Antiques—as if oceanic affiliations might prove an adjunct to sales and lure visitors, before tasting the pleasures of the seaside itself, inside their doors. Rewards to be harvested from these oblique, even subliminal appliances of market research had fallen below expectation. The faint air of unease routinely discernible on the outskirts of English coastal resorts gave suggestion that not only was trading in the general run of things far from brisk but that slackness of economy was being bolstered by furtive, perhaps downright crooked transactions taking place this very moment behind grimy net curtains that obscured the interiors of upper storeys: fortune-telling; the procurement of children; misappropriation of elderly residents' life savings; infinitely shady trafficking among car salesmen, loan sharks, pawnbrokers, dealers in stamps, bric-a-brac, out-of-print books.

It was, in any case, early closing. Establishments had barred their doors as if against the plague. A scattering of people, day-trippers driven from the beach by the rain, frustrated shoppers like myself, tramped the pavements outside these impoverished, seemingly quarantined premises, staring disconsolately into the windows. A cafeteria, capriciously open for business among those other ominously shuttered bazaars, and disgorging rock music at high volume through an open casement, harboured a few mackintoshed figures similarly thwarted. This bivouac, such as it was, posed temptation to explore no further. Familiarity with the tune carried on the wind blowing more fiercely than ever up the hill may have made me pause; and the sudden requirement, too, since it could well prove the staple brew of the place, for an exceptionally strong cup of tea such as Sgt Barker used hourly to produce—rust orange, heavily sugared—in those army days found beneficial for symptoms of a hangover that, after last night, still blearily obtained.

It was ponderable whether Sgt Barker would have classed this particular misfortune—the choosing of an early-closing day to visit a shop that was almost certainly going to be shut like the others—as a 'Titless Susan': an expression of his for each and every unavoidable stroke of fate. I had never asked him the derivation of the phrase, whether in times past he had indeed known a woman of that name who had proved troublesome, perhaps because I preferred my own vision, devastatingly clear, of a squadron of villainous, 'po-faced' women diving out of empty skies—like, I suppose, the Furies—seeking whom to harry and frustrate. In all likelihood, today's piece of bad luck would not have ranked as a 'Titless Susan.' It was something of a rarity for Sgt Barker to admit any at all of life's ups and downs (mostly it was the latter that came under discussion) to such exalted categorisation. When called upon to arbitrate between human folly and divine intervention, he would sift every scrap of evidence with the fastidiousness of a devil's advocate: only after all possibility of personal mismanagement had been eliminated would he allow the event to qualify for 'Titless Susan' status. In this case, it had been my fault and mine alone for not checking on early-closing days before making the journey ('prior to entrainment,' as Sgt Barker would have put it); for drinking too much the night before, come to that. A grave mistake had been made in my suggesting to Lindo we should go to the Rum Cove. Sgt Barker would have made much of those lapses in forward planning.

Lindo, in retrospect, would have been just as happy to have stayed where we were, imparted his news in the basement laboratory of ALEMBIC; happier, perhaps, because what he had to say turned out to be a private matter and his two colleagues had already absented themselves for the place I unwisely put into his mind. We had been alone. Lindo could have spoken freely. In excuse, though, I never felt at ease in the laboratory, keen as always, yesterday evening, to cut my visit there as short as possible. Hushed, vibrant, intensely lit, it reeked of formaldehyde, sulphur, ether, and other unidentifiable chemicals stored in massive carboys along the tiled walls. Partly as a joke and partly as testimony to the antiquity of their line of work, the cooks had strung from the rafters an accumulation of dessicated, for the most part unappealing objects: a stuffed crocodile, a clutch of huge, blown eggshells greenishly tinged, a human skull, the mottled foetus of a four-legged animal—a pony or a calf. On exhibition too, on a high, roughly carpentered shelf just below the crocodile, they had set up a display of outmoded chemical vessels in forcible contrast with modern technical equipment in daily use below: cucurbites, *balnea Mariae,* ampullae, leather bottles, iron cauldrons—all now covered with the dust of ages. The towering, bulbous, hourglass-proportioned steel crucible, built for us by APEX (Alternative Power Executive), threw out waves of fierce internal heat that conflicted with an air-conditioning system of equal efficiency. In the resulting dry, crackling, abnormally cooled air, sounds were magnified: the rustle of straw as the rats and hamsters moved in their cages beneath the test-tube littered workbenches, the insistent hum of the crucible's motor, an occasional choke of a liquid-filled retort like a cough from a patient's bed; and, despite the laboratory's practical if unusual accoutrements, it exemplified for me the sort of mysterious, sinister futility for which ALEMBIC had been founded: the transmutation of base metals into gold.

There were reasons to suppose ALEMBIC a government department of some antiquity, existence in its library of a ledger for the minutes of a year or two's early meetings proposing a date of foundation circa 1797; and it was stimulating, if finally unrewarding, to speculate who on earth could have argued, let alone extracted funds, for a scheme that the 'Age of Reason' ought by rights to have laughed out of court. Pitt? Fox? Burke? Surely they could be ruled out. The King himself in one of his fits of dementia or casting frantically around for ways to pay off his son's debts? Wilkes perhaps? We would never know. It was not altogether fanciful to ascribe origins to a group, close to the throne, who had caught themselves up in the 'Gothic' revival, found inspiration, as had William Beckford and Horace Walpole before them, in the mediaeval period not only because of an antiquarian curiosity—the sort of unhealthy application to the novels of Mrs Radcliffe or the paintings of Salvator Rosa they might also have pursued—but because they believed the Middle Ages held 'secrets' long forgotten; and to assume that these people, whoever they had been, had managed somehow to persuade the Treasury that there might be something 'in' alchemy and to put up the money for further research. I, who subscribed in private to the school of thought that alchemy was more akin to psychology, a way of spiritual enlightenment as opposed to one of chemical elucidation, had by chance lit upon a likely candidate for one of ALEMBIC's founders: the first Earl of Eldon.

Successively solicitor general, chief justice of common pleas, lord high chancellor, he was given in private life to drinking too much port—'over-sampling,' Sgt Barker would have called that sort of indulgence—in public to a draconian administration of his own legal decrees. There could, on the surface, be no less likely contender for the advocacy of alchemical doctrine, yet the initials J.S.E.E. (John Scott, Earl of Eldon) were among those who had cryptically signed the early minutes and only recently I had heard of a flourishing occult society to which His Lordship regularly, and with lengthy commentaries on the spirit world wherein he had dwelled for nearly a hundred and fifty years, 'came through.' The coincidence was disturbing.

Doubtless in Victorian times ALEMBIC's survival was due in part to the activities, covert as much as exoteric, of Freemasons, or to that branch of Freemasonry that concerned itself with 'Rosicrucianism,' a word much bandied about by the earlier, Gothic aficionados. Certainly, in the 1890s, there had been an unsavoury lawsuit involving a government official who, entangling with occultists of a dubious nature and forced into legal action, had had to admit in court he was a practising alchemist. There had been questions in the House. Things were hushed up. Then, early this century,

APEX, our rivals, had been set up, though under military, as opposed to ALEMBIC's civil, control, dedicated to the very latest scientific discoveries, nuclear power these days of course its almost sole branch of research. APEX conflicted violently with our own hermeneutical delvings into the early literature of science. There was an uneasy alliance between us, but how soon it would crumble nobody could tell. We all at ALEMBIC felt from time to time it would not be long before the axe fell, our masters that secrecy was of the essence for continued existence, not any more because of an incipient breakthrough, after centuries, in the recovery of the formula for the Philosopher's Stone, but because of possible exposure to ridicule, the sort of public ridicule that had been experienced by one of our number in 1896.

Much of the laboratory's unpleasantness—those feelings that what went on there was contrary to the laws of nature, a 'selcouth thing' as a mediaeval alchemist, Thomas Norton, quaintly put it, from which we might all receive some psychic kickback—was alleviated by the decidedly 'earthy' qualities of the three chemists, or 'cooks' as we called them after alchemical tradition, when they were in attendance there: Lindo, Bastable, Goodwin. Like me, in their early twenties, though recruited not from the army as I had been but from the universities, they were in looks more or less dissimilar. Colin Lindo was dark, stocky, fresh-faced, apple-cheeked, even in the pin-striped suit he revealed by the removal of his white laboratory overall looking as if he had spent the day at the plough or the helm. Blood, and English blood too, warmed by sun, invigorated by wind, pumped lustily through his veins. Stephen Goodwin was darker, shorter than the other two, an upturned, almost snub nose belying Jewish origins; bespectacled; bearded. His shuffling, bowed way of walking endowed him with a professorially absentminded demeanour that suggested, quite incorrectly, an uninterest in the matters that engaged the greater part of the trio's waking hours. Richard Bastable, the tallest of the three, like Lindo, looked the picture of health, yet a certain overblueness of eye and redness of mouth and a thinness, indeed an incipient recession of a head of frail golden hair gave to otherwise rude—though Scandinavian more than English—vitality a touch of dissolution and presented the only clue to the psychic bond that held the three together. As well as exterior, there may have been intellectual divergencies. Indeed, it was later revealed there were: Lindo's passion for modern music, for instance, and Bastable's enthusiasm, not far short of obsessional, for chemical research the other two were inclined to skimp; but these individual traits had been ruthlessly suppressed the better to pursue a single shared ambition: to get into bed as many girls as humanly, or for preference, superhumanly possible.

In pursuit of their quarries, there was none of Sgt Barker's somewhat rumbustious approach but an uncompromising seriousness of purpose that bound the three of them together and struck up between them the sort of intensely loyal camaraderie observable among small bodies of fighting men.

They were, indeed, a force to be reckoned with. Action, fought in many arenas, was tough, time-consuming, relentless.

When not going to plan, which was all too often the case—a rarity certainly that all three had satisfactory affairs in progress at the same time and even then some urge akin to wanderlust would provoke the need to broaden horizons and seek out new conquests—these operations demanded minute, searching analysis of tactics. Discussion took place in the laboratory during working hours and took away, as I have said, much of the alien, distinctly unnerving atmosphere that obtained in the cooks' absence, or when, not very often, they were too absorbed in their work to be engaged in conversation. From time to time I was called upon to contribute to these symposia and it was I, I think, who had proposed a shift in the cooks' theatre of war. This had been confined for too long, the way I saw it, to a few pubs, clubs, discotheques, places of that sort, where they were well known and from which talent had been overamply tasted. Fortunes were at a low ebb, manoeuvres on all fronts at a virtual standstill. Although I had not been there, I put forward the Rum Cove. Situated a stone's throw from ALEMBIC, it had only recently opened its doors, the night in fact I happened to pass by. Laughter and music floated, at considerable volume, up a poorly illuminated basement staircase. The suggestion had received an enthusiastic welcome; and with the call of battle again ringing in their ears, the cooks were exploiting the establishment for all it was worth. Goodwin and Bastable, Lindo reported, were already in attendance. He was delighted at the idea of joining them for a drink.

'Provided we can have a little chat in private.'

'Of course.'

As it turned out, privacy had been at a premium. Despite its name, hinting at an alcoved, Devonian, rather piratical ambiance, a chance too that drink on offer could have been smuggled in or, distilled on the premises, be dispensable at bargain prices, the Rum Cove had proved the very opposite of eponymous speculation. Fitted out in shiny chrome and scarlet plastic from which all corners had been streamlined the more easily to project along its cigar-shaped length the frenetic 'disco' music issuing, so it seemed, from a battery of neon tubes assembled at what might be described as the 'sharp' end of the room that impelled themselves on and off more or less in time to the beat, the place resembled more than anything else the hull of some vast intergalactic space-craft, one furthermore off course, out of control, perhaps on its death plunge. Every so often the lights disconcertingly changed colour, grew brighter or went out altogether and threw us briefly not into darkness but into a lurid, hazy glow as if we were on fire. All things considered, the bar struck me as an unlikely hunting ground. Love, if that was what the cooks were after, seemed here a hopelessly outdated concept, its physical concomitants—desire, passion, orgasm, even conception of children—available at the touch of a button or telepathically communicable along one of the strobic beams that, from time to time, impinged across lines of vision. Goodwin, however, disagreed. It was his theory that the ritzy, vulgar, utterly specious modernity of the place could attract girls in the modeling profession. These ranked high on a list of young ladies, as far as I knew uncommitted to paper, only tabulated mentally, that he classed as 'goers.' There was also a good deal to be said for the strength of the drinks on offer, Goodwin had added. Very likely he meant they either buoyed up or substituted for expectations of amatory success. All of the cocktail variety, listed on the arm-length tariff with names that conveyed the sort of damage they could be expected to wreak upon the human frame—'kickers,' 'stingers,' 'sockaroos'—their active ingredients, rum, of course, for the most part, were commingled with freshly pulped fruit juices endowing the mixtures with a deceptive, nourishing, vitamin-packed quality of which, after a sip or two, it seemed tissues had for all too long been deprived. Two of them stood before Goodwin and Bastable. In each floated slices of assorted fruits and a small green plastic umbrella. Bastable demonstrated the workability of his, opening it up and plunging it deeply into his glass. Gamboge bubbles rose to the surface.

'I'll get you one of these, Colin,' he said to Lindo. 'You too, Tom. They're called Tallulah Twisters. Guaranteed to put wool in your needles.' He wandered off in the direction of the bar.

Goodwin raised his concerned, bearded face. He began to polish his glasses and to speak in a low, serious voice. 'Colin and I have been puzzling over that German passage you've just done for us, Tommo. Are you sure you've got it right? *The blood of the lion and the gluten of the eagle?* What the hell's he talking about? It sounds as if he's trying to make some disgusting pudding.'

It was my job to acquire old alchemical texts—books and manuscripts—translate them where necessary and pass them to the cooks to interpret chemically. It needed to differentiate between the scientific treatises, those offering practical instructions which could be followed in ALEMBIC's laboratory and those that spoke only symbolically: the 'unsatisfactory' ones, as Rastus called them. This one, German, early eighteenth century, seemed to fall between two stools. Receipts were offered, the reason I had translated it and passed it on, but those passages had been linked by other, vague, possibly sexual interpretations of the 'art' that perhaps gave a clue to the author's own psychological makeup. Goodwin seemed to have spotted this. Beneath wolfish exteriors ran a philosophical, rather a psychoanalytical turn of mind. He looked this evening not unlike an analyst, dark, earnest, the young Freud perhaps, turning matters over in a café with medical acquaintances: sex-obsessed too, it could unkindly be said. I replied I thought the text not without merit.

'I agree with Tom,' Lindo said. 'It has its points. It corresponds with the Chinese idea. They thought the elixir of life, the *prima materia,* the precious substance we're all slaving our guts out to produce, is the same as the human menstruum, the beginning as well as the end of life. The passage is allegorical, you see. It veils a scientific truth.'

'Now, Colin. Naughty, naughty. No talk of allegories. Rastus wouldn't care to hear anything like that. Loudermilk, either.' Bastable had returned with our drinks. In the ever-changing light he looked more cherubic than Scandinavian, fair hair and pink skin babyishly aglow. His small round rosebud mouth, now moistened with a draught of his Twister, gave him the appearance of some scaled-up putto, the sort that hovers in the corners of oil paintings cooperatively plucking aside bed curtains to reveal reclining nudes. Use of our chief's new nickname aroused considerable mirth—between Lindo and Bastable, that is to say. Goodwin had not heard it employed before. He asked for enlightenment. Bastable launched into the story of its derivation. I pondered Bastable's remonstrance. An allegorical interpretation of alchemy would indeed have been frowned upon by Rastus, anyone proposing such an hypothesis likely to be pronounced upon as 'unsatisfactory.' It was an adjective he greatly favoured. We had all on occasion found ourselves indicted under its all-embracing banner for faults ranging from what Rastus saw as ingrained criminality to the sort of lapse of which we were all from time to time guilty: poor timekeeping, idleness, inefficiency: in this case, if it came to his ears, a muddleheadedness verging on clinical imbalance. Until today Major William Cleave had been known as the Owl. All features on his round, moon-shaped face were very close to the surface. Had it not been for a paralysing illness that, at forty-six, had left one of his hands knotted and twisted to skeletal, clawlike proportions, he would still be pursuing the army career from which he had been seconded to run ALEMBIC and over which, in the five or six years he had been there, he had grown so fiercely proprietorial. His disability, of which he was peculiarly unembarrassed, often waving his bad hand pointedly about in front of people's faces, was no doubt the reason for occasional bouts of sulking, hot temper, lofty inaccessibility, leading when all experienced together to what Ma, his secretary, described as a 'two-and-eight.' His hearty, aggressive, filibustering methods of command were dictated by a virtually complete ignorance of what we were about, his beholdenness to Loudermilk, the other name Bastable had mentioned, a further source of annoyance. About Loudermilk, presumed to be ALEMBIC's tutelary genius, encountered by myself on only one occasion and that before my recruitment, I was not able to agree with Bastable. A spectral, stooping figure, he suggested acquaintance with darker sides of alchemy than any of we 'hewers of wood and drawers of water,' as Ma categorised us, would have cared to contemplate.

Perhaps I was the only one who did contemplate them. However, our general lackadaisical attitude, Frederick Palin excepted, the tissues of lies and deceits we wove (and were sometimes encouraged to weave under the protection of the Official Secrets Act) and the sort of mockery of our superiors that was still giving rise to amusement at our table, seemed to me to be not simply manifestations of rebellion against incompetent leadership and constricting regulations but expressions of the same basic insecurity that I felt within the throbbing aseptic laboratory that should, by rights, have affirmed our exclusively scientific lines of research. One of ALEMBIC's rules was even now being contravened: the discussion of alchemical matters outside its walls. Because of the music, we were all talking quite loudly. Goodwin called us to order:

'Keep it down, lads. Place is filling up.'

'How is Stephanie?' I asked Lindo. Lindo's honest face clouded over.

'Oh, fine,' he said. 'Fine. A lovely girl. One more of these and I must get back to her. After we've had our little chat, of course.'

I went over to the bar for more drinks. Stephanie was Lindo's girl of the moment, quite a steady one, described coarsely by Bastable, perhaps because loyalty to her was keeping Lindo out of active service, as it were, as a 'living-in poke.' She in fact had inspired Major Cleave's nickname. She had persuaded Lindo against his will to sit up late watching a minstrel show on television. In the course of this, which Lindo, other diversions in mind, had watched with increasing impatience, a member of the cast with a blacked-up face that had borne nevertheless striking resemblance to our chief, and wearing a jacket of similar strident pattern and colours to one he sported on Saturday mornings, had delivered himself of a song entitled 'When Rastus Plays His Old Kazoo.' Speculation on Major Cleave's launching himself at ALEMBIC into a song-and-dance routine of this kind—there had been some accompanying 'business,' Lindo reported, with a walking stick and a straw hat—had been keen; not when I returned to the table with a tray of drinks laid finally to rest. Lindo stood up and gave us a few steps from the dance he had seen performed. He doffed and waved about an imaginary boater. We all laughed afresh. Then quite suddenly over Goodwin and Bastable there fell a pall of silence. Their eyes were focused on the gap between Lindo's chair and my own. The room's pinkish light flashed on Goodwin's spectacles, permeated Bastable's plump cheeks with an even rosier glow.

'Girls?' Lindo enquired.

'Um.' Bastable manoeuvred himself a fraction to one side so he was hidden from whoever he observed past Lindo's curly head. He slid down a bit in his seat. Under his jacket his ribs worked in and out like a panting dog's.

'Models?'

'Could be. Only two though. Steve and I were wondering if you and Tom . . .' Bastable twitched slightly one corner of his rosebud mouth and made a barely perceptible movement of his head in the same sideways direction.

'. . . Push off?' Lindo got the idea at once. 'Certainly, Rick.'

Bastable gave him a thumbs-up sign. Gratitude, promise of reciprocity, acknowledgment of adhesion to the 'cause,' were all implicit in the man-to-man gesture. I got to my feet. Lindo, however, was not quite ready to make a move. He rapped sharply on the table as if calling a meeting to order.

'Ah.' Bastable reached in his pocket, found his wallet and extracted a five-pound note. He placed it within Lindo's reach.

'Steve?'

Goodwin jumped. He wiped from his face a beaming smile he had from under his beard been projecting into the far reaches of the wine bar. He looked thoroughly put out.

'Oh, do sod off, Colin.'

Lindo beat his knuckles on the table again, more peremptorily this time.

'Hell. Sorry.' Goodwin scrabbled in his trousers pocket. His note joined Bastable's on the glass-topped table. Lindo scooped them both up. He and I moved over to the bar.

As an example of the cooks' method of operation, this could hardly have been improved on. Only Goodwin's momentary forgetfulness of his contribution towards Lindo's and my departure had marred an exhibition of tactical skill of the highest precision. More than that, it had revealed in the best possible light the comradeship that existed between the three men, the chivalrous, almost samurai-like selflessness with which actions over the years had been conducted. No illiberality, intrusive on Lindo's part, financial on the others', had been allowed to taint the execution of what would almost certainly turn out a successful campaign; and not even when we had seated ourselves at the bar, perched ourselves up on high stools lit from inside with a ghostly, cyanosed glow, and established what we were going to go on drinking, did Lindo cast so much as a single envious glance over his shoulder to ascertain how his friends were faring.

He was, of course, anxious to talk. That had been forgotten in the excitement. It would most likely be about Stephanie. Her arrival had initiated worries of an intimate kind. Faithfulness was proving difficult, Lindo had confided, sexual performances not always up to scratch. After a fair amount to drink, which we had now had, he was disposed to enlarge on these problems, to see in them psychological malfunctions on a larger scale, impotence, an inborn fear of women, a deeply suppressed preference for his own sex one day perhaps bursting shockingly to the surface. I feared reiteration of these themes. Lindo was slumped gloomily over his drink, poking at the bits of fruit he found there with his plastic umbrella, obviously deep in thought. The fourth—or would it be fifth?—Twister would be efficacious if reassurances were once more to be given. However, he said:

'What do you know about Thomas Norton?'

'I'm very keen on Norton. He's a dear old chap. The Chaucer of English alchemy. His *Ordinall* was written in much the same period too, give or take fifty years.'

'Is there anything in him for us? Anything to work on?'

'Not very much. Chemically, he's extremely vague. He's got plenty to say about the setting-up of a laboratory; apparatus required; costs; cooks as well, come to that.'

'Really? What's he say about cooks?'

'*Some be drunken and some much use to jape.*'

Lindo gave a hollow laugh. 'Us in a nutshell. You know your stuff. I have an uncle who owns a sixteenth-century manuscript of *The Ordinall of Alchemy.* From what you say, though, there wouldn't be any point in buying it for ALEMBIC.'

'There might be. There are several manuscripts extant, of course, but they all have variations. Your uncle's might yield some clue not in the others, especially if the copyist were himself an alchemist. Remember the Khunrath manuscript?'

'That put us on to carbon, didn't it? Rick's still messing about along those lines. If we buy it, I wouldn't want it known it was from Uncle Hamish.'

'Why not?'

'Because I'm in for 10 percent.' Lindo put a finger to the side of his nose and winked an eye.

'I see.'

'One more thing. I'm pushed to hell for money right now. I wondered, if you had nothing on tomorrow, whether you could go down and give it the once-over. Clinch the deal if you like the look of the thing.' Lindo named the seaside town. It could be done in a day. The journey rather appealed. We needed, then, to talk about money. Lindo had that pretty well in hand.

'We were thinking of five thousand.'

'That's not out of the way. You've done your Norton homework too.'

Lindo nodded. 'Cash-o, cash-o?' he asked.

'Your uncle'll have to sign for it. And assuming Freddy's got that much on tap.'

'I should think he would have.'

'Probably.'

'You could slip me my cut as soon as you get back, if things work out.'

Lindo looked more relaxed. He sank the rest of his drink and called for more. 'Stephanie's not cheap, you know,' he remarked. 'There are expenses incurred, hidden extras, you might say. Let me fill you in about Uncle Hamish. He was something in bauxite.' Lindo waved his umbrella grandiloquently at this disclosure of his uncle's profession as if he had revealed that he had a title or was on intimate terms with the royal family. Thomas Norton would not have approved. For some reason, he disliked merchants as a class. I asked Lindo if his uncle had read the text. He thought not.

'The old boy bought the manuscript as a sort of investment. Merely because it mentioned mining, or so he thought. I'm sure he never deciphered the text.'

'That's right. Norton leans heavily on Agricola.'

'There you are. I'm glad to be able to do something for Uncle Hamish. In a way, he procured me my first girl. He used to saw her in half. Not a twice-nightly job, you understand; Uncle Hamish's legerdemain or rather leger-de-some pretty suspicious-looking magical apparatus was on a strictly amateur level. The odd Rotary do, Masonic evening, that's when he put on his act and sliced through Wendy's midriff. And a very neat little midriff it was too, I can tell you. Anyway he's never really grown out of his rabbit-and-hat capers. Now he's retired, he's opened a joke shop. Marina Novelties, it's called. Itching powder, exploding cigars, Captain Belcher's Tea. That's rather a good one. You might score me a packet if you think of it.'

'Certainly. I'm looking forward to meeting your uncle. And to seeing the manuscript.'

Lindo slapped me on the back. 'Stout fellow,' he said. 'Thanks a lot. I really appreciate it. A thoroughly useful application of public funds.'

'Another drink?'

'No, I must get home. Stephanie's waiting.'

We slid off our stools. As we passed, none too steadily, their table, Bastable's and Goodwin's laughter mingled with other, feminine voices. Bastable had opened his miniature umbrella and was holding it above his head. Droplets from his Tallulah Twister sparkled in his golden hair. The girls shrieked their approval. As if to signal the evening's likely denouement, the lights in the Rum Cove discreetly dipped.

▪▪

Marina Novelties, like the other shops, was firmly shut. Its window was festooned with evidence in plenty of Uncle Hamish's grim trade, flags, favours, grinning papier-maché masks, noses with spectacles or moustaches attached—both on occasion—things to wear, to rattle, to wave, to blow. Underneath them had been laid out in serried ranks the practical jokes, stink bombs, latex sick, dribble glasses, whoopee cushions, the product Lindo had mentioned, all neatly boxed. Each package was crudely illustrated with little black-and-white drawings of perpetrator and dupe at their zenith of respective mirth and bewilderment. Eyes popped, hair stood on end, teeth were bared in rictuses of laughter. The victim of Captain Belcher's Tea writhed as if in his death throes. The whole window mocked and leered at my error of timing. I would have to come back tomorrow. Freddy would very likely suspect me of pocketing half the double train fare. It began once more to rain.

Presentiment of some problem the day might bring had been vouchsafed early that morning. On my walk through the park to ALEMBIC's headquarters, there had been no sign of the herons. Most days they could be spotted, perching on wooden mooring posts sunk into the lake-bed a few yards off their island, rearing their long necks to the sky so that, from the shore, they could be mistaken for tapered extensions of the posts themselves, or hunched like grumpy schoolmasters in chalky gowns beneath the island trees where they had built their nests. That the presence of these sinister, silent birds brooding across the water, as I had seen Loudermilk brooding over the barometer at his club, could augur good luck and not bad, ordain by their presence undefined but incontrovertibly benign auspices for the next twenty-four hours, had been implanted in my mind by Tamara Benke. Quite possibly, before I turned out of the park, she might have passed me on one of her morning runs.

Miss Benke was given to all forms of divination, by cards, the crystal ball, the Ouija board, yarrow sticks—tea leaves if no more formal equipment were to hand. She had once opened her door to me with arms bloodied to the elbow as if she had been interrupted in the middle of an haruspicy, revealed disappointingly as she had led me into her kitchen to have been only the early and messy stages of the assemblage of a liver pâté. She gave yoga lessons each Wednesday evening in a church hall not far from ALEMBIC which I attended both for exercise—librarianship being for the most part sedentary work—and for the purpose, not altogether unrewarding, of picking up girls. The cooks had given some thought to the question of enrolling in Miss Benke's 'Wednesdays' but, rather to my relief, had decided against it, energy needing conservation for what Goodwin had airily categorised as 'later on' and because of the unlikelihood of achieving, let alone maintaining, some of the *asanas* they had seen illustrated in a book on yoga somehow finding its way, before my recruitment, into ALEMBIC's library. Considering her bulk, Miss Benke performed these Eastern disciplines with maddening ease. Heavy, tall, rawboned, in her sixties, she resembled when she let down her tresses of copper-coloured hair a circus acrobat of considerable daring; with her hair piled up and spiked with a number of jewel-incrusted combs, the votary of an obscure cult. Images, equally potent, were offered of Miss Benke aloft on some precarious rigging acknowledging a cheering crowd or alone before a moonlit altar holding to the heavens a flaming dish. Her exercises which she demonstrated to the accompaniment of instructions shouted in a middle-European accent that over the years she had been in England had thickened as if to emphasize bonds with the country she had been forced to abandon reflected these twin physical and spiritual qualities of her personality. Indeed she was fond of making the point that her teachings had as much to do with mind as with body, due attention to both the path to spiritual perfection. Thomas Norton in his *Ordinall* made much the same point about alchemy:

> *Therefore, in our work, as authors teacheth us,*
> *There must be Corpus, anima, & spiritus.*

This was Miss Benke's philosophy precisely.

Naturally I could say nothing to her of alchemical connexions. Had I been able, she would undoubtedly have had much of interest to impart, positing arcane as well as practical goals of the science: 'art,' more likely, the word she would employ. Even her runs through the park, when, with her hair ablaze with her combs and clad in a white robe, she took on aspects of an Egyptian priestess absconding with temple funds, were not for the purposes of physical fitness alone. Her eyes peered from side to side in search of the Master of the Orange Robe. He had made several appearances in her life, had been briefly present at her birth, surprising mother and nurse, on the crowded train, reeking of fear, that had carried her as a child to the safety of Britain, once or twice more in adult years. He never spoke, merely gave signs. The last sighting had been in the park. He had been seated on a bench, had risen when he caught sight of her and had pointed to the herons on their island.

I had been rather impressed by this story, perhaps because 'masters,' prophetic-looking sages at least, getting on in years and pointing dramatically into the distance, cropped up from time to time in illustrations to alchemical texts and I found myself growing ever more reliant on a daily sighting of the herons: then, of inventing all sorts of elaboration on the superstition Miss Benke had implanted in my mind. The more birds, for instance, that were visible—maximum number thought to be twelve—the more fortunate the day would be. If one were glimpsed in flight, never in fact yet witnessed, there would be hardly any limit to the prosperities of the next twenty-four hours. Failure to make a sighting, on the other hand, could only bode ill, but since the herons' absence from their lakeside shore was of extreme rarity—for they were creatures of habit—my mind began to seek excuses for behavioural divagation and so ward off sensations of anxiety that would have otherwise impinged. Human presence on their island was just such an excuse. In early autumn park-keepers rowed over to thin the undergrowth and to lop the trees. Sometimes I saw them at work over there or glimpsed through the trees smoke from the bonfires on which they burned the detritus of their labours. Once or twice the only evidence of their presence was the small blue wherry they had rowed across and had left moored to the bank. Then of course it could not be expected the herons would show themselves, for, unlike the other water birds with whom they shared the lake, they disliked the proximity of man. Noise, too, could scare them away. There had been a time during some cleansing operation of the lake-bed that involved the use of heavy machinery—diggers, dredgers, cranes—when they had vanished for weeks on end; but today, in late summer stillness, their absence had been disturbing. Other birds swam lazily in the water or padded on clowns' feet across my path. Gulls soared in the sky. Something unlucky was going to happen.

ALEMBIC lay ten minutes' walk from the park in the centre of the part of London devoted to the practice of private medicine. Adjacent to brass bell pushes the circumference of soup plates, front doors gleamed with burnished plaques engraved with the names of doctors, surgeons, specialists, dentists, to whom visitors—'patients' seemed too coarse a word—were admitted by 'leggy' receptionists (admired as a class by Goodwin) into flower-filled halls. The quiet streets breathed hope and concern for the well-off and the privately insured. The excellent upkeep and solidity of the houses proposed, after money had changed hands, similar dignified longevity for the human frame. We were quartered in an eccentric, flat-fronted building, once a block of flats, with a much fussed-over stuccoed exterior in a sort of pinkish-beige colour like icing on a cake, coffee and strawberry flavours mixed, its eye-catching, almost edible, exterior disguised to a certain extent by being sandwiched between two taller, more modern blocks. Within, all exoticisms had been ruthlessly obliterated. The hall was bare, the floor covered by dark green linoleum, deeply pitted, the walls with a bureaucratically thin coating of whitewash, application far from recent. At the far end of the hall two sliding gun-metal elevator gates reflected light from the open street door. On their either side a pair of asbestos doors with Yale locks provided, or rather barred, access to the staircase in whose well the lift had been accommodated. I used my passkey on the left-hand door and started up the stairs. I passed my library on the first floor and climbed another flight. On the second landing, I paused. All was quiet. Only the throb of the air-conditioning system that was pumping the chemical-laden air from the basement laboratory suggested activity of any kind. We might have been cut off from the world. ALEMBIC often gave that impression. Amoebalike, we floated in the teeming ocean of ministries, many of whom would deny, probably were genuinely unaware of our existence; protoplasmic; alien; barely functional. Two years ago, a year before my recruitment, ALEMBIC had been, I gathered, in an even more parlous position than it now maintained, in imminent danger of being closed down because of failure to produce practical results and the suspicion by more sophisticated operators (APEX for instance) of eccentricity in its pursuance of experiments long abandoned by men of science. To successive governments, those members of them who knew about us, we appeared to hover between the footling and the expendable and the axe would in all probability have fallen had not a defecting agent hinted at our flourishing counterpart behind the Iron Curtain. Funds had been hastily reinjected, new blood, mine among it, impressed, Major Cleave, 'Rastus,' given command.

Evidence that we were, after all, 'attached' could be observed from this landing window. Behind one half of our rococo façade was a government department devoted to the restoration of furniture and fabrics adorning official buildings and royal residences, so that one day might be seen being loaded into the lift, along with our vats of chemicals, pulpits and pews and elaborately carved thrones, on another day Union Jacks and royal standards and regimental colours and hangings from Courts of Justice, conveyance in and out of these exotic artifacts occasionally drawing the attention of passers-by. Pedestrians sometimes briefly rested on the pews. On one occasion an office worker had been observed perched on a gilded throne, 'knighting' with his umbrella a companion who knelt on the pavement before him. Furthermore, our neighbours, seldom encountered since the building had been divided down the middle, convergence in the hallway whose right-hand door was theirs the only meeting place, were in the habit of suspending out of their windows some of the draperies and banners in their care in order to speed up drying processes or to remove creases. Quite a few had been hung out today.

It was probable that whoever had worked out security arrangements considered this bedecking of the building and the surrealistic cluttering of the pavement, the pungency, too, of the cleansing fluids for the flags and compounds arresting worm or decay in woodwork that, along with our laboratory smells, was pumped through serpentine shafts and out over the doctors' roofs, as being excellent cover for ALEMBIC activities; yet sight of the banners which were fluttering quite bravely in today's moderate wind enraged and alarmed Rastus: if dwelt upon too deeply could bring on a 'two-and-eight.' Perhaps for that reason, the view from his secretary's office of the elevation the most often to be found caparisoned had been totally obscured by a variety of plants. Plants grew in luxuriant, jungly profusion almost up to the top of the window frames. In fact, vegetation of one kind or another took up almost all of Ma's office space. As well as on the window ledges, plants in various stages of growth were scattered all over the floor in painted tubs. They occupied stools, chairs, filing cabinets, and a large part of her desk. Sturdier varieties, not far short of trees, burgeoned in each of the room's corners. A wire basket with an umbrageous creeper rooted in moss was suspended from the ceiling. Outside, on a flat roof to which a fire escape on the landing gave access, still further evidence of horticultural abandon could be found. In the daylight these specimens grew ever more lushly and to greater heights than those indoors where the light was dim, bosky, rendering Ma, who favoured flower-patterned garments, difficult of location. Today though, she had been clearly visible as I made my way along the passage to Freddy's office. She had her back to me and was tending one of her species, a sticky, olive green contraption, impressive even by Ma's standards. She spun round as if I had caught her feeding it a small woodland creature.

'You gave me a turn, dear. I thought it was my lord and master.'

Ma's Christian name, used only by Rastus, was Violet, indicative perhaps of parentally shared gardening enthusiasms. Ample, grey-haired, in her fifties—more, Goodwin said, past pensionable age—she had a very small, dead white doll's face with a beauty spot on one cheekbone. Those looks and a rather roguish manner of speech called to mind the sort of widow portrayed in Restoration comedy, past her prime, morally unsteady, in the course of the action to be 'discovered,' consequent upon the dislodgement of a firescreen, in the arms of a parson. It was said she was deeply in love with Rastus, feelings despite his being married—to a mousy woman lax on her *ou* sounds I had briefly spoken with at an office party—possibly reciprocated. Lindo went further. He had found them once, 'discovered' them, as it were, in a restaurant over a candlelit supper. They had not been talking, he said, but gazing into each other's eyes.

The breadth of Ma's steadfastness to Rastus extended only to personal affections, work she had to do for him taking rather a back seat. When his door was shut as it now was, she was generally, after nurturing her plants, ready for what she called a 'chat.' By that she meant assimilation and diffusion of gossip on a fairly lavish scale. If she required information, more often the case, she would settle in her typing chair and breathe in expectant tones,

'What news on the Rialto?' Exegesis of events, expected to be in considerable detail, was then devoured with little upward movements of her eyebrows and the clapping from time to time of her hand in front of her mouth as if those secrets with which she was being regaled threatened already to find means of escape. She was prepared on occasion to trade information in equally ample measure, signal for its delivery a placing of her forefinger to her lips and an indication with the same finger that the only chair innocent of plant life be drawn up facing her desk, on which she would then lean dimpled elbows and begin her story. That, this morning, she had done.

'Tell it not in Gath, dear,' she said in a whisper.

I sat, only half listening, concerned that what she had to tell might only be barter for some gossip of my own. There was nothing very much to report, except news of Lindo's 'living-in poke.' Expressed another way, that might be fee enough. The burden of Ma's news, not really of much interest, revolved around trouble between Freddy, whom I had to see to get Lindo's uncle's money, and his daughter over a pop group called Celestial Praylin. On television last night, the group's appearance had clashed with another programme, *Ferguson on Thursday,* a favourite of Freddy's. There had been a quarrel.

It was a Praylin 'tune,' if the thunderous assault on the senses could be so designated, that had been blasting forth from the café jukebox where I had taken shelter later in the day. Nicholas Spark, the group's singer—there again exception had been taken in some quarters, Freddy's especially, to the use of traditional phraseology to describe the crazed, shrieking attack on lyrics deployed by Nicholas more or less as a matter of routine—was an old school-friend of mine. We had been in the same house. Celestial Praylin had made considerable progress in their career since I had left the army. Whereas a couple of years ago they could fill only average-sized dance halls and cinemas, these days they played to arenas, stadiums, football grounds packed with capacity crowds. They went down well in America. They sold records in their millions. Nonetheless, it was a surprise to learn that Nicholas had agreed to their appearing on television for he had become fastidious, even pernickety, about the quality of the band's sound—deep-textured, ominously chorded, abominably loud—that set them apart (many said above) the usual run of 'pop' bands but which, he had told me, was untransmissible other than in the recording studio or through the band's personal, hugely complicated loud-speaker system. More peculiar was the band's invitation on air at any time of day when children were likely to be watching. Celestial Praylin's brand of strutting, indeed rampaging, sexual braggadocio could be compared with some enormously rumbustious, enormously protracted 'rock'-inflected interlude in a thoroughly 'unsuitable' Restoration comedy of the type in which Ma could also have made her flirtatious appearance—that period of the arts proposed as much by the length of the band's hair as by its accent on fornication—in which cast and stage crew had miraculously found themselves blessed with electric guitars and the paraphernalia of modern amplification.

Mid-seventeenth-century imagery, though of a slightly earlier period, subsisted too in Freddy's—many other people's—Cromwellian bigotry against Celestial Praylin, their species of 'cock rock' (Lindo's phrase) held in as much disesteem as the stage play under the Commonwealth and for much the same reasons: that they promoted lasciviousness, godlessness and anarchy in equally lavish measure. Misgivings were not without foundation. Celestial Praylin's behaviour both on and off the concert platform was resulting these days in tangle after tangle with police, customs men, airport officials, local councillors in places where they played, one incident involving drugs, the smashing-up of hotel accommodation, trouble over a couple of girl fans found to be on the run, once landing Nicholas in gaol for a day or two while matters were sorted out. There could be no doubt that Nicholas, or his agent, collaboration of both more likely, turned such incidents to advantage, perhaps even deliberately orchestrated these clashes with authority in order to publicize the band, increase record sales and inspire an ever-burgeoning retinue of faithful, indeed fanatical, admirers. As a result, 'stuffier' members of the public, provoked by a uniquely hostile press, entrenched themselves more deeply into positions of disapproval matching in intractability the sturdy allegiances of the musicians' manifold and passionate devotees. Oddly enough, Ma was by no means to be counted among any dissentient faction.

'I tore Freddy off quite a strip, I can tell you,' she announced. ' "Get with it, man," I said. "Where's the harm in a little honest rock and roll? You should let your hair down once in a while." ' She raised her plump arms and swayed violently from side to side in her typing chair as if she heard the more brutal of Celestial Praylin's chord sequences cascading round the room.

'You're quite right, Ma. Parts of *Gibbous Moon* are pretty stunning.'

'Death stalked my spore, a spectre
I tore him out my heart.'

Ma made no attempt to imitate Nicholas's stricken, almost falsetto coloratura as she rendered this extract from 'Love's Mansion,' Praylin's first song in the 'charts' and the reason, most probably, for last night's television debut. She had made a better job than I of making out what Nicholas was saying, at no point in Praylin's body of work a guaranteed bonus even after repeated listenings. The lines raised syntactical points of interest, whether for instance Death were the spectre or Nicholas himself. Nicholas was, had been even at school, pale; ill-looking; spectrally thin. There again, was Nicholas relinquishing his life to this persistent revenant: desirous of yielding up his heart: of experiencing, like Verlaine, his favourite poet, as it happened, the *divin final anéantissement?* Or were we to accept the second line as elliptical? Preferring life, Nicholas could be avaunting the baneful presence of Death by tearing him out of his heart and sending him packing. Showing Death the door would be another way of forwarding this alternative interpretation. Either way, aspects of early English drama, Jacobean now in their thoroughly gloomy preoccupation with mortality, still held sway over musical prowess. Regardless of conflicting definitions, Ma's even knowing the lines from the song was far more impressive than were the words themselves. I congratulated her on the expert translation of the lyrics.

'Oh, but they're on the T-shirts, dear. Haven't you seen them around?'

'No.'

'You will. All the kids are wearing them. As I was saying, if Freddy goes on at Joanna all the time, she'll up and become a chorus girl. You mark my words.'

Ma's specification of career had not just been picked out at random but derived from alarms Freddy himself expressed that Joanna might one day 'go on the stage.' Distrust of the theatre was not held with the Cromwellian zeal that fuelled anti-Praylin sentiments, after last night most likely burning fiercer than ever. Indeed, if pressed for reasons for his antipathy to the stage, Freddy would merely remark that the profession was 'overcrowded,' Joanna's talents unlikely to secure her a steady future as an actress. That was what he put about. For my part I was not so sure. In my earliest days at ALEMBIC I was still ignorant of Freddy's anxieties and, by a quirk of fate, contributed to them. The first time Freddy asked me home, some family difference had arisen, because of my presence been brought under control. Nonetheless, there was endemic in their small flat what Sgt Barker would have categorised as an 'atomosphere.' Joanna, then coming up to thirteen—a 'difficult' age, in Ma's estimation—had done all she could to exacerbate prevailing tensions and had spoken hysterically to her father over the supper table. Quite simply to prevent the evening's becoming a bore, I answered her in Freddy's place with a similarly dramatic turn of phrase. Brought to her senses and scenting, perhaps, some kind of 'game,' Joanna countered with a more impressive rejoinder still. A sort of melodramatic dialogue had ensued. The party had been saved.

The trouble was, it had set a precedent. Soon, some kind of fanciful interchange had come to be expected, in fact grew 'traditional,' Joanna expending a good deal of thought between my visits to what we should next 'do.' Performances became ever more challenging. Prince addressed princess, Chekhovian couples exchanged gloomy confidences, protagonists with drawn swords spat pre-combattal repartee. Joanna, very likely, used these dramas as a way of antagonizing her father who, as well as disapproving her penchant for playacting, could become amusingly censorious at some of the language employed or at the revelation, every now and then, of a reprehensible, rather Ibsenesque steaminess of relationship between the characters we were making up. Much conscious of people's ages—she had once drawn attention to the mathematical fluke that all our years rose in exact multiples of two—hers twelve, mine twenty-four, Freddy's forty-eight—she may have been using me as a sort of buffer state between her own adolescence and her father's antiquity, much as she used my friendship with Nicholas Spark to demonstrate to her father that Celestial Praylin must be 'OK.' Perhaps, for my part, age came into it as well. It was easier to lapse into realms of fantasy with a girl that age than to have to answer her bombardment of questions about Nicholas or to attempt conversation about schoolwork—or anything else, come to that—about which she exhibited a profound uninterest. Vis-à-vis Freddy, too, I never felt entirely at ease. Kind though he was in regularly asking me to supper, first because I was a 'new boy' and later because he found out I lived on my own and might lack company, he could never quite conceal the resentment he felt at someone (as Joanna had pointed out) half his age being in a senior position at ALEMBIC and taking home, as he well knew since he was responsible for drawing my salary cheque, more money than he earned himself. For that reason too, Joanna's and my 'dialogues' were a means of escape.

Actually, I did not think Freddy had anything against me personally. Frederick George Palin was rather an institution at ALEMBIC. That was where resentment lay. Possessed of a lower security clearance than some of his juniors, the cooks for example and myself, and, like Rastus, unacquainted with the theory and practice of alchemy, he had never received nor could now expect preferment. The death of his wife, whom Joanna I assumed must resemble since she did not look a bit like her father, five years ago from cancer, meant he had to bring up his daughter (who attended a fee-paying school) singlehanded; and money was important. He was fearful of being dismissed, made redundant, seconded on a lower salary to another ministry; and a resultant conscientiousness in ALEMBIC matters, founded though it was on the quicksand of necessity as opposed to the rock of allegiance, made him envious not only of me but of almost everyone else in the organization who, more uncaring of their future, grasped the opportunity of doing the least work for the most money.

Ma concluded her story of the 'row'; and began to talk about her recent holiday in France. It had included a visit to the birthplace of Frédéric Auguste Bartholdi, an expedition that, for some reason I had missed, perhaps the heat of the day or remoteness of location, had been punishing in the extreme. She produced a photograph of the Statue of Liberty, perhaps on sale at Bartholdi's house.

'I was glad to have made the effort,' she said, 'my tootsies notwithstanding. It's instructive seeing where people are born, don't you think, dear? One feels somehow an . . .'

'Ma, look, I've got to go. I'm off to the seaside. On ALEMBIC business of course.'

'Of course.' Ma looked hurt. She withdrew her picture postcard. Placing it back in her desk she lit on another object, a further souvenir I thought at first, one more evocative than the card, a pressed flower perhaps, from Bartholdi's garden, which brought from her a little sigh of pleasure. What she had located was a box of chocolates. She lifted the lid on which two rickety puppies with bows around their necks looked beguilingly as if they had already availed themselves of the contents.

'Fancy a choc, dear?' she asked.

'Ma, it's a bit early.'

'Go on, be a devil.' She slid the box over her desk towards me with the conspiratorial air of a procuress manoeuvring towards a client the ripest of her charges.

'Save it for Ron,' she said.

'Ron who?'

'Later-Ron.'

'That's good. I'll remember that. Good-bye, Ma.'

'Go in peace and not in pieces.' Ma waved a hand and settled to her chocolates. As I walked along the corridor I could hear her fingers rustling among the papers like the rats that rustled in their laboratory straw. I entered 'D & D.'

'D & D,' 'Dizzies and Dokkies,' Disbursements and Documentation, an awkward angular room in a turreted corner of the building, must have aggravated Freddy's apprehensions about being passed over. Uncarpeted, roughly shelved to hold the ledgers and files over which he and his colleague, Loder, held sway, furnished only with a vast partners' desk across which they now faced each other, and a cast-iron safe, the room had a bare, stripped look suggestive of only temporary accommodation. Its narrow latticed window disallowed daylight to enter in quantity enough to allow work to proceed. An overhead fixture, the sort that illuminates billiard tables, bathed the surface of the desk in soft white light.

A fourth person was in the room, one of the filing clerks, Janet, Janice, Janine, some name like that, to whom Goodwin had made unsuccessful overtures. A query about her pay packet was under close investigation. I started to go away.

'You stay put, Thomas Graves, Esquire,' Freddy said. 'I've got a bone to pick with you.'

He sat tidily at his desk, silver hair shining in the light, his pink scrubbed face that only Joanna could light up composed, half smiling. He wore the darker of his two grey suits and a brilliantly white shirt that Joanna herself would have laundered and ironed. Loder, dumpy, bespectacled, with a rapping voice, began a lengthy explanation to Janine of the figures arrived at. I wandered about the room.

There was not much to inspect. Two pictures, though, hung on the walls, a coloured print of Annigoni's portrait of the Queen, statutory issue perhaps for all government offices or donated by our banner-cleaning neighbours; and an alchemical engraving in a Hogarth frame. The picture was not new to me, had been met with at the outset of my interest in alchemy. I had been at school, no older than Joanna. Now, as then, the scene, an historical one, aroused a faint repugnance. As in its neighbour, a monarch was represented, a king this time. Bewhiskered, advanced in years, his crown on his head, he occupied a canopied throne set up in a draughty ground-floor apartment in his palace that through Gothic arches gave on to an altogether meaner part of his city. Men trundled handcarts and dogs ranged along narrow alleyways. The king was in the act of embracing his son, also crowned, who leaned lovingly over him. A third figure who held a staff, a species of chamberlain as far as could be made out, also bearded, surveyed this familial encounter, very much the sort of touching homecoming Robert Ferguson liked to engineer in front of cameras for the television programme Freddy so much enjoyed. When I had first seen the print, it had seemed to have nothing to do with alchemy. A caption added in manuscript had been virtually illegible, only the title, *Filius Regis* and part of the Latin word for 'published,' *edit. . .*, readily discernable, but as I had given it closer attention to try and discover its meaning I saw there were three features I had missed, peculiar in the extreme. The benign old chamberlain sprouted a pair of neat, clipped wings. The king's son, curly-headed, not much more than a boy, was stripped to the waist. Perhaps because of the precipitance of his entry into the palace and up to his father's outstretched arms, his only garment, a kind of pleated skirt cut rather short, had slipped perilously low over rotund, almost womanly haunches. In a moment he would be naked.

One more detail caught the eye. The engraver's skill, evident as well in the grave acquiescence on the face of the chamberlain, the feminine rotundities of the boy and his bubbly curls, the composition's general architectural perspectives, had not failed him in the portraiture of the king. His mouth was open. Not just half open as if expressing joy or surprise at this perhaps unlooked-for visitation but agape, like a roaring lion's, the jaws a great 'O' in the hoary face. I realized I had mistranslated *edit. . .;* it meant not to publish but to consume. All became horrifyingly clear. This was not a delineation of a father welcoming home his son. Before a passive, indeed an approving audience, the old man was about to devour the boy alive.

Disgust lasted only a second. The chamberlain's ridiculous appendages took from the picture much of its obnoxiousness. Clearly a symbolic interpretation was to be sought. It was of course merely an allegorical representation of life, death, rebirth, its placement in the book therefore perfectly explicable. Nevertheless, whenever I looked at it, the original shock—that the old man would in the next moment be crunching in his whiskered jaws the effete curly head inclined so deferentially towards him—never failed in some measure to repeat itself.

'Your noisy pals blew up our ruddy telly.' I turned round. The girl had gone. Freddy had said nothing to Ma about an explosion as far as I could remember. It seemed unlikely, even given the volume of sound to which Celestial Praylin could attain. Sgt Barker would have accounted electrical failure at that precise moment a 'Titless Susan.' Sometime in the future Freddy might be amused to hear his theories on fatidical intervention into human affairs: not now, though. His words, jokingly spoken though they had been, were intended to be taken seriously.

I commiserated with him on the accident; and explained my mission.

'Five thousand quid,' Freddy expostulated. 'What wouldn't I give for a handout like that. All for a miserable old dokky.' He opened the safe and began to count out the money. The sum involved was large, not however unusually so. ALEMBIC was prepared to pay highly for alchemical manuscripts in the way police pay for information: 'cash-o, cash-o,' as Lindo had put it, a necessity, on occasion, for unencumbered acquisitions. Documentation, however, was elaborate: 'no disbursement without documentation' was a catchphrase of Loder's. He employed it now as he set a sheaf of papers before me. While I filled in the forms Freddy demanded from Loder a rundown on last night's sabotaged programme.

'Now, Harold, the greengrocer, first of all.'

'One thing's for sure,' Loder said. 'He'll never sell so much as a pound of spuds again.'

'Accused him to his face, did he?'

'There was no need for that. That's where Ferguson's stage training stands him in such good stead. He called the bloke a cheat without calling him a cheat, if you catch my meaning.'

'And the old girl with the chicken farm? Did Ferguson produce her brother for her?'

'Indeedy-doody,' Loder said. 'Thirty-four years they'd been parted; ever since the Saltdean polio scare. There were tears, I can tell you that, tears on both sides.'

'That was to be expected.' Freddy looked as if he might cry himself. Loder, too, admitted to having been moved. Well-intentioned though it might be, the programme also sounded vaguely indecent, petty criminalities, private griefs, tearful reunions ruthlessly exposed to a maximum audience. Nicholas, who thoroughly disliked Robert Ferguson, had turned down an invitation to be interviewed, his refusal causing yet another stir in the newspapers.

'I'm not having that fucker cocking his eyebrow at me,' Nicholas had told a reporter. 'Besides he'll only hint we're immoral, disgusting, symptom of a nation in decline. What about his boring plays with everyone pissed on cocktails. He's handily forgotten those.'

That may have been true. Thirty years ago, Ferguson had stormed London with his cocked eyebrow, his cigarette holder, his quizzical smile, a certain polished charm. Comedy had succeeded brittle comedy but, like the cocktail, he was no more to the public taste. He ought not to have worried too much about loss of favour, his plays having made him extremely rich, but missing apparently the adulation in which he had once basked, he had begun to use his money, and to be seen to use it, in support of various charities. Bountifulness had returned him to the public eye, some among his older fans interpreting his new role as atonement for past cynicism. Now he was at the top, as Nicholas had put it, of the 'compassion market.' In *Ferguson on Thursday* families were reunited, lovers fell into one another's arms, victims of society recounted their plight, those who battened on the unwary and the poor were hounded out of business (like the greengrocer of last night's episode) by Robert Ferguson's cool exposure of their guiles. The class he appealed to these days was the one that, from the footlights, he had once been in the habit of mocking. All in all, Nicholas's strictures appeared justified.

I had been wandering about the town thinking of these things instead of returning to London straightaway because of a handwritten notice attached to the window of Marina Novelties. It had read *Silver Palace. 4.30.* I could not think what it meant. A racing tip? Message for a friend of somewhere, a cinema, restaurant, drinking club, where Lindo's uncle might at that hour be found? It had seemed worth hanging on until the time came round. I wasted half an hour in a bookshop, succumbed finally to the allures of the noisy café. As hoped, the tea would have been much to Sgt Barker's taste. The waitress, a rather plain girl with no chin or rather with a chin that looked to have been bound up at birth to restrict growth in later life, the way the Chinese bind feet, bore resemblances to Valerie Latham, the girl we hoped might effect changes, civilian and military, on Pte Potts.

Valerie's lookalike had clad herself, almost enshrouded herself, so far down a figure of indeterminate girth did the untailored, ill-fitting garment descend, almost to the level of a summer dress, in one of the Celestial Praylin T-shirts from which Ma had learned by rote the two lines from 'Love's Mansion.' Pictorially, the clothing resolved the textual difficulties offered when Ma had recited the lines in question. Nicholas had done himself to death. That was unequivocally stated in the garish red and black drawing depicted above the lyrics. In a grotesque parody of Ligier Richier's funerary monument at Bar-le-Duc of the skeletal knight holding out his heart to God—possibly viewed by Ma during her historical tour of Alsace-Lorraine—Nicholas had been delineated in the same mortified yet exultant posture. The original figure was macabre enough, in the flaying of the naked body and the exposure of leg and arm muscles not yet rotted from the bones, to command attention, but the figure was imbued by Richier's art with an enduring majesty that, though his design had been closely followed, was utterly overturned by the specious caricature of Nicholas Spark emblazoned down the waitress's white cotton vest. Like the engraving of the king's son in 'Dizzies and Dokkies,' the statue, whenever I had seen photographs of it, had for quite different reasons always been impressive: the fearfully putrefied yet magnificently poised corpse offering to heaven the heart he had plucked from his breast quite suddenly endowing elements of faith—aspiration for, almost conviction of there being a future life on high—with which, as a general rule, I remained altogether untouched. To be sure, the artist, whoever he was, had retained some aspects of the grandiloquent statement of piety inherent in the sturdily upright, even in death supremely triumphant, man-of-arms. Nicholas, too, stood straight enough, flung his head upwards in the manner of the statue to emphasize the few still uncorrupted tendons straining to hold neck to shoulders for the examination of the organ he had extracted from his bosom across which he, like the knight, had thrown his other fleshless hand to mask from view the cavity its extraction had made in the rib cage: but there similarities rested. Nicholas had been given a full head of black hair depended from the cranium of a deeply socketed, crassly grinning skull that still tenuously secured gobbets enough of flesh to present a reasonable likeness of the singer who contemplated, shrieking with undisguised mirth, a blood-soaked chunk of butcher's offal he looked at any moment he might pop into his mouth. Blood, totally absent from Richier's sculpture, cascaded in gallons both from the seriously mangled entrails that Nicholas squeezed in bony fingers like a bathroom sponge and from the gaping wound he had gouged in his chest. More blood coursed down his torso and across draped though heavily emphasized genitals; and, finding its way between toes elongated like eagle's talons, coagulated, as a kind of hazardously unsteady pedestal on which the figure maintained its footing, into the words of the song:

Death stalked my spore, a spectre
I tore him out my heart.

This was typical of Nicholas. Probably he had fashioned the design himself. He always liked to twist artistry of whatever period to his own, again undoubtedly artistic, ends: fairly horrid ones on this occasion. The waitress, oblivious to having her torso subjected to a searching examination, placed beside me another cup of tea. Thoughts wandered off elsewhere, turning this time on how preferably army life—much in my thoughts—stood up to current, civilian employment.

Once, in a 'two-and-eight,' or a mood bordering on that condition, Rastus had accused me of dilettantism: of exercising connoisseurship in the formation of ALEMBIC's book collection—overattention to wideness of margin, sharpness of impression, quality of binding, aestheticism along those purely bibliophilic, tactile, visual lines—rather than assembling a working alchemical library; of an antiquarianism that ran counter to the scientific principles on which ALEMBIC was run; in fact of a general 'unsatisfactoriness.' Its root cause was hereditary, he implied, or at least environmental, fault of my parents for being, as he saw it, 'bright.' For this harangue, he had adopted a high rasping tone of voice usually reserved for homosexuals or the aristocracy from neither of whose ranks he came. His moustache, the only un-owlish feature of his round beaky face, was flecked with droplets of spittle; his eyes started out from below hooded lids; his 'bad' hand sawed the air. Looked at frankly, a point or two had to be conceded, hysterically though they had been made. Specialization in the literature of alchemy may indeed have been a pose but it was one assumed as an antidote to parental influences, not as a result of them.

My father, a concert pianist by profession, composed in his spare time musical pieces that consisted for the most part of an arbitrary, not especially pleasant series of sounds that I, for one, found beyond my grasp. My mother, too, thought poorly of his work but then he in turn had little time for her novels of which she unburdened herself at regular intervals—one every two years or so. Of some length, turning on emotional entanglements among the moneyed classes, they were nevertheless widely read. Her success riled my father who considered his branch of the arts and his own gifts within it of a superior order. This was disputable, certainly by 'popular' standards because my father made practically nothing out of his music and my mother more than enough to keep us all in reasonable comfort. Differences of opinion led to intellectual breakfast and suppertime banter, far above my childish head. I saw, however, the importance of making my way in some sphere of learning which would be quite incomprehensible to them so as, at least, to be able to join in the family squabbles. Chemistry, later alchemy—the engraving of the king's son contributing to a change of direction—was an admirable choice. As it turned out, it was more rewarding than expected, not only because it had the effect of fomenting parental bewilderment but because progressive investigation revealed that predecessors in the field, especially on the bibliographical side, had been extremely careless. At almost every turn, mistakes had been made, items overlooked, editions wrongly recorded, authorship incorrectly ascribed, and much amusement could be gained by being seen to be good at the subject for the simple reason that everybody else had been rather bad at it. By the time I was fifteen, I had begun to contribute articles to learned journals that corrected, on occasion advanced, earlier researches.

My father and mother, however—and this had not crossed my mind—had no wish whatsoever that I should turn out, in the way they saw themselves (though not each other) as 'exceptional.' Recognizing the exclusivity of their gifts and the undesirability of their manifesting themselves in their son under whatever guise, they selected a middle-of-the-road educational regime. They packed me off to a draughty preparatory school in a coastal town not unlike the one where I was now drinking tea and, after that, to a less austere and much-esteemed establishment, inland this time, where, in a freer atmosphere than they must have wished for, I began my annoying habit of contributing to academic periodicals. Formal education, though, had begun to bore me and my parents' wish that I proceed to university goaded me to fairly violent action. I joined the army.

Legally enlisted, I could not be legally removed. Distress, anger, incomprehension, whatever emotions raged over the breakfast table, had by the time I came home on my first leave more or less abated. At first I suppose I had vaguely thought of taking a commission, that ambition perhaps having the effect of calming my parents finally down. Duties in the Orderly Room, however, changed all that. Existence—life-style, one could go so far—in the warm, noisy, wooden hut became far too pleasurable to exchange for the Officers' Mess.

It was through the army that ALEMBIC got to hear of me, or rather through a twist of fate coming to pass during army service which, even with all his knowledge of the ways of divine inevitability, would have given Sgt Barker food for thought. I reluctantly finished my tea and began to make my way back to Marina Novelties. Duty called, as Cpl Kinnell used to say, duty no more, certainly no less, irksome than military routine, the often futile aspects of current, civilian chores setting off again trains of thought of the advantages, come to that the disadvantages, of past employment when weighed against today's.

This time I was luckier. The door to Lindo's uncle's premises had been unlocked. I found myself in a long, twilit, deserted shop. In the silence objects moved gently in the draught my entrance had made. Japanese lanterns and paper parasols strung from the ceiling began to stir and rustle, tall flowers of green and red feathers that ornamented a shelf behind a glass counter dipped and waved in the current of air. The counter, running along the left of the shop, held a collection of toy spiders in transparent cubes that emitted little clicking noises as they scuttled aimlessly in their perspex cells. On the countertop stringy plastic ducks with long stilted legs like the herons' canted up and down to take sips from tumblers of water placed under their beaks. In a capacious glass phial lit from within, a swollen green amoeba floated soupily about, changing every so often a gelatinous fatness for an elongated mucilent ribbon. On the other side of the shop, glass-fronted cabinets held puppets and ventriloquists' dolls that dangled contortedly from hooks and nails, murkiness of light giving the impression of some sort of mediaeval effigial tableau set up in public as a warning to evildoers. One of the dolls sporting a monocle and a sharp suit bore a disturbing resemblance to Pte Potts. It wore his 'Goddess of Mercy' look, a phrase Sgt Barker used to employ as descriptive of Potts's habitually contemplative, on occasion comatose, approach to his tasks; and was hanging by the neck.

When my eyes grew accustomed to the gloom I saw that the shop was divided into two halves: what I had taken for the back wall a pair of curtains concealing further premises beyond. I passed through them and found I was not alone.

I was in an altogether smaller room. Darkness here was even deeper but broken at the far end by a brightly lit cabinet about three feet by two elevated just above eye level and draped in folds of crimson satin. Before it, occupying the three or four rows of chairs that only just fitted into the cramped space a scattering of people had been gathered or impressed. Pink light glowing on upturned faces showed them to be elderly for the most part. The women wore hats or headscarves, the men's bald pates shone in the sickly illumination. The atmosphere was hushed, respectful, even reverent, as if they contemplated a shrine or tabernacle behind which, curtained from view, a holy relic might repose or a disembodied head—Uncle Hamish's perhaps—would, when the time came, be revealed speaking in tongues. Something mystical, anyway, vaguely unwholesome, seemed to be afoot. There was a decidedly 'churchy' feel about the place underlined by the design of the chairs on the end one of which, in the back row, I tentatively took a place. Of plain wood, each was equipped with a trough at the back for hymnals, psalters, orders of service. Some leaflets had been stuck into them and I was about to try to read one when the lights around the shrine were extinguished. We were now in total darkness.

Anticipation, heightened briefly by this signal, negative though it was, began after a few minutes to tail off as we sat in silence and the dark. People began to cough and to scrape their feet. I felt now that I must have strayed into premises let off by Lindo's uncle to some sect—spiritualists, I now suspected, the tasteless little curtains representing the 'Veil'—in whose observance this week there had been a hitch. A fuse could have blown, the mechanism for pulling the curtains failed, the celebrant not yet arrived or taken ill. Perhaps a member of the congregation would lead us in a hymn until things had been put to rights. The protracted delay seemed the moment to make my escape and watch whatever was going to take place from the curtains at my back; and I was about to grope my way towards them when a loud cockney voice rang out through the darkness.

'Ladies and gentlemen. *The Silver Palace: A Water Pageant for the Miniature Stage.*'

I turned. The shrine had been re-illuminated. A vivid green light now shone on the satin curtains. Music began to play. The curtains parted. On a tiny dazzlingly lit stage an underwater scene was revealed.

Silver Palace. 4.30. That had been the notice on the door. There had been toy theatres displayed in the window. We were about to see a production, to promote sales most likely, although it was doubtful if Lindo's uncle would find a ready market among this particular audience. The tiny cardboard figures he began to propel onto the stage would be a challenge for failing eyesight. Close as we all were, they were difficult to make out. There were two of them to start off with. They rode in chariots pulled by sea horses and blew on conch-shells the sound of which Uncle Hamish faithfully reproduced from apparatus concealed behind his curtains. Cardboard billows lapped their chariot wheels. They were adroitly manoeuvred through the waves and around an elaborate tinseled grotto to the focal point of the stage where a baroque coral arch afforded the only space where action could develop. In contrast to the smallness of the figures, Uncle Hamish's voice boomed out the first lines:

Hark! the wild tide gushes, our task is o'er;
Speed, brother, speed, to the crystal palace shore.

The play, its action subaqueous throughout, was of some length. The burden of the plot, not really much more than a vehicle for various cutout set pieces—caverns, waterfalls, grottoes, the Silver Palace itself—revolved around a series of attempts by Prince Volcano, a sort of satanic Neptune, heavily bearded and flourishing a drawn sword, to recapture and bear off, for good this time, a flaxen-haired maiden, Lady Luminia. She, to escape his clutches, had fled to these submarine havens in every expectation of marrying Coral Crown, the Water King. He too had flaxen hair: his weapon a trident. Lindo's uncle did his best with the voices, a cavernous baritone for Volcano, a contralto for Luminia, a punchy tenor for the Water King, and slid everybody around with commendable skill. As the plot unfolded, he even managed to infuse the minuscule figures with a certain depth of character, Coral Crown at any rate. It was hard not to bring in a verdict of cowardice. He was never at hand for Prince Volcano's repeated forays, one in each of the five acts, and it was left to Quicksand and Waterspout, the charioteers who had opened the play on their conches, to fight rearguard actions while Lady Luminia cowered behind a stalagmite. Despite his size, I could discern in him, too, an effeminate quality that put me in mind of the king's son in the alchemical engraving. Perhaps before long, Prince Volcano would eat him alive. He bore certain resemblances to the king as a younger man. Thoughts turned on further symbolism to be observed in the pageant—the elemental clashes between fire and water, which Lindo's uncle conveyed by dimming and raising the stage lights and hammering on a drum, perhaps corresponding with Thomas Norton's 'fire of humectation'—and to relating the little coloured silhouettes to the archetypal figures Jung made play with in his psychological writings on alchemy. Coral Crown could be the Psychopomp, the 'id' in other psychoanalytical schools, Lavinia the *anima* that guides mankind not to the material gold we sought at ALEMBIC but to what could be called the 'light.' At ALEMBIC Rastus and Ma (a shortening of *anima,* I now wondered, invented by a deceased colleague thinking along similar abstract lines?) could be looked at in the same way. I pondered which archetypal figure fitted my position at ALEMBIC. Perhaps the Egyptian god Thoth, god of libraries I seemed to recall, ibis- or was it heron-headed, often pictured reading or with stylus and writing tablet. It could be that our secret experimentations, our empirical muddling with outworn, simplistic, surely by now demonstrably false branches of physics, might at last, rather than yielding gold or a universal medicine, instil in us instead a form of spiritual superhumanity. If so, the cooks, I too, had a long way to go.

These contemplations, 'unsatisfactory' in the extreme to Rastus's way of thinking, coupled, despite changes of pitch, with the singsong nature of Uncle Hamish's delivery, glimmerings too of the headache that had been with me all day, made me close my eyes. I may have slept for a while. I was roused by a roll of thunder as loud as any yet produced. It was Volcano's final assault. Uncle Hamish was pounding his drum and switching his lights on and off in a frenzied imitation of the thunderstorm the Prince, by supernatural means, had called down on his enemies. Smoke—some sort of chemical, the sort that Celestial Praylin released at the close of their concerts—billowed out through the proscenium arch. When it cleared from the stage, although residues clung ectoplasmically around the heads of those spectators in the front row, Coral Crown, to refute my charges of irresolution, entered stage left to face his bearded foe. There was an impressive clash of arms. Some sea horses were ruthlessly despatched. Volcano was drawn off in disarray. Sea nymphs, tritons, mermaids, Waterspout and Quicksand joined the couple for a celebratory fire dance. Dark tongues of flame licked at the backdrop. Bars of Ravel's *Bolero* gave suitable accompaniment. Coral Crown declaimed the final lines of the play:

Go! Threat thy fire-born myrmidons, but here
'Tis mine *to threaten, Prince, and* thine *to fear.*
Come! To the water-gate with me advance.
Meantime my subjects here resume the dance.

The curtain fell. It was not a moment too soon. It had all been rather noisy: bewildering too. Afterimages of the final lightning flashes still danced before my eyes. Wisps of the Prince's chemical weaponry lingered in the air. We filed out.

'I hate all forms of puppetry,' Lindo remarked when I reported on the performance. 'As a child I could never watch Uncle Hamish's Punch and Judy. I always thought they were alive, like homunculi popped back after performance into stoppered jars. Is the manuscript any good?'

'Better than expected. It's a late-seventeenth-century transcript. In itself, that is unlikely to excite. Reidy collated about twenty of them when he edited the *Ordinall* for the Early English Text Society and they yielded only one variant reading between them, but what we have is a whole prose section, presumably by the transcriber, on the Red Dragon. The *Ordinall* barely hints at that.'

'I don't think I've come across the Red Dragon.'

'It's the use of blood in the Great Work. Norton veers off almost as soon as he mentions it: calls the experiment a "selcouth thing":

But my heart quaketh, my hand is trembling
When I write of this most selcouth thing.'

For some reason, I rather spouted these lines: awarded them the same declamatory vigour with which Lindo's uncle had tackled some of the more stirring couplets in *The Silver Palace* earlier in the day.

Lindo raised his eyebrows: 'Wow.'

The words were not unimpressive, even less histrionically delivered: among Norton's best. They conveyed much of the sinister side of alchemical tinkerings.

'Perhaps Loudermilk would donate us a pint or two of his blood, for us to boil up. Be on the thin side, though, wouldn't it?'

'It wouldn't do at all. Blood has to be virginal, menstrual for preference.'

Lindo cheered up. 'I say. Do you think we'd be allowed to cage up the odd virgin along with the rats and mice? Would that ever be permitted? Of course, with Goodwin and Bastable around, status would be subject to daily confirmation. Anyway, send us down a transcript when you've got a moment and we'll have a look at it. Was the old boy pleased with the money?'

'Very. I'd like to have found out more about the manuscript's provenance, but there was some trouble in the street. Your uncle had to hurry upstairs ready to douse the offenders with a pail of water. I felt, at such short acquaintance, I didn't have to stay and fight at his side.'

'Quite right. It's the local yobs. They walk in and pinch stuff. Uncle Hamish usually lets off a stink bomb and they all disperse. The war has obviously escalated. By the way, did you remember . . . ?'

'Yes.'

'Thanks. I'll give you fair warning. Morning coffee break, I think. Tomorrow or the next day.'

'Keep me posted.'

Impressions of Uncle Hamish had been vague for the reasons given. A beanpole of a man had thrashed his way through the satin curtains, with grey hair, wiry like his nephew's, hornrimmed glasses and a potbelly that seemed unsuited to a man so tall and otherwise thin and gave him the look of having stuffed a small cushion under his waistcoat prior to giving a comic turn. Financial problems may have been acuter than Lindo believed. He seemed nervous as we sat among the ventriloquists' dolls and clacking spiders that the manuscript might not suit: after I had handed over Freddy's bulky envelope far more at ease. We had begun to talk of other things: his dexterity in *The Silver Palace,* his days 'in bauxite,' guttering problems at the back of the shop that could be resolved with the cash now in hand. I had purchased Captain Belcher's Tea. Then we had heard a commotion in the street outside. Youths were shouting. There were sounds of running footsteps. Lindo's uncle had sprung to his feet and secured the shop door trustingly left ajar for late arrivals to the water pageant. He dragged over a stout steel grille and clamped it across the frame with chains and padlocks.

'Punks, skinheads,' he said. 'Get a lot of trouble with them. They come in here, nine, ten at a time and pull the stuff about. Think nothing of slipping things in their pockets and making off. Little buggers. I'd tan their hides for them if I could catch them. Listen, I'm going to leg it upstairs and watch they don't start breaking my window.' He caught hold of a metal bucket and gave a threatening rattle. 'If they do, they'll get a drenching.'

Despite perturbation, some quickening of the blood was in evidence. Uncle Hamish's eyes had gleamed menacingly behind his heavy spectacles. Battles, in the past, had clearly not all gone the way of the local youth. He hurried me through the curtained alcove that led to the auditorium and out into the backyard. There he had given me a glimpse of the gutter causing trouble and then opened a gate leading into an unpaved lane. He waved good-bye and hastily barred the gate behind him. The lane led to a side street that would take me, with a turn to the right, into familiar territory. In the road, part of the 'gang,' six or seven of them, came into sight. Another knot of youths similar in dress and buoyancy was running up behind me. They passed, shouting excitedly. Others followed in their wake. They were making for a whole army of their number some fifty yards in front of me, milling about a tall red-brick building, the back of some warehouse or department store, that dominated the left-hand side of the street. To begin with, Uncle Hamish's tactics appeared to have been justified. The atmosphere was tense, febrile, aggressive: trouble of some sort not far from the surface. The hoarse male voices we had heard were continuing, punctuated now by shriller, female cries. Behind me the crowd was now as thick as in front. I was propelled forward.

Had Rastus been present he would have accounted most of the throng as 'unsatisfactory.' There was an unruliness of hair styling, widely divergent though it was, too long, too short, eccentrically waved or trained up in spikes, shaven, dyed, that spoke of a distaste, even of an open defiance, of authority, uniformity of clothing—T-shirts, leather jackets, jeans—emphasizing the indelible stamp the crowd had impressed upon itself of being 'young.' Non-conformity too was advertised by designs, patches, labels, transfers, metallic badges, that had been printed or sewn or pinned to garments, proclaiming allegiance to radical causes or calling attention to environmental problems and the endangerment of larger mammalian species. Chains, necklaces, finger rings, earrings, safety pins and strings of beads decorated the wearers as if they had been some savage tribe who had fallen on the offerings of missionaries and decked themselves out with all spoils at once in some frantic share-out. As I forced my way along or rather, after an effort to do so, had stepped into the road where the youngest among the crowd, no more than children, were leaping up and down in a vain attempt to catch a glimpse of whatever was the focus of attention, I came to feel that the climate, charged though it was, reversed original impressions of menace, the jeers of the youths entirely good-natured, the girls' cries pleasurable yelps. Ripples of applause alternated with louder outbursts of cheering. Nonetheless, some alert must have gone out to the local police station because, nosing his way through the crowd behind me which had now thickened to the point when retreat was impossible and which was sweeping me inexorably on and into the thick of the rally or demonstration, there came a policeman on a motorcycle. Directions from his radio and the throbbing of the machine he navigated along at walking pace caused people to turn their heads and when they saw his insignia to make a path for him; and while this parting of the multitude could not be deemed respectful and a few 'boos' and catcalls went up, the policeman's beaming mouth, which was all that could be seen of a goggled and helmeted head, proclaimed that whatever the meeting was about, it was both peaceable and to be condoned. As he passed me, he slewed his machine round to the left and, sounding his horn, rode up onto the pavement. By following behind him so that my feet nearly touched the rear wheel and I could feel the heat of the exhaust against my legs, I was able to inch along in his wake until he had penetrated one side of the solid phalanx of swaying youths and girls and come to a halt in the very front row.

I saw that everybody was surrounding, boxing in and preventing from getting on its way a low-slung black limousine of transatlantic design parked outside the warehouse entrance. There was much that was admirable about the dimensions of the gleaming, chrome-fanged vehicle, ostentatious though it was, an inspired deployment of opulence and sleekness to their very farthest limits that one more inch on radiator or on boot, one more blinking light added to the banks of head- and tail- and wing-lights all of which were flashing steadily on and off, would have rendered merely absurd. Because its windows were of smoked glass and no steering wheel was visible within, it was impossible to tell from viciously streamlined contours which way the car was facing, whether the elongated coachwork nearest to me, still further emphasized by razor-sharp fins, defined trunk or bonnet. It was not beyond the bounds of possibility that the automobile could split itself in half and be driven off in both directions at once. Leaning against this vehicle stood a figure so grotesque—in quite a different way from the mode of transport it was attempting vainly to enter and being prevented by having autograph books and scraps of paper thrust at it to sign and pass back as fast as possible—that it could have stepped from some nightmare painting—Bosch, Ernst—or from the pit of hell.

First glances signaled some red-skinned saurian creature, long extinct, half lizard, half bird, but the horny, scarlet hide of the body turned out on closer inspection to be a seamless robe of grained leather, red leather boots also just visible below the ankle-length hem. Thick red gauntlets sewed to the sleeves of the robe clutched awkwardly at the waving pens and papers being thrust at him—if masculine the creature was. For the head was encased in a grey melon-shaped globe of metal attached to a scarlet cape, again of leather, that pulled down over neck and shoulders, from the front of which protruded a substantial parrot-shaped bill, bright yellow in colour. Two small bulbous eyeholes made of perspex completed the macabre avian aspect of the head which had been topped with a red leather hat, its wide brim jauntily curled upwards and attached by two threads of string to the pointed crown.

Yet to my mind there was nothing in the least jaunty about the monstrous figure whose origins, familiar after all, were not to be sought in either mythological or demonological pantheons. An historical textbook used at school had reproduced just such a creature. This was the garb of the Plague Doctors, the yellow beak stuffed with aromatic herbs against infection, who stalked the city streets in the time of the Black Death in vain administration to the dying. They had been held in awe, I recalled, final hopes pinned on their fraudulent skills. Indeed there was an expectation about today's clamouring mob, whom three or four other policemen stationed along the far side of the car dissuaded from scaling over its roof to touch the swaying nodding figure whose eyes could be seen through the transparent peepholes swivelling from side to side, that spoke of wonderment, idolatry, blind faith. Even if that were going too far, the actor (or actress)—that had at least been established because a sign on the building read *Stage Door* and what I had joined was simply a press of young fans around a film star or star of some television series—by dressing up in this antiseptic way, the way royalty used to sniff at oranges as they processed among their people, seemed to offer to his (or her) admirers a deliberate insult. That was of course too melodramatic. Obviously whoever it was featured in some science-fiction adventure I had never come across. Joanna would probably know if I remembered to ask her. Yet, feelings of distaste persisted; and when the creature all at once stopped signing the 'books' and waved its great gauntlets at the crowd that it was time to go and moved over to the mounted policeman so I could clearly hear the creaking of the stiff leather robe and focused its bulbous eyeballs directly on my face, I would all too gladly have turned tail and run. But the crowd behind me, some twenty deep by now, who must have envied me my front-row vantage point, made escape impossible; and I watched helplessly as the figure stripped off its gauntlets and raised white, bony, almost skeletal fingers to the side of the ponderous diver's helmet of a mask and hauled it and hat and cape in one movement up and off his head. I caught a glimpse of raven black hair, a long white hatchet of a face, a gleaming wide-mouthed smile. The thin fingers grabbed my hands and wrung them up and down in a greeting of the utmost solicitude and pleasure.

'Tom.'

'Nicholas.'

A great roar had gone up from the throng. Perhaps they too had been a bit overawed by Nicholas Spark's bizarre disguise. Shouting and yelling his name, they began a great surge forward, rocking the limousine that divided them from their hero. Struggling with police, a man in a leather jacket with a multi-coloured serpent entwined on the back broke free and, with the help of friends, clambered on to the car roof where he broke into an abandoned dance. His steel-capped boots rang out on the polished bodywork. He yelled down to Nicholas: 'Rock on, Nick. Celestial Praylin's the greatest.'

Nicholas looked up and bestowed on the capering figure another of his sweet, beguiling smiles. One of the constables began to pull the man down.

'I think we'd better get you out of here.' The policeman on the motorcycle revved up his engine. 'They're going to wreck your motor.'

'They paid for it. Let them wreck it,' Nicholas said. He pulled a zip at the side of his heavy robe and struggled from its folds. He opened the rear door and stuffed the outfit onto the back seat. The cheering grew louder. For a moment he stood motionless, as I had seen him stand before the microphone at rock concerts, arms raised, painfully thin, clad now, like his fans, only in shabby jeans and a sweatshirt. Then he turned back to me.

'Where are you going, Tom? Or are you just loitering with intent?'

'London.'

'Me too. Jump in.'

I followed Nicholas into the back and slammed the door. Outside, the policeman activated his siren and eased his machine forward. Nicholas's chauffeur, his head just visible through the smoked-glass partition, engaged the gears. The limousine began to move. Hands thundered on the roof, smacked on the gleaming bonnet. Pressed against the darkened windows, distorted faces stared wildly in at us. As the wails of the siren increased, we quickened our pace. At walking, then running speed, still pursued by some of the fans, we descended the hill to the sea. A last, despairing, waving girl darted across our bonnet. The policeman turned in his saddle to see if we had extricated ourselves from the mob; saluted; and veered off to the right. We were alone.

2

Never an especial fan of rock, though by rights the atonalities of my father's music could have sent me fleeing to the sanctuary of its altogether simpler harmonic patterns, I had taken a long time to come to terms with Nicholas's enormous popularity. That he was going to be, in some way, marked out, even notorious, had been borne in on me at school, our housemaster remarking one day as Nicholas hared across the playing field, ball under arm: 'Spark must be the only man alive capable of imitating, with passable precision, the shade of Aubrey Beardsley pursued by a satyr.'

By the time I was about to leave the army, on the disastrous night that had, in a way, led to my appointment at ALEMBIC, I discovered by chance that Nicholas had already skyrocketed to fame. I hadn't meant to impress Pte Potts's girl by dropping his name in conversation although I had been trying to impress her by every other means in my power, but when I mentioned I knew him and knew him very well she had thrown back her head and closed her eyes and sighed a great lascivious sigh as if at that very moment she was abandoning herself to his caresses. Cpl Kinnell, too, who was still of our party at that stage of the evening, had expressed interest in our acquaintanceship and, for a minute or two, I had been rather the toast of the assembly Sgt Barker had convened for Pte Potts's initiation into what, in the former's view, was the adult world.

Potts, Cpl Kinnell, Sgt Barker and myself made up the staff of the Company Orderly Office. Unlike the cooks at ALEMBIC, we never managed to infuse our ranks with what might be called an *esprit de corps,* any sort of spirit, come to that, other than one of fostering idleness on the most luxurious scale we could muster, certainly not with the sort of solidarity required to neutralize disagreements about liability for the incident—the most sensational of my three years' service—that affected for a time such a dramatic change in our sybaritic routine. Each of us very different, we held conflicting views on who had brought the tragedy about. As often as not, I was the one held responsible: that was the general opinion during some of the postmortems, at least. I saw that well enough—with reservations—and bowed, I hope, my neck to the yoke, but looking at things another way Sgt Barker should have taken some of the blame for committing the first of the many errors of judgement with which the evening had been beset. Cpl Kinnell and Pte Potts could sometimes be called upon to agree with that alternative standpoint, Sgt Barker never. Pulling rank, or so we said in alleviation of his indiscriminate assault on the three of us in turn, he accused me of insobriety, Kinnell of defection, Potts of all-round hopelessness. In fairness, though, when, after a long time, Sgt Barker had sifted all the evidence and laid it out in his mind as he taught other ranks to lay out for inspection the mechanism of their rifles, he reached the conclusion that what had happened could not, when all was said and done, have been humanly avoided. His adjudication, solemnly delivered, was that the incident had been written in the stars. There was no other explanation. Any further arguments would be a waste of time, their continuance up to now deriving from ignorance of certain arcane factors about which he alone, an old hand at the affairs of gods and men, was qualified to speak *ex cathedra.* In his final words, we had been visited—and it would be very improbable if ever again in our lifetime we would be the central figures in such a spectacular example—by a 'Titless Susan.'

Square, with a bulbous nose and a toothbrush moustache, Sgt Barker resembled in mufti the sort of henpecked husband portrayed on seaside postcards. A selection was very likely on sale in Lindo's uncle's shop. In uniform, on the contrary, he was immensely smart, militarily correct, 'shit hot,' to use his own words. Domestically (he was a married man) there may have been bedroom problems of the nature such postcards invariably depict—last-ditch failures, insufficient endowment or too much of it, ardency, possibly out-and-out randiness, not to his wife's liking—since in off-duty hours he was much given to 'swiving.' I was not familiar with the word, discovered by Cpl Kinnell in the course of reading the collected poems of the Earl of Rochester, and had asked him what it meant. 'Copulating,' he had explained bluntly. The word's onomatopoeic qualities conveyed to me additional implications of going about that practice fairly noisily, much drink taken, a sort of long drawn-out carouse, night-long, and although Kinnell denied etymological ramifications along the lines I proposed, they described pretty well Sgt Barker's method of approach to the matter in hand. Preferring quantity to quality, the sort of ample, peroxided, rather on-coming brassy lady to be found in plenty in the garrison town pubs, herself not particular about looks, Sgt Barker would ply her with drinks until closing time, so, as a rule, they left for a barrack room illicitly commandeered for the purpose rather the worse for wear. Sometimes a bottle, port one night, cherry brandy another, was purchased for home consumption, so that when eventually it was reached, the 'swiving' part of the evening may not have always been entertainment, at least to an onlooker—a forbidding notion—of any particular fruitfulness.

What was important to Sgt Barker, a creature of habit, was that this sort of wassail should constitute part of a weekend leave, a treat to punctuate with reasonable frequency the tedium of military chores. Indeed he looked on these evenings out as part and parcel of army routine, a duty therefore into which all of us should put our backs with very much the same panache and precision Sgt Barker liked to witness on the drill square. Kinnell and I occasionally accompanied him into town, picked up a girl and took her back to barracks. That gave Sgt Barker great pleasure and, for my part, absolved me from strictures about 'bookish' ways—I had by no means abandoned study of alchemy and read a fair amount during working hours—which he conceived as odd, undesirable, even effeminate, a trait he found particularly disturbing.

'Not 'umpty-dumpty, are you?' he had enquired when he had first looked over my shoulder to see what I was reading. Strangely, it had been Thomas Norton's *Ordinall,* its *mise-en-page,* narrow ranks of rhyming couplets, adumbrating to Sgt Barker a willowiness of mind that might extend to unorthodox preferences: choir boys, other private soldiers, even Sgt Barker himself. Those fears had been allayed. Pte Potts, on the other hand, had been by no means passed as fit. Not that there was any question of 'humpty-dumptiness.' What disturbed Sgt Barker was the overall cleanness of Pte Potts's sheet. Tall, with a pale, spotty face and long wrists protruding from khaki sleeves, Potts was given to mooning about and staring into space: 'like the Goddess of Mercy dishing out wanks,' Sgt Barker said obscurely. Addicted only to sport—we discussed cricket quite often—and to crossword puzzles which he would buy in book form so he could have two or three going at one time, he neither drank nor appeared to care for women. That caused Sgt Barker great anguish.

'Look at Spots now,' he said one day when Potts was out of earshot, busy on a puzzle. ' 'E'll have spots on that phizzog of 'is until he's 'ad crumpet and a drop of the 'ard stuff. Spots is brought about in two ways and two ways only: chastity and haerated waters.'

Soon afterwards, cutaneous and psychological cures too urgent to brook further delay, Sgt Barker found an opportunity of having a word with Potts on the question of his initiation into female company. Reaction, he reported, had not been unfavourable but unenthusiastic. What had come over was a lofty and, as Sgt Barker put it, 'lacksadaisical' attitude to what was a more than pressing matter. Potts's reply was that he had yet to see a girl in the town he considered even remotely attractive. There was some truth in that estimate of local talent, conceded even by Sgt Barker. Obviously a woman such as he 'went for' would not do at all. Eventually, since he knew a quite pretty and demonstrably affectionate girl, Cpl Kinnell agreed to lend a hand. So far, I had not been involved, but the day before the scheduled assignation which Sgt Barker had expressed a wish to oversee in person, it was found that I, too, would have to be of the party. It was at Potts's insistence. 'The fact is,' he confided, 'it's the alcohol bit worries me. I can't take the drink, you see. Not even the one.' Alcohol in any form went, he said, to his stomach. I saw the problem. In different company he would have been able quite simply to refuse drinks—temperance a quality that Cpl Kinnell's girl might well admire in a man—but under Sgt Barker's eagle eye that would not be feasible. 'Sampling,' in his book, was every bit as important as getting Potts off with a girl. Refreshment and quite a lot of it would have to be seen to be taken. That was where I was to come in.

An arrangement was struck up between us that, on analysis later in the day, involved me in considerable financial gain. The plan, the first part of it anyway, was simple enough. I was to polish off each of Potts's drinks as it was purchased whether by himself or another companion. The plan's corollary was vastly convoluted, exact details never precisely clarified. It involved the use of an extra glass, switching around of other glasses, the addition of Sgt Barker's vilified 'aerated waters' to the drink of my choice that Potts could consume unadulterated without Sgt Barker's being aware it was innocent of alcohol. The colour of whatever we were going to drink would therefore look roughly the same with or without spiritous accompaniments. Very probably we settled for rum and Coke or whisky and ginger ale. Cpl Kinnell's connivance was sought, also a barmaid's. We could have done with a dress rehearsal but matters had been left too late. We could only hope for the best.

The evening was a disaster. Haste in conception spelled failure in execution. For once in his life, Sgt Barker had chosen ill. His companion, outwardly the nonpareil of his fancies, blonde, buxom, eager, it seemed, to guide him, when the time came, to the very pinnacle of his desires, whatever they might be, turned out to be rather crotchety in the evening's early stages, later, after a few drinks, disposed to break into song. Content for a while with the odd few bars, snatches plucked at random from an extensive repertoire in the hope that we might be familiar with the offerings and join in the chorus, she settled finally for a keening ballad which, in the teeth of our continued resistance, she delivered solo and on her feet:

'Lonely rivers flow to the sea, to the sea,
To the open arms of the sea,'

she sang. Her plump, beringed hands flailed the air in time to the refrain. Her light, confident voice, from which she had curbed a certain stridency that had marred earlier, more tentative efforts, wafted gracefully across the pub. Others, not of our gathering, began to sing along. A piano was struck up at the other end of the saloon bar to which people beckoned her to make her way. Soon she was surrounded by ten or so drinkers, several of whom had lined up on the top of the instrument enough drinks to sustain her through what they hoped would be a sing-along protracted enough to last until closing time. To musical accompaniment, she now repeated each verse of the love song that had first caught the attention of her new, altogether more appreciative audience and then began, in contrast, a very different 'number,' turning, admittedly, on love—or 'lerve' as she had pronounced the word whenever, with reasonable frequency, it had cropped up in the previous song—but of far more spirited, even frenetic, tempo that made me wonder if in due course she might essay something thoroughly up-to-date, more 'with it' as Ma would have said—perhaps even a Celestial Praylin song—to round off what had developed into a more or less formal musical evening.

'I know a boy called Bony Moronie;
He's as skinny as a stick of macaroni.'

The change of pace and the violent swing from sentimentality to knock-about farce was received with noisy approval by the drinkers, now quite a mass of them, around the singer, a shift in mood reaching, almost subliminally, senses Sgt Barker had acutely attuned during the singing of the ballad to how properly or otherwise we all were comporting ourselves in the various roles assigned to us for Pte Potts's baptismal night on the tiles. Now he rose to his feet. He may have stood up and begun to elbow his way through the crowded bar merely to clarify with the chanteuse those plans for 'later on' he had not made quite categorically plain to someone he expected to be by his side throughout the evening and which he could, as the hours leisurely passed by, reveal a bit at a time. There again, it may have been the words of the second song that finally goaded Sgt Barker into action, perhaps because he conceived of this surely nonexistent tubular boyfriend, Bony Moronie—in a way to be compared with his own 'Titless Susans' as figments of imagination, his and the lyricist's, on the same uniquely mythical wavelength—as a rival for his affections, whereas in her first offering much play had been made by the songwriter and embellished—indeed overembellished—by its interpreter on a craving for the sort of tenderness Sgt Barker may have assured himself, when the moment came for embraces, he would be able to satisfy in full measure. At any rate, he forced himself through the crowd and whispered something in the singer's ear while she was still in full voice. Nobody at our table heard what he said. Perhaps he went a little too far in itemising amusements for after closing time. Whatever his words were, they found little appeal: and the chanteuse dealt him a severe blow in the side with her elbow, causing him to reel backwards into the throng who, incognisant of previous acquaintance and apprehensive perhaps he had been sent to break up what had developed into an unlicensed public performance contravening pub regulations, subjected him to considerable verbal abuse. The singing recommenced and Sgt Barker, in some pain, returned to our table in poor temper. With nobody now to distract his attention, he set himself on an even more searching reconnaisance than before of how relationships were progressing between Pte Potts and the girl, Valerie Latham. He delivered two awful winks and dug Potts sharply in the ribs, a sort of retaliatory blow for the one he had taken by the piano.

' 'Ow do you like Valerie, Pottsie,' he said quite loudly. 'Is Jack jumpin' in yer breeches?' He raised his glass in salute and sank a quantity of ale. In his reciprocal toast, automatic, deeply embarrassed, Pte Potts made a bad blunder. He drank from the wrong glass.

His confidence to me that drink went to his stomach had not been one to include notice of how long it could be expected to stay there. It was uncannily brief. Only a minute or two had passed before Pte Potts clapped a hand over his mouth and made for the door.

He was gone some time, during which Cpl Kinnell decided to return to barracks. He had little cause to stay since he was not benefitting, like me, from Potts's abstention and, if Sgt Barker's plans were to come to fruition, would in any case have to make himself scarce sooner or later and deliver Valerie Latham to whatever attentions Potts might be able to muster on his return from the lavatory. He bade us good night. This further reduction to our number, now half dispersed, had the effect of reducing Sgt Barker to a sullen silence and to cast around, even at that late hour, for some substitute companion for his night of 'swiving.' He raked all corners of the pub with boot-button eyes. He must have spotted a likely victim or maybe discerned some flagging among the community singers that might release his original partner from her musical commitments. At any rate, with another of his fearful winks, he rose and vanished into the crowd. That left Valerie Latham and myself alone at the table.

Throughout the evening, on a scale exactly commensurate with the number of Pte Potts's drinks I had, along with my own, consumed, my feelings towards her had been steadily ascending. First impressions of prettiness in a chinless sort of way had, by the time Sgt Barker left us, been elevated to the realms of total infatuation. I had never seen such a beautiful girl. Furthermore, since she had been answering me quite politely and had even laughed at one or two of my jokes as well as responding with suitable awe when I mentioned how well I knew Nick Spark, I was now assured that feelings were mutual. Unspoken messages of affection, love, passion, were, I was convinced, humming between us along invisible wires: messages it would be madness for a moment longer to ignore. Through the haze of this unforeseen, quite glorious dawning of romance that Fate, with a prodigality unrecognized by Sgt Barker, indeed in resolute contradiction of his ideas about 'Titless Susans,' had so bountifully bestowed, I too made a hideous mistake. Rising to my feet in order to occupy the chair next to her that Pte Potts had vacated, I slumped unconscious to the floor.

It was Sgt Barker's claim in the thousand and one postmortems we held afterwards that his brush with the woman singer had gone unnoticed by 'the world at large,' as he put it: my alcoholic collapse the sole decisive factor in the landlord's calling for the Military Police and having our party, such as remained of it, thrown out. Here, help was forthcoming from Pte Potts, his return from the lavatory coinciding with their arrival and with the exit of Valerie Latham, who pushed past him, fed to the teeth with the lot of us. As two policemen manhandled Potts into the waiting van on the floor of which I already lay spreadeagled, the landlord had pointed to Sgt Barker now lustily singing with his arm around his friend and given the order for his removal also. Instructions were plainly delivered: 'Get that old tit-groper out of here before I do him a serious mischief.'

The three of us always managed to stifle our laughter. Sgt Barker would again protest about my 'over-sampling' at which Pte Potts would interject and remind him of the 'arrangement' between ourselves that had been its cause. Cpl Kinnell would go on to iterate relief it had not fallen to his lot to take on board refreshments of a quantity that might have felled him to the ground instead of myself. Everyone, Sgt Barker apart who, to save his own skin, was already throwing out hints upon the placement of the incident into the 'Titless Susan' bracket, felt—indeed expressed—guilt about their part in an evening that for a certainty reflected little credit on anyone involved.

What was seldom discussed were the events, taking a horrific turn, enacted in what Sgt Barker had called 'the world at large' while we were being transported to the guardroom. As it happened, I was the first to learn of them.

I had awoken the next morning frozen to the marrow covered by a thin sour-smelling blanket by the unlocking of my cell door and entry into it of a 'squaddy' dressed in fatigues who set down on a rough trestle table in the middle of the floor a tin mug of coffee.

'Wake-y, wake-y, hands off snake-y.'

The soldier swung his legs over the bench on one side of the table and sat with his chin in his hands watching my staggered movements as I made progress, still shrouded in the blanket, into the seat facing him. Generally delinquent cast of features—ears set well down a shaven skull, eyebrows meeting on the bridge of a flattened, probably broken nose—was enlivened by an enchanting smile, the smile often to be observed among the criminally insane when evidence of their wrongdoing is planted before them.

'They're letting you go back to barracks after you've had your coffee, and without a military escort. Seems they might deal with you quite lightly, as such. Any case we've got bigger trouble on our hands than you lot will keep us here all day. Like to see a pretty picture?'

He extracted from a tunic pocket a garishly coloured snapshot and slid it across to me with a slightly trembling hand. A more radiant smile than the first now accentuated rather than belied ingrained criminal habits. 'Have a squiz at that.'

I felt hideously ill. The very last diversion I wanted to engage in so early in the morning was to examine a pornographic photograph, perhaps a whole series of them each to be plucked from the soldier's clothing and passed across the table for inspection and comment. That was certainly what was on offer. I gave it therefore only the most cursory of glances, hardly enough to confirm suspicions of the art form my gaoler found so intriguing even at this hour of the day. Some comment, though, was needed, if I were to be allowed to drink my coffee in peace. This would hardly be the moment to quote Herrick's poem beginning

A sweet disorder in the dress
Kindles in clothes a wantonness

but even in my present condition—perhaps because of it, retentive fumes of alcohol still censing altars of desire however otherwise thickly palled in headache, nausea, mortification, misery—the girl's disturbed clothing, skirt vigorously hoisted, blouse torn open, arms thrown outwards back onto the bed as if the model required to be taken then and there without further disrobing, engaged just for a second attentions almost immediately re-besieged by physical pain.

'If you want my opinion, girls like that are crying out for it,' the soldier said. 'Better slip this back into the CO's office before he notices it's gone AWOL. He had time to shoot his load, look, lucky bugger, even if he was a bit off target.'

I had not so much as glanced at the girl's face. 'You don't look at the windscreen when you're cranking the car' (an old adage of Goodwin's) was cause enough not to have done so, disarranged garments appeasing (no difficult matter as I have said) whatever stimuli still reacted in the intense cold of the prison cell to consideration of amatory pursuits. Now I saw that the girl's face, harshly colour-photographed by flashlights that revealed she was not lying on a bed but somewhere out in the open on the bare earth, was lividly bruised, gashed, swollen almost beyond recognition. Not quite, however. The unconscious, perhaps dead, girl was Valerie Latham.

In the vast arena of sexual matters, the flotsam and jetsam of uniquely fleshly preferences that may turn out not to be unimportant after all but bear upon our choice of a wife and the rearing of a family—my father, for instance, who was fond of announcing he had only married my mother because she looked very 'Sixties'—there resides a discreditable attraction for rough-housing of a playful kind: 'a slap and tickle,' in Sgt Barker's outdated vernacular by no means unapt phraseology for favours granted only after some mild form of struggle. Perhaps the reason the attack was so seldom mentioned in the Orderly Room in after days, so far as I knew, was not because each of us, in our hearts, knew that he should have seen the girl safely home but because our treatment of Valerie Latham had been preparation for some sort of misusage, demarcations of callousness Pte Potts or I, given the opportunity, might have observed overstepped—that was for sure—by her attacker, yet no less calculatedly nor unjustifiably meted out. I said nothing about the photograph which I am sure none of the others ever saw, my misconstruction of its image, first time around, when I had been briefly stimulated by a girl, in my gaoler's words 'crying out for it,' haunting me for some time to come.

We did send flowers though, not unexpectedly returned by Valerie's father with a curt note. They sat about the Orderly Room for a week or two. Then one day Cpl Kinnell tossed them into the wastepaper basket and poured the water—brackish, evil-smelling—out of the window. Its miasma floated back into our work area. Sgt Barker proposed a cup of tea.

Before my escapade, we used to see little of Major Hamilton, our CO. A bluff, sandy-haired man, rather broad in the beam, unmarried, suspected by Sgt Barker of being 'humpty-dumpty,' he took not the slightest interest in our work, or so we thought; and his sudden appearance in our Orderly Room on the Friday afternoon following my month's confinement to barracks was originally construed by Cpl Kinnell and Pte Potts as a direct result of our escapade four weeks before. In their eyes, that had alerted Major Hamilton to the possibility of poor behaviour's spilling over into duty hours: hence the raid. To our relief, Sgt Barker's analytical mind had already got to work. Consultation with others of his rank confirmed that our bit of trouble had been no isolated tremor on Major Hamilton's seismograph of 'unsatisfactoriness,' no more remarkable an oscillation, in any event, than many others he had been recording in the quiet of his office. It was the opinion of the Sergeants' Mess that Barker had become too 'pally' with the other ranks: slack too in details of administration he was charged with overseeing: a 'visit' had for a long time been on the cards. There remained, however, the timing of Major Hamilton's inspection. That was where Sgt Barker was so vastly impressed; and worry the evidence though he did, recomposing the afternoon again and again in his mind's eye, there endured for all time the inexorable hand of fate, the monstrous ill-chance of all of us sitting idly about that, reticent though he had been on some of the aspects of 'Titless Susans,' unwilling up to then to expatiate on what he held to be a universal truth, whenever afterwards anyone asked him exactly what he meant, this particular example was held up as illustration.

Friday—'Poet's Day,' Sgt Barker called it, acronym for 'Piss Off Early, Tomorrow's Saturday'—tended to drag in the morning, work to be eventually dispensed with shortly after lunch, although, in case of emergency, we could not actually shut up shop until five o'clock. It must have been around half-past three when the blow fell, the afternoon autumnal, sunny, on the cool side. Sgt Barker had remarked on the fall of temperature and had helped Pte Potts to get the Orderly Room stove going. Then he had 'brewed up' and settled down with the newspaper. Mugs of his orange tea steamed before us. The fire burned and crackled. Cpl Kinnell was turning the pages of his collected Rochester; Pte Potts, wearing his Goddess of Mercy look, brooded on a puzzle. I was drowsily reading Thomas Norton's *Ordinall of Alchemy,* with not a shred of the concentration the author demanded from students of his text. *Not once or twice but xx. times it would not be over-saying:* that was Norton's estimate of the number of readings necessary for anything like serious application to his poem. The line swam mistily before my eyes. Its exhortation fell on deaf ears. Or not quite deaf ears. Music from our radio, sinuous, Oriental, composed for the accompaniment of veiled dancing girls in a languorous measure, impinged on the only faculty not exactly dormant. Fumes from our cigarettes and the aromatic wood we had found to burn on the stove, that by now heated the Orderly Room to a temperature in which dancing girls, had they been present, would cheerfully have stripped to the buff, swirled narcotically around, abetting Eastern fantasies. Major Hamilton, when he burst in, may too have found himself overcome. He stood, at any rate, motionless for quite a while. Around his silhouette, bands of sunlight pierced accusingly into the dim recesses of the office. The temperature dropped. A gust of wind plucked Sgt Barker's newspaper from his grasp. We rose bemusedly to our feet.

He bore down on each of us in turn. He peered into Sgt Barker's cup; into all our cups come to that. He picked up Potts's puzzle book and flung it high into the air. In recognition, it might have been, of a higher level of scholarship that engaged Cpl Kinnell's attention and my own, he resisted similar urges with our reading matter but nevertheless whipped out pencil and notebook from his tunic pocket and jotted down the titles, together with the time of day which he ascertained from his wristwatch. The Orderly Room clock, I noted, was wrong. Then, with the same keenness of eye that Sgt Barker employed to rake public houses, he set off on a thorough inspection of the hut, opening drawers, peering in cupboards, prodding objects with his swagger stick, scraping dust out of corners, adding the while to the notes in his pocketbook. His face had taken on an unhealthy, choleric hue as if the atmosphere, rapidly clearing though it was, threatened him with suffocation.

The raid, which took a long time, was carried out in total silence apart from the music which nobody ventured to turn off. The wonder was that its gingerly meanderings—ever more redolent of bazaar, caravanserai, harem—should have for so long gone unnoticed. When he eventually heard it, Major Hamilton could not believe his ears. He marched over to the shelf where the radio stood and snatched it up. He peered hard at it and twiddled various knobs, succeeding only in increasing the volume that rose to unsuitable, almost Celestial Praylin, levels of sound. He opened his mouth to speak but he must have realized he was being rendered inaudible by the din of his own creating. Passion in any case would have hampered a coherent sentence. Visual confiscation of the apparatus there and then, he seemed to reason, would at least convey displeasure if that continued to escape us. He tucked the radio under his arm, turned on his heel and bore the instrument, still loudly playing, from the room.

We crowded to the door. Blasts of a northeasterly across the barrack square augured in their chill winds of change that would come sweeping across our lives and carried with them too the diminishing notes from the portable radio: flute, gong, cymbal. In a fearful travesty of Sgt Barker's suspicions of Major Hamilton's 'humpty-dumptiness,' his departing buttocks undulated to the serpentine rhythms.

Retribution came at once, brutal in its effects. 'Good-bye to crumpet, good-bye to sampling,' Sgt Barker commented when he brought the news: 'and for some time to come.' We worked as we had never worked before. Leave was canceled; extra duties imposed; cleaning materials issued for a thorough overhaul of the Orderly Room; the radio, books, other personal belongings, Sgt Barker's teapot and milk jug, banned from our place of work. It was a period of cruel, merciless graft, during which only Sgt Barker's philosophy gave any cheer. The effects of a 'Titless Susan' expired, he explained, with time. Karmic laws, of vigorous application, were, notwithstanding, scrupulously fair. Sooner or later we could expect fetters to be unchained. Cpl Kinnell, Pte Potts and I struggled to accept his faith. Days passed; and surely enough, together with measures we had contrived for cutting corners, came an easing of the pressure. Leave-passes were renewed; inspections became less frequent; some kind of compromise reached about making of tea; there was a general lifting of the 'atomosphere'; and when one day I was again called up before Major Hamilton, Sgt Barker was able to declare with absolute confidence that it could have nothing to do with the past. Admittedly, he could find no reason for the summons, mulling that over for some time, finally giving out that there would be revealed at last tangible proof of our CO's proclivities, his 'humpty-dumptiness,' as he again put it.

'That'll be it, lads,' he opined and gave one of his terrible winks. ' 'E fancies 'im. It's 'is lily white body the Major's after, lily white body and thighs. 'Is kettle's whistlin', Pte Graves, and 'im being your superior hofficer, 'e'll look to you to take it from the boil.'

Major Hamilton greeted me with the surprised grunt of a master acknowledging arrival of a summoned butler, appreciation shown for the speed with which a staircase has been negotiated or a sobering-up in the pantry seamlessly achieved. To my concern, he had adopted a pose of extreme informality. His beefy frame reposed on his bed in shirtsleeve order, his belt was undone, his feet were tucked into soft leather moccasins. His big, freckled head was supported by a number of snowy pillows. Books, none of a military nature, lay all around. Whitman's *Leaves of Grass* did nothing to relieve agitation. I saluted in the doorway.

'Ah, Pte Graves. Shut the door.' Major Hamilton eased himself up the bed. 'You're leaving us shortly?'

'Six weeks, sir.'

'Any ideas for the future?'

'Not really.'

'Ever thought of staying on?'

'No, sir.'

'Why not?' Major Hamilton swung his legs off the bed and sat up. 'We treat you well here, don't we, unless you're getting smashed out of your head. We don't drive you too hard, give you plenty of time to find the Philosopher's Stone or whatever it is I caught you looking for. I own I'd feel a certain pride if I could boast the elixir of life had been discovered in my Orderly Room by one of my men, but,' he levered off a slipper, 'I can't actively encourage it. Others might. Others I could put you in touch with.'

'I'm open to suggestions, sir.' It seemed, as I said it, an unfortunate phrase.

'I'm suggesting nothing. I'm a soldier, pure and simple. But I dine with colleagues occasionally, in other lines of country. They ask me about my staff: any loners, cranks, geniuses. I can't very often say yes.'

'Which category did you place me in, sir?'

Major Hamilton chuckled. 'I may tell them you are open to suggestions, as you put it?'

I hesitated.

'Half open, then?'

'Yes, sir.'

He held out his hand. I shook it. 'Good man,' he said. 'It's useful work, I'm told.'

3

Just before my demob, Nicholas had bought Carpenter's, a country house in Sussex, where he had invited me to a party. Perhaps because Pte Potts's girl had been so impressed by our acquaintanceship, I too began to see its advantages, to bask, as we met every so often, in his fame and to take much pride in being seen in his company. Encapsulated in the warm, dark, luxuriously appointed interior of his limousine, which the tinted windows bathed in a torrid amber luminosity like the sand-coloured light that, in summer, presages thunder, I particularly enjoyed being able to examine, through the glass, the faces of the girls who, whenever we drove in and out of his gates, would cluster round and gaze in on us with lovelorn eyes. That little knot of fans was another indication of his growing popularity. For my part I had no idea how I was going to make my way in the world on any level of glory or success. My father bought for me a tiny flat in London, near the cricket ground. It would, he remarked with an expansiveness that suggested he had used my mother's money to make the purchase, give me 'time to look round.'

Alone for the first time in twenty-three years, I began to calculate for how long this period of idleness could be spun out. I pictured my little flat filled up with girls or at least visited by a procession of them in single file, no very great time gap between calls; long days watching cricket; riding holidays at Carpenter's; hours at the British Library at work on Thomas Norton whose *Ordinall* I had finally decided to edit. Such dreams were short-lived. Not very long after taking up residence, a terrible lethargy began to enter the soul. As the walls fell away of the various civilised prisons in which I had been raised, my mind emptied itself of everything except a strange introspection, a critical examination of each and every action I performed. At first I hardly noticed anything was amiss, felt only an occasional unease, a tiny dark presence of foreboding, perhaps of evil, but the very act of acknowledging this lone, baneful cell that floated every so often to the surface of the mind was enough to nourish it and nurture its growth. Soon it flourished fatly on the increasing attention, the regular daily feeds that, ever more lavish in my contemplation of its nature, I bestowed upon it.

Work became impossible since I was merely watching my pen move over the paper. Alternatives, cricket, riding Nicholas's horses, set up an immediate suspicion that I could no longer experience happiness. Happiness, a sensation perhaps in any case only to be acknowledged in retrospect, continued to elude me because of my watchfulness to see if I could again attain to it. I became two people, a person who performed certain mechanical functions to achieve that happiness (as a drunkard will down drink after drink in the effort to reach euphoria) and a watcher of that person, my own melancholy critic. Certain alarming sophistications of this fragmentation of personality began to manifest themselves: sudden swirling panics, a fear of fire or of an unspecified tragedy in which I would cause harm to innocent people. I believed madness would strike suddenly, bloodily, in an attack on an elderly woman or on a child. I entertained suspicions that it was I who had raped Valerie Latham; that I had not passed out in the pub after all but lured her outside the building, beaten her up and returned to my seat: and when very quickly I recalled the 'squaddy' had hinted they were holding the culprit in custody I only slightly modified my train of thought and recalled my shameful excitement at the photograph of her injured body which, in my present state, I conceived had been the catalyst—as early sexual experiences are supposed to be—for aberrations of a sadistic kind to which I could, at any time, fall prey. I threw out from the flat all potentially dangerous weapons, carving knives, a hammer, a pair of kitchen scissors. I could see only their menace and their capacity to wound.

For a while, there were periods of respite. My doppelgänger had strange habits, some predictable, others less so. It was curiously prudish, laid low if I were drinking or in bed with a girl: activities, to keep it at bay, I began to overindulge. A night's sleep dispelled it for a while the following morning, as if, like a gaoler who knows his prisoner is shackled and does not rouse himself when he hears the rattle of chains, it was assured I was still at its mercy; but those times when I did forget, when the watcher and the watched merged into a healthy oneness, became less and less frequent until, after an incident on an October morning, they halted altogether.

I was in the park, on the path I would later take to ALEMBIC, that skirted the lake with the herons' island, when, some hundred yards in front of me, I saw a mother and her little girl. They walked towards me hand in hand. Hardly close enough for more detailed observation, I noted only two things about them. The woman wheeled an empty pushchair, conveyance obviously for the child although she looked too well-grown for it. Apart from that, the only other thing that struck me, a contrivance that I, any other passerby for that matter, was intended to inspect, since the child was slouching along and peering from side to side in the hope of finding someone to alarm, was the grotesque pink rubber mask with which she had covered her face.

There was, unusually, nobody about. The mother, upon whom the disguise might have been tried too often, stared blankly ahead. Reaction was up to me. It seemed a pity that the artifact, which certainly had splendidly ghoulish qualities and had most likely been an expensive acquisition—perhaps the reason for the mother's rather stony aspect—should not receive some acknowledgment of excellence. This could be most rewardingly testified by my pretending to be scared out of my wits. As we passed, therefore, I assumed an expression of horror and shock every bit as exaggerated as the mask itself. I gave a scream and clapped my hands over my mouth. Too late to alter my absurd reactions, to wipe from my face the mock terror in my popping eyes and snatch my hands away and set shut my gaping mouth, I saw that it was not a mask that so dreadfully contorted the small girl's features but her own skin and bone. The child was a mongol.

For hours I contemplated my appalling mistake. The child's misshapen features had seemed to register dismay. The mother's eyes had turned on me in as much agony and disbelief as if, with one of the knives I had thrown away, I had stabbed her in the neck. I could not erase the incident from my mind. I spent the whole day trying to work out how I could atone for what I had done, communicate in some way with the mother and explain my real intention. Not until the evening, when some of the poison had at last begun to drain away, did my mental censor return. The entire day, the first for weeks, had passed without its insidious presence. Now, however, it gave the event its own interpretation, twisted it and worked it into radically different shapes that, while they relieved the shame and confusion still uppermost in my mind, presented sinister and far more worrying significances. It made me wonder if anything had happened at all.

The park had been abnormally empty. From beginning to end, from the moment I had entered it by the boating pool until I left it again, almost at a run, past the seat where Miss Benke had encountered the Master of the Orange Robe, I had seen absolutely nobody except the mother and her daughter. That could hardly be. Furthermore, I could not comprehend how I could possibly have taken the child's head, deformed, too big for her body, hideously ugly, to have been a mask. I saw it all now, or my censor did, as an hallucination.

Yet, despite the fact I was now convinced I was 'seeing things,' the lesson learned was that, to dismiss my censor, I would have to seek out regular shocks of this kind: try to set up, day after day, until I was cured, the sort of raging torment the incident in the park had brought about. Only in such circumstances, locked out by the fierceness of other mental preoccupations, could I once more be at one with myself.

I had no clear plan how to initiate this revolutionary life-style except, as a start, to go and stay with Nicholas. I had, in any case, fallen in love with Carpenter's, a long, low, comfortable grey Sussex house and its rambling grounds and although I could not expect, as on my first visit, it would bring me peace, I believed I would find a foretaste of the perils I had made up my mind to embrace. There, since Nicholas's music was their constant celebration, would be girls, drugs, drink, but there was also a powerful black stallion, named Vindictive. When Nicholas had suggested I should have a shot at breaking him in, I had nervously refused. Now it seemed exactly the challenge I sought.

In a way, I struck lucky: in a way not. Vindictive turned out to have gone lame, was unridable for a month, in any case thoroughly broken in. On the other hand, the first night coincided with a party, at my arrival—by no means late in the evening—already in full swing. Nicholas was nowhere to be seen among revelers, all of them unfamiliar to me, who thronged the whole of the ground-floor accommodation and overflowed a spacious entrance hall onto the lawn in front of the house. Music, uniquely Celestial Praylin music, blasted across the shouting, laughing, quarreling components of an assembly that, had the newspapers been present, would have been designated an 'orgy.' Perhaps that was why the musicians themselves were nowhere to be seen. A certain newfound unsociability coloured Nicholas's life these days that could well be attributed to wishing to avoid publicity of an adverse kind—unless deliberately orchestrated to get him into the news—but on the other hand now he was so enormously rich there was no longer the necessity to mix with all and sundry. Probably it was the latter reason that had prompted Nicholas's absence, for nothing resembling an orgy was in progress. To be sure, Carpenter's was full to bursting with young people having a good time: eating, drinking, dancing, embracing, out cold. A couple, perhaps not man and woman, exchanged languid caresses under the portico of the main entrance. Another visitor, indisputably male, stripped of all clothing apart from shoes and socks, was being dragged upright but deeply unconscious by two shrieking girls who nearly overturned me on the driveway as they hurried their sleeping companion, feet trailing, into the night air. Within, in a small dining room through which the same music was being piped at equally tumultuous volume, a silent intent group sat cross-legged in a semicircle passing round a joint and consulting the I Ching. At the far end of the crowded vestibule some sort of game was in progress. Another splinter group of the party, predominantly male, jumped wildly up and down around the perimeter of a monstrous brass urn much their own height set at the foot of the stairs and employed as a general rule as a dinner gong, its deep, immensely satisfying reverberations when struck with a mallet penetrating into the farthest recesses of the house, even of the garden, at times when meals were to be served. Now some object or other, perhaps quite valuable, prize for whatever competition was in progress, had been hurled into the cavernous depths of this gigantic metal receptacle, the irretrievability of which was frustrating to the point of frenzy the ten or so participants who more or less in turn in obedience, it might be, to an obscure ruling of this indoor sport, propelled themselves into the air and thumped heavily, sometimes overturning in the process, back to the ground.

These divergencies from absolutely perfect social behaviour, in no sense to be accounted orgiastic, constituted only the smallest section of a get-together no more than rowdily convivial. People—with the exception of the young man in the garden perhaps given to such extravagancies or suffering some kind of fit—were not going to tear off their clothes at the touch of a button and grapple on the carpet. I was conscious of a certain disappointment that this was not going to be the case: infected too, despite a draught of Nicholas's brandy someone had offered me, with whatever factor it is in the human spirit, not easy to dislodge, that generates a deep depression at the sight of other people having a good time. I pushed my way through the merry-makers around the urn and began to ascend the staircase. By an unwritten rule of draconian stringency that reflected, I dare say, the aloofness now beginning to colour his life-style although (obviously) not to the extent of denying hospitality to myself and, if the guests downstairs were legitimate ones, to scores of others, Nicholas forbade all but personal friends above ground-floor level. I reasoned it would be in order, as a houseguest, to go up and see if the first-floor bedroom, allotted to me on an earlier visit, had again been put to my use. I stopped on the landing and peered over the banisters. The cause of the commotion round the gong was immediately apparent.

Three or four girls, perhaps more, had clambered or been precipitated into the bowels of this enormous receptacle, its spun concave interior making egress troublesome if not humanly impossible. As a gloomy accompaniment to the music, muffled echoes, screams, one assumed, of pleasure or terror, issued at intervals from the gong's inky black recesses, upon the surface of which occasionally broke a head or a stockinged foot betraying as feminine the otherwise unidentifiable mass of partially clad flesh that seethed in more or less regular undulations as though, at a cannibals' feast, the girls, undissected, were being cooked up alive. The crowd, cannibalistic too in their glee at the girls' plight, to which in fact the rhythmic rise and fall of their bodies suggested, despite their cries, they had become fatalistically resigned as if, of poor moral fibre in their lifetime, they found their souls despatched to some Dantean hell-pit, continued to leap up and down in attempts to verify who of their number was among the entrapped. Some broke away to pursue more orthodox forms of party-going. New arrivals took their place. Because of the embargo about going upstairs, nobody had as good a view as I of this stew of girls, the richly simmering *daube* which, culinarily speaking, had been set on just too high a burner, so that whenever one of the constituents arched her back or shot out an arm, there threatened a lack of final delicacy from the concoction's being brought a little too rapidly to the boil. At least, for a while I was alone. Then I was aware of someone's joining me. A man had made his way up the staircase and along the landing. He took his place next to me and leaned over the banisters as if he had been taking an after-dinner 'turn' on the deck of an ocean liner.

It would have needed to be a liner maintaining prewar standards of excellence to have lured on board the man now standing by my side. To judge from appearances, he was the very last person to have been asked to come along to a cacophonous assemblage of the sort now in progress, its hosts, guests as well (rock music's adherents as a class, for the matter of that) inclined to denigrate those who have achieved the riper years my companion owned in full measure. Still harder to imagine were the kinds of inducement other than some unsavoury errand—perhaps the retrieval of a wayward grandson or goddaughter found to have absconded here at an infuriatingly late hour of the day—that had persuaded this man to have put in an appearance at a gathering for a certainty violently opposed to the sort of function which he would have willingly graced with his presence. A royal garden party: a box at the Eton and Harrow: an embassy soirée: the promenade deck of a private yacht: those were this man's stamping grounds. Dressed in a dark three-piece pin-striped suit, stiff collar, club tie, he owned touches of the onstage 'breeding' of Robert Ferguson, but his features, heavily etched both vertically and perpendicularly in contradistinction to the actor's boyishly smooth skin, were untouched by the almost fictional *chic* upon which Ferguson drew to ascend—in the end of things only to run a poor second—to this person's impromptu mannerliness. A full head, nearly a mane of hair but without any hint of being coiffured—another affectation of Ferguson's it was said by Nicholas—trained back from the deeply lined forehead matched in clinical whiteness arching eyebrows and a brusquely clipped moustache. In point of fact, I was uncertain why Robert Ferguson should have sprung to mind at all: perhaps only because of a retrospective—'Thirties'—suavity that at first sight could be taken for a mutual possession. My neighbour's demeanour, old-fashioned though it was, seemed after all to owe nothing to stagecraft. Dissembling of any sort had been called upon in what I judged to be an ambassadorial past only on occasions when, against his wishes, he might have needed to defer to, more likely bring firmly round to his way of thinking, other officials as high-ranking as himself, or higher ones if such existed, by the deployment, almost a second nature, of the charm, diplomacy, good sense, courtesy, native wit, with which my one casual glance sufficed to assure me he was imbued. His craggy, distinguished face displayed no emotion at all—humour, surprise, distaste, impatience—at the bizarre scene below on which steady grey eyes were impassively focused as if on Old Boys' Day he had paused around familiar walls to watch a few seconds of a rugby scrimmage, although a slight flaring of the nostrils gave away that one at least of the keenly honed senses with which he appreciated life was attuned to fragrances and, for that matter, less agreeable odours wafted up the well of the stairway from the gently seething, sighing vesselful of girls beneath our feet.

For fragrances there were in plenty, subtly though they were, from this height, diffused: a potpourri of perfumes and toilet waters and the natural sweetness of young girls' skin, soap suds used on singlets and jeans by those, by no means all of them, who had donned clean clothes for the night's entertainment, across which cut from time to time ranker odours that entered the nostrils along with the scent of flowers and musk as if a child, rather a variety of children, had run under our noses fingers dirtied in the course of play or in private exploration to disgust, it might be to tempt, responses already stirred by the more congenial essences, by far the more prevalent, we also inhaled.

'Ah,' the man said, 'a coven of witches. But for a change entrapped in their own cauldron instead of dancing around it giving trouble.'

' "Double, double, toil and trouble." '

'That is theirs with a vengeance. How I would love to kiss each one of them in turn upon the seven entrances of her body. Rapture, rapture.'

The man released his hold on the banisters and turned slowly to ascend with care, as if a little lame, the staircase that led to the second storey where Nicholas and the band had their private stronghold. Assurance that he was in one way or another 'privileged,' British ambassador perhaps in some country—America, Japan, West Germany—where Celestial Praylin had cut up rough and whence he was bearing news that, through his own personal intervention, the incident had been smoothed over, was in no respect undermined by this casual ascension to levels of the house under an even more stringent interdict against trespassers than those on which we had been exchanging our few words. On the other hand, the sudden, not far off prurient, revelation of sexual preferences by this 'diplomat,' as I continued to think of him, even taking into account the unlikelihood he might, after all, have been infected with the party spirit downstairs and found it alleviative to an otherwise exhaustingly formal round of duties, rather demeaned him in my eyes. At least, it made for difficulties. Activity in this, at times, flippant arena, should be supposed to have gone altogether against the grain: been 'beneath him,' as it were. It was hard enough to imagine this immensely distinguished personage lying down, even sitting down, let alone naked in a state of arousal. To be sure, amusements along the lines he had ventured as 'rapturous' did not require that he should take his clothes off, yet they adumbrated, certainly in part, a servility, even an abasement, totally alien to his nature. It had to be admitted, though, he had made his point clearly enough. Appetites had been sharpened by the tableau he had observed from on high. There had been some quickening of the blood. There was no question about that. The answer might be that he had perceived in the undoubtedly erotic spectacle of a whole lot of girls one on top of the other demonstrations of lesbian affection so stirring almost as a rule of thumb to any heterosexual male—even a man 'in his position' by no means indifferent to this virtually universal stimulus—perhaps because of the double (in this instance, multiple) chances of seducing the combatants from their sterile endeavours, most readily brought about, to this man's way of thinking, by the implantation upon each and every partner in turn of his septenary of kisses. Be that as it might, impassivity, as a long-exercised discipline in life, continued to hold the upper hand: directed the diplomat upstairs upon whatever mission he had with Nicholas and his musicians.

There again, it was possible to dismiss priapic motives altogether. His insistence upon the number seven might have held occult significance, rather in the way alchemical texts often infer, on a first reading, an almost pornographic connotation that veils exegesis of far loftier esoteric precepts. His reference to the seven entrances of the body perhaps led on from the idea of witchcraft propounded in his reference to the brass gong as a cauldron, each of those orifices to be ceremonially sealed with a wizard's kiss against the entry of unwitchlike, presumably Christian, pneumata, part perhaps of the initiation ceremony of a budding sorceress.

Among Nicholas's official and unofficial entourage could always be found a fair sprinkling of new-lifers, simple-lifers, vegetarians, magicians black and white, spiritualists, Buddhists of the crankier kind, among whom too witches were very possibly also to be numbered. For all I knew their ranks also held the odd alchemist or two perhaps because rock music, when not being self-congratulatory and applauding its own efforts like performing seals clap their own tricks, or celebrating—though less specifically—the sort of pleasures the diplomat—now vanished into the fastnesses of the house's upper regions—had admitted were his own, proposed an alternative life-style that, even if not along the sectarian lines, however divergent, adhered to by Nicholas's followers, nevertheless threatened to topple by its insidious invasion into the established order of things the constitutions whereby society had for many years been jogging along. The diplomat could be an exponent of the 'craft,' high priest (he would have accepted no less exalted a post) within a coven giving trouble: blighting crops; blasting enemies; casting spells; generally running magically amok and ripe for a taste of their own thaumaturgical medicine.

Thoughts were interrupted by a commotion below. All of a sudden a man burst through the crowd of revelers assembled round the gong and strode up to the rim. At least a head taller than even the tallest of the men through whose company he was so roughly scything a path, he was comfortably able to peer into the bulbous vessel and ascertain the cause of a rumpus that might have been disturbing this man's enjoyment of other aspects of festivities in progress in an adjoining room. Not that he looked in the very least angry, nor for that matter was any of the crowd especially put out by the intrusion of this powerfully built, well-nigh musclebound giant who, as he wrapped his arms around the gong's circumference and hung a luxuriantly whiskered face over its interior, gave appearances he might raise the capacious *objet d'art* bodily above his head and upend its squirming contents onto the carpet. This was Celestial Praylin's drummer, Scotty, encountered a couple of times in Nicholas's company. On both occasions, he had barely contributed to the conversation, general though that had been. He looked then and now utterly, irradicably miserable. Reticence, all but total silence, had proposed—still did propose—his was a life overshadowed by despondency, even clinical depression. Loudermilk, when I eventually met him, was overladen—again occupationally as it turned out—with very much the same woebegone cast of countenance but this was Loudermilk's lugubriousness multiplied a hundredfold. Even pounding away at his drum kit, which he attacked as if he were singlehandedly fighting off a body of men swarming over castle battlements—bashing them over the head, kicking them in the teeth—Scotty's habitual careworn features remained unlit by any trace of demonstrativeness transcending this absolute hangdog misery which the recent cultivation of a heavy black drooping moustache now amplified to almost comical proportions. This evening, he looked like a very old-fashioned, gigantically structured, suicidally disposed grocer selected to illustrate in a book of Victorian photographs the consequences of falling trade in some urban area of acute financial recession.

Like the diplomat before him, Scotty was vastly unconcerned, except with the insurmountable problems of his own forever perpending, at what caught his eye. Blackest, deepest gloom still uniquely overlaid features overhanging the brass gong, as if, by a tarn of unfathomable deepness, he had at last decided to take his own life. Then again suggesting proximity to water, this time a water tank containing marine life, he rolled up his sleeves and, plunging bare brawny arms deep down inside the receptacle, scooped out over the rim the girl that moment uppermost in its depths. He held her kicking and yelling at arms' length until, like a netted fish, her struggles died away. Pushing his way back through the crowd, he slowly ascended the staircase to where I was standing and, not for a second allowing to dissolve from his face his customary expression of terminal melancholy, so that, to look at him, he might have been carrying the lifeless form of a loved one, he dumped her at my feet.

'Here you are, squire,' he said. 'Have this one on me.'

Scotty set upright on the carpet a small thin girl dressed in one of the band's 'official' T-shirts, the one with the skeletal portrait of Nicholas extending to the heavens his blood-soaked heart, and a pair of baggy purple 'Turkish' trousers. The girl rocked back and forth on her heels without otherwise moving a muscle like a showroom dummy dumped sharply down in a window by a shopfitter anxious to get off to his lunch; and then collapsed in my arms. She stood on tiptoe and covered my face with kisses. Scotty stared disconsolately over her shoulder not as if he regretted parting with a gift demonstrably to his advantage to have kept for himself but as if he abhorred bitterly and to the depths of his soul each and every second of time that extended a life span on earth already saturated in misery. He trudged morosely away upstairs.

His ascent, almost as if he had depressed a button concealed under the stair carpet with one of his huge feet, coincided with the switching-off of the music. The hubbub of conversation on this level, high above the hall, barely intruded into a silence as unexpected as it was chillingly lowering of temperatures a moment ago conducive to hugging and kissing: activities which, if the girl's enthusiasm could be a little bit toned down, I was eager to recommence. We began to whisper.

'Hi.'

'Hello.'

'You're Tom, yeah?'

'Yes.'

'I'm Phyllidula.'

'Are you with the band?'

Phyllidula threw back her head and raised her eyes to the roof rather as Potts's girl, when I had mentioned I knew Nicholas, had ventured in that same despairing gesture the ecstasy and the hopelessness of such a dream's ever coming true.

'No. I hang about the house sometimes. Occasionally I get lucky. Well, twice, actually, Scotty's asked me in.'

This, then, was one of the girls who stood vigil at Nicholas's gateway. He had spoken warmly of these fans of his. 'They are an enormously valuable section of society. In my more eclectic days they had, of course, their obvious uses. But they also sew on my buttons. I can find nobody else, nobody at all, who will sew on a button for me. Like King Lear, really, although, naturally, I am much more famous. Cordelia would have risen from the grave to ply her needle on one of my buttons.'

'Lear wanted to be unbuttoned actually.'

Nicholas had made light of this example of literary pedantry. 'Did he? Oh, well, in that case there would have been no difficulty whatsoever. Unbuttoning people is second nature to those girls.'

That seemed true enough. Phyllidula threw her arms around me once more. We began to caress to music once more thumping upwards from downstairs, at which a terrific cheer had gone up as faulty mechanism had been set to rights or someone—Nicholas himself, perhaps, storming in and switching it off because he wanted everyone out of the house—had been persuaded to allow revelry to continue on its way.

There was much to be said for kissing to rock music. Bass pulsations reverberating like earthquake tremors through the body heightened proceedings already pleasurable enough in embracing someone 'new.' In a way, especially now I craved regular indulgence with women to keep at bay those fears of madness that, as I traded kiss for kiss with Phyllidula, beat their expected retreat, that was probably why, later on, I always got on well with the cooks. Early on at ALEMBIC, before we got properly acquainted, Bastable had been grumbling about a current girlfriend: 'Sometimes I think I'll make a complete change.' 'To what?' Goodwin had asked. 'Goats? Monks? Watermelons? The dead?' Bastable explained he meant only that yet another change of partners was at the back of his mind. That seemed far more understandable when I reflected on nights such as these when I felt that to be 'in love' with a girl could arouse in me feelings of cruelty towards her—towards anyone 'cherished' for that matter: alarms to be compared, though less rationally, with Lindo's apprehensions of impotence unless companions were replaced—like Bastable's—with reasonable frequency. Perhaps Phyllidula too was driven by forces deriving from similar insecurities. Certainly it was hard to divine from where effervescence originated: passion; ingestion of drugs; a shrewd business sense.

A phrase of Ezra Pound's then came to mind: 'Phyllidula is scrawny but amorous.' Pound's girl had been a prostitute, I seemed to recall. This dispiriting trade did not seem to fit the girl in my arms, although hers was as sad, even as desperate, an existence. Sewing on buttons, twice sharing Scotty's bed, if that had been the fee for her double admittance to the house, requirement now to make love to one of his friends (as she quite incorrectly labeled me) consequent upon the band's newfound lordliness that forbade her any more their fellowship, was as much as she could hope for.

Nevertheless, enthusiasm had not waned. She broke away momentarily and, fumbling in her trousers pocket, produced a door key.

'Scotty said we can use his room. Come on. We can get naked.'

We hurried up the stairs and traversed a wide, thickly carpeted corridor. I began to feel anxious, friendly though I was with Nicholas, that intrusion into his private territory with a girl in tow, intimate with Scotty or not, might give rise to annoyance. Phyllidula stopped in front of a stout mahogany door. 'They're in there,' she said. 'Let's listen a sec.'

'Suppose they come out?'

'They won't. They've got Tex Ringenberg in there. It's an important meeting.'

Phyllidula pushed back her bunch of wild, wiry, black hair and pressed her ear to the woodwork. From where I still uneasily stood, I could hear the muffled, cultivated tones of the diplomat—implausibly now identified as 'Tex Ringenberg'—suddenly interrupted by Nicholas's higher-pitched, no less 'grand' accents.

'Just because some fucker goes "twang," ' Nicholas was shouting, 'and we happen to go "twang" the same way, those cripples who go under the name of rock critics complain all we're doing is being derivative, imitating some crap band like the Experimental Rumble Strips. God in Heaven, there's only seven notes, A, B, C, D, E and whatever the other two are called. Somebody's got to repeat something somewhere along the line. Can't they get that into their heads?'

Phyllidula pursed her lips in acknowledgment of the acrimoniousness of the conference in progress. We tiptoed onwards: turned a corner. Another flight of stairs of a meaner kind led to an attic. She pushed open the first door she came to and ushered me inside. Locking the door behind her, she threw herself onto an unmade bed and beckoned me to join her.

Desires had very much subsided on this foray into personal premises, authorised though it seemed to be by her possession of a key to the slant-ceilinged quarters on which Scotty had set his own infinitely disheveled mark. Dirty clothes, pieces of drum kits, records, dumbbells, comic papers, lay strewn all over a carpet heavy with the dust of ages. Indeed as I joined Phyllidula on the bed and dissuaded her from stripping her gory T-shirt over her head, Tex Ringenberg's comment (if it had been made by him) concerning Nicholas's music, rock and roll in general, he may have meant, seemed applicable to lovemaking as well: love's progress, like the music, a circumscribed journey, to Tex Ringenberg's way of thinking, around the seven 'entrances' of the body and, if one were to accept his equation, of startling coequality, mathematically speaking, with the seven musical notes itemized by Nicholas in the course of the 'row' downstairs: every so often returning to the place where one first ventured out: a tour of duty in Sgt Barker's military jargon.

Certainly, Phyllidula, prevented from undressing, had set herself upon a course of action automatic enough of stimulation yet cheerless other than physically in a drilled execution to be thought of, disappointingly, as performed under orders. In the days before fastidiousness had coloured Nicholas's way of life so far as girls were concerned, the chore on which she was now engaged and which expertness of technique other than a certain watchfulness as to its eventual fulfillment was unable to disguise as anything other than routine, had become, so Nicholas said, the unique means of the band's gratification with one of Phyllidula's kind. Reasons for its popularity very likely sprang as much from ease of execution within cramped, cold, outdoor as well as indoor conditions when time was precious—just before the band hit the stage or took to the road—as from any diversion attributable to the sensation—exquisitely pleasurable though I was finding it—or from the servility—even humiliation—of womankind engaged in an active yet altogether demeaning role. Nicholas enjoyed relating an encounter of this overhurried nature in a backstage 'gents' when, just after its completion, his bass player had come in and, unaware of events, greeted the young lady—well-known to him as well—with a smacking kiss on lips that still glistened with Nicholas's so-recent achievement.

So far as I was concerned, speed was no longer of the essence. Between Scotty's walls—plastered with posters of football teams, fast cars, enlargements of characters from the comics lying about the floor—realisation I might be found as estimable as he made me, in a way, 'become' Scotty, because I suspected Phyllidula's enthusiasm was compounded by the stricture of Nicholas's and perhaps Scotty's own declining catholicity of taste. Within this new regime, girlfriends, even at this moment perhaps sitting in on the meeting with Tex Ringenberg, were drawn from echelons of society to which those girls at the gate, of inferior age, breeding, looks, intellect, could lay no claim. Starved of affection from their heroes, the closest they could now get to sleeping with the band was to sleep with the band's friends. This acceptance of second-best may very well have also been the root cause for Goodwin's passion for models, at first directed towards an individual from those ranks found especially desirable, but now broadened to include any one of that profession or their hangers-on who could remind him by their talk and demeanour of the departed girl whom he had so inordinately adored.

This shape-shifting, taurean rather than lycanthropic to fit with Scotty's bullish image, resultant upon Ringenberg's observation that some sorcery might be afoot and, for the matter of that, upon the vampiric act from which I had finally disentangled Phyllidula from bringing to its conclusion, an occult enchantment on her part as well as on mine, for all I knew, that transcended fantasy and motivated her as well into the assumption of some other persona, Europa, perhaps, given Scotty's shaggy Highland-cattle aspect or that of the whore in Ezra Pound's *Lustra* whose name she may have adopted as a magical motto for the attraction of the men she desired in the way alchemists were known to clad themselves in robes appropriate to the colour of the element or the planet they were invoking, emboldened me to believe she was having a reasonably good time rather than going through her paces on Scotty's orders. There again, looking at things more rationally, she may have cast herself into the mould of courtesan as some sort of protest arising from the same disaffection with life that attracted droves of similar girls to Nicholas's concerts where more fun was to be had from going out against their parents' wishes than from any intrinsic musical excellence the evening might provide. She was quite probably as 'well brought-up'—the decisive factor in her revolt, it could be argued—as other girls I knew keen on the band: Joanna Palin, for instance, or Potts's girl, Valerie Latham. In any event, this brazenness, synthetic though its mental constituents might have been on both our parts, calmed us down. Phyllidula lay quietly in my arms and ran her fingers through my hair. I did no more than stroke her thin body. Moderately happy now, when most often I was driven to doubt if I could ever again experience happiness and could grasp its meaning only by contemplating those days not overclouded by the storms of mental anguish, it came to me that a fair proportion of the time spent making love is given to mulling over the past insomuch as it has brought the girl into our arms whether by good luck or good management. Perhaps for the same reason that lovemaking, like rock music, inclines to the repetitious, there is much excitement to be gained (as well as time tacked on) by self-congratulatory roaming back over the strokes of chance and the sharp judgements that have brought us where we find ourselves. The future, too, is a back-slapping affair, for we give consideration to who will be impressed when they hear of our 'adventure.' The cooks proved to be that way inclined, dedicated 'listers'—Goodwin, anyway, even if tabulation only existed in mental form—who liked to count up conquests in the way Cpl Kinnell would strike off days of service on his wall calendar or fighter pilots, upon their machines' fuselages, chalk up little images of the enemy aircraft they have despatched from the skies.

Scotty's bedroom was overladen with his own unambiguously masculine miasma, vigorous exercise long in the past unaired by tightly shut lattice windows, abetting Phyllidula, it might be, in her fantasy that it was the drummer with whom she lay entwined. As I lifted my face from hers and nuzzled against her shoulder those odours were obliterated entirely and I inhaled again, much more richly effused this time, those essences of the nomadic tribe of girls at Nicholas's gate that had wafted up the stairwell to Tex Ringenberg and myself.

How lucky that I had dissuaded her from taking her clothes off. Her ridiculously baggy T-shirt with Nicholas's fleshless portrait, the pair of equally shapeless trousers, retaining not only the scents of the launderette, establishments for some reason always imposing images of sexual congress—soap, steam, textiles soaked in warm water, dried in hot air—but of rain, leaf-mould, the campfire, the groundsheet, the morning dew and of her own dews at which, over how long a period since she had left home—days, weeks, a full month? (there were grounds for supposing that)—they had so luckily sipped, enflamed passion far beyond Phyllidula's original ministrations and instilled in me—a fugitive like herself, if not from family, then assuredly from mental strife—the keenest desire to conjoin with her on a regular basis, outdoors as well as within. I longed to lie with her beneath the stars, far, far away from her unhappiness and my own tortures.

As my nostrils paused at a junction on their fastidious journey where this symphony of aromas tussled with more personal ones that smelled of carelessness, more likely hurriedness, among the bushes affording the only shelter in the area of Nicholas's gateway and that cut across the sequences already discerned in the fabric of her T-shirt as fiercely as certain atonal chordings in the more lilting passages of Celestial Praylin's music, I began to anticipate the initiation of other precipitations I sooner or later could also inhale: those that Nicholas declared came uninduced in girls attending his concerts and in which the tiniest of an unrevealed garment my fingertips measured only from its elastic ridging at waist and thigh might already be steeping. As if to signal their flux, Phyllidula, who had been giggling quietly at attentions she probably saw as amateur in the extreme, suddenly fell silent and a minute later gave a great convulsive heave. From head to toe, her body was wracked with a convulsion of such violence I took it to be climacteric until I heard her snort out one word: 'Pardon.' I looked up. Phyllidula had productively sneezed.

That it was those results, emergent from twin entrances probably not the most highly esteemed in Tex Ringenberg's septenary, upon which I pounced and, from their saline cordage, achieved sufficiency of my own I thought only other moistures effusing into the purple satin could expedite, was attributable, I dare say, to the same masochism by which, when riding Nicholas's fierce stallion I had hoped to substitute physical pain for immaterial suffering. Maybe, too, when we first see and violently fall in love with a girl, we would not, because every facet of her seems so inviting, shrink from attending at duties, perhaps in our eyes becoming ceremonies, performed behind locked doors: only when we get to know her, that is to say upon her very first utterance of any import that extends our knowledge of her and contributes to a 'personality' which original appetites have not taken into consideration, becoming revolted by the daydreams conceived by physical seductiveness alone. Phyllidula now made just such a comment:

'You must love me to do that.'

If I had answered at all instead of getting off the bed, stumbling over Scotty's belongings and unlocking his door, I could have replied 'Yes, passionately' or 'No, not in the very slightest' and both replies would have been true, looked at in a certain way. Yet because I trembled at the thought of the injuries I might inflict upon someone I came to love and because I was revolted at what I had done with someone who, now, because of those demanding words at which I felt both flattery and terror, had evolved from the silent enchantress who would have allowed me all those liberties we long for from a strange girl we pass in the street into someone who would require and, I had no doubt, donate affection, I could say nothing at all. I slammed Scotty's door behind me, found my room on the first floor, fell across the bed and slept.

▘▗

It had not been made clear that my visit would coincide with a period of intensive work by Nicholas on Praylin's new album, the previous night's party some sort of climax to a successful tour of America which, rich as he seemed to be, needed to be capitalized upon. When I awoke in the morning, Nicholas and I were alone in a house absolutely deserted, miraculously rendered spotless, work, like the replacement of Nicholas's buttons, he might have set the girls on, Phyllidula included perhaps, at some godforsaken hour before the dawn. Everyone now was banned from Carpenter's until further notice.

Thwarted by Vindictive's lameness and deprived of the companionship of the girls who, when allowed, followed Nicholas wherever he went, I sank into deeper gloom. Lack of company that, after the hurly-burly of army life, had seemed so desirable, now led to loneliness: loneliness to isolation. To begin with I went for long walks but as I wandered through Nicholas's woodlands gaunt against wintry skies and across his fields fallow under December frosts, the countryside took on unsteady, dreamlike dimensions. I would grow alarmed by the crack of a twig I broke underfoot or a bird set up by my passing; and the surges of panic instilled by sound and motion set the earth atilt under my feet and the sky swirling in nacreous eddies of cloud that sent me scurrying for home. If, as occasionally happened, I met anyone along the way, I feared I might be shouted at or attacked; and even when I remained unmolested and the passerby gave me, as Sgt Barker would put it, 'the time of day,' I dared not look him in the face for fear of seeing the same monstrous, mongoloid features I had conjured up in the park. Illusory configurations encroached on every mile of the silent dead land through which I wandered. Expeditions became shorter. Eventually, they stopped altogether.

At those times of the day and night biorhythmically linked—as some of Nicholas's irrationally disposed retinue would have interpreted—to the fluxes of desire that swept intermittently over me, I longed to find Phyllidula again and to tinker with even crasser exercises on the scale of love that now seemed to include violence as well as depravity. Her behaviour, rather her playacting in pretending that I was Scotty, trod the thinnest line between compliance and whoredom and beckoned further experimentation along lines of other than orthodox coupling. Yet those images of violence during which I recalled the stimulation the military police photograph of Valerie Latham had so shamefully induced when I had had to admit I would have enjoyed tearing her clothes and torturing her flesh closed down the sluice gates of passion and made me pray I would never set eyes on Phyllidula again for fear of what I might do to her if we found ourselves again on our own. Nicholas, on the few occasions when we had any kind of conversation, denied knowing who she was, repudiated her very existence, as if I had made her up. In my current state of anxiety that seemed a credible and a very dreadful supposition.

Nicholas's methods of work, unenviable to steadier minds yet productive of the clamorous, anarchical music he composed, seemed eminently desirable. I longed for such total immersion in alchemical studies. He had shown signs of the same intensive concentration at school, examinations pending to be found in his study with his hair soaked in cold water and with a drawerful of illicit pills to keep him awake. The fever had begun to grip him before I arrived. Soon it was at its crisis. He started to lose sense of time and place. He wandered from room to room, thumping a few notes on the piano or plucking one of the many guitars left lying about, scattering sheaves of music, filling a brandy balloon to the brim because he had forgotten where he had put down another one equally full. Night and day became one to him. When it grew dark as it did, early, he switched on every light in the house and, when daylight came, left them blazing ready for the next darkness to descend. His hair and beard grew at a strangely fast pace, his hands became filthy, he ate voraciously at odd intervals from an enormous pressure-cooker full of curry he had prepared at the onset of the siege on his genius, often without bothering to heat the pan; swilling the food down with coarse red wine straight from the bottle. I would discover him slumped in a chair or crouched on the floor always with a page of music in his hands. Sometimes he slept where he sat or had drunkenly fallen, to awake minutes, hours, once a whole day, later, to continue the monstrous battle with the chords he heard within him. He reeked of perspiration and brandy and the abominably hot curry that was his only sustenance. Then, to cool his skin he had inflamed with the spirits and the spices, so that it began to break out in sores and blisters and to cause him the utmost irritation, he threw off his clothes and put on the long spangled robe he sometimes wore in performance. With the hood over his head like a dark, scheming magician, he stalked his cold bare garden.

One afternoon that coincided with the climax of his pernicious fever, I looked out of the window and saw him in the paddock where his great black horse stood cropping grass. Apprehensive that he might try to ride him, when surely Vindictive would sense the tumults that raged within his soul, I kept watch. For a long time Nicholas stood motionless in the grass while Vindictive, who had indeed sensed something amiss, pricked up his ears and began to cavort around him. The two figures, starkly set against the dying sun, silhouettes against indigo and gold, took on a mystical, fairylike quality. Suddenly the huge horse, whose shape had become barely discernible against the dark ledge of the hills beyond the paddock, reared on his hind legs to paw the flaming sky. Nicholas's cowled head dipped—the only movement he had made within the half hour I had been watching—in pagan obeisance to his ebony beast. He turned and re-entered the house. That night no corner of it remained undisturbed. Doors were opened and slammed shut again; furniture was dragged about; china smashed. Occasionally Nicholas's voice rent the air with a terrible scream. Everywhere was the sour, sharp smell of his sweat.

In the morning all was over. I had long been kept awake to the frightful noises—the more alarming since I could never be sure from which quarter of the house the next disturbance would erupt—but towards dawn they had died away and I had slept until aroused by the booming of the great brass vase at the foot of the stairs. There was a smell of frying bacon. Nicholas sat at the table in the small paneled dining room. He wore a clean linen suit. Eggs and bacon were set on the table and bowls of steaming coffee. He waved a fork at me. 'Eat hearty,' he said. His left hand was pressed on a pile of manuscript which he riffled with a long thumb. 'There we are. Done. Finished.'

Some sort of celebration seemed to be in order for the evening. I suggested a few drinks at the local, taking him on to a restaurant newly opened in the next village.

'Not the pub, if you don't mind. You forget, Praylin's fame has seeped even into these remote areas. Beethoven means nothing: a bewildered scratching of the poll with a gnarled hand. Praylin, though, sends the yokels running for their toddlers' autograph albums. Besides, the landlord is a shit: a very palpable shit.'

I had not recognized this particular inconvenience to Nicholas's life as a country 'squire,' assuming that the stout wrought-iron gates at the bottom of his driveway and the electronic eye that had swiveled round to survey the taxi bringing me from the station had been erected to discourage non-indigenous intruders, Phyllidula for instance, who assuredly did not live in the vicinity. I rather regretted not being allowed to go to the pub and, while Nicholas was signing autographs, being surrounded myself by eager fans and questioned about our relationship. For some time I had fallen into the habit of letting drop rather than letting slip that I was a friend of Nicholas's, especially, as with Pte Potts's girl, if there were any hope of cementing feminine friendship. The incident with 'scrawny but amorous' Phyllidula had now proved the efficacy of mixing in his circle. As much in the hope of finding a similar companion to ward off anguishes more or less put at bay by Nicholas's crazed behaviour as by the unworthy pleasure in basking in his reflected glory, I wished now I had suggested eating somewhere noisier, more crowded, less formal, than the restaurant to which the chauffeured car, that evening, began to make its way. Stifled both by private terrors and the vicarious delight in being driven along beside someone so enormously grand, I found it difficult to talk to Nicholas, himself torpidly uncommunicative. The limousine halted outside the restaurant. We got out.

As it happened, he was spotted at once. The cloakroom girl caught her breath, made a dive under her counter and waved a pencil and a crumpled envelope at Nicholas as we went past.

'I hardly like to ask,' she said. 'And on such an awful scrap of paper too.'

She was the sort of healthy girl with bouncy hair often to be found leaping up and down in the first row of Nicholas's concerts, not unlike, either, a girl at Miss Benke's yoga class I was rather keen on, and as Nicholas, with one of his ravishing smiles, asked her name and scrawled his signature across the paper, a pang of jealousy shot through me at the thought of how easily he could pick her up, bodily if need be, and carry her off in his car. There was the consideration, too, that if Nicholas had not been a rock star, the girl might have supposed that he looked, if not ugly, then certainly odd: menacing; faintly criminal; someone at any rate who might give trouble. Goodwin once went further about Nicholas's ill-aspected appearance. On seeing a press photograph of him, surrounded by a crowd of girls very much like this one whose eyes were aglow with love and admiration, he had remarked that, facially, Nicholas combined the most unsavoury aspects of Savonarola and Richard III. The comment had not been unkindly meant, passed only to convey the sort of surprise we all, from time to time, experience that one person can 'see' anything in another, but his words carried with them just the sort of petulance at Nicholas's luck with girls that I continued to harbour as we sat down at our table: incredulity, too, that he could be accounted in any way sexually attractive. A small lamp set in the wall above him isolated him in its beam. His high pale forehead was half shielded as always by the lock of hair that fell over his eyes, one of which he had half closed against the smoke of the cigarette he held in lantern jaws. Goodwin had been correct in assigning figures from the past to draw his comparisons. An aura of fin de siècle ravagement, tubercular, absinthe-induced, overlaid Nicholas's features and awarded to the hollow cheeks and sunken eyes the half-suffering, half-worldweary languor it would not have been uncharitable to say he actively cultivated; and when he put his elbows on the table and slumped forward over the menu and cupped in his thin fingers the elongated skull that, despite erosions, seemed too heavy for the rounded, almost hunchbacked shoulders, he resembled one of those despairing figures at café tables depicted in sketches by Toulouse-Lautrec.

He lit another cigarette and stared exhaustedly around him. The restaurant breathed discretion in heated, perfumed gusts. It had about it all the attributes of which the guide where I had read of its existence made such play. I had called them out to Nicholas: 'Polished mahogany, sparkling silverware, soft-footed waiters in immaculate evening clothes, gleaming napery, imaginative dishes tastefully served. . . .' All these qualities were much in evidence in the hushed, dark, mirrored room. Nicholas, on whom the guidebook's words had

had an acutely depressing effect, in which he had spent the day pleasantly muffled, looked gloomily about him.

'That book's right,' he said. 'This place is so fucking discreet it'll drop dead before we've had our . . . what?'

'Tartes de fruits de mer à l'estragon.'

'Dear God.'

'It'll make a change from your disgusting curry.'

Nicholas grunted. He relapsed into his state of exhausted incommunicability. Despite the quiet, the dining room was comfortably full. Mainly middle-aged and elderly couples intently ate and drank. There was a low hum of conversation, none of it audible, the clatter of knives and forks, the occasional pop of a cork. On the fringes of the room, however, in the lobby where the girl had asked for Nicholas's autograph and opposite which we sat, there were signs of a rather unseemly bustle, a constant *va-et-vient* of the staff that, at first, I could not understand. Then I realised that the cloakroom attendant must have apprised her colleagues of Nicholas's presence. They came out one by one from the kitchen and stole a glance at him through the double doors that led into the restaurant. Two giggling maids in flowered overalls were replaced by the chef in cap and apron, then by a burly kitchen porter still clutching the potato he had been peeling when called upon to take his turn, two or three other members of staff more or less in succession. Each peered in and darted away again before, so they hoped, they drew attention to themselves. Finally, though, the unauthorized forays into public areas, which had taken on the features of a game of Grandmother's Steps, everybody daring, as turns came round, to approach a little closer and stay a little longer, were remarked on by one of the two owners who floated gracefully around their candlelit domain.

Engaged with a chafing dish, he alerted his colleague, an altogether younger man, who almost ran across the room, wrists flapping, to drive the invaders, like geese from a barnyard, back where they belonged. The vegetable cook whose 'go' it was, found himself trapped, riveted to the spot by the descent of his master and forced to explain the cause of the general disobedience of which he now appeared the spokesman. He pointed dramatically with his potato-peeler in our direction. Explanations were more than sufficient. The young man spun round to confirm correctness of identity. The servant made off.

Soon everybody in the restaurant knew Nicholas was among their number. The owners may have had two motives in alerting other diners to his presence. Of recent establishment, very probably the place had as yet attracted few public figures. There again, it had to be said that part of Celestial Praylin's notoriety had been achieved by the band's poorish behaviour in public places and it may have been to advise guests of the possibility of a 'scene'—not much of one necessary to overset the restaurant's muted calm—as to inform them of the celebrity within their midst.

Under the ensuing bombardment of eyes, it came to me that Nicholas's 'act,' his way of looking as if he were on his last legs and of refusing to speak when he was spoken to, had become less affected than at school where he often had unreasonably fanciful, willowy days in which it was impossible to get a word out of him. Fame had now set him apart. It could not be expected that he should withstand constant plaudits and deprecations, in neither case far short of hysterical, nor for that matter the torments of musical composition from whose throes he was only just emerging, without mental adjustments of one kind or another. Outpourings of energy not only in writing but in the wild, bleak, endlessly prolonged concerts where very often Celestial Praylin had to be driven from the stage by management's killing of the lights or disconnecting the amplification, would require replenishments of vigour that food, sleep, drink, even the drugs he occasionally took, could not, on their own, supply. Now I was a witness to how he went about recharging run-down batteries. He was not unaware of the sensation he was causing as he sat so apparently listlessly eating and drinking wine. Just as at the end of one concert I had watched him raise his head and close his eyelids against the spotlights and let beat upon him as lazily as if he had been basking on a sun-baked beach all the searing, stamping blasts of adulation, he was gathering now the small shocks of inquisitiveness that were sparking off all round us and absorbing them quietly into himself. By this strange, peaceful, salamandrine feeding, he recuperated his strength.

There was nothing in the least arrogant about this attitude. Fame had come to him. It might as well be usefully applied. It was I who was guilty of the sin of pride. I stared about me quite bloated with glory. To be fair, to continue to suppress my doppelgänger who, when we first sat down, had observed me or I it—it had never been easy to fathom which way about it was orchestrated—in this discreet room and had planted in my mind that it might be I in a fit of madness and not Nicholas in a Praylin-inspired frenzy who would set about smashing the place up, I had been drinking rather a lot of the wine; and now I had become moderately 'myself' I desired more than anything else to be observed by everyone in spirited conversation with my famous companion. Instead, I was sitting wordlessly beside him while he moodily picked at his food: someone with whom he had only to get through dinner before he could decently take his leave.

I began to try and draw him out by talking about the band.

'What are you going to call your next album, Nicholas?'

Nicholas glanced up at me contemptuously as if he found himself being asked by a pious cleric whether he descended, very often, to self-abuse. In a voice ravaged as much by boredom as by the constant strain on his vocal cords, he intoned various words:

'*Dreams, Waking Thoughts and Incidents.* That is how life is made up, would you not agree? Each the hinterland of the next, occasionally indistinguishable one from the other. It is the title of a book by William Beckford. Have you read it?'

'Author of *Vathek*, a novel, written like your music, in self-inflicted incarceration.'

'The title takes on ever more pertinent overtones. However, Beckford surrounded himself with little boys, didn't he? That gives me cause for concern. We don't want a scandal. Not another.'

'Only one little boy. Or one at a time. There were girls as well, on and off.'

'Oh, well, that's all right then. Scotty gave me the idea.'

I wondered if the drummer's attunement of sentiments had been what had dictated his seeming generosity in handing me Phyllidula who was still much in my thoughts, but Nicholas did not respond to that enquiry: not immediately, anyway. During his long silence, my censor returned. Omnipresent but far from dominant because of the wine, it leaped back with one of the basic torments it used to distress my other, my 'real,' half. It observed in the crowded dining room a manifestation of unalloyed happiness, a spontaneous, therefore unselfconscious display of enjoyment of which it refused me, nowadays, even so much as a foretaste.

A woman had come in. Middle-aged, overdressed in a sweeping emerald gown and a little leopard-skin toque, she was casting round the room to find her dining companion. No hint of worry clouded a painted, beaming, rather greedy face that her friend might not be waiting or could have been delayed or, worse still, forgotten their engagement altogether. There was in her gaze as she took us all in, the waiters who hurried to and fro, the trolley with a baron of beef, the candelabra in which the silver winked and gleamed, a look of such intense delight at what she saw and of anticipation of the deliciousness of the evening ahead that it wrung from me the acutest despair because I could never again partake of the oblivious exhilaration that rushed headlong out of her. Her companion, two tables away from us, saw her at once. Considerably shorter, older too, or so a grizzled pointed beard and rimless glasses made him appear, he too had dressed up. He wore a white tuxedo and a frilled shirt. He rose from his chair and waved his arms extravagantly up and down to attract the woman's attention; and before they spoke, indeed before they were close enough for speech, each began an elaborate mime of joy, he by drawing his hand up and down in the air to emphasize how stunningly from top to toe his friend was dressed, she by great expansive gestures of disbelief that embraced everyone and everything to convey her wonderment at how all this was being afforded and of her host's prodigality; and when, at last, they did meet and kiss and clasp hands, they still found no words to say but breathed long silent brays of pleasure into each other's faces and swayed their bodies back and forth to afford themselves the sight of each other from all angles, and the woman did a little dancing pivot to show off her dress.

Nicholas had been watching the small happy commotion through inexpressive eyes. I could not tell whether it had passed him by or whether he were considering its import. When he did not speak, I decided to do so.

'What revolting people. They can't be that glad to see each other.'

I regretted my remark at once. It was tasteless, unkind, more revolting by far than the innocent couple who had prompted it. Almost for the first time in the evening, Nicholas turned to face me, stared me straight between the eyes. He spoke his next words tonelessly as if he picked them from an autocue in the centre of my forehead.

'When you are miserable,' he said very slowly, 'there is always something indecent about other people enjoying themselves.'

I had indeed never felt so miserable. His tart, almost vicious retort dispelled anything that remained of my smugness at being seen in his company that, together with the wine, had been fending off the misery and fear with which my days were filled; but then, as if he divined some caving-in of defences, as if I had been standing or kneeling before him in tears instead, so far as I knew, of staring calmly back into his dark, searching eyes, he took my hand and prised it from the wine I needed to refill my glass and drew the bottle towards him out of my reach.

'What's wrong, Tom?' he asked. 'You might have the decency to tell me.'

I made a despairing effort to retrieve the wine bottle. Nicholas pulled it further away; and deep within my soul relief burst cascading like the waters of an underground geyser, long pent up; and in the restaurant from which now all hubbub seemed to be subdued and the diners to have withdrawn their attention from our table and where for all I knew or cared we sat alone and unobserved, I began to tell him.

4

'I'm going to buy shoes in my lunch hour so we may as well have fish for supper.'

Sylvia threw her cape over her shoulders and looked at herself in the bedroom mirror. She tucked a wisp of hair under her cap. Fair, freckled, snub-nosed, she resembled in her nurse's uniform those devastatingly pretty stereotypes of the nursing profession represented on paper covers of romantic novels about hospital life. She came over and kissed me good-bye.

'Don't bother with fish if you're going to buy shoes. We can eat out somewhere tonight.'

'Oh, there's always a fishmonger's next to a shoe shop.'

Sylvia spoke her words mechanically, even with an inflexion of boredom as if the triteness of the axiom, as she supposed this, to my mind, quite remarkable piece of information, were hardly worth the repeating, at least to anyone of moderate intelligence. In all likelihood her shopping expedition would confirm these two vastly dissimilar lines of business's precise, if surrealistic, abutment, already established in her own mind—judging from her tone of voice—as one of retail trading's more categorical juxtapositionings. She had come out with dicta of this sort at regular intervals over the weeks we had been together. Imponderable though each of them sounded, they had all been found to present incontrovertible truths.

'A neurosis shared is a neurosis halved,' she had said when I told her how Nicholas had 'cured' me of my mental anguish. That adage too had seemed accurate enough. Nicholas had in fact done little more than listen. 'Good lord,' he had said when I had done and the waiter had brought coffee and brandy. 'Don't you suppose that we all, from time to time, think of bashing babies' skulls in or knifing the woman asleep at our side? You are suffering from the common cold of the introvert, the urticaria of the contemplative: uncomfortable, yes; disturbing, certainly; but a fleabite on the back of mental imbalance. Mad, I can promise you, you most assuredly are not.'

At the time his words had been of the greatest comfort but, as Sylvia had pointed out, it was by the mere voicing of my distress that I had most effectively banished my 'censor.' As if enraged at being exposed, it had slunk sheepishly away. In the calm, empty, trouble-free void its departure had left, I began a furious onslaught on Norton's *Ordinall of Alchemy.* I fell in love with

Sylvia. Life was again worth living. At the back of my mind, there was still the question of finding a job. I should, as my father put it, 'be looking round.' Enquiries as to progress in that direction accompanied the handing over, every so often, of 'something to be going on with.' In fact expenses were minimal since Sylvia's off-duty hours were spent indoors, sitting by the fire and talking; later on in bed. Goodwin once offered an explanation for this predilection, a fairly common one among nurses, in his opinion, who, as a class, took pride of place on his list of 'goers.' Nurses' professional concern for the unfit, he argued, brought out a desire, in moments of leisure, for healthy physical passion. It was a natural reaction against seeing so many unwell people. It gave reassurance of their own bodily vigour. It contributed to their researches into human anatomy.

'Did she wear those rather special black stockings? Mmm, what fun. I wonder where they get them. Some sort of hospital issue, I presume. One doesn't run across them in shops. Mind you, you could count yourself lucky to have got in there. Nurses usually go for heftier types altogether than you and me, footballers, scaffolders, people of that sort.'

I had been able to put forward some rival interpretation of Sylvia's rewarding infatuation. She was a devoted fan of my mother's fiction. She devoured her novels as soon as they came out, intervals between publication taken up by rereading ones especially enjoyed or catching up with those issued, as my mother, greatly flattered, put it, 'before she was born or thought of.' Every so often she would take my head in her hands and gaze penetratingly into my eyes—like the dustcover nurses she so much resembled—and seek to divine there traits she believed were reflected in some of the young male characters moving unsteadily through my mother's gloomy narratives.

'There's a lot of Caspar in you,' she once commented, 'the cost accountant in *Cry, For We Are But Angels.* You've got his jawline and the same way of spreading marmalade.'

I had not read the book: unfamiliarity with its text demonstration, in Sylvia's eyes, not only of a deficit of literary acumen but of family pride. Blood in her opinion, for once unoriginal, was thicker than water. It was in fact the cause of our first argument.

A couple of months after I got back to London I spent a weekend at home where I promised Sylvia to collect a proof copy of my mother's 'latest'—rather a longer one than usual it turned out—of which publication day was still some time off. Unanticipated bulkiness and the fact that my mother, in one of her rare practical moods, had insisted I pack a winter overcoat, disallowed the book's fitting into my bag and, separately carried, it got left on the train. Recrimination took the form not only of my delinquency's robbing Sylvia of a 'good read'—a series of night-duty rosters giving ample time for getting to grips with the most recent addition to my mother's body of work—but of just the sort of filial disloyalty she found so reprehensible. I invoked my father's distaste for his wife's books: several established critics' also. Sylvia remained unmoved. Words were exchanged. There were tears: eventually, in the way of things, conciliatory moves. I promised to go to the lost property office first thing in the morning. At last Sylvia kissed me.

'Never mind, darling,' she said. 'Beautiful people are always losing things.'

Not only flattering, this was a maxim of considerable subtlety, beyond even Sylvia's range, enigmatic though that had proved to be. I looked forward to putting it to the test.

Eight or ten people had already gathered outside the office when I arrived. None had a companion. That itself was unusual in any assemblage—if such a word could be applied to so fragmentary a company—testimony, perhaps, of entirely personal responsibility for the mismanagement of their lives that had brought them to this place, a wish not further to discommode friends or relatives by asking them to come along as well. Some distance towards repentance had already been covered by the fact we had all shown up before the place opened. Nobody wanted to compound his felony by another one of lateness. Even I, last but one to arrive as it turned out, was still five minutes ahead of time. We stood, or rather hung about, around a faceless, begrimed building, its larger part occupied by more important departments of transport administration, entrance to those offices gained elsewhere. A grudging attempt had been made to advertise the sole means of public ingress. In a window where, after some statutory interval had passed, more desirable of unclaimed items within were displayed for sale, was stationed a blue plywood elephant. Of considerable size and garish execution, it was bestowing upon us all from under heavily mascara'd eyelashes the most unambiguous of winks. Suspended from a howdah on the back of this chastening image, management had hung a placard announcing hours, not especially convenient ones, when it was open for business.

The forbiddingness of the building's frontage, its still closed doors despite, now, the passing of scheduled opening time, the wintry chill of the day—flurries of snow along the street confirming my mother's prediction of a change in the weather—the uneasy, almost shifty demeanour of all of us foregathered, evoked memories of a Russian film Nicholas and I had once stolen away from school to attend. Truancy had very likely intensified atmospheres of tension, uneasiness, suspicions of our fellowmen, nervousness at being spotted hanging around in public, that the film had admirably conveyed. Similar inquietudes appended in the dark, cold street. Although naturally in a much lower key than in *Comrade or Foe,* that mutual wariness allowed me, since we were all eyeing each other, a reasonably free examination of faces in an attempt to prove or disprove Sylvia's paradoxical utterance. Certainly nobody could be described as physically repulsive. There was one stunning girl. By and large, though, we were a dull-looking lot. Perhaps by 'beautiful' Sylvia had meant spiritual beauty. That of course could not be judged.

All at once, though, a newcomer joined us who, at first glance, ruled out body and soul any possibility of endorsing Sylvia's axiomatic declaration. He was a boy, about sixteen, dressed in jeans, a studded leather jacket, stout brown boots. All had seen service. He passed very close to the pretty girl, appeared even to brush up against her, made straight for the entrance of the lost property office, propped himself up against the stonework and lit a cigarette. His coarse simian features reflected the sort of capacious contentment with which stupidity, on its crassest of levels, endows the human mind. Fair hair, cut *en brosse,* accentuated a low, sloping forehead. Tired, swollen eyes of the brightest blue appraised the small gathering of which he had made himself a part, focused lasciviously on the girl and then, as if in that one glance he had consummated the act he had so unequivocally contemplated, began an inspection of the bitten fingernails of his left hand.

It was not the first time I had seen him. Far from it. It was the first time, though, he had stayed long enough for me to examine him closely. With fear and loathing I forced myself to do so.

Despite coarseness of features, he had skin of the translucency of alabaster, pale, glowing as if lit from within, attribute that, with the brightness of the eyes and the eccentrically shorn, corn-coloured hair, took much from the ugliness of bone structure and stamped him, indeed, with an ethereal strikingness none of us, even the girl, was able to match.

There was much that was enviable, too, about his self-possession, his spare, neat, gathered economy of movement. No external circumstance nor interior insecurity was allowed to disturb the white, vacant mask of his face. His lounging attitude conserved energy needed for later in the day. This discipline—hardened like his muscles in some tough school of life, such as it had been—this totally unabashed, loose, calmly waiting stance announced, was designed to announce with the utmost clarity, that he had not lost anything. He had merely been sent, very likely also paid, to retrieve it.

I sought reaction from the others. As I expected, there was none. Nobody objected to his jumping the queue. Even the girl, although I was now quite sure he had touched her as he passed, paid him no heed. That of course was to be expected. For he did not really exist.

Although not convinced until now, I had for some time suspected he was a figment of my imagination, an extension of the visions I had been experiencing before I believed myself cured. Previous sightings had not been peculiar in themselves, except perhaps for the boy's unearthly pallor and the fleetingness with which he had always crossed my line of sight. I had seen him in the streets, smoking his absurdly long cigarettes; on a bicycle, his stubby hands defiantly removed from the handlebars and swinging by his side as he pedaled along, smoking; once on the steps of the British Museum. It was the last occasion that sowed the seeds of doubt as to his real existence because, when I got on the tube a few minutes later, he was already on board when it pulled into the station. Aloof, expressionless, feet in his big boots propped up on the seat opposite, he had seemed unconscious of my presence as I, feigning unconsciousness also, took a place as far away as possible. When I looked round, he had vanished. This morning, however, he had gone one better. Across the road from the bus stop where I had waited to get to the lost property office was another, a fare stage for coaches traveling nonstop to London airport. I had watched the boy boarding one of those coaches and being carried off in the opposite direction. He could not, therefore, twenty minutes later, unless he had stopped the coach and asked to be set down and then doubled back on his tracks, be standing where he now was.

I knew then as the doors opened and we all filed past the boy, who made not the slightest move to go inside, that I was again condemned to the pattern of anguish I had known before. In the vain hope that he might still be hanging around, that I could go up to him and beg him to leave me alone, I turned and broke through the small knot of people and went back outside; but, as I knew in my heart, he had disappeared.

Somehow I managed to retrieve Sylvia's book and make my way home. All the time my doppelgänger stalked triumphantly beside me. He would not again let me so lightly off the hook.

For weeks I lived in fear of this new symbol of my illness. The creature, as I now called him, discarding the mean physicalities of his adolescent jauntiness, the dirtiness of his clothes and the ever-present dangling cigarette, and isolating, whenever I caught sight of him, only the uncanny opalescence of his flesh and the unnatural powder blue eyes, was far more fearful than any other cerebral disturbance that had plagued me in the earlier stages of my unrest. I saw him all the time; daily, twice a day sometimes. There were other incidents of bilocation when he watched me off from my place of departure and had been awaiting me at my destination, coolly loitering. It was as if I could summon him at will.

How innocently, by Nicholas's reassurances, I had been lured into underrating the deviousness of my censor. Its double-dealing, its relentless exploitation of my mind's resources, now became apparent. I had not mentioned my hallucinations to Nicholas—the mongol apparition by the herons' lake, the swirling vortices that had enveloped me on my country walks, my doubts of the reality of those who peopled his estate—but I was now convinced that, had I done so, there would have been no miracle cure. Nicholas would have given a very different interpretation of what was wrong with me. The sane do not see visions. It was as simple as that. I was, as I had always feared, mentally deranged.

Then, one day, Loudermilk rang. Freddy, my first morning at ALEMBIC, expressed surprise at this informal method of approach. Personal appearances by Loudermilk were rare enough, he pointed out; telephone calls virtually unknown. It was his first hint that I was somehow and to his own disadvantage preferentially treated.

Loudermilk's voice had sounded uncertain, suggested unfamiliarity with the method he had chosen for communication. I too may have sounded wary. By that time I was testing every event to ensure it was not part of another hallucination. All that I heard and saw passed now through a mental filtering system of appraisal. Of only a split second's duration this new barrier could be compared with the brief delay in a transatlantic telephone conversation before a friend's voice is heard in reply, nearly but not quite long enough to ask if he is still on the line. Loudermilk may have been disconcerted by the hiatus. He repeated his name, then spelt it out letter by letter so there could be no mistake.

'Francis Loudermilk here. L-o-u-d-e-r-m-i-l-k. I'm a friend of your ex-CO, Major Hamilton. He mentioned your name.'

I waited for him to go on.

'Are you still there?'

When I said I was, he set about delivering his message in a loud voice and at breakneck speed as if equipment he already believed untrustworthy might at any moment break down altogether and cut me off before he could finish what he had to say.

'I'd like you to have dinner with me tomorrow, the fourteenth. Seven o'clock at my club, the Hertfordshire. I have a proposition to put to you you may find not without interest. Time and place will suit, I trust. May I ask you to be prompt? Lateness raises certain problems I should prefer not to have to face, that you yourself would not wish to be burdened with. You can? Good. I look forward to our meeting. Good-bye.'

He hung breathlessly up. I pondered the message. Despite nervousness, the voice had been efficient, commanding, dictatorial even, only a faint difficulty with *r* sounds indicative of some softening of an otherwise autocratic personality. Age could not be judged: youthfulness, though, out of the question. I wondered at the nature of the problems lateness could cause. Another engagement probably, a rubber of bridge after dinner, a late-night film. Later in the day I recalled Major Hamilton's words, the first he had spoken to me after admonishing me for getting drunk: 'I dine with colleagues occasionally. . . . They ask me about loners. . . . May I tell them you are open to suggestions?'

Punctuality, underlined as of the essence, made me rather too early and I hung about outside Loudermilk's club for some time, eventually going inside a few minutes before seven o'clock. Entrance was made along a draughty passage tiled in black and white marble squares. Rows of pegs held members' hats and coats of uniformly dark colouring and of an anthropomorphic forlornness that signaled total abandonment by their owners, not in favour of newer fashions but because earthly raiment of any kind was no longer required. Beyond these sinister tokens of mortality and abutting the swing doors of the interior entrance lay the porter's office. It seemed polite, even obligatory, to present myself there. Not having the least idea what Loudermilk looked like—mutual ignorance indeed appending—announcement of arrival to the porter for communication to my host when he got there would prevent any preliminary awkwardness of recognition. There again, Loudermilk might be already inside, ensconsed in some remote corner of the club or at the bridge table where he planned also to end the evening which, without guidance, I could never hope to locate.

I peered through the glass hatch. Visibility was at a premium. The chill of the passageway where I stood and heat generated on the inside of the porter's sanctum had misted the glass completely over. Through the condensation, two dark forms could be made out. They stood gazing up at a glowing orange disc high above their heads. Each grasped in an outstretched hand some sort of implement, a staff or wand, that he kept for the most part pointed steadily upwards to the source of the light. Every so often, though, the figures would lower their arms and then fall for a few moments to their knees as if in obeisance, prior to rising up again and re-adopting with upturned faces and wands held aloft the fixed attitude of salutation that occupied by far the greater part of their time. Slowly, purposefully, the mist-swathed officers dipped and stretched in rhythmic succession. Impressions were that I had stumbled across an observance of ritualistic nature worship, a hailing of the dawn—the fiery globe representative of the rising sun—for not only had the figures assumed for me the role of priests, hierophants well versed in whatever stylized, pre-Christian mysteries they celebrated, but shadows thrown onto the ceiling along with their own spectrally elongated images, astral shapes, *kas,* it could be conceived given what was in progress, demonstrated that the badges of office they wielded possessed spiked trifurcations at the apexes not dissimilar to the tridents with which Lindo's uncle's sea creatures had been equipped throughout his underwater pageant; and it seemed, by flourishing these aquatic weapons in the face of the molten ball of fire and then by directing them through the atmosphere to touch the ground beneath their feet, the pair were seeking to bring about by ritual a placation, not otherwise to be looked for, of the quaternity of warring elements—fire, air, water, earth—by means of which the Almighty, the godhead, anyway, of their decidedly pagan pantheon, in lightning, tempest, rainstorm, earthquake, instrumented his displeasure.

Intriguing though the ceremony was, time was getting on. I hardly liked to interrupt observances by no means at their climax, yet it was now precisely seven o'clock. Loudermilk's strictures about tardiness had not been forgotten. As luck would have it, a club member then came hurrying down the flagged corridor to where I was standing. With a clenched fist, he came down on a burnished bell push screwed to the counter of the hatch that I had overlooked. Its effect was immediate. One of the celebrants spun round, made for the hatch and flung it upwards. Illusions of having been privy to an act of conjuration, exorcism, enchantment, mumbo jumbo of any subdivision whatsoever, were precipitantly dismissed from consciousness as the blast of hot air that swept almost like a tornado out of the grossly overheated porter's sanctum filled my nostrils with the appetising fragrance of toasting bread. The two officiants, revealed in identical blue serge uniforms, had been engaged in running up a snack. The one who had not answered the member's summons, still kneeling on the floor, applied butter to a substantial doorstep of bread, richly browned, that he plucked from an expandable toasting-fork, elongated to its fullest capacity and added the morsel to a plate already lavishly filled. His colleague, the senior of the two, features hotly suffused from the filaments of the circular electric fire suspended high on the far wall of the sanctum that I had mistaken for the image of the rising sun, endeavoured to conceal behind his back kitchenware of similar footage and manufacture, the prongs of which, however, stuck up behind a pate as darkly reddened as cheeks by the fire's rays and gave the illusion—the only one of mysteriousness that for any longer perpended—that he had imbedded in his cranium the three sharp metal spikes that formed the necessary adjuncts to the instrument put to use in the preparation of his meal. He answered whatever question the member had to put: then addressed himself to me.

In other circumstances, he might have proved difficult to deal with. His troubled, congested face reflected a truculence that could only be appeased, in the normal course of events, by 'slipping' him a coin. Now, however, caught in a rather schoolboyish, possibly also illegal, act and eager too, most likely, to get on with his tea, he replied with perfect civility. Mr Loudermilk was in the Flower Court. He indicated that was to be found immediately beyond the swing doors.

Within the club, floral arrangements had been restricted to straggly, tropical-looking plants embedded in brass pots set on tall, thin, bamboo stands. A tiger-skin, head still attached, carpeted a section of the floor, flagged like the passageway with marble slabs. These colonial influences, such as they were, did not extend to the walls on which a selection of slaughtered elk gazing mournfully down as if they awaited their feed from stable doors imposed Scottish-baronial overtones. A wide staircase plunged from indeterminate heights into the cavernous and distinctly chilly forecourt. It was hardly less cold than in the street outside. At the farthest end of the room, a man examining a scientific instrument beneath one of the elk heads could have been confirming this thermometric likelihood. As the hall was otherwise deserted, this must be Loudermilk.

When he saw me, rather when he sensed my presence, he turned and started to make his way slowly across the floor towards me, staring at his boots. He appeared rapt in thought. Graver matters by far than the room's temperature weighed him entirely down. His head was so bowed, his chin so deeply tucked into his collarbone, his shoulders so highly hunched around his ears, he resembled one of the men mentioned by Othello whose heads grew within their chests. He had on a plain, heron grey suit which appeared to have been worn through a rainstorm and allowed to dry on the body. There had been considerable overall shrinkage. Trousers revealed not only thick grey socks but a quarter inch of Loudermilk's waxen shins. Equally white wrists extended far below his jacket sleeves.

Progress, though slow, thoughts patently elsewhere, was nonetheless purposeful, set in a dead straight line between the door and the barometer that had been engaging him when I came in. In his own distracted way, he could be said to be making a beeline. After an age he drew abreast. Sparse grey hair parted exactly down the middle was all I could see of the sunken head.

Obedience to his instructions notwithstanding, my arrival had obviously been ill-timed. It could not be shyness alone that was maintaining a painful, brooding reserve. Some immense problem, suddenly arisen, by no means resolved in the course of his journey across the floor of the Flower Court, was continuing to rack his tall, sparse frame. I said some formal words.

Pitched as far as I could judge at reasonable standards of audibility, they could, in normal circumstances, have been expected to have drawn some sort of a reply but by a freak of chance they exactly coincided with the commencement of the stertorous and quite unmistakable sounds of the flushing of the club's lavatory system. Behind an archway to my left, in gargling, swirling cataracts of sound, magnified tenfold by echoes generated around the deserted Flower Court, gallon upon gallon of water began to be discharged from a vast, secreted reservoir, a copious, endlessly prolonged rushing and coursing that, had it not been accompanied by groans and rattles and whistles and a final soughing cough that identified all too plainly its unhappy source, I would have feared was being projected towards us and would sweep us, the next moment, pitilessly away.

It took no effort to comprehend that, even in the highest of spirits, Loudermilk would not have been amused by any reference to what I was later to hear Major Giblin call the 'gubbins,' even its merely mechanical aspects of which we had just been so clamorously reminded. In the silence that followed, the poised chill silence that succeeds a car crash or the explosion of a bomb, Loudermilk visibly shuddered. Distress at my having been a witness to this particular shortcoming of his club's facilities may have overtaken the problem, whatever it was, that had been uppermost in his mind when first he had come up. He was, at any rate, now at a complete loss for words.

There was nothing I could do. Repetition of what I had said could only draw attention to the elements of farce that were threatening to overthrow, before it had begun, our evening appointment. We stood, therefore, still longer, all hopes of any kind of agreeable preliminary exchange apparently dashed until Loudermilk, despite his acute embarrassment, sensed that the ball was squarely in his court. For the first time, he drew himself up to his full height. There was a glimpse of a wide, pink, carefully barbered, infinitely careworn face. Then he turned round and shot out one of his long arms and pointed to the staircase that descended into the middle of the Flower Court. He turned its indication into a gesture of the highest dramatic quality. Designed to put paid to the unhappy incident that had marred our first moments together, it succeeded in overriding mundane matters of any kind at all. As he stood gazing upwards, arm outstretched, he might have been displaying to me limitless uncharted lands to which, after months of danger and privation, we had finally attained. Thus Cortez must have pointed, Hillary on the final thrust up Everest. Millais's sailor in *The Boyhood of Raleigh* burned with these impassioned fires. In the sweeping arc he had made with his arm, in the light that flashed from his soulful eyes, in his shining uplifted face, Loudermilk captured the essence of the loftiest, most noble ideal with which mankind is inspired: the Spirit of Adventure. His first words too, when they finally came, served, in their simple way, to underline this same pioneering resoluteness that would now drive us on to grander, happier times.

'Here lies our woad,' he said.

He led the way to the foot of the staircase and commenced the ascent. We trudged slowly upwards. It was hardly to be expected that he should maintain for very long either in speech or gesture the forceful images with which he had prefaced our climb towards (it was to be hoped) the bar, but at least he did not allow himself to sink back into rumination of whatever it was that had been troubling him earlier on. By the time we reached a landing where the staircase divided, tensions were easing.

'Things don't look too good down under,' he remarked.

This could not be a reference to the plumbing. In view of what had gone before, it would have been entirely out of character. He must, I thought, be referring to another refreshment area situated in the basement, inferior in catering to the one we were heading for.

'Our batting is very bwittle.'

He was talking about cricket, a match in progress in Australia, appraisal of England's feats mournfully correct. This was safe ground. I started to give reasons for failure to which he seemed to be listening attentively as we ascended to another level. After I had finished he took a few moments before venturing his next comment.

'Your mother's last novel was very clever.'

I said I had not yet read it.

'The woman magistrate was very well dwawn. I can wecommend it.'

'I must try and get round to it soon. Did you perhaps read *The Tinker's Cuss?* That's always been my favourite.'

Loudermilk paid no attention to that opinion. By now we had reached not a bar but the club dining room. It was deserted except for some grim-faced waitresses who stood sentinel by various of the empty tables. Loudermilk once more inclined his head as if, despite the room's height, he might crack his forehead on a beam and stepped over the threshold.

We were, then, going 'straight in,' words I recalled Nicholas dreaded hearing from his hosts. A drink beforehand would have done much to improve matters, at least so far as I was concerned. Loudermilk's two disconnected fits of speech, his further gloomy lapse, and now, as a waitress broke from her mould and came up to ask if he would have his usual table, an uncomprehending frown as if he had been addressed in a foreign tongue, implied all too clearly he was still far from relaxed. Perhaps, though, drink, for his part, was not the answer. Walking behind him as, with head bent, he raked the carpet for obstacles placed in his way, I wondered if he were ill, perhaps terminally so. As a fit man he must have been very tall indeed, capable in those days of almost touching the archway under which we had passed with the crown of his head. Now in the twilight of his years, it could be pain that was crumpling him up, efforts at speech attempted only during temporary respite. He seemed, as we reached our table, a man broken in spirit and body.

Once settled, he began to gather himself somewhat. He snatched at some bread and crammed it into his mouth. He waved the menu aside.

'Dwessed eggs,' he said. 'Those are the best bet. And the veal fwicassee. You will enjoy the club claret,' he went on as the waitress was replaced by a sommelier whose sudden appearance and cadaverous features proclaimed he had risen, transiently, from the tomb. 'Then when you've polished that lot off, you shall have some of our famous whubarb pie.' He paused while the wine waiter left us, then spoke in lower tones. 'Frankly that was the weason I had to insist upon your being to time. Some nights, dining only shortly after this hour, I have known the pastry to be quite limp. Cwispness in a pie is all, I think you'll agree.'

I said I did.

'And how goes Thomas Norton,' he asked as the eggs were put in front of us.

'Quite well. How did you know I was working on the *Ordinall?*'

'I shouldn't waste too much time on it, if I were you. Norton has little to offer.'

'He's vague, certainly. No more so than the alchemical references in the "Canon Yeoman's Tale." I often wonder what Norton would have made of that piece of work. He might have appreciated Chaucer's style but he would have been very upset by the characterization.'

Loudermilk gave this no more consideration than anything else I had tried to put forward. He was eating his eggs at tremendous speed.

'I believe in coming stwaight to the point,' he said when he had done, 'as well as requiring as a wule an early night's wepose. I work for a governmental department. That is a fact you will wish to confirm and I shall give you opportunity to do so. I dine occasionally as I mentioned on the telephone with Hamilton. Your name cwopped up. I am here to invite you to join us.'

I tried to ask a question very much on my mind ever since Loudermilk had rung up, but he stopped me. 'Allow me to finish if you will be so good,' he said. 'There'll be time for queries later. It is ware to find a spagyrist of your calibre among the young. I was vastly impwessed by some of your articles. We have scientists aplenty, this age seems to bweed them, but we need a humanist, a scholar who can collect the old texts, twanslate them, scwatch about for rarities generally, a hand to feed the cooks, as we laughingly call our lab boys. You're just the man.'

The veal arrived, attendant vegetables in plated dishes. The ghoulish wine waiter poured claret. Nothing that Loudermilk had said had come as a surprise, although I was uncertain why not. I suddenly felt very calm, ravenously hungry. As soon as we were alone again, Loudermilk picked up the thread of his words. He talked into his plate to which he gave close attention, ferreting out meaty pieces of the veal to convey to his mouth, forming a small pile of discards—bones, gristle—over to one side.

'We do a thoroughly necessary job. It is absurd to suggest that we do not wish to become again a stwong, a mighty power in the world and it is therefore pwesumptuous for a nation so desirous to ignore the ownership of gold. Its artificial manufacture could pwove nothing but beneficial. I do not have to tell you that the evidence for success in alchemical documents is considerable. We are under fire, naturally, for being quaint, but successive governments have, after consideration, left us to our own devices; provide, as it happens, quite substantial funds. Naturally as our wulers become more wadical, we in ALEMBIC, as we call ourselves, are at pains to underline to them the other goal of the ancient alchemists, the elixir of life, so while our masters still hanker in their own way after world domination, they are ever more eager to discover a panacea. You can see evidence of that anywhere you care to look: accent on physical well-being, mental health, anti-smoking campaigns, adequate intake of vitamins, homeopathic techniques, acupuncture, a new concern for the elderly, the cwippled, the infirm. I myself, courtesy of HM Government, twaveled here fwee of charge this very evening. I am nearly eighty, you may be surpwised to learn.' Loudermilk allowed himself a little shrug of the shoulders: pride or resignation, it was hard to tell. 'All this is very costly. Medical wesearch is slow and expensive. We in comparison are cheap. We are worth the money. Imagine if we did come up with a miwacle? If I may, let me prompt you again on the documentary evidence, plenty of it, that the elixir has been found: even though once again lost.'

'Gold is often thought to be part of the elixir's formula.'

'How wight you are. A point I might take up with our detwactors. As I was saying, a Universal Wemedy is what they would like us to turn up. Fortunately, some would say unfortunately, we are not alone in the pursuance of these wesearches. There are competitors. That is the word favoured, "enemies" nowadays taking things a little too far. For this weason we are placed under a canopy of secrecy, whose it matters not to you. We pwefer, no, we insist on secrecy.' Loudermilk looked round to see if he himself were not breaking this particular rule. A few members had come in to dinner but there was nobody within earshot. 'Wegardless of your decision therefore, you will say nothing of this meeting to anyone. Is that understood? Now then, have you any questions for me?'

Loudermilk's work was done. He fell once more into his own slumped, contemplative world. Not even the pie roused him. He pushed fruit and pastry wearily round his plate. The evening had either exhausted him or, more likely, bored him to tears. The topics of personal relevance he had so laboriously trotted out were obviously the result of a last-minute briefing. The question remained, by whom? Major Hamilton, whose literary tastes ran to Walt Whitman I recalled, might well have known my mother was a novelist and, in the raid on the Orderly Room, have made a note I was studying a modern edition of *The Ordinall of Alchemy,* snippets of information passed on to Loudermilk who had mugged them up in a half-hearted way to make me feel 'at home'; but it was quite certain that Hamilton had had no idea that I—or Pte Potts either, for that matter—was interested in cricket; and nobody except Sylvia and Nicholas knew I was still at work on Norton's text. There could be only one possible informant: the alabaster boy. I racked my brains to recall if I had glimpsed him among the spectators at the late-season matches I had watched just after leaving the army. I had certainly sighted him outside the British Museum where, armed with some sort of authority Loudermilk had been able to procure for his personnel from other departments, the police perhaps or the Ministry of Information, he could perfectly well have elicited from the librarians details of the books and manuscripts for which I had indented. His strange, almost ghostly appearances seemed explicable now simply because of his efficiency at sleuthing, no longer a sort of bilocatory miracle. I had therefore only one question for Loudermilk, one that would for all time dispel the fears of madness that had once more enswathed me. I asked it:

'Are you having me followed?'

Loudermilk gave a start as if he assumed I had already taken leave of him and returned suddenly to the dining table after saying good night to make this final enquiry. He grappled as best he could with after-dinner fatigue now impinging on conditioned exhaustion of spirit.

'What you have to bear in mind is, the application of chemistry can produce whimsically unchemical wesults. Nature abhors a vacuum but she positively courts an unlooked-for occupancy. Science ends in chaos, so we are told these days, but in its halfway house wesides a delicately organized iwwesponsibility.'

Loudermilk raised his eyes from the tablecloth and spread open his arms as if to refresh aphorisms rehearsed more than once before various audiences. Almost as an afterthought he replied to my request for information.

'Followed, you say? Yes: possibly. It is sometimes done. I twust you have not been incommoded.'

5

ALEMBIC confirmed my appointment the next month, February. Eighteen months later, a short time after bumping into Nicholas dressed as the Plague Doctor, I spent my first holiday at Carpenter's. Unlike other visits, punctuated by the sort of party where I had met Phyllidula or overshadowed by Nicholas's frenetic methods of composition, it was very peaceful. There were no musicians, hangers-on, girls, newsmen. A housekeeper looked after us, a gardener tended the lawns and groomed the horses. We rode one afternoon listlessly through the heat of the day.

'Oh, he killed her at the brook, the brute, for all the world to see.'

Nicholas turned his long bony face towards me, one eyelid closed against the smoke of the cigarette that drooped as always from his lips.

'And no one but the baby cried for poor Lorraine, Lorrèe.'

Nicholas acknowledged my continuation of the poem and tossed away his cigarette. Dropping Vindictive's reins, he rocked in his arms an imaginary infant:

> *'She clasped her new-born baby, poor Lorraine, Lorraine, Lorrèe,*
> *"I cannot ride Vindictive, as any man might see,*
> *And I will not ride Vindictive, with this baby on my knee;*
> *He's killed a boy, he's killed a man, and why must he kill me?"*

'Why did she have to ride the race with the baby, Thomas? Couldn't she have given it to someone to hold while in the saddle? A nursemaid? A passing butler? Or just left the brat in its perambulator?'

'It was the cruel whim of a blackguardly husband. She was killed, of course, in the race, the "capping" race as Charles Kingsley calls it, quite how is unclear. At the brook in one line, "against a pollard willow tree" in another.'

'I see. It's not a very good poem, is it?'

'Kingsley was dying when he wrote it.'

'What sort of excuse do you call that? Proximity to the invisible choir should have aided inspiration, not thrown it out of the window.' Nicholas picked up the reins again and bent over the horse's neck. 'You wouldn't kill me at the brook, would you? Or against a pollard willow tree, even if we knew what the fuck that was.' Vindictive snorted and flicked a shiny black ear. We began to canter.

To an onlooker who did not know the two of them, the eventuality of some sort of accident could not be overlooked, even a fatal one such as Kingsley's poem, vague though the details were, all too vividly described. Vindictive's arrogant strength, Nicholas's frailty, more than that his almost culpable vagueness when riding the stallion, could well conspire to some sort of misunderstanding between man and animal, or so I thought when I came to ride the horse myself. Last September when I had been ill, I would have welcomed the dangers, or what at the beginning of that first ride seemed to be the dangers, in trying to control him and would not have particularly cared, so miserable had I been, if he had thrown me into the water or dashed me against a tree trunk. Now, cares forgotten, I was apprehensive and unsure of my skills, such as they were. Sensing uneasiness, Vindictive was mockingly lively from the outset. His tossing black head that set his bridle jangling and the reins sawing through my fingers was working out what sort of a rider he had on his back. He communicated his superiority in a series of leaps and curves and unpredictable sideways shuffles. Beneath the saddle I felt him twitch as if he were receiving small electric shocks.

We circled the paddock for a while and then, still content to let him air his patrician graces, I took him slowly down the drive. By now he was a little less difficult to manage, curving his neck to the simple snaffle Nicholas insisted he wore, brooding rather than mettlesome, as I, brooding too, began to learn how to curb his vivacity. I risked a slight loosening of the reins. He responded at once with a trumpeting snort of gratitude, accusatory as well of the freedom's not being earlier granted, and although he immediately recommenced his prancing, half-trotting, half-walking progress, I realised I had the hang of him. He was enjoying himself. That had not occurred to me. Under all the cavorting and arching of his neck and ringing of his harness, he was playing the part of a 'steed,' a charger, a story-book horse ridden, panoplied, by knights at joust or to the rescue of a flaxen-haired maiden. As I caught his mood, he relaxed still further and carried me dancing under the green arch of the trees that led to the end of the drive. His hooves clashed merrily on the tarmac. We reached the gate.

Beyond them, as if they and not we were incarcerated, the band of blue-jeaned Praylin fans kept their accustomed vigil. Numbers had grown since my night with Phyllidula. Of shifting membership, by no means drawn from solely local population—Swedes, Danes, Germans, French, once a party of Japanese, supplementing participants from all over the British Isles—they proposed an intriguing subject for a sociological, more correctly anthropological, thesis. There were distinct ethnic characteristics to be noted, nomadic, even *déraciné* though their numbers seemed, a banding together (like the cooks) for the commonweal, group behaviourism often bordering on savagery—fire-lighting, chanting—whose origins were obscure. Oral communication was hampered by the fact that the greater number thrust their heads between the iron bars of the gates and stared fixedly up the drive.

Speech seemed, in any case, unnecessary. Friends relieved friends in the automatic manner of sentries on duty, food was amicably shared, sometimes in inclement weather tents erected, as though these instinctive, almost tribal customs had been learned before arrival or were being atavistically obeyed. Their indefatigability, a sternness of purpose which signaled to passersby who did not know to whom the estate belonged that they were not sightseers but protesters, pickets, perhaps autochthonous owners of a tract of land at some period of history illegally confiscated, warranted, one felt, greater rewards than those with which they all, the girls in particular, were satisfied: a glimpse, however brief, of Nicholas Spark. Then sounds sprang from their lips as if the faculty of speech had for the first time in their lives been miraculously bestowed. They moaned; they yelled; they shook their pinioned heads frantically from side to side; and, when the great gates swung open and Nicholas was driven out in his limousine, they peered in through the car windows and pressed their lips to the windscreen so that the chauffeur, when eventually he had nudged the enormous motorcar between their ranks, was obliged, for the next mile or so, to turn on the windscreen wipers and erase from the glass the blears of lipstick and the condensation of human breath that fogged his vision. I enjoyed those episodes. When I sat in the dark car now further darkened by the girls' clambering bodies and gazed into the sea of laughing, weeping faces, it was as if I were in the throes of one of those dreams of incubi and succubi that disturbed the sleep of the saints. Nicholas sat impassively reading his letters or the newspaper. Once, at my suggestion, he opened the door and dragged in one of their number onto our laps but instead of throwing her arms round Nicholas as I supposed she would and, like Phyllidula at Scotty's request, embracing me as well, she had wriggled and squirmed like an excited puppy and had set up such a yelling and screaming that we were forced to slow the car and ditch her by the roadside after only a few minutes' journey.

I debated unlocking the gates and riding through this colony and up to the common a mile or so away but I was nervous that the girls might cluster around Vindictive as they clustered around the limousine—one or two were already pointing excitedly as they recognized Nicholas's horse—and scare him into bolting or lashing out with his hooves. I turned his head and took him back up the drive, past the house and as far as the gate that led to a field and to a distant wood. Last year I had not dared to set foot in that field. As soon as I had clambered over the gate and stood on the edge of the path trampled across the grass in serpentine undulations to the faraway trees, I had been besieged by agoraphobic terrors that tipped the heaven and the earth drunkenly around my head; and I had fled back to the refuge of the house. Now, as I swung the gate open and remounted Vindictive that path, as straight and broad as a metaled road, had lost its menace. The sky burned soft and blue above the flat plateau of the grass. We rode quietly, fearlessly, along. Vindictive had become ruminative, abandoned for good his restless prancing.

He gave an occasional shake of his head as if to rid himself of a residual, perhaps unworthy, thought. We came to another gate, punctuating a stout picketed fence that ringed the outer trees of a deep forest. It was padlocked. I took Vindictive along the fence's perimeter a couple of hundred yards in each direction in an attempt to find another entrance but none existed. We would have to retreat. I turned him back onto the broad path, shortened his reins and touched his flanks with my heels. The moment he sprang into the gallop I knew no malice rested in him. His back quivered in long sensuous ripples. He stretched for home in bounding strides that sent the path's brown earth pouring beneath his feet and tore us arrow-straight and so fast through the thick summer air that it struck winter-chill on my flesh.

He had made up his mind to jump the gate before I had decided to let him have his own way. He cocked an ear in a 'thumbs-up' signal of intent, slowed momentarily, danced almost on the spot in springing, high-stepping concentration at the obstacle that lay ahead. I settled forward in the saddle and leaned over his glossy neck. The high wooden palings hurtled towards us. He rose. He was up; soaring, as if, an ebony Pegasus, he would bear us high into the blue sky. Turf scored up by his landing rattled against the palings. The clash of his hooves as he hit the driveway cracked like pistol shots against the house's stone grey walls. He slowed to a trot: a walk: then stopped altogether, tossed his great gleaming head and, as I dismounted, rested his bright, brown, trusting eyes upon me and jutted his muzzle into my side. We had become friends.

We rode hard after that, long punishing rides through blazing sun or pouring rain. No terrain was too rough for us, no fence too high, no undergrowth impenetrable. The pace and exhilaration of those rides reflected pretty well methods of work on *The Ordinall of Alchemy.* When not riding or drinking with Nicholas, I went at it full tilt. Frustrated by the shortest interruption, I began to imitate Nicholas's methods of working that eschewed the mundane routines with which life is so cluttered. I stopped washing and shaving. My hair, long on arrival, grew longer, my fingernails dirtier, clothes, never changed, torn and disheveled. ALEMBIC seemed very far away, trivial, even contemptible. In the mornings, Thomas Norton's couplets fired my brain but when, at lunchtime, I sat back and looked over the lines I had revised and annotated, I could hardly wait to type them out before saddling Vindictive for another of our outings. Sometimes, on hot days, with the window open I could hear from the stable yard his hooves shifting in the loose box and I would shout across to him and wait for the whinny of pleasure he gave when he heard me call his name. We often had only each other for company for Nicholas was in London much of the time putting the final touches to *Dreams, Waking Thoughts and Incidents.* Most mornings the absurdly long chauffeur-driven car carried him out past his fans and brought him back only late in the evening. Then the two of us would get drunk on his fiery brandy or stoned on joints he deftly 'skinned up' in his skeletal fingers.

Sometimes, Nicholas added to a scrapbook he was compiling of Celestial Praylin news cuttings, chuckling every so often at articles, by no means uncommon, that expressed distaste for the band's raucousness, vulgarity, bad influence, poor example: 'unsatisfactoriness,' in Rastus's term. I decided to tell him about an incident that had occurred just after I had joined ALEMBIC that emphasized how widely this disapprobation had spread. I could not give exact details, as it had happened in the course of ALEMBIC duties (as far as Nicholas knew I worked for the Income Tax). Demonstration of his fame, notoriety in this case, had been brought to my attention in the most compelling way; and although, by then, it was commonplace to hear at parties or in public places—the Rum Cove, for example—Celestial Praylin's supercharged rhythms bursting out of radios and speakers and jukeboxes, their sudden intrusion into a day which, in other ways, had been decidedly odd, opened my eyes still wider to the sort of reputation his band was building up.

I had only been at ALEMBIC six weeks. Some sort of 'clearance' had been requested, perhaps by Loudermilk, of a character who had launched himself into print on the subject of alchemy. This happened now and again, causing a fluttering of dovecotes, the books, on perusal, most often turning out to be of a harmless, by and large dotty nature. Nevertheless, some sort of guarantee had been required about the author of this particular work, a certain Major Giblin, not up to then encountered, to be apprised of the author's name in case he might have something to tell us about his background. The book under notice was a curious one, more practical than most, recommending experimentation on farm land, due attention given to astronomical, more properly, astrological configurations. Coincidentally, it had been the day Rastus had chosen to sound off his accusations of dilettantism on my part. Ma, who had been asked to produce Major Giblin's address, had caught him in full flow, an expletive on his lips, crippled hand flailing wildly above his head. Seeing out of the tail of his eye another person on whom he might also turn his anger, Rastus had swung himself sideways in his chair to face the intruder head-on across the desk. His mouth opened to let out another oath. When he saw who it was, he froze, mouth agape. Ma too stopped in midsentence. Silently she contemplated from her vantage point her master's still twisted, suffused owl-face and bent on it the stiff, hurt, button-lipped gaze of a nanny who has stumbled upon a nursery tantrum. Rastus's oath became a strangled gulp.

'Ah,' he could only manage. 'Violet.' He tried a watery smile.

No benefit came or could be expected from its influence. Ma, who had observed all too clearly symptoms of passion that could easily develop, if left unchecked, into a 'two-and-eight,' was not prepared to leave the room until fires were altogether extinguished. These she now set about quenching. Icily calm, she stood her ground and repeated in carefully enunciated syllables her inability to locate the required information. That gave Rastus time while he assimilated the news to pull himself together. He scrabbled rather wildly at some papers on his desk.

'It may be in the green book,' he said at last, still with agitation in his high, cawing voice. 'That is my recollection, my distinct recollection. . . .' He arranged another smile. That too was pitilessly met.

'The one we compiled together, Major Cleave?'

'Precisely.' Rastus nodded with enthusiasm. Ma's use of the collective pronoun may have stirred within him reminders of a happy collaborative intimacy enjoyed in the compilation of the address book, a period, however remote, that if he could shake off his storminess of mind might yet be revived, but Ma's Junoesque, entirely stationary figure that still blocked the doorway gave no indication that such a time was at hand. He therefore tried again: 'Precisely.'

This time he was luckier. Despite quite a long pause, Ma said: 'Very well then. I shall take another shufti.'

'Please do, my dear, please do. Meanwhile I must, mustn't I, acquaint Mr Graves with Major Giblin's little peculiarities. Forewarned is forearmed, eh, Violet?' He smiled a third time, his best yet, a broad beaming confident smile, a pink and white crescent in his owlish face that had the effect of quite suddenly releasing from the crown of his head a little tuft of hair that sprang up and quivered in the slight draught Ma was allowing into the room. This appeared to be the very sign she sought. She returned his smile with a coquettish tilt of the head, made a warning moue with her lips—a sort of final reminder of the naughtiness she had observed but was now going for ever to expunge from her mind—turned; and closed the door.

Rastus lay back in his chair and sampled the great calm of which he felt the office and his so recently teeming soul were now possessed; and began in the most affable way to talk about Major Giblin. Very probably he suspected that Ma was listening at the keyhole. He spoke loudly, slowly and at considerable length. I had never known him so relaxed and man-to-man.

'A funny little fellow,' he said. 'Almost a dwarf. He may take to you, he may not. As a young man he was a first-rate officer despite his size. Sword of Honour, own command at twenty-six, capital record in Ireland. But even in those days—I'm giving it you as it was told to me—things were beginning to go wrong. Awry. Seemed to think the military was under some sort of left-wing control, that subversion of one kind or another was undermining the services. He'd been making notes on people for some years, anyone in the news or the public eye he thought was, ah, unsatisfactory. After he retired, he started plonking his findings onto the desks of his superiors. They ignored them for a bit until the stuff began to snowball, then started shoving the info round a bit. Contrary to expectations, it was often very illuminating.'

Here Rastus was forced to break off. Ma had re-entered the office.

Observable a few minutes ago only as confirmation of the intimacy between the two of them—analogous to Lindo's sighting of the restaurant tête-à-tête—Ma's ability to draw Rastus's fire now took on wider, more unusual, even metaphysical aspects. Rather like the curative powers of certain saints in olden days who were able to heal the sick by calling out their diseases and taking the suffering upon themselves, Ma was now being torn by the same uncontrollable passions she had so miraculously allayed in her master. She was in a towering rage. She shook, she was in tears, she stamped her foot.

'This is too much, Major Cleave,' she all but howled. 'I have to say I hardly expected these alarms and excursions. The green book, without a by-your-leave or a may I, that has not been asked for this twelvemonth. I,' she confessed, controlling herself for just a second, 'am all of a doodah.' She gave a great sniff.

Rastus stared at her in amazement, as if her healing art had not only totally composed him but had bereft him of any conception that human beings could experience suffering at all, let alone be prey to the racking upheavals he was witnessing before his eyes. He recognized soon enough that spirited action was called for. He took on a tone of upright, commanding, alert efficiency. He raised his right, his 'good,' hand like a smiling bobby admonishing a ravishingly pretty motorist.

'Now, Violet, now,' he said. 'Don't upset yourself. There is no hurry, not the slightest hurry at all. If need be, this is a matter that can wait until tomorrow, the day after, next week even. You must take your time. There are more ships lost at sea through panic. . . .' He broke off to observe progress. Ma pondered his words with another sniff. They were not, it seemed, without balm. Promise of time to initiate a thorough search might even have done the trick. Rastus risked lowering his square, capable palm. He bent his head as if offering a little prayer for the descent of peace. We waited in silence to feel its touch.

Ma, however, was not done. She gave a little warning blurt. Rage? More tears? It was hard to tell. Rastus rallied further forces.

'Violet, please. I tell you what. Give us half a tick more here and then I'll come out and we'll go through things with a fine-tooth comb. The two of us. Make no mistake about it, together we shall turn up trumps.'

Once more his smile beamed across the room. I saw he had delivered a masterstroke. The allure of a mutual hunt—there might be occasion for admiring a cactus or taking a turn on the roof garden—had finally quitened Ma's agitation. Now it was her turn to smile sweetly or as sweetly as she could while clouds were still dispersing.

'Very well, Major Cleave,' she said. 'I am sorry to have burst in. Perhaps some tea might set us all to rights.'

'Tea will be a boon and a blessing, Violet. And an assortment of biscuits. Biscuits would not come amiss.'

Ma considered this elaboration of her nostrum with every sign of favour. 'No sooner the word than the deed,' she said cheerfully. 'I'll leave you to your chinwag.'

Rastus gathered the thread of his thoughts. Talking, he idly began to clear papers to one side to make room for the tea tray.

'As I was saying, Giblin's observations were not without interest and certainly not without accuracy but he was kicking up far too much of a stink for his own good, fighting his own battles instead of leaving them to men more qualified. Finally, there was a lawsuit. The verdict went against him. There was a row outside the courtroom. He invited prosecuting counsel to remove his trousers preparatory to a horse-whipping. It was then that M.I.5 stepped in, pulled him out of trouble, sent him underground, made him their official informer if you like. There isn't a crank, queer or radical in the land he hasn't got a file on. He'll fill you in on this alchemist chappie, tip you the wink if there's anything—unsatisfactory.'

Foraging by Ma and Rastus produced at last, perhaps a little sooner than Ma might have wished, Major Giblin's address, one in North London. Behind a main road where the bus put me down full of kebab houses, travel agents, launderettes, the crescent of small semidetached houses was cluttered with skips of rubble from dwellings being refurbished, motorcycles under tarpaulins, shoddy, possibly abandoned cars. Major Giblin's house, before which stood a midget, bright green, eccentrically designed humpbacked little car that looked as if it would hop along rather than run on its four wheels, was small, pebble-dashed, pointed of gable, net-curtained, inexplicably striking in the way that houses which have been the scene of violent crimes take on forever afterwards a furtive significance. It was fenced off from the road by knee-high wooden palings that enclosed a pocket-handkerchief of a lawn through which a crazy-paved path cut a line to the peeling front door. On the sill of the front window a marmalade cat lay asleep. My approach disturbed the animal. It poured itself down the wall and vanished behind the curtains. I was about to ring, would have already done so had there not been several bells from which to choose, all unlabeled, when the front door was abruptly opened. The man who swung it right back on its hinges to the wall of the shabby hall it had revealed stood at attention by its side. Despite his size, hardly that to satisfy army regulations, a couple of inches shorter than Loder, not himself a tall man, he exuded a certain dry authority that made up for lack of inches. As soon as I stepped over the threshold, he banged the door shut again and adopted the 'at ease' position, wiry body erect, chin jutting out, hands behind his back, feet in tiny tan shoes set firmly apart. He was almost entirely ginger: reflected in his dress, his hair, even his freckled face, all shades of the cat who, unless Major Giblin had been looking out for me from some hidden vantage point, had announced to him my arrival. He wore a dark russet hacking jacket, sharply pressed gingery trousers of cavalry twill, an orange tie. His small egg-shaped head was bald, freckled like his face, surrounded by a clipped circlet of flaming orange hair. He gazed at me with narrow green watchful eyes as if he preferred somehow to confirm identification from circumstantial evidence rather than simply ask my name or announce his own. Satisfied, he snapped himself to attention again and strode off past me down the passage, halted before a door on his right, threw it open, thought better of it, half closed it again and spoke his first word:

'Gubbins?'

'I'm sorry?'

'Gubbins? Before we begin?'

I had not the slightest idea what he was talking about. I asked him once more to repeat what he had said.

'Gubbins. Lav, man, lav.' He barked out the words. 'Long journey. Never know. Down the passage, left turn, pull hard, pause of "two, three," pull again. No? Right. In we go then.'

He again opened the door and this time allowed me to pass. The cat I had seen in the window backed warily up across a small rectangle of Bokhara rug laid across the threshold. I bent to stroke it but it flinched and bounded away.

'Whoa back,' Major Giblin said. 'Friend, not foe.' I was relieved to hear myself thus spoken of. Nothing had yet suggested amicable relations of any kind whatsoever. Perhaps sensing discourtesy on his part, Major Giblin set about explaining his abruptness in the passageway:

'Sorry if I appeared somewhat edgy out there,' he said speaking in a brusque military voice that had in it something of Rastus's inflexions although lower pitched. 'Have to be a bit careful of what one says and does. Got some rum neighbours up aloft. Never know who's bending an ear, do you get it? Temporary billet this. I'm being found less cramped quarters, so I hear. One expands so fast if one's to keep abreast. They've promised me a computer but I doubt I'll be able to get the hang of it. In any case, you don't feel you've got the stuff at your fingertips with gadgets of that sort. They can be fearful asses sometimes, don't you find?'

'Computers?'

'Cats. I mean, they don't wait to take stock, sum a fellow up, they're off and away just as if they'd made up their mind they didn't like the cut of your jib and there was an end of the matter. Mind you, he'll come out again if you call him and be as nice as pie. Answers to the name of Cat. Seemed simplest. I'll rustle up some coffee if you'll give me a couple of ticks. Kitchen's down the passage. Sit on the bed, that's the best place. Only place, come to that. Hah.'

Major Giblin let a little smile whip across his pebble-smooth face, turned on his heel and marched away. I heard the sounds of a coffee-grinder. I was in a room of more generous proportions than I would have imagined from the house's frontage, but only because the two ground-floor rooms had been knocked into one. One saw immediately what Major Giblin meant about shortage of space. His hard, truckle bed placed across the far end of the back room was the sole item of domestic furniture. All other available space was taken up by row after row of gun-metal filing cabinets. They were not only set along all four walls and across the window bay into which the cat had somehow managed to insinuate itself but encroached in serried ranks across all available floor space. The narrowest of mazelike corridors linked these shining structures, across the taller of which had been balanced other, oblong receptacles, drawers containing index cards it was to be supposed, so they formed archways that ran like pit-props in some ghostly moonlit quarry away into every corner of the stacked, silent workplace.

A manilla file, extracted from one of the cabinets, lay on the bed. It was marked with the name of a labour councillor recently in the news, guest, so Freddy had told me, on *Ferguson on Thursday.* His photograph was attached to the outside. Overpoweringly tempted to investigate Major Giblin's system of documentation, I was about to peep inside the file when the cat, as he had predicted, stalked out from whichever of the dark passageways it had sought when we came in and sprang up beside me. It looked at me strictly with eyes much the same colour as its master's, emitted a chirrup of pleasure that had the effect of causing its legs to buckle from under its body and rolled over on its back. Its feet stuck up in the air. Its square, now completely relaxed body exactly covered the manilla folder. I tickled its stomach and it gave a delighted wriggle, at the same time managing to squash one ear under its head that gave it a cockeyed, untidy, rather mad look far divorced from the spruceness displayed on my arrival. Quite apart from the fact it was crumpling its owner's papers, I had the feeling Major Giblin would not care to witness the almost wanton abandonment of dignity any more than he would have wished me to come on him, pyjama'd, in his austere bed-space. Nor, when he appeared at the door with the coffee tray, did he do so. He rapped out an order for a change of position. The cat rolled over, arched its back, split its face into a wide pink yawn, jumped lightly down and took up a statuesque sitting position before us. Intent, inquisitive, eyeing each of us in turn, it seemed ready to listen, perhaps to contribute, to our conversation.

Major Giblin sat cross-legged on the floor and poured coffee from a tall copper pot into fragile, thimble-sized cups. The liquid was extremely strong, extremely sweet. He pointed to the file on the bed.

'Know him?' he asked.

I mentioned the reason for his television appearance, espousal, I recalled, of a minority cause, public money expended on its promotion arousing dismay in some quarters.

'He has a very poor track record,' Major Giblin remarked. 'A very poor track record indeed. An absolute wet. Sort of chap who makes canals in his morning porridge.'

He spoke the words with total disgust. It was all too abundantly plain that, in his eyes, there was no fouler stigma with which a man could be marked in a society with pretensions to table manners, anyone else, for the matter of that, in any other stratum consuming porridge of the necessary consistency to tempt this profoundly disgusting experimentation in irrigatory techniques. Major Giblin searched my face to ensure I had correctly taken in the full extent of his disapprobation. At last he seemed to thaw a little, as if conscious of having rendered himself too overwrought over so slight a matter or so I might have interpreted his outburst. He jerked his head away and turned to the cat. They stared steadily into each other's eyes, as if telepathically engaged.

'Ferguson's no great shakes, either,' the Major eventually said, looking up at me again. 'One of the Browning sisters, you know.'

For the second time I had to ask what he meant.

'Queer,' he said. 'Bugger. Homo. Trouser pilot.'

I had heard that before, probably from Nicholas, propensity stoutly denied by Freddy and by Loder.

'Humpty-dumpty,' I said. 'That's how my sergeant put it.'

For the second time Major Giblin allowed his tight little smile to acknowledge a pleasantry, a mere thinning of the lips before he settled his face once more.

'What was your sar'nt's name?'

'Barker.'

'I know him. A good soldier.' He got to his feet, adjusted the knife-edge crease in his trousers. He asked the name of the man I had come to investigate.

'Doesn't ring any bells. I'll have a look though. Would you mind giving the cat a little milk? Catch hold of that saucer, that fellow there. Put it in the corner by the door.'

He extracted from his pocket a pencil-torch and flashed it around the outskirts of his metallic domain. He marched in and disappeared. I heard drawers being opened, slammed shut, the low clipped voice muttering as he moved from area to area. I poured the cat's milk. It stood over the saucer, tail quivering. Two bubbles on the surface broke, making the animal leap in the air as if at a minor explosion. It waited guardedly, fearing further insurrections, before making another light-footed, more circuitous approach to its refreshment. Eventually it bent to drink.

Giblin meantime was crashing round his filing system. Every so often, the noise would cease, succeeded by a muted whistle signifying perhaps the location of pertinent material. A sharp beam of light from his torch flashed now and again across the darkened corridors. Once or twice I caught sight of his shadowy figure as it hurried under one of the arches and as quickly disappeared again into obscurer crannies of his elaborate workings. Over the slamming of cupboard doors and the sliding in and out of aluminium trays of index cards he began to call out questions about myself, perfectly friendly ones admissible of ready and truthful replies which I shouted back over the din. Although his interrogation was without apparent guile, it had to be considered that he already knew whether my answers were accurate. It seemed likely that, before my recruitment, somebody—Rastus or Loudermilk—had requested the sort of search he was now making among his files in case my own name were on record. It came to me too that it had been Giblin who had given orders for me to be followed by the boy with the alabaster skin. I thought of calling out to ask if that were correct but then, having reached some nook that lent to his voice a metallic resonance as if a robot addressed me, he rattled off a string of names, 'Adams,' 'Vanderplank,' 'Frith-Liddiard' —there were others, their tinny vibrations ricocheting against the cabinets like some strange roll call from outer space—in the hope, as he said, they 'rang a bell.' I had heard of none of them.

The cat, its milk consumed, face cleaned, rubbed against my leg. I scratched the small, snake-shaped skull. It tossed its head and began a purposeful throbbing purr. The noise seemed a reflexion of the steady pulse that beat throughout the strange, faceless room beyond the ascetic bed and the bright strip of rug where Giblin was at work. Rastus's description of him as a dwarf was a fair enough estimate, not only because of his stature but because of the gnomish industry he was applying to the task in hand. Agricola, enthusiastically noticed by Thomas Norton in *The Ordinall of Alchemy,* had written of men below ground in search of the Philosopher's Stone, troll-like creatures who never saw the light of day. There was in Major Giblin much of this diligent, elemental prospecting, the persistent mining of secret, productive seams that no discomfort, fatigue, hunger, cramped conditions, could be allowed to interrupt; and although his attitude, despite a characteristic bluntness of manner, was perfectly civil, Rastus's further observation—'He may take to you, he may not'—remained unresolved. Probably Major Giblin 'took' to no one. There was an abrasive quality about him, petulance not far from the surface, the grumpiness associated with dwarves in fairy tales. Malice, a capricious spitefulness rather, could not be ruled out.

At last his search was at an end. His records had not yielded the information we needed. He poured me another cup of his sweet, sandy coffee and announced he would accompany me to the bus. 'I feel like a turn,' he said. 'A breath of air. Cat will ride on my shoulder.' From one of his cupboards he produced a brown mackintosh and a loud ginger cloth cap. We went out into the street.

He walked quickly along taking brisk steps in his brown highly polished shoes. Both he and the cat viewed everything they passed with the deepest suspicion through green, watchful eyes. He chose a different route from the one I came by, along a deserted avenue of derelict houses that would, at its end, give onto the main road where the buses passed. Graffiti—violently coloured palimpsests of expletives, names of football teams, rock groups, street gangs, protestations of affection within heart-shaped frameworks—had been sprayed on to the peeling front doors, boarded-up windows, what remained of garden walls. It was a street of frigid gloom, gusty yet noiseless, overladen with a cringing expectancy as if the area had not fallen gradually into decay but had been pillaged by a marauding band for whom it now waited, trembling, to return. The major's steps rang out on the pavement. The cat, statuesque, lynxlike, clung to the shoulder of his mackintosh.

All at once, as if to soothe the almost palpable terrors the apprehensive, battle-torn street exuded, music somewhere began to play. Loud though it was, it came peacefully over the air: lilting, pastoral, a harbinger of better days for this stricken place. Giblin stopped; cocked an ear; seemed about to speak. I too had something to say.

This was Celestial Praylin music, the beginning of 'Light's Abode,' its melodies, like so many of Nicholas's, composed in a fairly advanced state of intoxication.

' "Light's Abode, Celestial Praylin," see, now?' Nicholas had said when he gave me the record. He had been in enigmatic mood. In the dim light of my sitting room great cavernous hollows under his cheeks had accentuated the gauntness of his bone white face. He stroked his long, ill-barbered chin.

'That's one problem solved; but I'm always being asked the origin of the name of your band. Is that another secret you're prepared to divulge?'

'A quotation from Rimbaud: a rough translation of *céleste praline.* The poem, one to which Verlaine also contributed, is not much read: not very often found in print for the matter of that. We spell it phonetically to convey an American accent, our music being founded, as I'm sure you have appreciated, on the blues. Otherwise, and correctly, it would be "prarleen." Aren't you going to play your nice present?'

The disc had not become a favourite. It demonstrated more forcibly than any of their previously recorded numbers Celestial Praylin's disconcerting speciality: the element of surprise. The band had a way of playing quite tunefully for a while and then of quite suddenly cranking everything up and blasting the listener, without warning, out of his seat. The prelude to one of these disconcerting 'pounces' now engaged Major Giblin and myself. The guitars' lutelike, almost Elizabethan measures trod with a stately tunefulness. Plangency would be short-lived.

'You know these chaps, you say.' The major was walking on, peering into houses as if set on locating the source of these formal cadences.

'Yes, I was at school with the singer. He . . .' I could get no further. Nicholas's drummer unleashed a thunderous percussive roll. The guitars struck two savage, ringing chords. Perhaps there was a second more of silence over which I could have issued some sort of warning; and then the whole street shuddered under the banked, merciless waves of amplified sound. The insolent, densely packed music struck against the shells of the houses and hammered in our eardrums. Above the great glissandi of noise Nicholas's desolate falsetto howled out his distorted message of hope and despair.

We had reached the corner of the main road. Over the din—its source now apparent, a group of five or six schoolboys assembled in the garden of one of the houses with a stereophonic radio-tape deck of epic proportions—I thanked Major Giblin for his time and trouble. He appeared not to have heard; very probably he had not. He touched his cap, bestowed on me a withering look only a little less expressive of the disgust he had signaled for the labour councillor's canalization of his porridge and thrust out a hand to be shaken. The cat stared balefully down as I took my leave. Giblin gave the curtest of nods. I turned away and passed the boys huddled about the recorder-radio that still pumped out Praylin music at deafening volume. They crouched around it like waifs before a warming fire. Despite wearing school uniform, by deft adjustments—ripping down of ties, unknotting of shoelaces, pulling out of shirttails—they had managed to make themselves look motley, unkempt, beggarly: 'up to no good.' The rapt attention on their small, white, hard faces had in it an element of revolutionary fervour as if they were tuned in to an inflammatory broadcast by a people's leader. Major Giblin may have been thinking along those lines as well. At any rate, he set himself upon a course of action to make his own stance regarding popular music quite categorically plain. From my vantage point at the bus stop, I was able to observe his every move.

The gang had broken up. All but one of the boys, the owner of the radio, slouched off down the main road, on the other side of which I was waiting for my bus. The boy with the 'ghetto blaster,' which he swung arrogantly from a chrome handle and which was still playing at earsplitting volume, struck off along the deserted street where Major Giblin and the cat still motionlessly remained. As they came together, Giblin turned to face the boy, as if to allow him to pass on the kerbstone side of the pavement. When they were exactly level, the Major drew back a leg and aimed a tremendous kick at the howling apparatus. His pointed leather toe connected with a crack on the polished casing. The boy, caught off balance, staggered and fell. The radio, still issuing music but shedding essential parts of internal mechanism, soared like a punted rugger ball high into the air; fell to earth; and shattered into a thousand fragments.

That was all I saw. A bus drew up, obscuring my view. I boarded it and hurried upstairs but it had moved too quickly past the intersection. I often wondered how the incident had ended. There and then, most likely. I imagined Major Giblin striding off, cat on shoulder, while the boy picked himself up and ran to see if the damage to his equipment was reparable. The major's deftly executed, thoroughly vindictive action seemed aimed not at teaching the boy a lesson in noise pollution but at Nicholas himself whom, like everybody else on his index cards, he had there and then marked down as a menace to law and order.

Nicholas liked the story very much; and indeed, whenever afterwards he came across derogatory press reports, he would read them out loud and fling out his foot as if he, too, were kicking a 'ghetto blaster' to smithereens.

One evening, he said, 'I'm afraid it's your turn to cop a little bit of Praylin flak.'

'How do you mean?'

'You and Vindictive. You're getting quite a reputation in the village.'

'Really?'

'Insanity, daredevilry, a menace to decent folk. Those words are on everybody's lips. Mothers draw their children to their breasts at your passing, old men shake their heads, young girls' hearts are strangely stirred. They no longer sleep at nights.'

'You exaggerate.'

'A bit. Someone did ask about you though.'

'Indeed? What did he say?'

'Word for word?'

'Word for word.'

' "Who's the mad cunt on your horse?" '

'Is that all?'

'Yes. Good-natured, if roughly spoken. I shouldn't let it worry you.'

It had not occurred to me that Nicholas's notoriety might redound on Vindictive and myself. It was a relief the enquiry had been of so casual a nature; that Nicholas, too, took it in good part. A more serious complaint, one from a farmer perhaps or a local apprehension we were becoming a sort of Dick Turpin–Black Bess duo, a threat, as Nicholas put it, to law-abiding citizens, might well have meant some curbing of enthusiasm, of the 'madness,' as the witness had interpreted it, of the way we thundered daily over the countryside.

I gave it no more thought; and it was not until the third from last day of my holiday that we were faced fairly and squarely with neighbourhood distrust. Rounding a corner of a narrow lane, we rode straight into the local riding school.

A neat uniform string of girls on horseback, two abreast, blocked our path. At its head a grim-faced woman dressed, like her charges, in cream jodhpurs, black jacket, velvet jockey cap, raised a yellow-gloved fist. Her sour powdered face stared into mine.

It was the first time we had been at such close quarters. Twice I had seen her in the school's paddock where she had been supervising manoeuvres with sharp cries of command, twice more strung out with her girls on the brow of a hill, a fifth time through the window of a tea shop. She had been seated at a table for two in acid contemplation of a sugared cake of adventuresome proportions. Its shape and colour, irregularly rectangular, unevenly surfaced, roughcast all over with pinkish-beige icing, had remarkably resembled a scale model of ALEMBIC headquarters. Crenellations, embrasures, turretings, together with overall dimensions and liverishness of colour had, in miniature, been precisely imitated. The way she towered above her purchase and the challenging gleam in her eye as she flourished the fork she would any second plunge into the very centre of the confection and open up great rifts in its stuccoed coating put me in mind of some allegorical cartoon—'The Temple of Superstition Destroyed by Rational Thought'—and kept me riveted to the glass in case I could have descried tiny figures, Ma, Rastus, myself, fleeing in terror from the wreckage.

Her face had seemed curiously familiar, that of some feared nursemaid temporarily employed by my mother or a hated piano teacher, names forgotten. Now it came to me that the flat, chalk white face, the red slash of the mouth, the thoroughly cross-grained expression and erectness of carriage were not attributes of anyone I had known but those with which I used to endow, whenever he spoke of them, the imaginary creatures of fate that disrupted, so he claimed, the life of Sgt Barker: his 'Titless Susans.' From this band of creatures that, over the time we had served together, I had been able, ever more clearly, to envisage and who, oddly enough, because I saw them dive-bombing, like scrawny superwomen, out of a clear sky onto his head, I had mentally provided with very much the same design of crash helmet that now protected the riding mistress's skull, she seemed to have been selected for an especial biliousness of countenance and sourness of demeanour to confront me, as Sgt Barker found himself so often confronted, with the unambiguity of fate. Not for one second, however, did I take her for an illusion. Icy though they were, I faced flesh and blood.

Words proved difficult to find. Even in less demanding circumstances they would not have come easily for I was, that afternoon, extremely hung over, possibly still a little drunk. For reasons that last night seemed desirable, even imperative, Nicholas and I had finished our drinking bout in a small summer-house full of rotting leaves where we had then fallen asleep. Their smell now mingled not unpleasantly with the fumes of brandy, quite a lot of which had got spilled on my clothes and with the cigarette I had lit up before this unlooked-for meeting, but in the warm air that had the effect of accentuating aromas, so that the scent of flowers that grew by the roadside overhung quite distinctly the narrow lane, I discerned for the first time upon myself another odour, the unmistakable rankness of unwashed flesh.

The riding mistress may have discerned it too. We were close enough. There was the faintest wrinkling of the powdered nose. Then the harsh red lips parted.

'Walk your horse on, please.'

These were words of command. I briefly considered their defiance. There was little question I was being made an example of, shown up by being made to run the gauntlet of her girls as a disgrace to the art of horsemanship, very probably to the human condition as a whole. I could have turned tail, urged Vindictive to the gallop and flung over my shoulder a parting expletive. Such an exigency seemed cowardly: unnecessary as well. The disapproval that swept from the riding mistress in gusty, chilling waves was finding no reciprocity among her charges. The girls' excited whispering, audible above the tinkling of harness and scrape of horseshoes on the tarmac as they respectfully began to divide ranks and afford me a passage between them, contradicted firmly their teacher's opinion of the stranger in their midst. Short shrift would be given to whatever lecture on manners and deportment she had in mind to deliver later in the day. These girls were Praylin fans, devoted and unashamed. I recognized several faces that made up the small colony of admirers at Nicholas's gate. For a certainty, I was a poor substitute for their hero, shabbiness of clothing and a few days' stubble a pale reflection of Nicholas's spectacular dishevelment. Nevertheless, I was riding his horse. For all the girls knew I might be a new member of the band or a replacement for one of its number. They were not going to miss the chance of a closer sighting.

I rode into their ranks and said good afternoon to each girl as I passed. Ideally, much could have been made of this necessarily slow, formal procession, bowing from the waist perhaps or doffing an invisible 'topper,' but I now needed to concentrate single-mindedly on Vindictive. His forbearance to other horses, of whimsical foundation, was being submitted in this head-on collision with a fairly motley selection of his kind to the very sternest of tests. He passed bay, chestnut, grey, a plump skewbald, none of them approaching his height and pedigree, with every indication of increasing acrimony. It was with the greatest difficulty we negotiated without incident or loss of dignity the parallel, seemingly endless pairs of chattering girls.

The ordeal—it had been little less—affected me as potently as Vindictive. My headache had returned. I felt decidedly ill. I was altogether unprepared for what happened next. The last girl in the line put out a hand as we passed and tugged at my sleeve. It was Joanna Palin.

'What are you doing here?'

Despite the jockey cap that covered her fair, shoulder-length hair and hid the fringe that was trained as a rule across the line of her eyebrows, she looked much as usual: neat, demure, half shy, half smiling, 'big for her age,' as Ma always said. There was some truth in that. It was as if she were experiencing a physical and mental misalignment, a failure of mind to run in tandem with a more rapidly growing physique, so that she exhibited on occasion the sort of awkwardness a subject feels who is suddenly faced with a camera and who senses, as Joanna was sensing now, she ought to be draping herself in some sort of pose and assuming a pleased half-smile at being 'caught' by the photographer's lens instead of just glowering into the aperture. Very likely she was finding things awkward, for although the object of her stopping me was for the kudos she would earn when I had ridden off of telling her friends just how well we knew each other and of retailing news about Celestial Praylin that could be accounted the very 'latest,' there was the problem of exactly what to say first of all. She could not very well, not politely anyhow, launch straight into Praylin territory. Formalities had to be got over, comment made upon the improbability of this meeting, news given of her father, preliminaries of that sort, and this was resulting in the same sort of battle with limbs I had seen her wage at home when, in order to look relaxed, she struck out with her legs and threw her arms behind her head and hurled herself backwards onto the sofa as if she had been lifted there by invisible hands, or, when showing her father some indifferent homework or a lukewarm school report, she went through great writhings and dips of her body as she stood beside his armchair in an effort to appear to be looking casually over his shoulder; and in these throes, not of embarrassment exactly, but of the same untutored locomotory bids for relaxation, she now began to tug at the peak of her cap, to stand up in her stirrups and fling herself to one side and tighten her girths in such a flurry of inarticulate activity that there seemed only one possible way to put her at her ease.

'I have a right to be here,' I said.

She gave a little eruptive giggle through her nose. The words had rung a bell.

'The hat,' she said.

'It was a tricky half-hour.'

'No kidding.' She giggled again.

What are you doing here? I have a right to be here. Joanna's disgruntled question and her father's equally tart response had been the very first interchange I had heard between them, prelude, as it turned out, to a 'scene' that had marred, for a while, the first evening I had been invited to supper with them. Freddy had been on edge all day. Perhaps after his wife's death he entertained little, Joanna's competence as a hostess all but untested. On the other hand, because he kept emphasizing they lived 'very simply,' he might have been regretting the invitation in case that life-style, whatever form simplicity took, might expose social differences on top of those of age and intellect already, to his mind, interposing. We traveled some distance on the underground; walked for a while through suburban streets. At length we reached a small modern house in a quiet crescent.

'We only have the ground floor,' Freddy said. 'What they call a maisonette. You mustn't expect the Ritz.'

He put his key in the latch and opened the door. Joanna was in the hall. Before a full-length mirror on one of the walls she was in the act of trying on an extraordinarily silly hat.

It was not only silly—almost any hat would have looked out of place on the head of a small girl still in school uniform—it was somewhat out-of-date, the style however not unfamiliar. Some twelve years before my mother had worn a model of basically similar design, colours a little more muted, to my prep-school sports day. In the course of the afternoon, my father had pronounced it 'tittupy.' It was a good description. Small, round, Joanna's version the brightest of cherry red, both boasted black veils. This, as we entered, Joanna was securing under her chin. In a fit of rage she had torn the object off her head and thrown it onto the floor.

'What are you doing here?' she asked. She had been close to tears.

'I have a right to be here,' Freddy replied.

I had not yet learned of Freddy's objection to a stage career. Ma's disclosure, when it came, went some way to explaining the distinctly chilly atmosphere that prevailed over the next half-hour. Freddy had very probably interpreted this propensity for 'dressing up'—if it had not been for our premature arrival it was conceivable she would have gone swanning round the empty flat pretending to be at a wedding or a garden party—as symptomatic of the dramatic ambitions he so feared in his daughter. He made no attempt to introduce Joanna who, in any case, plunged into her room and slammed the door. We moved into the sitting room where Freddy gave me a drink. He sat down in an armchair and picked up the evening paper. Tension hummed through the neat, highly polished room. Celestial Praylin, at their most rumbustious, throbbed purposefully from behind Joanna's door. I picked up a magazine. As I thumbed through it, a different interpretation of the incident occurred to me. The hat very probably belonged to Joanna's mother, not all that long dead. If that were the case, I could understand both sides of the argument, Freddy's for what he took to be disrespect, Joanna's that the hat, given fashion's habit of taking, every so often, a retrospective turn, might in a few years again become the 'thing.'

I decided to ask Joanna if I had been right. Behind me I heard the other riders begin to move off. Joanna made no attempt to follow. She turned her horse round, a pretty dun mare with a white blaze, and watched over her shoulder her fellow pupils as they tailed away. We were alone in the lane.

'Had it belonged to your mother?'

'Yeah.'

'That explains a lot.'

'Thanks for smoothing things over.'

It was my turn to smile. Rather like the early stages of my dinner with Loudermilk, the evening had looked intractable of rescue. Joanna had come in and given mumbled news about the progress of our supper. She had plumped herself down on the sofa with one of her great flurries of movement that made it look as if she had been hurled across the room by poltergeist activity and had begun to pick at the hem of her skirt. I had noted hints, even then, of childishness, even babyhood, in the plump, sullen face and the thick splayed fingers she seemed not yet able to control, but, as occasionally she had gathered herself in her jerky way and stopped fussing with the thread of cotton and sat upright with a great start and in the poise with which, before the glass, she had been adjusting the veil of the hat, there were elements too of an already womanly independence. Only her hair, cut boyishly short, her white blouse, the skirt she fiddled with and her heavy 'sensible' shoes had pinpointed more or less her exact age. As if reading my thoughts, she had suddenly asked:

'How old are you?'

'Twenty-four,' I said over Freddy's remonstrance.

'You look younger.'

'So people say. How old are you?'

'Thirteen, as it happens. Almost, anyway.'

Freddy had roused himself. 'I'll see to the potatoes,' he said. 'No more personal questions out of you, please, Miss.' He left the room. We were, then, going to eat. That was a comfort. Unless they actually threw it at each other, food could well prove the antidote to their quarrel. Alone with me, Joanna resumed fiddling with her skirt. I found nothing to say. All at once, she looked up, raised her eyebrows and gave a little, exasperated shrug of her shoulders. She smiled. This seemed a breaking of the ice, the opportunity to enquire further into the episode, perhaps to ask the provenance of the hat, but that would hardly do as the kitchen was within earshot. Freddy could be heard rattling plates and banging saucepans. Some acknowledgment that I was on her side, or at least not against her, was, however, called for. She may have asked my age with that in mind, a recruiting, to her way of looking at things, of someone comparatively young, looking, as she had said, younger still. A middle course had to be found if I were not to upset Freddy: sympathy without connivance. Curiously, the words they had exchanged at the front door were precisely those taught to a friend at drama school as an exercise in inflexions, emphasis on one word or another radically altering the sentences' meaning. I launched laboriously into an explanation of all that. Joanna listened with interest, then with excitement, drumming her heavy shoes on the carpet. She began to rehearse permutations.

' "*What* are you doing here?" "I've a *right* to be here." "What *are* you doing here?" "I've a right to *be* here." "What are you *doing* here?" Yeah, that's brilliant.'

Freddy came back bearing a tray with dishes on it. He was beaming. Some period of adjustment in the kitchen had reaped a bountiful harvest. He beckoned us to the table laid in a corner of the sitting room. We took our places.

All, however, was not over. I had reckoned without Joanna's stupidity or her willfulness. As soon as we were settled, she once again confronted her father with the same question.

'What are *you* doing here?'

Freddy looked up, suprised. 'Serving the supper, dear.'

She gathered herself to repeat the question. Whether she were goading her father to prolong indefinitely their disagreement or continuing to experiment with the sentences' nuances for her own amusement now seemed immaterial. Another repetition could hardly fail to remind Freddy of the original altercation in the lobby. The food that was now before us looked rather good, Freddy's wine, from the label, not undrinkable. I was both hungry and thirsty. If equilibrium were to be finally restored, I would have to switch, once and for all, the direction of Joanna's attack. I decided to humour her, to change her provocative question into some form of dramatic dialogue between the two of us. I pointed histrionically at Freddy.

'What are you doing *here?* Unbidden and unconsecrated, thou cans't not enter our sacred hall.'

Born of desperation, delivery of this phrase, read I suppose in some Freemasonic ritual, had been striking in the extreme. Its pompous formalities rolled across the table with Churchillian vigour. Mercifully, Joanna picked up the idea at once.

'Stranger of darkness, thy feet sully our holy portals.'

Despite faintly adenoidal delivery, these words were excellent. They could almost have been part of the ritual, whatever it was, that had stuck in my mind. I pressed home the advantage.

'Honoured sister, lay the instrument of benediction on this, our hapless brother.'

Joanna rose to her feet. She gave one of her nasal giggles. She picked up the spoon used to serve the potatoes and raised it aloft. Processing slowly around the table, she laid its bowl reverently on her father's silvered pate.

'*Aum,*' I intoned.

'What's "orm"?'

'You say "*Padi.*" '

'Paddy.'

'*Aum.*'

'*Aum,*' Joanna intoned after me. 'OK, Dad, you're consecrated now and allowed to eat with us. Isn't he, Tom?'

'White as driven snow.'

'Well,' Freddy said. A small lump of mashed potato adhered to the crown of his head. 'I don't know where you two learn these things.'

Now in the lane, conversation, cheerfully enough begun, had once more dried up, but Joanna was clearly in no hurry to join her companions. She had brought her mare up beside Vindictive. She sat fiddling with the reins and staring at her yellow-gloved hands, still half smiling, half bashful. I began to think about means of getting away. My head was still aching. I wanted very much to get back to Carpenter's and lie down. The easiest method of escape would have been to invite Joanna up to meet Nicholas—it would have to be tomorrow or the day after, my last—but the invitation could prove inconvenient. It might interrupt work, riding too, perhaps. Moreover, as I had once discovered, Nicholas could be extremely offhand with his fans, even downright offensive. There was the question too of introducing someone so young into Carpenter's which, although now empty, could fill up at any moment with the other Praylin musicians and their hangers-on and the sort of wild party develop where, like the 'gong' evening, carousing got out of hand. It had been instructive to have gained confirmation of my hat theory. If conversation were to continue, it would be best kept along similarly reminiscent lines. The fact was, though, that Joanna and I had never had anything much to say to each other, had never met outside the confines of the maisonette, the sort of theatricals we always fell into, of which Freddy's 'initiation' ceremony had been the precursor, a substitute of a kind for polite conversation at which neither of us had proved much good. Without Freddy as an audience, however, there seemed little point in setting up a dramatic dialogue. Play-acting would in any case have been superfluous. In this unexpected meeting, in the story-book improbability of our both being on horseback, in our oddly disparate disguises—Joanna's spotless formality and my own dishevelment made them hardly less—there were features enough of a little melodrama every bit as contrived as any our imaginations had previously given rein to: 'meeting like this' a coincidence indeed. I felt a sudden curiosity to know how it had come about.

'What *are* you doing here? Seriously?'

'I'm on a riding holiday. Didn't Dad tell you?'

'No.'

'He's awful. He never tells anyone anything. He's in Scandinavia.'

I remembered that. Ma had spoken enviously of the projected holiday, Loder less so. He had envisaged problems in obtaining hot meals. 'Glorified sandwiches, that's all you'll get. Raw fish too, I shouldn't wonder.'

'I didn't want to go,' Joanna went on. 'It sounded boring.'

' "The lure of the fjords." That's what the brochure said.'

'They didn't lure me. Can I tell you something?' Joanna let go of the reins and allowed her mount to crop the long grass on the verge of the lane. Vindictive, uncharacteristically, watched with equanimity and jerked his head to suggest he too would like to graze.

'What?'

'You won't mind?'

'No.'

'Promise?'

'Promise.'

'You smell.' Joanna made the point in an amused, matter-of-fact way as if telling me that my tie was crooked.

'It's the horses.'

'Horses don't smell of toe cheese.'

'You work better when you're dirty.'

'Who says so?'

'Norman Douglas.'

'Who's he?'

'A writer.'

'You look gloriously shabby too. Like a tramp. You smell to high heaven, and you look like a wino and you can't have shaved for yonks.'

'You must excuse me. I wasn't expecting to meet . . .'

We were interrupted by a clop of hooves behind us. Joanna swiveled in her saddle to see who it was. I looked back too. A plump girl on a barrel-shaped skewbald was trotting urgently along the lane. Her solid, determined face was overlaid with the cheerfulness of one who brings bad news in some abundance. She stopped when she saw us turn round and called out to Joanna.

'Miss Speechley says you're to come at once. You're not meant to talk to strangers. Him, especially.' She pointed with her crop.

'He's a friend of my father's, as it happens,' Joanna called back.

'Oh.' The girl considered this in a disappointed sort of way. 'Oh, well, I suppose that's different then. You're keeping us all waiting, though, do you know that? This is supposed to be a ride.'

'Then ride,' Joanna retorted. 'Tell Speechy I'm going to do the circuit the other way round and I'll meet you up on the common.' Joanna turned back to me. 'Speechy's awful. We all hate her except Barbara: that one.' She gave another look back to see if her friend had gone. 'Will you go away? Now. Beat it.'

Barbara made a last desperate effort at discomforting her companion. Her fire drawn, as bearer of evil tidings, she could now only resort to their prediction. 'You'll get one hell of a talking-to,' she cried out shrilly. 'And serve you right.' She turned her pony's head and trotted off the way she had come.

'Good riddance,' Joanna said. Looking more relaxed, she gathered up her mare's reins. We began to ride along the lane. 'She's on Speechy's side, because she doesn't reckon Celestial Praylin. All the rest of us are mad on them like all really sensible human beings. Two or three have only come here to be near Nick Spark. They drool, they positively drool.'

'I know. I've seen them.'

'I think drooling's a bit daft. Mind you, I wouldn't say no to meeting him if you were thinking of issuing an invitation at all.'

'He isn't here very often. You could come up to the house one day on the off chance, if you like.'

'We could go riding if he's not there. I could ride his horse perhaps. He's lovely. What's his name?'

'Vindictive.'

'Really. Some of the girls at school say I'm that.' Joanna paused. 'I'm not, though.'

The estimate seemed correct. There might have been something of slyness behind the bright, small, perhaps calculating half-closed eyes—the offhand way she had angled for the invitation to Nicholas's some indication of that—but there rested in her too an almost sleepy complacency like a cat's before a warm fire, a sort of inward purring, which signaled that, without recourse to revenge—by which she probably meant only a kind of teenage cattiness, a 'getting back' at someone who had done her wrong—things went along much in the way she desired.

'Mine's called Artemis.' She patted her mare's neck. 'You could ride her if you liked.'

'Would Miss Speechley allow that?'

'Oh, yes. She may hate Praylin but she's scared stiff of them. You see, it's Nick she rents the stables from. He's the big landowner round here as you must have discovered. I bet he'd clear her out if he knew what she thought of him. Anyway, she can't stop me seeing my friends, can she?'

I wasn't so sure. Beholden to Nicholas or not, Miss Speechley had looked a formidable taskmistress. Besides, some parental sanction would be required for what she would consider a thoroughly unsuitable visit, Freddy unobtainable for its provision. In a way, that would be for the best. I was not sure that Joanna would be able to manage Vindictive and I was not anxious to ride Artemis who, even now, as we went along, began trailing her hooves to indicate displeasure at the extra mileage this diversion was incurring. Joanna goaded her back alongside. Vindictive, who had taken a liking to her, nibbled her ear. Joanna fell silent, perhaps in consideration of the problems I myself had been turning over. We walked slowly on. The hot gold afternoon poured down upon us, the long straight lane shimmered in the distance.

'Look at our horses,' Joanna said suddenly. 'They're like lovers.'

As a rule, Joanna employed a bored, rather irritating, almost 'unwell' way of speaking as if she had a cold or were pinching her nose while she talked, a tone of voice she adopted, it seemed to me, because it countermanded her father's precise, almost elegant inflexions that had once prompted Loder, much to Freddy's pleasure, to compare his accent with Robert Ferguson's. Now, although she had spoken quite softly—the words had almost rustled over the air as if she had run her riding crop along the topmost shoots of the untrimmed hedge at her side—her articulation carried with it a new resonance and projection, so that I turned to look at her in case she were falling into a character role in our of our extempore 'plays.' I found she had been fixing me—for how long, I wondered—with a sly, sidelong, almost avid stare of concentration, as if trying to divine my thoughts and draw them out along the lateral beam of her eyes while pretending to keep fixed watch on the lane ahead; and although our eyes did meet, her pupils bored so deeply into my own that that outward clash, the conjoining focus of eyeball to eyeball, the fact that we were staring at each other as if each thought the other one mad, passed her by completely. She went on gazing at me, through and through.

'I wouldn't know,' I said.

My reply broke whatever spell she had fallen under. Her eyes lost their strange, urgent gleam, flashed now with undisguised anger. The muscles of her face tautened. I thought she was going to cry out. As she had torn her mother's hat from her head, she now tore off her velvet jockey cap and hurled it to the ground. She had grown her hair. At least, it was less boyishly cut. It gripped her round head and the nape of her neck like a golden helmet shining in the sun.

'Neither would I, actually.' She spat out the words. She tugged her mare's head round and rode her roughly on to the grass verge. There she stopped, turned deliberately away from me, her spine ramrod straight. She was in a sulk.

I was glad of the opportunity of collecting thoughts. Her distinctly odd behaviour, which I hoped, with back turned, she was making efforts to rearrange, was not the only reason to welcome this hiatus. I had suddenly recalled—the scene was as clear as if it had been part of the events of the afternoon—I had seen that look on her face before. Then, she had not known I was present.

We had heard of some alchemical books for sale in Freddy's vicinity. He suggested I should drop in after looking at them and stay for supper. It had taken only a few minutes to see that they were worthless and I had found myself with about three-quarters of an hour to kill before Freddy got home.

It had been about half-past five. I could find no pub (Freddy later confirmed their scarcity). The late afternoon, cool, still light though with rain impending, was not one in which to tramp the maze of residential streets of his neighbourhood. The answer seemed to be to go to the house, if Joanna were in to spend the time listening to Praylin records, if not, to shelter in Freddy's porch against the rain which, even as I made the decision, had begun to fall. The window of Joanna's room—her 'nursery' I had once heard Freddy call it and be angrily corrected—gave on to the flagged pathway leading to the front door. She was inside, reading. When I saw her, I debated tapping on the glass, beginning, perhaps, a dramatic dialogue. Rather a good one could, without much imagination, have been initiated with one of us inside the house, the other in the open air. I saw, though, she was doing her homework. She was kneeling awkwardly on a yellow rug on the floor, her geography book which I recognized because of its bulk—Freddy complaining of expense, Joanna of its weight in her schoolbag—open before her, another, flimsier, pocketbook-sized volume on top of it. She supported herself with the elbow of one arm, the other crooked unnaturally beneath her weight. As she inclined her head sideways over her work, seeming at the same time to be slantingly perusing the text of the two books and cocking an ear for sounds she heard within the room or inside her tilted head, there had slid from under slitted eyelids the same conjoining rays of rapt attention, the identical piercing, tangential laser beam of curiosity from those almost hidden pupils that, a moment ago, she had aimed at me across the small distance between our horses. Her mouth was slightly open like an enthralled child listening to a fairy story. Her lips moved as if they formed the words she found on the open page. I had never seen anyone so deeply absorbed, nor could I possibly have allowed myself to ring the doorbell and break the spell under which she had fallen. I had retreated down the path.

At this point—Joanna still remained sulking, back turned—I recalled something else about that evening, a matter not at all to my credit. As soon as I had moved away and crept into the street, I was overcome by a compulsion to go back and look at her again. It was as if, at an art gallery, I had withdrawn from a stiltedly posed portrait only to realize there was, after all, in that very ingenuousness of composition to have made me dismiss it out of hand, a distillation of some essence—and a deeply troublesome one—of human behaviourism which a more painterly canvas would have failed to capture: only in its afterimage imposing its trenchant though thoroughly disturbing authority as a work of art. As soon as I decently could, I retraced my steps and, tiptoeing up to Freddy's front door, peered once more through the glass. In a way, I seemed to be experiencing the highly charged inquisitiveness and acute bodily discomfort with which Joanna herself, if she could be dissuaded from her studies, would have admitted her concentrated mind and awkwardly planted limbs were possessed, a spiritual feverishness and a physical distress that were perhaps the forces that had conspired to have made the first sight of her so intensely memorable.

This time I was unlucky. She had drawn her curtains across the window. By careful manoeuvring, I found a small gap and peered through. She had moved position. She lay sprawling across a large cabin trunk draped with the same patterned stuff as the curtains—toy soldiers in red uniform paraded across a white background—where she stored discarded toys. She had fallen asleep.

I had intended, over supper, to report to Freddy on what I had seen. Doubtless, he would have been cheered to hear of such application to studies even though after an hour or so they had cast her into slumber, but motives, still obscure, for having crept up on her a second time made me, after all, say nothing. Joanna, furthermore, by the remark she had made on awakening and answering my ring at the bell, suggested she did not want it known that she had dozed off. 'I hope I didn't keep you waiting,' had been her words. 'I was out in the yard.'

All this came flooding back as I stared at the nape of her neck and waited for her to gain her composure. I wondered which remark of mine of the few I had made was the one to have initiated that same alertness she had so memorably generated from the facts and figures absorbed that evening out of her school textbooks; why too, my offered comment on a remark of her own concerning the horses had thrown her into such a rage. I regretted, now, as I regretted that evening, not having had the opportunity to watch her more closely, to stare back longer into those prying eyes. Now the chance had gone.

At last she turned her mare to face me. She looked childlike again, shy, a little ashamed at having behaved so very badly. She raised her arm and pointed down the lane with her riding crop.

'I take the nether road to the Lion's Lair.' Now she was acting. Her clear, pitched-up voice disturbed Vindictive who tossed his head and jangled his harness in imitation of the ringing syllables she had proclaimed. She swung her crop behind her and, with bitten lip, administered such a crack on Artemis's flank that I felt Vindictive shudder beneath my thighs as if it had been he and not the mare who had sustained the blow. With a leap, Artemis began to carry her rider at speed along the grass verge. Joanna drove her heels into the mare's sides. As she drew away, she turned and waved. Did she beckon or was it a gesture of farewell? The open palm, the splayed-out fingers gave no clue. Faster and faster she rode, settled like a jockey over the mare's neck. The thin ribbon of her voice stretched barely over the distance between us.

'Do'st dare foll . . . ow?'

For a moment I hesitated as if the challenge she had issued held real not imagined dangers, the Lion's Lair, the nether road, places of unseen, unimaginable terrors. Vindictive, however, could no longer be restrained. It was he, not I, I told myself afterwards, who leaped in pursuit of the girl who bade to outstrip him and whose laughter flared out behind her like her golden hair in the summer sun.

Back at Carpenter's, in the bath I had run immediately after stabling Vindictive, a great lethargy overcame me, not as if I had just had a hard night's drinking and an eventful afternoon's exercise, but as if some monumental task had been completed—*The Ordinall of Alchemy,* for instance, which in fact was far from ready—or one that lay, unappealingly, still before me. Something at any rate seemed to have happened or to be about to happen. Considerations, like the grey, opaque water I floated in, swirled listlessly around how I should pass the rest of the day, what I should eat for supper, why I was bothering to tidy myself up. Eventually, I got out of the bath and, in front of the mirror, began to hack impatiently at my unkempt beard with nail scissors, finally to shave it off altogether. I found clean clothes among my luggage, put them on and lay down on the bed. I stayed there a long time.

About seven o'clock, I got up and wandered into the dining room to see if, among Nicholas's array of bottles, there were any soft drink to offer Joanna if she decided to call. The reason for her sudden tantrum continued to elude me as much as explanations of my own edginess and inability to settle. I was deeply ashamed to have confronted her in rags and smelling, as she said, 'to high heaven.' Born of that embarrassment, my remark about my ignorance of lovers' ways that had followed up Joanna's rather vapid comment about our horses had been made in order to get away and into a bath, not to cast 'nasturtiums' (as Ma would have said) on her naïveté in that direction, although that was how it had been interpreted. Perhaps she had been about to tell me that she had fallen in love, was stricken by some hopelessly unrequited passion for a boy, as daredevil as Vindictive, in whom there might lie, if she could find it, the same unforeseen compatibility the stallion had exhibited to her mare. She might have gone on to ask my advice on how she could best deal with the situation. My refusal to discuss the matter, or, as she may have seen it, naïveté on my part, must have been the explanation for the flinging off her cap, still lying in the lane for all I knew, to show me that she was no longer a child, its similarity to the other hat episode explicable by the fact that she had then been observed wearing something too grown-up, today something too childish. At that point, just like that time she had dived into her bedroom to recover her dignity, she had turned her back and 'counted to ten,' as it were, and made up her mind that I was only worth playing games with: perhaps not even that. After our gallop up to the common, she had just said 'See you, then' in her nasal voice and trotted off to the string of girls who had duly made their way by the other route. Yet, in that moment of her anger, which had revealed the burnished helmet of her hair and altered completely the plain, almost expressionless face and, afterwards, in the daring run she had set me to the Lion's Lair, another facet of her personality had been exposed, the one that held me now so poised and expectant for her visit, whenever that might be: her quite undeniable attractiveness.

The great surge of desire I had felt for her as she rode away, tearing through me like the scream with which, in the lane, I feared she was going to rend the air, had passed as quickly as it had come, but, in the way a searching gust of wind through a hallway door will leave in the papers it has strewn about and the detritus it has swept in from the street evidence of the storm still raging outside, my mind was filled with disordered fragments of past events. I could no longer be certain that I had not found her attractive from the very start when, for a split second, I had intruded into her private world and caught her 'dressing up.' Perhaps my motives for enjoining her to participate in our dramatic sketches, when I was able to manoeuvre her into roles of adulthood, not especially virtuous ones on occasion, had been for the purpose of observing her features once again becoming overlaid with the unnatural sophistication of that first glimpse of her, of trying to recreate for my personal enjoyment the juxtaposition of woman and child that had struck me so forcibly as she had preened herself before the looking glass in a grown woman's hat. If, in those games, I was willing her to reach an age, still two years away, when I could legally take her in my arms and kiss her and, by prompting her to mouth certain speeches in those of our 'plays' with amatory undertones, I was seeking confirmation that she was giving thought to 'one day' having an affair with me, motives, though disreputable, seemed moderately harmless. Had such a signal now been despatched? And if so, what had it been and how had it been recognized? Or had she merely, by a glance or a word, surreptitiously reiterated an earlier message equally surreptitiously delivered which I had failed, at the time, to interpret? The harder I tried to recall the confused images of her, the less distinct they became as if a curtain, like the girls' misty breath on the windscreen of Nicholas's limousine that clouded their faces and transformed them into the wild, chimerical phantoms of a nightmare, kept them just out of focus. Surreptitiousness, if any there had been, seemed, after all, to have been on my part. I had the feeling I had all along been secretly savouring her and that the sudden, overt burst of passion that overcame me in the lane could herald a liking, as time went by, for other girls as young as she, or younger still. With the thought that I was harbouring a forbidden taste of that sort, there arose a quite different picture of the incident, no longer than a minute's length, when I happened upon her reading in her room. I saw myself now not as a reasonably presentable young man of twenty-five striding up a friend's pathway and glancing in the house to see if his daughter were at home to give him shelter from a rainstorm, but as a decrepit haunter of parks and playgrounds who had stationed himself outside a child's window in the hope of catching her bare or in her underclothes.

As I applied the chemicals of thought to the two paltry negatives of the scene—Joanna reading, Joanna asleep—that were all I owned (when what I really wanted were full-length feature films and slow-motion ones at that, which I could microscopically analyze frame by frame) and swirled them around the developing tank of memory, there swam into consciousness the very sharpest image of her that, throughout the hours of pondering, I had yet been able to capture. It brought with it conclusions of a startling kind.

Although she had immediately started up to answer the door, I had had time to wonder if, after all, she had not just fallen asleep but had been taken ill. Perhaps that was why I had hesitated before ringing the bell. About her pale, damp skin, upturned eyes, half-open mouth and the disposition of her limbs and clothing as if she had not arranged herself on the toy chest but collapsed across it, there were indications of exhaustion, of strength sapped beyond endurance. Yet, if suffering there had been, it had already passed over. If I had not seen her half an hour earlier, perfectly well, had she been in bed and not sprawled across a temporary resting place, I would have taken her prostration not for the commencement of an illness but of its abatement, sleep from a fever shaken off after a long fight, its dews still on her brow. Then, as I continued to stare in at her, I had been struck by yet another aspect of this sudden fatigue. Before I unglued my eye from the gap in the curtains, I had detected a satiety about her face, almost a smugness, as if she slept after a heavy meal. For some reason, I had been trembling. Now, I realized why.

At the time, I took her sleep, torpor, prostration—I did not know how to think of it—as the outcome of too close an attention to her books, of 'overwork,' simply. Now, another cause, not at all unrelated to those books, at least to one of the two books, presented itself. What had been absorbing her attention was not the bulky geography book but the paperback volume of smaller format she had set on top of it. Its grubby, well-thumbed appearance had originally adumbrated it to be some kind of crib, passed covertly from desk to desk or smuggled in pockets to examinations, Joanna's avid perusal of its contents discouraged, very likely forbidden. Accompanying definitions of its somehow clandestine dimensions came the revelation of its true nature. Joanna had been reading an obscene book. Nothing else could explain that fixed, hypnotised, hungry devotedness with which she had seemed to be drawing up along the beam of her eye, as an addict syphons up with his needle the drug he is about to inject into his veins, passages that flushed her cheeks and set her lips repeating in a whisper their intoxicating phrases.

Anger now possessed me, an inarticulate, seething, frustrated rage at not having, for longer, kept my position at the window and drunk in every detail of her kneeling shape and of the neat, bright room that gazed down upon her, for I understood at last why it was that she had drawn her bedroom curtains. It was to veil from the world some activity, some getting to work to alleviate the fever the book had roused in her; its delicious throes, that she had perhaps already been inducing with the bent left arm she had trapped between her thighs and which, now, in the semidarkened room, as she once more kneeled down and resumed her reading, she could implement as flagrantly as she liked, draining her ultimately of all strength and casting her in exhaustion over her toy box.

What form did those rituals of self-initiation take? How regular was their occurrence? With what thoughts, rather with what wild, lascivious conceits, were they accompanied? Now that I had missed my chance and abandoned the chink she had left in her hasty tearing-to of the curtains which would have made such a convenient vantage point for measured observation, there was no means of finding out. I racked my brains to divine how it could be brought about, how I could become, with her permission, a privileged watcher, to whose presence, as she gave herself up to the ragged little book and drowned herself in its story line, she would become as oblivious as she was to the dolls and toy animals that peopled her nursery and to the poster of Nicholas in his monkish robe that stared down on her from her bedhead.

Perhaps, though, she did not ignore that poster. Despite the turmoil of my thoughts, enough coherence remained to accept that her preoccupation in the lane, when she had been overtaken by some salacious fancy and had stared at me through and through as if she had been reading her secret book, had been directed at Nicholas and not at myself. I wondered, in those solitary interludes of hers, if she did not deliberately reveal herself to that poster, sit herself before it in pose after pose and clamber up on the pillows to press her small breasts to the cowled, scowling face. Her adoration of Nicholas was admissible, as I knew well, of being turned to considerable advantage; but I dared not risk it. There had been an occasion when, with very much the same ideas of seduction in mind, I had introduced a girl to Nicholas. I had never seen her again.

I had met Belinda at the yoga class. She had expressed a desire to see Celestial Praylin, then performing in London. A call to Nicholas had procured tickets. We found ourselves in the bowl of a vast, cold exhibition hall, staring down at the stage. The clutter of amplifiers, cabling, microphone stands, the glittering chrome tangle of the percussion, the scaffolding on which the stage had been erected and which rose high above the platform to accommodate the battens of lights that flashed on and off, imparted to this focal point, on which all eyes were turned, a ramshackle, makeshift, totally untheatrical appearance as if scenic effects were still being unloaded. Now and again the P.A. system emitted an anguished howl. Electricians, seemingly in the very earliest stages of wiring up equipment, flitted like rick-burners from power point to power point. Belinda hugged me excitedly. 'This is sweet of you,' she said. She left her arm around my shoulder. We sat on. The hall filled up. Despite the mounting excitement—people stamped their feet and whistled in anticipation of the commencement of the performance—it seemed to me unlikely, on that meshed island of metal where the lights burst forever on and off and the electricians, caught in the glare, continued to scurry about their business, that the concert could be expected to begin at the appointed time. Apart from the audience, which was every minute becoming more and more feverishly aroused, nobody else seemed remotely mobilized to participate in the event everyone had paid to attend. There was no sign of the band. Quite suddenly, however, the two great chords that announced 'Love's Mansion' thundered out from the loudspeakers. Three limelights shot their beams over our heads and illuminated in their shimmering circles that shook to the noise Praylin's guitarist and bass player and the drummer on his rostrum. Dressed like their stage crew, who had now melted away, in jeans and singlets, their skin already shining with perspiration under the arc lamps, they must after all have been in position for some time.

Despite my fear, in the next few minutes, that I would go deaf, that those repetitious explosions of chords that built layer upon layer of sounds inside my head were inflicting permanent damage on my eardrums, I became intoxicated by the amplification which was the loudest I had ever heard the band use. I turned to see whether Belinda were similarly impressed. On the contrary, she was in the deepest distress. She sat clutching her head and rocking backwards and forwards in her seat. She was mouthing something I could not hear. At that moment, the music died away.

This was a passage of lutelike guitar playing, anticipatory, as I knew well, of an even more bludgeoning assault on the hearing than the overture that had gone before, but it enabled me, though my ears still rang from the band's preliminary onslaught, to ask what the matter was.

'Where is he?' she moaned. 'Where is he?'

'Who?'

'Nick. He's not coming. Oh, he's not coming.' Her wild eyes raked the tangled stage.

That indeed could be judged the case. The guitars meandered meditatively along. Scotty, the drummer, morose as ever, sprayed soft rippling patterns of cymbals over the lilting chords. Perhaps Nicholas was unwell. It had been some time since we had been in touch. Belinda was now crying unrestrainedly. She brushed off the arm I tried to put around her.

She was by no means alone in her anguish. A seething discontent started to permeate the whole vast auditorium. Hisses, catcalls, a sullen drumming of feet on the tiered planking like rolls of distant thunder overlaid the guitarists' ruminative improvisations to which, however, they gave not the slightest heed. Indeed as the noise grew in intensity, almost drowned now the sound of their playing, their faces were set in masks not of impassivity but of disdain both at the audience and at their own efforts now dwindled into almost total inaudibility. Scotty looked half asleep at his kit. The bassist stopped playing altogether, put his instrument on the floor and lit a cigarette. Some sort of protest, even a riot, appeared a very serious threat. I pondered how Belinda and I could best make our escape in the event of the audience's storming the platform. It was inconceivable, even taking into account the haphazard arrangements, that someone had not announced Nicholas's indisposition and offered us our money back or that the instrumentalists made no effort to quell the increasingly mutinous atmosphere by striking up again the ferocious exhilaration of their opening sequence.

Just then, among the myriad stars and sparkles that sprang from the band's equipment, I discerned three or four tiny dots of light, violet and green. At first I could not understand how they could have caught my eye since they were pinpricks among all the others, but then I realised it was because they were in motion. From the pool of darkness where, behind the drummer's right hand, they had first appeared, they now vanished behind him and revealed themselves again on his other side and continued their floating journey. Somebody was groping his way in darkness across the back of the stage. Then everybody saw him. There was a roar from the crowd. The guitars struck up again their great ringing chords. A fourth spotlight sprang out. Stage centre, in his spangled robe, Nicholas's crooked figure stood bathed in light. He allowed the tumultuous welcome to beat down upon him. Then, with a flick of his wrist which sent the lead of his microphone snaking across the stage, he raised the white wedge of his face to the heavens and howled out the first line of his song:

'Death stalks my spore, a spectre
I tear him out my heart.'

With all her might, Belinda howled back at him. The whole audience howled. The concert went on its way.

Afterwards, backstage, to which ingress was barred by a number of security men who challenged us at every corner and by whom clamouring fans were being roughly pushed back, the atmosphere had been unbearable. It was as if Nicholas and I were strangers. He ignored my congratulations; declined to shake hands with Belinda when I introduced them; resisted all efforts of mine to catch up with his news. As I made one last effort to get him to talk, Lindo's words came back: 'Don't know what people see in that chap. He combines the most unsavoury aspects of Savonarola and Richard III.' I wondered if, in the wretched dirty cell he had commandeered as his dressing room, Belinda had come to the same conclusion. Disillusionment, as much as adoration, could have been tying her tongue. From where he had vaguely waved us to sit down, a caved-in, foully upholstered sofa behind the chair he sat in that faced his makeup mirror, she stared expressionlessly at the back of his neck and at her own reflexion in the glass. Nicholas bounced ferocious glances off the mirror at the two of us. I had never seen him in such a mood. He might have been drunk or drugged, 'coming down' from something taken to improve performance. His ravaged voice snarled an occasional monosyllabic reply. At last, I said we should be going but Belinda shot me a look every bit as furious as those that Nicholas had been delivering. I could take no more. I walked out. The concert, one of Praylin's more protracted ones, had ended late. Tubes and buses had stopped running. I began to walk home.

In the taxi I eventually found, I judged that Nicholas must have suspected he was being used as an intermediary in my seduction of Belinda and had taken umbrage. He was of course quite right. I cared little for rock and roll, a labeling in fact he hated being applied to his own brand of 'popular' music which he put on a far loftier, even a transcendental plane, a sort of 'music of the spheres.' 'When Celestial Praylin plays, we rock the very angels at the gate of Heaven,' he was later to remark, only half in jest. He had very likely detained Belinda to chide me for my irreverence. I doubted whether he would sleep with her. In a way, that consideration made me more rather than less uneasy. Girls in Praylin circles, as Scotty had demonstrated in his procurement for me of Phyllidula, were treated much as disposable objects, passed from hand to hand like the joints everyone around them smoked all the time. Even before the taxi had dropped me at my door, I had made some sort of vow not to make the same mistake again, a vow sealed by subsequent events that, unclear as they were, bore in upon me the unwisdom of what I had done.

Belinda completely vanished: never to be seen again. Miss Benke lamented her loss from the yoga class: 'It is so *sodden,*' she said in her deepest accent, 'and *soch* a pity. She would have been *teep*-top.' A month or so after the concert, a pupil there reported some story she had heard of Belinda's having gone 'downhill.' There were rumours of drug dalliance, she reported, magic rites, initiation into some fanatical religious cult. Miss Benke had confirmed its existence: 'They are *bleck,* very *bleck.*' The story, like many others involving the band, had very likely been blown up out of all proportion. Nicholas was surrounded by the sort of crank who tampered with occultism and became dependent on drugs. The more I thought about Belinda's abduction, if that was what had happened, the more it seemed to be the fault of her own empty-headedness. Nevertheless, remembering Freddy's strictures on Celestial Praylin, derived from precisely that sort of half truth, half fiction, it would be most unwise to introduce Joanna, if it could be avoided, into the house. In any case, the dangling before her of the prize of a day spent in Nicholas's company would yield no benefit. I was not in love with her. Speculations, restless though they were, eventually convinced me of that. From the many torturing desires woven, that wakeful night, from images both of fancy and veracity—the 'dreams, waking thoughts and incidents' of which, as Nicholas had said, life is made up—I had by morning discarded all but one, one that, powerful though it was, because of its unconventionality and hopelessness of achievement, seemed impossible to have been engendered by love or passion, by lust even: a thirst for knowledge, a great yearning hankering to be apprised of what had gone on behind her curtains. This tantalization, no less sterile than her own administerings and, for that reason, manifoldly repeatable, threw me into planning all sorts of ways of wringing from her, perhaps after all with a promise of introducing her to Nicholas, some sort of confession. That, though, would not be sufficient. My enflamed imagination began to impose on her amusements a criminality every bit as abominable as the old king's cannibalistic immolation of his son in the alchemical engraving at ALEMBIC and I came to see that what I really desired was not a verbal confession but an optical demonstration which, like the benign old chamberlain in that scene and with the same unobtrusiveness, I must be permitted to invigilate.

None of that could ever be. Even if somehow the subject could be broached, it would either be vaguely shrugged off as 'only natural,' or denied with one of Joanna's furtive giggles. At the very best, perhaps, were I to make her a little drunk, all I could expect would be some dreadful dashed-off shimmying striptease, performed to honour as fast as possible her side of the bargain: fumbled, perfunctory, uncompleted. I would have to content myself by feeding on her face, staring at her as she had stared at me, on and on, and ingesting all her various aspects and mannerisms, many of which I believed would betray her as the victim of her malpractices. By gorging myself on the sleepiness under her eyes and the slyness of her smile and the way in which, if the talk turned to love, she might part her lips and slide her hand to her lap as if a kitten, sleeping there, had stirred, I might be able to reconstruct at least a minute or two from that squandered half hour I could have spent outside her window and of which, more than for any other period of my life, I yearned for the restitution.

She showed up just after three o'clock the following afternoon. Nicholas had departed for London. I had been prowling aimlessly through the empty house trying to settle to the *Ordinall* when the buzzer sounded on the closed-circuit television system in the hall. The screen recorded a shimmering image of treetops and a diagonal slice of the sky. I pressed the SURVEY button and the camera on the gatepost panned over a circular sweep of its domain. Joanna, mounted on Artemis and surrounded by a few loyal fans, gazed into its traversing eye. I pressed ADMIT and watched to see that no one else slipped in behind her but, as usual, everyone fell politely back as the gates reclosed. I ran from the house and took up a position at the front porch where she could see me as she rounded the corner. As she came in sight and waved her hand all the night's fantasies drained away. It was as if the events in the lane had been experienced under the aftereffects of some drug Nicholas—not above such willfulness—had introduced into the evening's brandy, its influence only now dispersed. I beheld not the impure maiden of the night's lucubrations, within whom there burned the choking fires of her budding carnality, but a plain, slightly plump girl on a plain, plump horse; and in the way that, once, a girl with whom I had hoped to spend the night had said 'I must go early,' those enforced hours of solitude, that the night before and the night before that and all those nights since the last time she had stayed, had been passed in the oblivion of sleep, had strung themselves out like an interminable prison sentence before me or when, one Test match morning, I had awoken to find it raining and, unable to give countenance to occupying myself in any other way than in watching cricket, I had sat the whole day staring at the waterlogged ground where there was no hope of play, so now, because Joanna seemed so 'ordinary,' the day—and I had no idea how long she intended to spin it out—took on almost unbearable aspects of irksomeness and waste.

As she trotted her mare round the sweep of the drive and up to the porch into which I had retreated and stood huddled in its farthest corner like a stage-frightened actor who dares not break from the darkness of the wings onto the hot golden apron of the afternoon, she peered at me with eyes half closed against the sun that beat down over the roof of the house. 'Am I being a nuisance?' she asked.

She had abandoned her spotless riding habit of the day before for a plaid shirt and a pair of worn jeans she had tucked into scuffed brown riding boots. She was hatless. Her fair hair, no longer the burnished helm of yesterday, fell lifelessly over ears and forehead. She took her eyes away and made some adjustments to Artemis's harness, then, when I still did not speak, she said: 'I obviously am.'

She tugged at her near rein and brought round her mare's head, pivoting her on the spot in a full circle so they faced the way they had come. Her heel drove angrily into Artemis's side. The mare's flanks quivered, her goaded hooves scattering a shower of gravel as she leaped two paces into the gallop that would carry them away down the drive.

'No.' My voice, resonated by the wooden walls of the portico, cracked out like gunfire from a sniper's post and Joanna, as if shot in the small of the back by the bullet of my command that had sprung unbidden from my lips, lurched back in her saddle and hauled at Artemis's bridle. She spun the leaping mare round once more which, in her flight and in the sharp oval she had been flung by Joanna's vicious reining-in, reared like a cowboy's horse high in the air. Joanna, like a cowboy too, flung up an arm and whirled it over her head as if she were spinning a lariat and, as the mare landed in a cloud of dust, swung her right leg high over Artemis's shoulder; at the same time disengaging her left foot from the stirrup. She landed lightly on the path. By this time I was by her side.

'Are you all right?'

'Are you trying to kill me, Alastair? Is it my death you require, to leave you free to marry that, that . . . harpy? It is crew-ell. Too, too crew-ell.'

She threw herself round and buried her face in Artemis's neck. Her body shook with fake, impassioned sobs. The relief I felt that she was unharmed, when I had envisaged her being thrown to the ground and cracking her skull open or the mare's bolting and dashing her against the trees that flanked the drive, dispelled the gloom that had overcome me on her arrival. Her distinctly flashy piece of horsemanship, of which Miss Speechley would have strongly disapproved, revived excitement at the chance, after all, of an afternoon's riding as spirited as Vindictive's and my own perilous expeditions. She was going to be a good 'sport.'

'Keep silence, Gertrude,' I spat at her heaving shoulders. 'Thy unsnaffled tongue tarnishes the lustre of God's given daylight. Know thou not, thy sainted father and My Lord the Cardinal await even now within the palace? Wilt thou sully them also, sufflate upon them as well the foetid odour of thy calumnies and slanders?'

Joanna looked round.

'That's very good. Shouldn't you add an "Egad"?'

'Egad, then. Look, I'm sorry, Nicholas isn't at home.'

'Tell me about it. He was spotted on the London road. Two of the girls saw his limo, two of the real droolers. There's nothing to stop us going riding, is there? I've got hours and hours.'

'Would you like to have a go on Vindictive? That is, if you promise not to pull any more wild West rodeo stunts?'

'I promise. Good though, wasn't it? Artemis and I have been practising: when Speechy's not looking of course. God, that woman is a pain in the bum.'

She walked Artemis round to the stables. I saddled Vindictive and gave her a leg up into the saddle. Artemis trotted willingly enough beside her new-found friend. 'Shall we go up and down the drive a couple of times, so he gets used to you?'

'OK.'

We started off. His usual prancing self, Vindictive demanded Joanna's full attention, but she rode him expertly, quelling his quick, lateral dances with calm precision, smiling to herself as if she had predicted this kind of behaviour and knew perfectly well how to cope with it. Whatever her faults, Miss Speechley had done her job well. A hand taller than Artemis, Vindictive brought Joanna's face on an exact level with my own and I was able, as I had so much wanted to do, to search its every line and contour. There was nothing in its dreamy placidness to provoke the suspicions with which I had been so oppressed and enthralled; and if, in the faint puffiness under her eyes, there was evidence of a girlish excess or, in the satiety that composed her features and hovered around the edges of her smiles, of a tabooed gratification, it could be the contemplation, only, of the successful bringing-off of this ride or the memory of some treat last night, a box of chocolates or a hamburger consumed beneath the bedclothes. I rode, after all, alongside an unexceptional fourteen-year-old girl. That was a relief.

'Which way? Back to the gates and on to the common or through the field and into the woods?'

We had done our practice, ridden down the drive, turned, and come back past the house. Now we had arrived at the wooden gate leading to the emerald disc of the field through which the loamy path, where I had galloped Vindictive on our first outing, cut its diametrical line to the forest's edge.

'Oh, the woods, please,' Joanna replied. 'The school may be up on the common and we don't want to bump into them.'

I dismounted and opened the gate for us. This was the third time I had stood on the perimeter of the field. I had felt terror there the first, the second a great calm. Now there swept over me a feverish excitement at the thought of crossing, once again, this shimmering saucer of land to some unexplored destination that, in a fairy-tale way, as if it were scenery in one of our 'plays,' I conceived of as 'yonder,' its traversal about to break boundaries not only of space but of time. Pedantically, all we were about to break was the law. Set in three circles, like a double figure-of-eight, the land, Nicholas had explained, was his own from the drive entrance to the edge of the field.

Ownership of that was in dispute, the woods categorically not his property. Uncertainty about the field's correct assignment, prolonged by the absence of relevant deeds the claimant's agent held to be in Nicholas's possession and, to a certain extent, by Nicholas's dilatoriness in answering correspondence, had led to a tetchiness and, in Nicholas's opinion, an illegal denial of access to the forest area. The padlocked gate I had seen at its edge proclaimed purposefulness of that edict.

My thralldom was accompanied not by the kind of indefinite thrill with which unauthorization can sometimes spice enjoyment but by a leaping of the heart and a pounding of the blood and a redefinition of light and colour. The umber path we rode on led through heraldic golds and azures and verts. The dense mass of the wood brooded sable black in the distance. I considered asking Joanna if she had squared matters with Miss Speechley but it seemed no longer important except as some undesirable link with the outside world that, in this hallucinatory landscape, even stranger now we had reached the hub of the field and the grass, mown in swathes, revolved in ever-widening circles around us, had already been fractured. Neither the woman who kept house for Nicholas nor the gardener who doubled as groom had that day put in an appearance. Nobody in the world, therefore, knew where we were.

As we reached the forest edge and rode around the coronal of light and shade its outermost branches cast like a precious ring of gold and sapphire above our heads, impressions of gyration set up by those swirling emerald swathes of turf persisted: if anything intensified. Our horses were taking us side by side around the wood's fenced perimeter so measuredly that the aureole of light, under the incandescence of which we passed, constantly plunging us into shade and back into the sun and flecking us simultaneously with black and gold dustings, gave the impression of itself revolving, the breeze in the boughs the air displaced by its circumvolution. We might have been aboard some vast carousel where the painted steeds turned but slowly and in a contrary direction to its glittering, vaulted canopy.

I had to force myself to attend to what Joanna was saying. She had taken up again her annoying, nasal manner of speech; was coming to the end, I realized, of another diatribe against Miss Speechley.

'She isn't half the horsewoman she thinks she is,' she was saying. 'She's far too tense. The horses are scared of her, her of them more likely. She keeps on about the discipline of man and beast, lady and beast she means, of course. If you want my opinion, hers is a deeply frustrated personality.'

Just then a rabbit broke cover, coursed past us and vanished into a burrow. The tiny commotion it made in the grass, the sudden spoke of life it pitched across our mechanical, bejewelled merry-go-round—not enough to ruffle my mare nor to cause Vindictive more than a jingle of his harness—shattered the spell under which I was falling. I answered Joanna in a Southern drawl.

'Ah have to tell yew, Ah'm in accordance, Cindy Lou, with jist every word Ah have heard yew declime, jist every wurn.'

Joanna was not to be deflected. 'No, I'm serious,' she said. 'Discipline is very important.'

'Then tell me, why hadn't you had a bath yesterday?'

'Ah.'

'Ah,' she repeated. 'I mean, you don't smell as a general rule. Dad would have said something. "Quite frankly, Joanna, I work with a young man who, well, I'll be blunt, stinks the place out." '

It was an excellent imitation of Freddy in serious mood. Joanna removed imaginary spectacles, breathed on them, pinched the bridge of her nose. 'This holiday has made you undisciplined. You have thrown discipline to the winds. You hadn't had a bath for hours, days, weeks, months, years, centuries. You had a long beard. And I think you were drunk.'

'I told you, I work better when I'm dirty.'

'Do you? I wonder if it would affect me like that. I'd love to try it, sitting doing my homework, ponging away.' She giggled at the thought. All at once, she leaned over, shot out a hand and pushed me on the shoulder as if to distance herself as far as she could from me. 'Pig,' she said. 'Dirty pig.'

Our horses sprang apart. Vindictive pulled away on one of his pirouettes. Artemis lunged forward. We began to canter.

We had completed almost two-thirds of the wood's circumference before we found the second entrance. Beyond a yawning gap in the fencing and the undergrowth, a sloping track struck far in among the trees. The distance along its dappled shaft, embedded, like a lance, in the very heart of the wood, could hardly be judged nor where, if anywhere, it would finish up. Tall banks of bracken and gnarled roots rose high on our either side, impeding all but the view along the one way open to us. I asked Joanna where she thought it might lead.

'To the Lion's Lair, of course.' She edged Vindictive in front of me and leaned over his neck. I heard her whisper his name. He threw up his head and with a great bound, as if invisible tapes had sprung up from a starting post, he rushed her off along the path.

Artemis galloped after him willingly enough. The trees tore by. We plunged ever deeper into the wood's sequestered darkness. Gradually, Vindictive began to pull away. Joanna was riding him well. She sat poised and motionless in the saddle, allowing the horse to ripple and glide beneath small, hard knees. Soon she was lost to sight.

To judge from its exterior foliage, more or less of one height when viewed from across the field, it was to be assumed a forest had been planted or had sprung up on level ground, but this was not the case. The densely packed tree trunks were the perimeter only, some fifty or sixty yards deep, of a vast, undulating bowl of woodland no more widely spaced, through which the path descended ever more steeply and then cut suddenly off to the right and climbed again between deeper folds and pockets and craters of land in which the tops of clumps and groves of smaller trees, woods within the wood, appeared and disappeared between the ivy-covered boles that lined our route and, steepling to the heavens, plunged us into the deepest shadow.

Although I could have pulled across and ridden either up or down one of those many slopes, precipitous though they were, slowed Artemis to a walk and threaded her at walking pace through any thicket of my choice among one of which, for all I knew, Joanna had already taken it into her head to explore, I decided to maintain our brisk forward journey. I drove the mare on at a steady gallop. Feelings of exhilaration returned in full measure, our destination, the Lion's Lair, to be sought out with the speediest despatch. Despite its loops and turns and alterations of height, so that sometimes we seemed to be careering upwards along a high rampart of earth that might bring us soaring above even the tallest of trees and back into the sunlight and, a minute later, through a subterranean tunnel slanted through the very bowels of the earth, the pathway was always broad enough to maintain the forceful acceleration that bowled us deeper and deeper into the heart of the forest.

Suddenly, though, our road took the sheerest yet of its downward plunges. Artemis tried to pull up but, carried along by her own momentum, rushed us down through overhanging branches for the first time on our journey low enough to whip our faces with their leafy tendrils. Half blinded, I perceived a shift in the colour of the light ahead from a dark green to a rich, glowing purple. As the branches thinned out and the path widened, Joanna came into view. She had halted Vindictive in front of this curtain of light. I trotted Artemis up to her side. We had stationed ourselves on the fringes of a grove of flowering trees. Planted in neat, serried ranks, they overhung our way with thick, clotted blossoms.

Hallucinatory impressions were hard to dislodge. The rich, bursting bladders of colour throbbed with an interior life of their own. It was as if we had coursed through some main artery of the wood and touched now on its crimson, pulsating heart. Even when I had taken my bearings, assured myself that what I observed was real enough and that we stood at the edge of a grove of blossomed trees planted in the deep hollow of an encircling wooded ridge, their almost ceremonial colouring, the scented air they wafted, as though from censers, along a central tunnel through which the path, now luxuriantly grassed, ran like a sombre, deep-piled carpet laid out for a procession, the formal, tented shape in which they flourished or had been cultivated like some elaborately hung pavilion, seemed not only nonumbrageous but phantasmagoric. Progress, if we were to make it beneath this spectacular purple baldachin, would need to be stately, deferential too, as far as could be managed in our shabby clothes, to those unseen watchers who had erected this display. Indeed, as I stared along the path, I had the feeling we were awaited. Within the hangings of this glowingly panoplied marquee, dignitaries, even royalty, could be enthroned for our reception.

Joanna, too, sensed something of pageantry, something too of the presence of human beings.

'Are they making a film?'

She could almost have been right. The quality of the illumination, diffused through the blossoms as if through acetates, suggested a stark, artificial source. The ranks of trees looked 'put up.' Even the springy turf, absorbing the blossoms' colour and taking on an achromatic, velveteen gloss, resembled a maroon carpet laid in a formal drawing room as the only sort that would 'go'; but as we dismounted and led our horses towards the grove, disbelief in its existence and impressions of its artificiality were replaced by wonderment at its survival in the heart of the green, choked forest.

Why had the blossoms not fallen? A few petals drifted onto the horses' backs as we tethered them to two of the outermost trees and dusted our shoulders as we made our way into the interior, but by rights their season should have been long over. The air, heady and oppressive at the same time, as if the trees both engendered warmth and then conserved it under the dark extravagance of their flowers, was hushed, torpid, poised for a shifting of the seasons that had never come. Perhaps the stockade of trees on the ridge, which allowed the sunlight to pour down upon the grove, rendered protection from wind and weather and, by some process of incubation, had forced on this unnatural luxuriance. The grass too, where I joined Joanna and sat down, was of an abnormal succulence, tussocked here and there with small round humps of earth from which taller blades were extruding. I poked my finger into one of them. Something sharp was embedded just below the surface. I drew out a small whitened bone. I thrust it quickly back into the earth. It unpleasantly crossed my mind, each one of the hummocks could mark a grave, the grave of a bird or woodland animal choked to death on the thick, scented air and from whose putrefying flesh the heavy trees drew their nourishment. This new, sinister aspect of the grove—as a place not of life but of death—changed again the direction of my thoughts. I stole a glance at Joanna in case she might have seen my disinterment of the bone; if so, to ask whether she wanted any longer to rest here. She sat silently hacking at the ground with the heel of her boot, sending divots of turf scudding through the grass. Suffused with the colour of the blossoms, her slightly furrowed face reflected a preoccupation not with what she was doing but with thoughts that as, still frowning, she looked quickly across at me and then back between her knees, she seemed about to communicate. Whatever they were, she was not yet ready to put them into words. She ploughed deeper with her heel, burrowing, it seemed, as deeply into her mind, for ways of expressing what she wanted to say. She could be regretting the expedition, worried now she would be missed at the school, or feeling, as I was, that there was something baneful in the air. Waiting for her to resume conversation, I lay back and gazed upwards. The massed blossoms shut out the sun, diffused no light other than their own purple hotness, the sheen of a contused, infected wound. The sense that the grove was peopled had long since dissipated yet the feeling of a presence lingered on, a shape not wholly benign who brooded, like a miser on his gold, over this sick, stayed place.

Joanna rolled over on the grass. She said one word: 'Let's.'

There could be no question of what she meant. She straddled herself across me as, in her bedroom, she had crouched over her forbidden book. The same fierce sideways look sprang from her eyes. Her elbows rested on my either side, one arm around my neck, the other awkwardly caught between our adjoining bodies. Her knees closed on my thighs as if they gripped Vindictive's saddle. Our lips touched. Shifting her weight from her arms and legs, she fell heavily on top of me. Her trapped left hand scrabbled at clothing, mine, her own. There was a scrape of a zip-fastener. Over the odours of the grove, I inhaled the smell of airing towels, of the harness room and a bland, cheap, vanilla sweetness, the sweetness of crumbled biscuits.

When we had done and she had screamed out and rolled over exhausted and shut her eyes, her features were overlaid with that same expression of satiety, of flesh teased beyond endurance, that I had once mistaken for sleep. The vaulted canopy of the blossoms dappled her naked body with jagged purple bruises as dark and as dreadful as the blood that stained her thighs. With the animal cry I had wrung from her, that held in it as much of the triumph of the huntress as the anguish of her quarry and had sent a great clatter of birds soaring into the sky from the heavy trees on the ridge, a great silence fell, the same attentive silence that succeeds a gunshot, as if death had indeed struck in the deep heart of the wood. I felt as much terror as if I had killed her. Her crooked body lay in the stillness of death. As layer after layer of panic rose inside me like the dark birds from the woods and beat about me like their startled wings, I thought now of taking her life. To wring her neck and commit her to the rich dark soil for the trees to gorge upon her flesh and fill to bursting their fat, red blossoms, seemed no more bloodthirsty a crime than the one I had committed, its guilt no harder to carry. As if I had actually done the deed, I thought then to flee, to abandon the horses, tiptoe away and seek once more the bright, round disc of the field, then vanish for a while, perhaps forever, from the face of the earth. Then, hard on the heels of those murderous concepts that included my own suicide, hanging myself from one of the tainted trees, arrived new deliberations on ways by which I might buy Joanna's confidence: begging for forgiveness: promises never to see her again: engagements to see her constantly, all the time, until she came of age and I could make her my wife. Like a prisoner already behind bars who ticks off on his cell wall the days of his sentence, I began to calculate the number of days to her sixteenth birthday. I sidled away from her and stealthily began to put on my clothes.

She stirred then and unrolled her eyes. Emerging from the cataleptic somnolence that had overtaken her and assuming, or trying to assume, the exteriority of herself that—how long ago?—she had lost and in which, like a dress slashed to ribbons, she could never again enrobe herself, she exacerbated feelings of dread and despair. From the frowning girl who had kneeled over me and whose burning flesh had twisted in my grasp, from the half-drugged plaything whose limbs, while the birds wheeled about us, I had manipulated in my fists and wrenched from side to side as if she had been one of Uncle Hamish's articulated puppets and whom, in a wildness to revive the tableau of her that day upon her nursery floor, I had forced to her knees a second time and entered from behind, she had reverted to a half-puppet indeed, a creature barely of flesh and blood but one to whom, nonetheless, I had now to devote the service of a lifetime. She moved again; and her movement caused those livid wounds that played on her body to expand and contract, so that she seemed both larger and smaller, leaner and grosser, longer and shorter of limb: like the Mongoloid child in the park quite terribly deformed. In its slow progress over a small gap in the blossoms, the sun burned full on her upturned features and revealed them set not in the sort of bashfulness of a girl who has just screamed out in pleasure and may be feeling she has demeaned herself in this excess but in a bland and prettified babyishness: as if, atop the pliable cast of mottled limbs, at once swollen and of a dreadful thinness, a sculptor, with a final mocking proclamation of disgust at his own work or at humanity as a whole, had mounted a cheap waxen prefabrication of a dolly's head.

Joanna became aware she was being watched; and, in an effort to appease whatever distaste or rage or anguish she found in my gaze, rolled her eyes and cast them up at the purple trees in a travesty of remembered ecstasy. Her mouth opened in a silent 'wow.' She fell back and surveyed me from under slitted eyelids. This cheap, rather revolting display, designed, I suppose to put me at my ease or to make light of what had happened, imposed on me very different sensations. It was then that I again began to contemplate her murder, doing away with the culpably adolescent girl who, by our brief and violent coupling—of which, unlike her, were there any part of honesty in what she so tawdrily expressed, I, for my part, recalled no moment of enjoyment whatsoever—had devastated the tranquillity of my life.

A cloud obscured the sun, muffled the grove in a brown, engealing light that, while it eradicated the mottled staining the blossoms' radiance had imparted to Joanna's skin, could not blot out the dark wound in the hollow of her thighs.

Then is the fair white woman married to the ruddy man. Thomas Norton's words rushed unbidden into consciousness. They were no part of me. They came as if sacerdotally intoned or oracularly delivered. Pertaining to the 'Red Work,' the use of blood in alchemical transmutation, Norton's 'most selcouth thing,' priapic as well as alchemical symbolism was shockingly apposite. The manifesto seemed conveyed over telepathic airways as ratification that a change of some sort had indeed occurred within the red crucible of the grove, the sort of atomic mutation the cooks might one day bring about within the womb of ALEMBIC's blast furnace, a shift in the order of things, blood spilt for its attainment. In the sudden withdrawal of the sun and in the deep brooding shadows of those incandescent trees, I sensed that the wood was not mourning a death but celebrating a sacrifice and leaned in contemplative approval over its bleeding victim. If so, if the reigning silence held the savour of propitiation, what dark gods had Joanna, by her cry, contented? For how long would they remain appeased?

As if in answer, the forest began to stir. Branches rustled as bodies thrust them aside. Footsteps tiptoed in every corner. An invisible army—how many strong?—was moving into position at the grove's edge. Joanna, who had lazily started to get dressed, sprang up at once and tugged on her boots. She took my hand and stared at me in panic. She yanked at my arm, urging, begging us to flee. Her slack mouth opened and shut in silent, beseeching cries. Quite suddenly calm, I resisted her, glad that she too understood the meaning of fear. Her fingernails dug into the skin of my wrist. She almost dragged the arm from its socket. I held my ground. The rustling among the trees grew louder, more importunate. Then, a drop of water, warm and heavy as the tears that had started to roll down Joanna's cheeks, landed on my bare arm. It had begun to rain.

▪▪

'It was the wood made it happen.'

'You feel nothing for me, then. I could have been anyone, anyone at all.'

'Don't be silly. I'm saying it seemed right there. It was so beautiful, all the scent and the flowers. It was our bridal bower.'

'Supposing I'd been someone else. Nick for instance.'

'You're not Nick. I chose you specially for you.'

'Like a doll off the shelf.'

'That's silly too. I don't play with dolls and I'm not playing with you.'

'If that is true, your relinquishment of playroom fetishes may, in terms of months, be precisely calculated on the fingers of two hands. Charitably, we will include the thumbs.'

'I think you're horrid. Horrid and unromantic and dadlike. Age has nothing to do with it.'

'Public opinion would say it had a great deal.'

'The public's not going to be asked its opinion. Can we watch *Ferguson on Thursday?*'

'If you like.'

Joanna got up and switched on the television. Light from the set fell bleak on her pale body, flickered across the ceiling in swathes of grey shadow. Introductory music played and faded. She came back to the bed and sat on it, cross-legged, in front of me. She put her arms behind her, groped for mine, drew them about her waist. I leaned my chin on her shoulder. Half hidden by the intricate mesh of her hair, Robert Ferguson's features filled the screen.

Torments of a very different kind now possessed me. Time was fast getting on. In an hour, she would have to leave. How, when, where to see her again and to be able to observe once more the hungry gleam in her eyes, to explore her when she fell back in her deathly trances, those were now my only thoughts.

The few depressing words we had exchanged—as trite as any in our extempore dialogues—brought me no closer to knowing when that might be, or whether, for that matter, she desired another meeting at all. Her concept of the grove as our 'bridal bower,' although it failed to revive, anymore, my feelings of remorse—all too readily discarded for the desire to possess her that swept devastatingly over me every few minutes—prompted suspicions she had made love for a bet or a dare. An hour ago, that concept would have calmed me down, gone some way to exonerating me from blame for what had occurred. Now I was tortured by the belief that I was just a plaything to be discarded forever when Nicholas's door shut behind her. I felt sure one of her friends—perhaps a gang of them, those who swelled the ranks of Praylin fans at the driveway gates—had told her it was high time she lost her virginity and that in an hour's time she would be boasting to them that she had achieved that status. In the telling, she would very probably substitute Nicholas's name for my own; make much of the 'bower' where they had lain and of the description of the house within the walls of which she now sat watching television. Even if this were not the case, if she did in fact, as I had archly put it, 'feel' something for me, the practicalities of engineering future meetings seemed insurmountable. Plans, as urgent as the vow of silence I had so much yearned to wring from her in the forest, needed, before her departure, to be definitively laid.

Assurance of that silence had already been given in full measure. She was plainly terrified of anyone's finding out. Her fright that we were about to be ambushed by hidden watchers, whose stealthy approach had turned out to be only the patter of the rain and the soughing of the wind in the trees, was proof enough of that. I had cause to be grateful for the few moments I had desisted from joining her on our headlong flight to the horses. I, too, had taken the noises for human footsteps but, as I waited for whoever it was to break cover, had welcomed the outcome, however shocking, of being found with a young girl, half naked and bleeding. If retribution had to come, I had reasoned, the sooner the better. Then I had felt the raindrop. At what point Joanna grasped what was happening, I still did not know. She must have felt the rain too but she had persisted in tugging me away when all I could do was to stare, rejoicing, at our interlocked fingers. That it was fear and not love that bound us, for the first time, together, concerned me not at all. A link had been forged. That was what counted. Elatedly, I ran with her to the horses. She rode Vindictive at full tilt up the shaft of the forest track and into the open field. I followed as hard on her heels as Artemis could manage. Rain drove down on us and enveloped the land in a grey, choking mist. She had still been trembling when we stabled the horses. 'I thought there was someone there,' she kept saying over and over, 'I thought there was someone there.' I could not let her go back to the school in such a state of nerves. In any case, it was too early for her to do so. Time, which seemed to have been stretched to its limits, had in fact progressed by only three hours. Two more remained before she needed to be on her way. We were both soaking wet. Joanna shook without cessation. We went into the house; and climbed the stairs to my room.

By taking her in my arms again and kissing her hair in which, like confetti, some petals from the grove were still entangled, I intended only to warm her icy skin and abate, as I gripped her more tightly, the shivers that still racked her body and set her teeth chattering in her head. I ordered her into the bath. She pulled my arms from around her waist. Within seconds, she had wriggled out of her clothes and stood before me, the same half-sly, half-smiling beam in her eye that she had darted forth in the wood. She kept on only a white wisp of cotton through which a speck of blood shone blossom bright; a garment not in its intimacy, although its revelation was as touching to me as if she had run her fingers through my hair or returned my kisses, nor in its costliness, for there was nothing about the serviceable, even a little ragged, article that had the touch of lingerie, but, because of just that inconsequence, its having been purchased without thought, tugged on, kicked off, didn't, as it were, 'know its luck,' that assumed, for me, the treasurability of a sacred relic, a fragment of a winding-sheet or the napkin used to wipe a martyr's brow, to which my fingers, as I led her to the bed, were hagiolatrously impelled.

Her detached, untutored way of lovemaking—the frenzied activity when, with burning eyes, she crawled all over me and exasperatedly pushed my hands from her body as if I disturbed her at her books and the succeeding cataleptic passivity when at last I could manipulate her at will—conspired to shore up, however precariously, belief that no blame could be laid at my door for what was in progress. She seemed to be engaged on a cross-examination of her own flesh or on an extension of the journeys she put herself through in the solitude of her nursery; and this independence, inexperience it might be, or selfishness, the fact that she seemed to be careering, then meandering, across some unimaginable landscape, rekindled many of last night's wild imaginings. I desired now, more than ever, to confess that I had been watching her that afternoon and then to listen to a confession of exactly what she had been about.

Joanna stirred restlessly. On the screen, a child in calipers clambered out of Robert Ferguson's white Rolls-Royce and hobbled painfully towards an ugly block of flats. Microphones tracked the sound of his footsteps, the squeal of his harness. The camera changed angles, closed in on Ferguson himself. All smiles, an eyebrow cocked, he watched the boy's laborious progress until he vanished through a doorway. The plummy voice spoke words of comfort. The manicured hands stretched out towards us. Credits rolled across the urbane, ageless countenance. The programme was over.

So now was the day. Joanna swung herself off the bed and picked up her clothes. I longed to take her on my knee, to ease her slowly into the damp garments, to caress her as I questioned her about her solitary debauches. I watched helplessly, afraid to speak. She finished dressing and opened the curtains. She leaned on the television set that stood before the window.

'Can we have colour next year?'

'Next year?'

'Yes. A whole fortnight. You'll be here, won't you?'

'Yes, of course.'

'Stop looking like that. And get dressed. We can't make plans with you like that.'

'What plans?'

'I shall arrange it with Stella. My best friend. I've told you about her. We shan't be able to meet in London, worst luck.'

'Why not?'

'It would be far too dangerous.'

'Couldn't Stella fix that as well?'

'We mustn't ask her any more favours. She'll have an enormous responsibility on her shoulders as it is. Quite the sternest test of fealty she has ever had to bear. I'll keep you abreast of developments when Dad brings you over to supper.'

'You will telephone?'

'There'll be no need. Don't you trust me?'

'I can't wait a whole year, my darling child.'

'Tom, I am not your darling child.'

'My darling girl; my darling woman; my darling, darling angel.'

'That's a whole lot better. Yes, a year is a long time. We could write each other letters, but I think that would make it worse. Now, quick, before I go, we must arrange about the playacting. We must keep that up in front of Dad. I know it was only wooing and now we've wooed and we're lovers and we don't need to do it anymore, but it would look funny if we suddenly stopped it. Let's do the scene out of Ibsen. That's about love, so we won't be pretending, only pretending to pretend. We'll be making true protestations of affection; and Dad will never guess.'

'Kiss me then.'

'There. Oh, and one last thing. Next year, I shall get as dirty and ragged and as smelly as you were.'

She jerked her head forward as if she were going to bestow one last quick kiss. Too late I turned away. The warm globule of her spittle trickled down my cheek.

6

Passion, in the way of all bodily exercise of any very strenuous kind, depends upon a more or less systematic recapitulation of its attendant functions if forces are to be kept in trim. This is a thesis that should give no surprise, since passion derives from physical stimuli as much as from galvanization of brain cells which, when mustered in isolation towards its reenactment, only results in overtaxing, finally tiring out, resources deprived of the bracing corollaries of the touch, sight, smell, taste of passion's original stimulus. To be sure, these uniquely mental gymnastics, to be bracketed in their contortions with the physical, yogic ones taught by Miss Benke, may be—indeed, are compulsively—practised on one's own (some of the sensuous details re-implemented by persons such as Joanna in the quiet of her bedroom upon which my mind frustratedly turned over much of the time); but the self-communion of unrequited passion, like the rehearsals at home of Miss Benke's complex *asanas* which seemed beneficial enough in her classes with the accompaniment of her thick Slavonic accent (and lately, because of a young man there keen on their music, to Celestial Praylin records) and, in the old days, through the presence of girls whom, by the toning-up of physique, I used to feel might be the easier to seduce, became a sterile pastime in the solitude of my flat. As for succumbing to Joanna's addiction, a remark of Goodwin's confirmed fruitlessness of that, by and large, acceptable cathartic: 'Have you noticed, when you're having a wank, you never fantasize about the girl you're in love with? It's always tarts you call to mind or casual acquaintances or girls you've seen on the telly. I wonder why that should be. Respect, I suppose. I mean, you could hardly go up to the girl of your dreams the next morning and admit you'd come all over your pyjamas thinking about cleaning your teeth with a mugful of her pee.'

My mind, sturdier by far than the muscles even when overtaxed, overtired, was not proportionally exhaustible by its own callisthenics but drew upon excitants outside its rumination on that one session of lovemaking which it first registered as happening yesterday, then a week ago, then a month, finally as 'last summer' and, like ever heavier dumbbells, pumped them relentlessly up and down until, thoroughly massaged, it picked up still more challenging gymnasium apparatus and set to work on that as well.

When it was no longer able to detail the ecstasy of that one hour alone with Joanna in Nicholas's spare bedroom, it gave itself up most often to the hideous hour among the apple blossoms—if apples they had been—and to the scrutiny of the unnaturalness of my passion for Joanna: activity again to be compared in its painfulness with the abnormal twisting of limbs required to formalize Miss Benke's Eastern postures. I was terrified of Freddy's finding out about us and having me arrested for raping his underage daughter. I made efforts to steer clear of the cooks who often used to talk lustfully about young girls, but that very avoidance seemed to have given them opportunity of piecing together behind the hermetically sealed laboratory doors whatever shreds of evidence they had been able to amass of my secret obsession. 'Ah, there you are,' Goodwin said one day. Underneath the stuffed crocodile suspended from the rafters, he was bent over a rat pinioned upside-down on a cork matting strip which he flicked at with a scalpel so that extinct limbs, or so one devoutly hoped, were reactivated by the probing blade. The hourglass-shaped crucible, heated to furnace point, blasted out waves of scorching, dehydrating fumes. Beside his colleague, Bastable applied a pair of worn leather bellows pointed through the aperture of a glass receptable at a besmeared, fungoid excrescence which, as he lifted the dome to ascertain progress with his experiment, emitted a foul gaseous odour of decay.

'We're having a bit of fun with the Red Dragon line of approach,' Goodwin said, 'the scheme annotated in that manuscript of Norton's *Ordinall* you let us have.' All at once, he pursed his lips and drew the scalpel swiftly along the underbelly of the dead or dying rodent. 'Gracious me, this little bugger's been firing on one cylinder all its life.' He picked up a pair of tweezers and deposited in front of Bastable a tiny gobbet of bloodstained flesh.

'Well, a one-eyed man isn't blind,' Bastable said. 'I expect he had as good a life as any of us. Come on, Tom, any more on the "blood" front up in your library? What was it you said Thomas Norton called it? "That most selcouth thing?" '

'No, I haven't. Do you need me any longer? This is making me feel rather sick.'

'Only for you to hear Lindo's latest bit of news.'

Lindo now stepped from behind the pulsating crucible. He was grinning from ear to ear.

'Guess what. I've got a date tonight with a sixth-former. We're meeting in the Rum Cove. Bit of luck really. I was in the park minding my own business when this whole hockey team in grey flannel skirts and white socks came dashing past me, dropped their ball at my feet and then clustered round as they fought to be the one to pick it up. Some of them—not my assignation, of course, who's a big girl now—couldn't have been more than twelve. I was absolutely buried in schoolgirls. It was like being slowly and deliciously asphyxiated in menstruating bubble gum.'

In my current state of nerves, Lindo's almost certainly apocryphal story seemed aimed at wrenching the truth from me then and there. He had, I felt sure, only regaled me with this yarn because he had somehow got to hear about Joanna and myself. After a while, the mind took yet another turn, that of remorse, when I could hardly bring myself to look Freddy in the face, let alone mention his daughter's name on which I would have choked in shame and contrition had I attempted to pronounce its syllables. Then as day succeeded day and nothing after all seemed to have come to light, those reveries were swept away on the warm winds of complacency. At that point, physical desire for Joanna returned in full measure. I was racked with aching, debilitating longings to see her just once and then, somehow, perhaps through her friend Stella, to engineer regular assignations. In case that could be done or in case she might, one weekend, turn up unannounced at the flat, I asked Sylvia to take herself off. Mercifully, she exhibited only resignation: no tears, no anger, no recrimination, no regrets. Very likely, she had noticed a change in me, unalterable by any ministrations of her own in the foreseeable future. On the other hand, she may have been getting bored, experiencing something of the repetitiousness of lovemaking that, in bed with Phyllidula, I had compared with Nicholas's complaint about the restrictions of the diatonic musical scale, a circumscribed journey, to Praylin's manager's way of thinking, around the 'seven entrances' of the human body, every so often coming back to where she had started.

Musically speaking, I was now a convert to Celestial Praylin, heard all the time at Miss Benke's 'Wednesdays' and because it was Joanna's favourite band. Nicholas's music impressed me now as broadcasting a message that the hour had come for change, for sweeping out of the window timeworn codes of behaviour such as those that placed an embargo on my love for Joanna. Praylin's songs lent force to radical, even inflammatory principles of counter-culture of which that forbidden love was its most vital aspect. Other people's love affairs, even the cooks', now appeared deadly dull. Labours at ALEMBIC too became a means only of passing the time until next summer, the collecting and translating of alchemical tracts a fruitless grind, Thomas Norton's once intriguing couplets the hackwork of a third-rate mind; and had it not been that I was a servant of ALEMBIC, whose amorphous cell had the ability to extrude at will one of its punitive pseudopods to reclaim a defector or a renegade, I would have considered getting in touch with Joanna and running away with her until she was old enough for us to marry.

But, of course, we were already married. The gods we had awoken in the grove, who seemed after all wholly benign, had performed the necessary ceremony; given us their blessing, transmuted us to a higher plane of existence. Their trees, still unwithered—our sacrifice had seen to that—awaited, I felt sure, the time when they would enrobe once more, in their purple darkness, their two young initiates.

Perhaps this sensation of being privileged, transformed, the magical husband of a magical wife that, with the serenity of a pregnant woman, I cradled in my soul, was in fact love, but, like fear and like desire—doing nothing to satisfy a mind that still furiously rehearsed their every permutation —love too was an insufficient stimulus for its now highly tuned, endlessly vigorous athleticism. Like a painter before an unfinished canvas that no longer fills him with inspiration and on which overwork denies, any longer, a dispassionate analysis, I sought each day to touch up with new and false colours the composition of our entanglement and, by and by, to superimpose on the congested surface an untested, compulsively applied series of brush-strokes that, while they distorted still further the original contours, I worked on with a growing euphoria: the euphoria of deceit.

So much a part of ALEMBIC activities, deceit was not hard to extend into private life. We lied to everyone outside anyway. Nicholas believed I worked for Inland Revenue. The cooks put it about they were in pharmaceutical research. Ma's neighbours thought she was secretary to an M.P. Loder gave out he was in 'business.' We lied to each other as well. I felt sure that the progress reports the cooks submitted to Rastus for transmission to Loudermilk were optimistic précis, if not downright travesties of actual work in progress; and it was doubtful if they ever reached, anyway in the form they were submitted, the Scottish fastness of Alternative Power Executive. Rastus's blustering methods of command disguised an urgency to stave off ministerial enquiries with untruths or, at any rate, improvement upon such truths as ever came to hand. As I sat in the library, as often as not daydreaming the hours away, the reverberations of the serpentine air-conditioning unit out in the passage seemed to ring with the singsong taunt of 'I know something you don't know.' That same childish frisson of excitement crept over me ever more insidiously until I found myself almost audibly humming the little playground catch whenever I bumped into Freddy in those vibrant corridors or called in at Disbursements and Documentation; and when, at last, although not until February, I saw Joanna again and observed her father proffer his cheek to those lips that, last summer, had jetted her spittle in my face, it was as stimulating as if, while he watched, she had kissed me full on the mouth.

This new, almost delirious pleasure obsessed me only slowly. I could, however, exactly date its beginnings. For some time, I had avoided so much as a mention of Joanna to her father. Supper dates with Freddy, when I might have had a chance of a moment or two alone with her, had been suspended by a lengthy programme of redecoration in the Palin residence, the flat, Freddy reporting, in temporary upheaval. One day in late September, I realised I had been overplaying my hand. 'You never ask about Joanna these days,' Freddy said. 'She sends her love. I expect she's fishing for news of your pop-star friend.'

The month after, Freddy arrived bearing another message. The imminent issue of Celestial Praylin's record, delayed, as it happened, for technical reasons, until the new year, was Joanna's excuse for keeping in touch. 'The minute it's out, you're to bring it over,' Freddy said, 'even if we have to picnic in the spare room. It seems I'm not responsible enough to get the thing home safely on my own. They don't break these days, do they? By the way, we've got to call them "albums," not "records." I never knew that. Oh, and Joanna sent you this. It's not bad, actually.' He handed me an envelope. I tore it open. Inside was a watercolour drawing of a tree in flower.

The joy I experienced from the little painting derived not from the fact that Joanna had sent it to say she often thought about us but in the way she had despatched it: by her father's hand. If she had wanted only to say, 'looking forward,' she could have written to me at home. What she was really telling me, it seemed, the message behind the message, was that she too was deriving amusement from deceiving her father. It was as if, at a tedious dinner party, a strange girl had pressed her knee against mine: when I would have gained as much delight from the fact that we were in 'cahoots,' and bent, with pitying eyes, my gaze upon the other guests around the table because they were either bored or, when the evening broke up, would just be going home to bed, as from the anticipation that the girl and I would soon be in each other's arms.

Some time after that, I purloined a photograph of Joanna from her father's desk. Dressed in a riotous Fairisle sweater and blue jeans, she stood in one of her tortuously achieved poses before the front door of the maisonette. One day, just after Christmas, in the full flush of my delirium of being in collusion with her against her father, I had been examining the snapshot and had only just replaced it in my pocket when I became aware of someone standing at the library door. I found myself staring into the face of the alabaster boy.

He was absolutely unchanged. Last encountered nearly two years ago, the day before my meeting with Loudermilk, at a period of adolescence—fifteen, sixteen, no older, I felt sure—as a general rule subjected almost daily to violent physical alterations, the alabaster boy was perfectly as before. He had not grown in stature, lost or put on weight. His head was still amateurishly and closely barbered. The pale, glowing skin of his face sprouted no single hair of beard, moustache, sideburns. Most significantly, he still scared me half out of my wits.

To be sure, I no longer looked on him as an evil spirit sent—perhaps drawn from my own unconscious—to haunt me: even so, and taking into account a still more artisan style of clothing than that adopted in those days that should by rights have defused the eeriness his presence evoked—sweatshirt, dirty jeans, serviceable boots—his appearance, almost his manifestation, brutally jolted nerve ends already sensitized to the past by my contemplation of Joanna's photograph. Perhaps he had already been in position before I put it back in my pocket. That suspicion added the touch necessary, even though we were about to communicate for the first time ever, for reinvoking sensations of distinct unease.

Just as he habitually used to arrange things in the old days, he seemed to have materialized out of nowhere, an elemental of the elfin category summoned too urgently to have exchanged paint-stained overalls for more formalized folklorish raiment—winged sandals, gossamer tunic, a pleated skirt like the king's son in Disbursements and Documentation—or to have laid down a paintbrush for more magical, perhaps retributive, weapons. Certainly, the same disconcerting unearthliness of the past pointed to his visit's partaking of chastisement. The ice blue, calculating eyes spoke not of malice but of an admonishment not at all to be hurried in its administration.

He prefaced whatever sentences he would choose to bring me to heel with a courtly bow from the waist. Then he opened his mouth. It was as if an animal had spoken or a piece of sculpture. His well-nigh Neanderthal bone structure suggested that speech—anything but grunts and howls—would be beyond him, ghostliness of the white, translucent flesh and radiance of hair that it would be in an unknown tongue or beamed telepathically from a third eye secreted in the low, marble-smooth forehead. He gave the most engaging of deep-throated chuckles and addressed me in a strong, eminently grave and quite unexpectedly cultured voice.

'I tend my apologies, squire, but find myself in a state of being more than a little devoid of whereaboutness. Are you able, from superior knowledge of this edifice, and with the minimum of navigational discursiveness, to direct me to the office known as Disbursements and Documentation? It is in need, I am given to understand, of a lick of paint. Hitler,' he added more conversationally, 'started life as a house painter. There's not many people know that.' He waved his paintbrush. Then he set it under his nostrils so that the bristles hid his upper lip and raised his arm in a fascist salute. From the far end of the room, he initiated a slow, loping march around the perimeter of the library, staring at the books and employing his brush like the rotary blade of a helicopter, revolving it around his head as if the slow circulatory movements he described, rather than his heavy black boots, were propelling him along his course.

I told him where Freddy's office could be found. Quite suddenly, I heard myself asking him whether he had ever been employed to follow me. I could hardly bring myself to phrase the question. The words sounded accusatory, high-pitched, bred of panic. I feared he would not reply at all, at best give acknowledgment in the same absurd, convoluted way he had asked for directions. Even though we were now talking to each other, doubts as to his real existence were no less strong. His contradictory looks—boy, man, monkey, figurine—his improbably 'grand' accent, the overalls he wore that appeared not bespattered but psychedelically adorned, enhanced more than dispelled hallucinatory impressions still very much to the fore.

He thanked me for the directions to Freddy's office. '*Tanti* jolly old *grazie,*' he said; and not stopping the circumambulation of the library, increasing in fact his pace so that the bright colours he wore, which I grew more certain had been deliberately and far from inartistically applied, kept flashing past me as he began almost to trot round in circles, he went on:

'Yes, for a while I had the privilege of dogging your steps, stepping your dogs; trailing your scent, scenting your trail. The moment I came in, I said to myself, *sotto* most frightfully *voce,* "Here's a geezer what I once hounded the footsteps of. And about whom I may say I had daily and verbally to report to Him Who Must Not Be Named." '

'Loudermilk?'

The boy fanned the air with his paintbrush as if to rid the library of an evil smell.

'The very same. Mind you, skipper, I turned in the cleanest of sheets. You need have no cause for worry on that score. No rendezvous with gentlemen from East European embassies, no choir boys in the cupboard. No pawn shops with an "a.w." or porn shops with an "o.r." Evidence of alcoholism, arson, kleptomania, predilections for rubber, leather, boots, spurs, whips, corsets, knickers, there was most indisputably not.'

'Thank you,' I said.

'*Pas de tout.*' The boy sat down very suddenly in the middle of the floor. From his overalls he extracted a selection of packets of tobacco and cigarette papers and two or three boxes of matches. He set about the manufacture of a hand-rolled cigarette which he ignited deftly, using only one hand. I was about to ask him for more details, whether he doubled as an odd-job man when sleuthing assignments were thin on the ground or if his presence in ALEMBIC were for the purposes of espionage, when he picked up the threads of these considerations.

'One very interesting fact that did emerge from, if I may put it so grandly, my dossier, was that you're a friend of Nick Spark. Now, that guy is incontrovertibly the greatest rock artist it has been the world's duty to try to fuck up and sweep under the carpet.' The boy had exchanged a bantering tone for one of absolute seriousness of purpose. Smoke, in excess of the paltry proportions of his cigarette, wreathed around his head and made it appear more and more as if some disembodied voice gave utterance from a cloud or that what structurings could still be made out of his white face were, like a djinn's from a bottle, organized from the curling tobacco smoke itself.

'The point about Celestial Praylin, you see, is that each of their songs, quatropartite, you'll recall, the melodic strain twice repeated, a connecting bridge between, a final repetition of the melody, superficially no less elementary than any other popular song, "You Are My Sunshine," say, or "I've Got Spurs that Jingle, Jangle, Jingle," is in fact of far deeper significance. In their case, the song is an affirmation of the four letters of tetragrammaton, *yod, heh, vau, heh* (final), the four stages of a successful magical invocation, where the magician, Nick, rises on the planes and, through the employment of the four magical weapons, the wand of Darom, the chalice of Mearab, the dagger of Mizrah and the pentacle of Tzaphon—themselves attributable, as you must be aware, to the Divine Name—assumes at last the god-form he has begun by merely contemplating. Thus, Celestial Praylin's music is both the Serpent and the Lightning Flash. It coils upwards; it inflexibly descends.

There is no doubt in my mind that Nick is a Lord of the Paths of the Portal of the Vault of the Adepts. He may even have crossed the Abyss. One way or another, we are in the presence of a Master.'

This fiercely delivered exegesis, largely incomprehensible, appeared to have drained the boy somewhat, made him, if that were possible, paler still of aspect, as if he himself, rather in the manner he had described, had evoked some god of language who had chosen him as a vehicle of communication with the living. He rose from his crossed-legged posture, one perhaps assumed routinely for this particular vouchsafement of occult lore, and extinguished his cigarette in the ashtray on my desk. He did not appear to expect comments on what had been put forward. It seemed the moment, though, by picking up on his 'magical' allusions, to congratulate him on his perplexing methods of detective work. I was feeling a little more at ease.

'I often used to think you had magical powers yourself. Certainly an uncanny ability to be in two places at once.'

He gave another good-hearted chuckle. 'I move even more swiftly nowadays,' he replied. 'Our masters have provided me with a motorbike, a Norton as a matter of fact. Life is full of coincidences, is it not? The bike is a considerable aid to procedures. I had no idea, though, that you were aware of my presence. Dear, dear. Obviously I could not have then perfected the adoption of the Harpocratic Egg. These things take time, of course. And talking of time, I must be pushing my barrow.'

He squared his shoulders and goose-stepped stiffly to the door. Turning back, he repeated word for word my directions for finding Freddy's office. I confirmed them. He went out.

Much had come to light. It had now been established he was a dogsbody for Loudermilk, like Major Giblin perhaps permanently attached to some other department in the service, combining maintenance with surveillance duties turn by turn. The bonus of a motorcycle, upkeep of which may have been the reason for economising by rolling his own cigarettes, now he was old enough to ride one—from appearances inadmissible of substantiation except by the production of a driving license—would save much foot-slogging and pedalling around, as I used to see him, on a push-bike.

His description of Praylin's music had included symbolism not unakin to alchemical doctrines at more metaphysical levels: those disapproved of by Rastus. Loudermilk may have singled him out for that reason, leanings towards the arcane, like my own fondness for *The Ordinall,* interpreted as ALEMBIC material. Despite our confrontation, he seemed just as ethereal as before. Like Giblin, elemental qualities, mercurial in his case, contrasting with Giblin's earthiness, a sylph to Giblin's gnome, contributed towards insubstantiality. It was simple enough to envisage him as the boy Harpocrates, naked, foetally folded, finger to lip, within the blue-black egg of silence. The coincidence that he should ride a Norton motorcycle and I be working on an alchemical text by an author of the same name, separated in time by five centuries, was not especially out of the way; what was quite extraordinary was that he should comment upon the matter. I found it hard to accept that he had recalled that piece of information, fed him by Loudermilk, in his turn apprised by Major Hamilton following his raid on the Orderly Room when he had made notes on what we had all been reading, as a nugget of information that might prove useful during his three-month watching brief. On the contrary, it was further evidence of psychic powers, incompletely though he considered those developed. A week or so later, Freddy confirmed supernatural attributes. 'Came and went in a flash,' he said as he and Loder stood within the newly painted walls of Disbursements and Documentation. 'You hardly knew he was here. Look, not a brushstroke to be seen. I'm thinking of getting him round to help Joanna and me polish off the flat. There's some tricky cornices and things in the sitting room that'd be meat and drink to a chap like that.'

At the thought of that, of his being in the same room with Joanna and bestowing upon her the same cool look of appraisal he had bestowed on the pretty girl in the queue at the lost property office, of the possibility of her finding him attractive in his capricious way, a great new panic ascended into my soul. It would not be long before mutual enthusiasm for Celestial Praylin were established. Visions of the boy's hypnotizing Joanna with his rambling theories on their music, of their confronting each other while she listened cross-legged on the yellow rug in her room, of her inclining her lips to touch the alabaster cheek, of his deft fingers unbuttoning her blouse while, in his other hand, hung one of his smouldering homemade cigarettes, rose up in choking, jealous mists of alarm. Together with suspicions that, in his puckish way, he had rediscerned in me a predisposition towards mental imbalance on which he would now retributively play, it had to be considered that, with the same impishness, he would ingratiate himself with Joanna and set about sweeping her off her feet. Even when I heard Freddy had been unable to locate his telephone number and recruit his services with brush and paint pot, my mind was far from set at ease. The possibility remained that, over the months we had been apart, Joanna had met someone else, a boy, a youth—I saw him clearly, the antithesis of the alabaster boy's ethereal toughness: thin, gangling, bespectacled, like Pte Potts—who had usurped me in her affections; and so, when, one day in February, the long-awaited meeting finally came about, it dawned on me that, in two ways, by refertilizing the seeds of madness in my mind and by implanting there the new but no less baneful ones of jealousy, the boy had enmeshed me in thralls for Joanna from which I knew I could now never break free.

Joanna grabbed from my hand her copy of *Dreams, Waking Thoughts and Incidents* with every show of excitement. She had grown but little; changed, disappointingly, her hair style so that the fringe which had always emphasized the half-mischievous, half-sleepy eyes had been centrally parted and exposed the full ovalness of her face and, because it also revealed two frowning vertical lines between her eyebrows, imparted a certain hardness of expression, a sulkiness was perhaps closer to the truth, that its encircling coronal had of old disguised as a cautious curiosity. However her eyes, harsher though they had become as if, in the interim, she had 'suffered' or thought she had, were unnaturally bright: sparkled, it seemed to me, with remembrance of our illicit entanglement; and that pleasure, although eight months had passed, was enough to remind her of the little play we were to act out in her father's presence, the earnest, as it were, of continued affection. She began her speech straightaway.

'Eyolf, go quickly. In haste, to be sure. The steamboat just now moors up at the pier.'

'Now then, niece, your words come as a shock, all the same. It is not too much to declare I am trembling. Look, is Sub-Sanitary Inspector Manders aboard, as a matter of fact?'

'Yes, yes, that seems to be the case; and it would hardly do for him to find us together and that sort of thing. I fear repercussions, a kind of reprisal, so to speak.'

'Those days are over, Birgitta. A beard disguises this chin of mine. You catch up your hair no longer in the braids of girlhood. It was only when we were children that we did all manner of things and played pranks.'

My mother, commenting on the poverty of Scandinavian drama translations when she was a girl, had composed this conversation-piece. Joanna, who had learned it by heart, usually liked recitation in its entirety. Now she cut it short.

We stood in the cramped hallway where she had been caught trying on her mother's hat. Freddy beamed down on us. 'They ought to lock you two up,' he said.

'Come on, let's hit the hi-fi.'

'Not in our presence, young lady,' Freddy said. 'Tom and I want a bit of peace and quiet. Go and play it in your nursery.'

'Bedroom, Dad. Anyway, Tom does want to hear it.'

'Do you?'

'Very much.'

'*Et tu Brute,*' Freddy said. 'Shut the door behind you, then.'

Immediately we were alone, I took Joanna in my arms and began violently to kiss her. She fought me off in silent panic and pointed to the door. For a moment, she stood staring at me as she had stared at me in the apple grove, face filled with anguish. Then she broke away and ran over to where on a powder blue chest of drawers she kept her stereo. Much as I desired to hear her 'plan,' I wanted too to savour for a while the space she inhabited when on her own. Because of the matters I was going to question her about on our holiday, I needed, when she gave her answers, to be able to reconstruct in my imagination every detail of its arrangement. I gestured to her to delay putting on the record and looked about me. A bright bulb in the ceiling lit everything up with unshaded clarity. The pattern of wooden soldiers, red against white, still marched across the drawn curtains and the big cabin trunk where she kept her toys. It was understandable that Freddy found it hard to abandon the appellation of 'nursery.' Its glossy, sweet-smelling tidiness seemed designed to house a girl half Joanna's fourteen years, the red school desk and matching (and attached) chair both splashed with floral transfers, the narrow bed across the counterpane on which the red soldiers also formally strutted, too miniature now for her easy accommodation. None of her 'things,' either, a heap of furry animals and a row of dolls on two shelves of an apple green bookcase, the books they supported, a framed print of fairies in a wood, reflected any process of getting bigger, any shift of the girl who lived among them from childhood to adolescence. Even the garish poster of Celestial Praylin where the band, pulling hideous faces, cavorted round a cloaked and scowling figure of Nicholas whose hatchet face, gleaming evilly from under his hood, peered out over the bed like a baleful icon, seemed drawn there of its sting, in the cool asepsis of the room rendered no more sinister than the dancing elves in the woodland picture by its side.

As the room embraced me and my senses absorbed its frivolous, almost dollhouse symmetries, mindfulness of the occurrences it, from time to time, beheld, aroused me as sensually as if its occupant had wound her arms round my waist and was pressing her body against my own. Joanna started the music. Praylin's predictable onslaught did no more to disturb the features of the room than the grimacing poster sellotaped to the wall. The little bright objects stood firm against the thunderous intrusion. I made signs that I wanted to listen to the first track from between her speakers on which she had arranged a pair of weeping Pierrots—their tears, pearls sewn to their painted cheeks, sparkled in the purity of the light—and sat down on the yellow rug, the one where, that late afternoon, I had lit upon her crouching on all fours. I dug my fingers into the springy fibres. It was here, then, that Joanna composed herself for her secret performances. As those desires took hold of her, aroused by means of the scrofulous paperback that lay even now, I was certain, within the confines of her toy box, and the time came when she could no longer be satisfied with its paragraphs and needed to disarrange herself and enter herself with her finger or with an object—and here I cast wildly around the room to see what it might be—did she sometimes look up from the rug into the dolls' faces and desist in shame from what she was about? Alternatively (and then I could scarcely refrain from leaping up from the floor and smothering her with kisses) I conceived that she might quite deliberately position those dolls where they sat, in a place of honour, as it were, and induce before their blankly staring faces and before the Pierrots' eyes from which tears descended at what they beheld, the final pangs of her achievement.

At the thought that I would soon be able to resolve all these problems, that at my bidding she would abandon herself under my gaze as she abandoned herself before her periapts of unchastity, I could not now wait to hear her plan. I sat down next to her on the bed where she welcomed me with a little kiss. She clambered up beside me and put her lips to my ear.

Of all the occasions when misgivings should have been confirmed and obsessions cured, those ten minutes or so were the most propitious. The fatuity of her scheme with its ramshackle contrivances of forged postcards, and telephone calls in disguised voices and with its stereotyped rewards of horses, romance, pop stars—all perhaps culled from one of her books in this very room—should have brought me to my senses. Her friend, Stella, was to spend a week's holiday in France, *en famille* with a friend her own age. She was prepared to say Joanna was with her. The French family, vetted by Stella's parents, approval communicated to Freddy who would himself be on holiday in Devonshire, was not on the telephone. Postcards, three in all, showing places of local interest, would be acquired, written and addressed to her father in the country. These Stella would despatch from France with correct stamps and postmarks. If I wanted, I could ring her father up, assuming a French accent, and put Joanna on the line. If I felt my voice would be recognized, Nicholas might be persuaded to perform this additional stratagem.

As I listened and nodded my head, which swam only with fantasies of her viciousness, one warning did not go entirely unheeded: *Dreams, Waking Thoughts and Incidents.* Its first side had come to an end before Joanna had finished expounding her idiotic plan of campaign for the summer. Played at moderately loud volume, the music had served only as a screen for her whispered machinations, its impetuosities barely impinging on consciousness. Praylin's other albums, *Look Slippy, Our Nightly Breakfast, Gibbous Moon,* despite the alabaster boy's thaumaturgical interpretations of the tunes, came across pretty much as a heads-down, high-voltage thrash. Now, however, as Joanna turned the record over, I sensed a subtle change in technique. Sullen insistent drumming, precursor in the past of nothing more than an incipient 'pounce,' introduced this shift of emphasis. Its brooding, tribal rhythms disturbed for the first time the matchbox-neat contours of the little bedroom. Guitars, entering over the beat and tuned not a whit less loudly than usual but to unfamiliar sonorities, heralded a new authority of music and of message. Then, in a moment of silence so deep, in such utter contrast to the massed banks of sound that it seemed as if Nicholas had been able electronically to endow silence itself with an audibility every bit as emphatic as his ringing guitars and his beating drums and redistil it into its clear, quintessential elements, his screaming blues-based voice howled out a new version of his most popular song:

Death stalks my spore, a spectre
I tear him out my heart.

The a cappella phrase, thrice repeated, beat about the room like a great wounded bird. Joanna jumped up. She tugged her hair back from her ears as if to let Nicholas's voice pierce her through and through. Her eyes were riveted to the poster on the wall; and indeed, when I turned to look at it, Nicholas's sculpted features and the three capering cohorts, who had seemed like everything else neutralized by the space they occupied, interposed themselves as violently as the music, threw, after all, a spectral shadow over the bright prettified interior.

As the song gathered momentum, Nicholas's discarnate voice chanted themes of pain, blood, defilement; and in its appalling confession, contritional or dithyrambic I could not be sure, shrieked out like a soul in torment or a demented ghoul against the mocking responses of the amplified guitar and monotonous drumming, the dangers in introducing Joanna to his circle were for a moment revived. Praylin's wolfish attitude to girls had changed direction, taken on new, sinister implications. Perhaps in the song we heard lay the key to Belinda's mental disintegration, to Major Giblin's disgust that compelled him to destroy the screaming radio in the hands of the schoolboy in the street. Listening to it then and, indeed, whenever I heard it again, it seemed to endow love, passion, sexual coupling, with dark, cruel significances, pleasures achievable for a certainty but only to be gained on the twin altars of degradation and suffering. In the song's words and in the awesome, calculated battery of instrumental assault, there had been enshrined a celebration of the secret abuses of the body and of the soul against which old Thomas Norton inveighed in *The Ordinall of Alchemy* and had passed over with a shudder: 'That most selcouth thing,' he had written; and had moved on to more bracing concerns.

The song began to die away, floated off on the strange nimbus of silence Nicholas's technical skills conjured from the recording studio, as if his pinioned soul took flight at last to its everlasting rest: or damnation. The needle slid into a new groove. The moment of danger had passed.

Nevertheless, as Joanna came and sat by me again, I could not at first shake off the portents of that song, and even though its echoes stirred now only practical anxieties—that Freddy might come in and complain about the noise and catch us whispering on the bed or that its satanic clamours had revived Joanna's infatuation for the man who sang the words—those few minutes offered a final chance to exchange illusion for reality. I did not take it. All too soon, before the rather mindless romp Praylin had set themselves upon as an antidote to the chilling opening of the second side had come to an end, Joanna's words, carried like caresses on her warm breath, took on again their message of her love for me and of her total compliance, when the time came, to my demands.

Then, when the record ended and silence, as palpable as any Nicholas had contrived, descended into the tiny room, she got up and smoothed down her skirt.

'We must go out now. Dad will be beginning to wonder.'

'You'll bring the book?'

'Which book?'

'Your secret book. The one you keep hidden in there.'

'I don't know what you're talking about. You talk in riddles sometimes. Please get off the bed. It needs to be tidied.'

She stalked to the door and flung it open; as roughly as if she had been acting in one of our melodramas. She looked extremely angry. For a second, I thought she was going to call out to her father to ask him to come and put me out of the house. In fact, she did cry out, twice:

'Dad, Dad.'

I heard Freddy open the sitting-room door. I jumped up from the bed. Freddy called something back in reply. Joanna turned back into the room.

'Want a sherry?'

Her anger had changed to amusement, presumably at the chain of all our voices she had so swiftly managed to link up across the small apartment; but if that was what her plan had been, to connect us all up again and so not to have to answer my question, she changed her mind. From the open door, she slid across to me, under lowered eyelids, the hungriest and sliest yet of her concupiscent beams, a shimmering metastasis of the sexual forces within her that dampened her forehead and drew from her a sigh as if all energy had been drained from her body for its projection across the room. She pressed her pale cheek to the doorpost as though she leaned exhausted against a departing lover and then, just as Freddy, who carried my sherry glass, entered the room behind her, she opened her mouth and stuck out at me her small pink tongue.

7

It had been raining. The platform at each end of the railway station shone glossily black. Within the central area, protected only incompletely by plastic roofing, pools of water had also formed, were breaking up now into meandering rivulets as they made their way to the platform's edge. The hypnotic effect of slowly moving water pacified to some extent agitation at Joanna's late arrival and the forebodings of the holiday ahead that rustled in the subconscious like the feathers of the birds, doves as far as could be seen, that moved fretfully within a wicker basket set down in readiness for loading onto the train. Every so often, certain of the rivulets changed colour. These did not emanate from the roof which, nonetheless, gave little expectation in heavier storms than the one just passed over of thorough resistance to the elements, but from a prolonged hosing-down of the station façade by the only visible member of the railway staff, their abstract, not at all unpleasing, kaleidoscopic variations the deposit from multicoloured chalkings, sprayings, and daubings-up of a myriad of graffiti on the walls, the advertisement hoardings, the paintwork, every available perpendicular surface, in praise of Celestial Praylin. These spontaneous, vividly applied testimonials of allegiance, the ones at least that had yielded to the porter's bucket and mop, had been ruthlessly erased: their liquefactions, flowing dreamily across the platform in combed random marblings, calling to mind the endpapers of the book of engravings where, as a boy, I had lit upon the illustration of the king devouring his son.

The porter could be observed at work on the adornments, no less plenteous nor colourful, on the platform opposite. A more aged version of Sgt Barker, ramrod-straight, moustached, 'put upon,' he managed to project, even across the double line of tracks, elements of loathing, and fairly deep-seated ones, for the whole human condition. I wondered how often he was set to perform this censorial duty. Judging from work in hand, not very often. The rich palimpsest he was attacking across the tracks, the multicoloured lake in which my side of the station was now engulfed, must have accumulated over a long period of time. Only a quarter of a mile or so from Carpenter's, the station was clearly a rallying point for arriving and departing Praylin pilgrims, too numerous, too cunning, perhaps also too hostile, to be kept, on a day-to-day basis, in epigraphical check.

As a bell announced, at last, the train's arrival, the porter turned off his hose and hurried over the lines to see to the loading of the doves and the collection of tickets. Each passenger—there were only four or five—was closely scrutinized for artistic propensities, mentally 'frisked' by the porter for brush, paint pot, spray gun: Joanna, as she ambled towards me, singled out for lengthier inspection. With good reason. She looked extremely odd.

She had dressed herself in a grubby camouflaged jumpsuit, its baggy trousers, tucked into the scuffed brown boots she had worn last year, slashed at intervals both horizontally and vertically with a bewildering number of zip-fasteners, some of which, partially open, revealed not pockets but expanses of bare flesh. Her fair hair, severely cut, had been done up in a series of tufts and spikes. She carried a canvas holdall into which, as I went to take it from her hand, she extracted cigarettes and a box of matches. She lit up inexpertly.

'Ticket, Sunny Jim.' The porter inclined himself menacingly over Joanna, a paint-stained hand outstretched. She handed him a crumpled slip of paper. He subjected it to a microscopic examination, turning it over and over for evidence of outdatedness, incorrectness of destination, other, more arcane symbols known only to him and his fellow employees. He inspected Joanna even more carefully.

'Half, be buggered,' he said eventually.

Joanna fixed him with a pitying stare. Perhaps she was emboldened by her one-piece uniform that she may have estimated a cut above the porter's rough blue serge coat and trousers, 'official' though those looked. Tailored for a guerrilla, very likely also an outlawed force engaged in jungle warfare, the jumpsuit had much of a no-nonsense look about it. Pockets, those that did not lead directly to Joanna herself, could well have been fashioned to accommodate knives, grenades, an automatic weapon. She set about running through a whole gamut of her habitual, vastly convoluted 'poses,' looking at her nails, sticking her hand into her trousers, exhaling gouts of smoke from her cigarette, tossing back her head and sending out challenge after challenge from under hooded lids, until finally she threw her cigarette down into one of the coloured puddles at the porter's feet and, as if she were going to kick him on the shin, ground it out savagely with the toe of her boot.

'I'm fourteen and ten months, if you must know,' she said.

The porter may have been impressed. His small, sharp eyes re-examined Joanna from top to toe. They revealed that, while hostility had by no means given way to deference, a lesson had been learned. Joanna's voice had held the ring of truth. This was the moment, a specimen before him, mistaken though he was about the sex, for a radical overhaul of his conceptions, gained it was to be supposed only at secondhand, of the somatic development of present-day youth.

Delineations were absorbed only gradually. Having measured her up from a head-on viewpoint, the porter began tentatively to ease himself a few steps to one side, alter his angle of vision so as to have a look at her sideways on, but in order to keep trained upon him those beams of righteous indignation that still darted from her half-closed eyes, Joanna, in her turn, rotated herself slowly in a contrary direction. Baulked of the lateral inspection of his passenger, wherein, by observing her profile silhouetted against one of the newly washed walls of his domain, he could finally work out in his mind the legality or otherwise of her traveling half-fare, the porter tried stepping up the pace a bit but Joanna saw his game and, as he increased his speed around her, accelerated her own anticlockwise gyrations; and although these circumambulations of the two of them endured only for two or three revolutions, there was in their attitudes—the porter's hands clasped behind his back, Joanna's arrogantly akimbo, two pairs of eyes locked in focus—all the makings of some fastidiously courtly, sensitively measured, gavotte: so that I half expected them, after a few more encirclements on the spot, each one, as those already executed had demonstrated, quickening gradually in tempo, to link arms and careen off in step along the platform.

Disappointingly, everything rather petered out; and the porter, who after all owned no kind of sprightliness necessary to put my whimsical notion into practice, contented himself with one last raking inspection that took in Joanna, myself and the offending railway ticket and stepped out of her path.

'Right, hop it then. The two on yer.' The porter stumped off along the platform. Joanna clenched her fist and extended her middle finger upwards at the retreating back.

'Breakdance on that one, camel breath.'

'Joanna.'

'Well, who does he think he is? Horrid old man. Why were his hands all different colours?'

'He'd been erasing Celestial Praylin graffiti.'

'Why didn't you do something? Stop him trying to chase me all round the mulberry bush? Let's get this taxi.'

I would have liked to walk to Carpenter's but Joanna's bag was heavy, mine as well. We piled in. Joanna got in front with the driver and struck up a conversation. His delight at being asked to go to Nicholas's was undisguised. 'We're old friends, as a matter of fact,' Joanna said. She lit another cigarette. I stared at the back of her head. Fair hairs I wanted to brush with my tongue glistened at the nape of her neck.

She seemed to have changed. Yet, how could I say that who did not know her at all? By that, I could only mean her spiked hair had displaced last year's close-cropped helmet, her mud-coloured clothes the pleated whites and greys and the worn blue jeans out of which her father made her change before sitting down to supper, that when we finally embraced, she would now come up to my chin. Of her personality I understood nothing, nor did I especially want to. What was alarming me was that I could not be sure if, from the commotive processes of growing up, she had not finally chosen how she wanted to go about it. I feared her smoking and swearing and donning of mannish clothes, her semi-punk and, here again, hermaphroditic haircut, were not imitations of the sort of scruffiness and dirtiness and antisocial behaviour she had observed in me the year before but a suppression, for other reasons, of her femininity, perhaps because, after all, she had decided she was unready for its experience; and that I, who wanted only to savour her in the state of flux, the child prinked up in her mother's hat and the deathly schoolgirl slain on the altar of her own vices, would, like her, have to make adjustments. Yet, in that awkward moment when she had been halted by the porter and challenged to make a choice, as it were, between girlhood and womanhood, she had ringingly proclaimed her age, truthfully and to the nearest month. It had been an example, I realised, of just the sort of flux I wished to invigilate. I judged, too, that the reason I had not interfered, 'done something' about trying to extricate her from the porter's mesmeric encirclements, was because I had been drinking it all in. It now dawned on me, the old man very probably 'fancied' her, though in his eyes she was a boy, and had been trying to position himself behind her in the expectation of a sight of a pair of firm buttocks on which he might have administered a dismissive slap if only he could have laid a hand on her.

We approached the tall wrought-iron gates. No fans stood sentinel there today. They might have been chased away by the gardener. That sometimes happened when they grew too numerous or too noisy. Soon, like faithful dogs, they would return. I got out and presented myself at the electronic eye. The gates swung inwards. We proceeded up the drive. Joanna and the driver were still in earnest conversation.

'Well, I never thought I'd see inside of these gates,' the man said. He looked a bit like Pte Potts, it came to me, though without glasses, stringy, poor-complexioned, a 'Goddess of Mercy' look not far from the surface. 'Are these all his acres, and that?'

'When you come back, just flash your headlights at the gates and they'll open automatically,' Joanna said.

'Is that a fact?' The driver looked distractedly all about him to the detriment of exactly linear progress. 'Every blade of grass his and a place in London I'll be bound and a million in the bank to go with it, ta very much.' He gave a low whistle, like Potts when stumped on a puzzle.

'I'll tell you something else interesting,' Joanna went on. 'Despite all his massive wealth, the last time I stayed here which was last summer actually, my bedroom, one of twenty or thirty of course, only had a black-and-white television.'

That nugget of information was too much for the driver. As luck would have it, we had come to a stop at the front door; otherwise his very severe shock at this piece of news could have caused us all to be dashed to death, reminiscently Lorraine Lorrèe's fate upon Vindictive, against the trees we had only distractedly negotiated along the drive. We were not to be let out of the car without elaboration upon this extraordinary penny-pinching aspect of our host's otherwise prodigal life-style.

'It was just a little portable, I think. Useful for watching the cricket if you wanted to sit in the garden.'

'Even so.' The driver reluctantly clambered out, gazed up at the house and opened the car doors for us. 'All those millions, eh,' he said as he dug into the boot and dumped our bags on the gravel, 'and a place half as big as Sussex and only a black-and-white telly. That beats cockfighting, that does.'

'It is strange, isn't it?' Joanna said.

'Strange?' he said as he examined the fare for assurance niggardliness had not been allowed reflexion among Nicholas's guests as well, 'I'll say it's strange. I don't believe what I'm hearing.' He climbed back into the car and started up his engine. Joanna and I turned towards the house.

'Here we are, then,' she said. 'At long last.'

'Happy?' I asked her.

'You bet.' She took my hand. We approached the front door. It stood slightly ajar, admitted light that illuminated only partially the dim recesses of the hall and its bulbous brass urn at the foot of the stairs. By its side, his face deep in shadow but recognizable at once by his hunched silhouette, Nicholas stood reading. He was talking to himself and gesticulating rather wildly like an actor engaged on learning his lines, those perhaps transcribed on a sheaf of papers he was waving in the air and which he brought up every so often close to his eyes. He appeared to have donned some kind of white, close-fitting hat, a rubber bathing cap, it might have been, that clung tightly to his skull, head-gear at any rate polished or of a shiny material since it reflected, like the metal of the urn, the band of daylight that streamed through the crack in the open front door. I called out. He came hurrying across the hall and opened the door more widely. He had rendered himself unrecognizable.

Sometimes at school, aware perhaps of his slight spinal curvature, Nicholas had quite enjoyed pretending to be a very old man. When the whim took him, he would hobble along corridors supporting himself with a walking stick or seat himself and bring himself back to his feet with elaborate care and a good deal of wheezing and sniffling. Addressed in this mood, he would cup his hand round his ear and produce a pair of gold-rimmed pince-nez through which he would squint shortsightedly at his interlocutor. Even these days, five years on, when we met at cricket, he was often to be discovered in the frowsty, clublike atmosphere of the pavilion examining elderly members behind their backs or contemplating the overpowering Victorian oil painting of the club's massively aged founders with every sign of fascination and respect; and, even on stage, although it would not have done to present himself as anything but extremely young, he made up his face to intensify natural pallor and painted great bruised shadows under his cheekbones and padded his shoulders to emphasize his crooked back so that, under the lights, he looked ravaged, bowed-down, a youth certainly, but one in the critical stages of some fell, wasting disease.

Now, however, he had attempted more far-reaching physiognomical alterations in pursuit, though, of neither the frailness of senility nor the sickness of youth, but of a dowdy, broken-down middle-age. What I had taken for a cap I now saw was the polished dome of his own shaven scalp. Of the luxuriant crop of raven black hair, much played up by caricaturists and featured on those T-shirts that depicted him as a mediaeval effigy, nothing remained but a narrow, semicircular tonsure. This remnant, severely barbered, he had dusted with what looked like flour or talcum powder. The pair of cheap wire-rimmed glasses through which he peered at us and which cut deeply into the bridge of his beaky nose and the toothbrush moustache, recalling Sgt Barker's, he had sprouted or more likely applied with glue, combined, with arthritic stoop, to imply tokens of abject seediness. Crippen, in the days leading up to the murder, must have looked as put-upon.

If, however, that were the impression he sought to convey, he had given no attention to an accompanying wardrobe that might set it off, a pinstripe suit, for instance, shiny with age, a watch chain across the waistcoat, perhaps a paper collar. Nicholas wore immaculate evening dress. Despite his hunched-up way of holding himself as if he were chronically rheumatic, the tailoring of his dinner jacket contradicted, in the most radical way, images of faded gentility he had so grotesquely worked into features and posture. I could not understand what on earth his game was.

Joanna too looked bewildered. Her fringe of hair, teased into sharp spikes, revealed a brow now furrowed with perplexity. She contemplated her hero with disappointed, nervous eyes which, as Nicholas continued to stand in silence, she turned on me for advice as to what she should do or say. Only a faint half-smile suggested she might be comparing the scene to her own frustration of 'dressing up' activities the day her father had arrived with an unexpected guest.

There were certainly analogies to be drawn. While neither angry nor discomfited, Nicholas had obviously been taken unawares, although I had, of course, asked if we might come to stay. At the time, he had enthusiastically assented. Coinciding with a period of Praylin inactivity, the fortnight had suited him well. I had forewarned him of the need for discretion. That, too, had been received with equanimity.

'Very young and very grubby,' he had remarked. 'A universal allure to which I used vigorously to succumb. Usually in the backs of vans.' He had kissed his fingers in a gesture of fragrant reminiscence. Now he appeared of two minds whether or not to abandon his impersonation, whoever it was meant to be. He produced a stifled giggle and hung his bald head in a sheepish sort of way as if he were about to come out with an excuse, and a pretty lame one at that, for vagaries of behaviour. Then he adopted once more his air of decrepitude and gave vent to a volley of ruminative 'mms' and 'ahs' and preliminary coughings and brayings with which the Crippen-like persona he had assumed, incommoded by the sudden arrival of two 'young people,' might itself have brought out. With his bundle of documents, he contemplatively stroked his now visibly false moustache. Then he began to speak—in a high-pitched, quavering voice—and to take our hands in some sort of welcome.

'Ah, Thomas; and his young friend, ah, Miss, ah, Palin. How d'e do, how d'e do.'

'I'm pleased to meet you—sir,' Joanna said.

'Nicholas, what the hell are you playing at?'

Nicholas brushed us aside and stared anxiously down the drive. Although it was to be assumed he was alone in the house and not engaged in making a film indoors nor posing for a comic photograph, there remained the possibility, although entirely out of character, that he had arranged in our honour a fancy-dress party. At any minute, fellow musicians, other guests, all in equally grotesque rig-out, might come bounding up the drive. It was a grim prospect.

'Nicholas.'

He spun round, and gave another self-conscious titter. Altered in appearance, he had also made radical changes to personality. I saw now that he was drugged. Pupils, vastly dilated, glittered in his dark brown eyes. His hands, as they grabbed mine, had been icy cold. Suddenly he brought out a loud manic laugh, a deep, cawing cry not unlike one of Rastus's equally unprompted outbursts when in a 'two-and-eight.' The sound echoed and re-echoed around the garden.

'Are you hiding from someone?' Joanna spoke excitedly. She seemed less put out than at first. She might have been examining similarities other than those between this confrontation and her hat one, the fact that, like Nicholas, she was also, to an extent, in disguise: in hiding too, for the matter of that. There had been no opportunity to ask if, as I did, she felt apprehensive now that our holiday had begun. Her aggressive clothing and shocks of hair were perhaps giving false impressions of adventurousness: devilment, one could go so far. Now, maybe, she was seeking to draw from Nicholas's handling of his own predicament whatever ones of courage she herself needed to see things through.

Nicholas bestowed on her a sudden beaming, totally natural smile. He looked, all at once, to have recovered: as if, on the wings of that great shriek of laughter, he had despatched some demon from his soul.

'On the contrary,' he said. 'I am entertaining colonials. And you shall help me. Thomas, too, if he brushes his hair and puts on a collar and tie. I should have rung to ask you to bring a dinner jacket. Colonials always change for dinner. Never mind, you shall be the one to strike the note of casual chic. How pretty you are, Joanna, so, so pretty. Have you a frock with you, something white, modest, not too short in the skirt? That would do very well.'

He led us into the house and into the big drawing room, not often used, the French windows of which overlooked the garden. I asked if we might have a drink.

'Certainly not,' Nicholas said. 'When the Baxters arrive, we shall partake of sundowners. That will be expected. Until then, indeed after their arrival, we shall maintain the utmost decorum in the face of strong liquor. The Baxters have "heard things" about me.' He prowled round the room and produced tall glasses of iced Coca-Cola which he handed to us. 'Hence my disguise. Do I not look eminently respectable?'

'You look like a murderer.'

'You do a bit,' Joanna said. 'The one who gassed his girlfriends and then did things to them. Or the other way round more likely.'

'Do I?' Nicholas searched distractedly round him for a mirror and, finding none, leaned over the grand piano that filled half the room and examined his face in the polished lid.

'Do you really mean that? Rubber tubing, deck chairs upholstered with string, femurs in the flower beds, that sort of thing? Is it the hair?'

'It'll take you ages to grow it again, Mr Spark.'

'Don't I know it. I shall have to wear a wig. I could put one on now, if you like. Yes, I may very well do that.'

Nicholas swept aside a pile of photographs scattered on the piano lid and rubbed the surface vigorously with the sleeve of his dinner jacket. He gave himself a further inspection. Perhaps, after all, he had not recovered steadiness of mind. He looked very wild.

'The Baxters are coming to dinner to sell me their land, to negotiate in a manner acceptable to all parties . . .'—Nicholas retrieved the bundle of papers he had carried in with him and began to read from them as if from a pulpit he were delivering a frenzied sermon on hellfire—' "all that tenement situate lying and being in the county of Sussex commonly called or known by the name of Miller's Wood together with all and singular the barns dovehouses ways paths passages trees woods underwoods commons and commonable rights hedges ditches fences liberties privileges emoluments commodities advantages hereditaments and appurtences or any part thereof belonging or in any wise appertaining or with the name or any part thereof now or at any time heretofore usually held used occupied and enjoyed. . . . In witness therefore the said parties to these presents have hereunto set their hands and seals the day and year first above written. . . ." '

Joanna threw herself into a chair and rocked with laughter. To an extent, matters had been clarified. The Baxters must be the owners of the wood, disputedly of the field that divided it from Carpenter's and concerning which there had been trouble about right of way. I asked Nicholas to confirm my recollections, more for Joanna's benefit so that she might understand the sale would include her 'bridal bower.' Across the room she sent me one of her small, sly smiles. When I saw it, I could not wait to take her again in my arms. I felt an excitement, an anticipatory keenness not experienced in such measure since her father had handed me her drawing of the flowering tree. In the turmoil of the day, a sign had come at last that plans were going to come to fruition, after all. She jumped up and went to look out of the window where, away in the distance, she would be able to see on the skyline the silhouette of Miller's Wood.

'There have been problems in the past because of "what they have read in the papers," ' Nicholas went on. 'The colonial press is no more respectful towards Celestial Praylin than its British counterpart, you know. Tonight, with your help, differences will be resolved. Mr and Mrs Baxter, you see, have decided, or will decide tonight after lavish entertainment, to spend their declining years in foreign parts where they are still actively at work, farming I dare say, among the lion and the hartebeest and to part, not for a song I have to tell you, both with tilth and with timber. Hence I have been at pains to appear before them as a respectable client, the type of Britisher they would expect to maintain the agricultural status quo and not to plough up the whole fucking caboodle and plant kohlrabi nor, for that matter, to raze it to the ground and erect an armaments factory. And now you tell me that "I will not do." '

'Nicholas, it's the moustache.'

'Truthfully? Are you quite sure? I thought it lent something, a *je ne sais quoi,* of . . .'

'No.'

'No. Oh, well, so be it.' Nicholas allowed himself a last wistful glance at his reflection in the piano, seized a corner of the false moustache and, with a great flourish like a grandee removing a plumed bonnet, peeled it from his lip. He gave it a lingering look of regret, then, bearing it between a bony finger and thumb where it seemed to tremble with a final, dying life of its own, he precipitated it into my glass of Coca-Cola.

'Fuck you then,' he said.

'The room ought to be tidied up,' Joanna remarked behind him. 'It's got into a bit of a mess, if you don't mind my saying.'

'Oh, this is too much,' Nicholas shouted, stalking about and waving his sheaf of deeds. 'I can be ordered about no longer. I am being treated like some half-arsed chorus boy instead of as a Star. For it's a Star I am and as a Star I should be approached. I should be indulged, cosseted, my every whim obeyed. I'm famous, for God's sake. Christ Almighty, I'm famous. I'm so fucking famous I can't walk outside my own front door without being torn asunder. I am nationally, globally, for all I know, intergalactically adored. When Celestial Praylin plays, we rock the very angels at the gate of Heaven.'

Joanna gave another shriek of mirth. Nicholas was patently enjoying himself. I doubted whether he really cared if he clinched the deal or not. It was more likely his 'gentrification' scheme had been conceived after he had swallowed whatever he had, rather than consumption resorted to the better to carry it off. Nevertheless, if he were serious about playing down his reputation, not all that far short of his own hyperbolic estimate, Joanna's strictures about the drawing room were more than permissible.

Little used for entertainment, it had been expensively carpeted and furnished, probably at one fell swoop. Its basically restful style, unpatterned carpet, chintz chairs and sofas, would no doubt appeal to the Baxters—cool after tropical heat, quintessentially British, masculine and feminine elements of interior decoration striking the nicest of balance—but in the paraphernalia that lay or stood or was piled up all over the place in a haphazard manner as if awaiting disposition elsewhere in the house, there was evidence of rock-stardom on a profligate scale. Television sets, vast coloured ones, three or four of them, dissipating instantly, if he could have seen them, the taxi driver's apprehensions of paltriness of expenditure in that area of personal possessions, video cameras, video recorders, stereo equipment, several electric guitars, stack upon stack of *Dreams, Waking Thoughts and Incidents,* spools of tape and coils of electric cable, unidentifiable gadgets in leather cases, lay all over the floor. On the enormous ebony Bechstein, that part of it which Nicholas had not employed as a looking glass, were strewn half-plate prints of Celestial Praylin personnel angrily, often obscenely scribbled over in Nicholas's erratic hand. The wall that faced the fireplace was adorned with Praylin's four 'platinum' albums in aluminium frames. The pair of bookcases against the opposite wall held Nicholas's collection of French symbolist poetry, each volume housed in a fitting black morocco box, among them presumably the questionable publication—'little read'—from which the band derived its name. There seemed no danger that the Baxters—probably not to be accounted 'booky'—would locate that particular work: literary interests, therefore, most likely counting in Nicholas's favour. On the same side of the room, though, attention was drawn from the shelves of leather spines and some 'good' pieces of china that might have taken Mrs Baxter's eye by a vast oil painting of Nicholas that had been suspended above the carved chimney-piece. It dominated the entire drawing room. Despite abstract, predominantly vorticist influences—great rearing angles of black, green, yellow—Nicholas's upturned white screaming face painted, rather poured by the bucket-load, diagonally across the twelve-foot canvas, was perfectly recognizable; and even if, under his disguise, the Baxters failed to distinguish the unique bone structure and striking pallor of the wedge-shaped features, the shock waves of colour it despatched to all corners of the room, its unmistakable message of rock and roll as 'anti-art,' violent, anarchical, no less disturbing than its own jagged lineaments, could not possibly be overlooked.

I suggested its removal. Together we clambered onto chairs, unhooked the painting, stowed it at last, face to the wall, behind the Benares gong in the hall. Joanna and I went upstairs and lay on the bed.

'He's not what I expected.'

'He's a bit the worse for wear, I'm afraid. He's not normally like that, unless he's composing. Then he's worse.'

'I do hope he can buy the wood.'

'Yes.'

'I wonder if he knows about the "bower." He might give it you as a present. Will you ask him?'

'If you're good.'

'How can I be good?'

'By being bad.'

'Like this?'

'Yes; but by yourself sometimes. While I watch.'

'I don't do that.'

'I think you do. In your nursery.'

'I haven't got a nursery.'

'You have. You've got a neat little, sweet little, clean little nursery with soldiers on the curtains and in that neat little, clean little . . .'

'It's a pity,' Joanna said as she pushed me away and got off the bed, 'that we've got to dress up. I mean, how can I get all dirty if I've got to keep dressing up?'

'It's only for tonight.'

'Yes, I suppose. And, after all, it'll be my first real dinner party. Where's the bathroom?'

'Second on the left.'

'Can we watch *Ferguson on Thursday* tomorrow?'

'You can. I shall watch the cricket earlier on, if you don't mind.'

'Cricket's boring.'

'You are a child in such matters.'

'That is a total irrelevance, as a matter of fact. I am eleven years younger than you. If I were a year and a bit older, we could get married. It would have universal approval. It is only mathematically we are frowned on. Do you know these Baxters at all?'

'No.'

'It's my distinct impression they will turn out to be daunting.'

When faced in the now portraitless drawing room, Mr and Mrs Baxter went some way towards confirming Joanna's forebodings. Their weather-beaten, reddened, curiously similar, rather bursting faces, Mrs Baxter's behind dark glasses, not only confirmed incipient retirement and colonial origins—not at all hard to imagine them in drill shorts bumping along in a jeep over difficult terrain—but prompted expectations of a conviviality if anything a touch overbearing. Now, for some reason, even politeness seemed at a premium. They stood ponderously in the middle of the carpet and exhaled columns of smoke from untipped cigarettes. At first, I wondered if they felt uncomfortable in their evening clothes—Nicholas's prediction about their mode of attire correctly sustained. That, however, seemed not to be the case. Mrs Baxter wore her long purple skirt, Mr Baxter a white tuxedo, with every sign of their nightly assumption—at a card table laid for dinner in a jungle clearing or, when quartered at home mingling with companions at the club—as a matter of course: a gesture of maintaining what Nicholas had called the 'status quo.' It had to be assumed, therefore, that discomfiture had arisen owing to a hiccup in the preliminary bargainings concerning the sale of their land.

At those I had not been present. Nicholas had led the Baxters off the minute they arrived, Joanna in tow, to survey the 'parcel of land' as he kept referring to it, he was hoping to acquire. I had watched their progress through the drawing-room window. The drugs Nicholas had taken appeared to be wearing off. He had dropped his snuffling, confused manner of speech and drawn himself up again to his full height. Even his shaven head and the wire glasses seemed, by that toning-down of the masquerade, not quite as absurd as at first. He was, however, still rather manic-looking. He had taken with him his sheaf of legal documents and, as the party made its halting way across the grass, waved it in the air or thumbed through it in search of a relevant passage with such enthusiasm that every so often a leaf or two would become detached from its fellows, flutter away on the evening breeze and send Joanna off at a run to intercept it and return it to his outstretched hand. She had exchanged her camouflaged jumpsuit for a cotton dress that reflected in its pinks and blues pale washes of Mrs Baxter's ecclesiastical purple; so that a uniform elegance of habit and the close attention the three were giving, as far as they could, to Nicholas who was forever halting in his tracks and reading from his papers and marching along again at variable speeds, suggested some formal reading party or a faction of a literary gathering of that sort driven, by the compelling quality of the spoken words Nicholas was reciting, out into the garden where quality could be better savoured under the evening and now rapidly clearing skies. The party had turned into the stable yard and been lost to view. When they came back, Nicholas had ushered the Baxters into the drawing room and vanished into the fastnesses of the house, taking Joanna with him. They had been gone some time.

'Some sort of picture has hung here in the past,' Mrs Baxter observed. 'Quite a large one.' She had plumped down in one of the chintz armchairs and was gazing through smoked lenses at the space Nicholas's portrait had recently occupied. Dust-marks on the wall delineated, as she had said, generous proportions.

'It has gone for cleaning. The smoke from the fire in wintertime . . . Nicholas burns whole railway sleepers in the grate. They give out a splendid heat.'

I turned to see whether this observation might have engaged Mr Baxter, fires not very often lit, probably never, in his corner of the globe, wherever that might be. He made no sign that it had done so. He had come to a halt by the piano from which, at the last moment, I had gathered up the annotated photographic proofs of Celestial Praylin and hidden them beneath the lid. Still in place, however, was my half-finished drink into which Nicholas had cast his false moustache. It was that that was claiming Mr Baxter's attention. He stared fixedly into its depths.

'Good lord.'

All things considered, his florid features displayed little emotion. He spoke his words of only faint surprise as if, although not on a day-to-day basis, he had seen false moustaches floating, perhaps now submerged, in soft drinks on a number of other occasions. Thoroughly saturated, the moustache could, by now, be proving problematical of exact identification, have turned sticking-plaster side uppermost or rolled itself into a ball like a furry spider. Creatures of that sort might, in the land the Baxters hailed from, turn up quite frequently in drinking vessels. It seemed the moment to ask exactly where that was.

'The Isle of Wight,' Mrs Baxter said.

This was too bad of Nicholas. Apprehensions were now that his 'getup' was only one of a series of trickeries which would punctuate the whole evening, Joanna, the Baxters, myself, successive victims of larkish practical jokes. They looked even more ill-at-ease than before. Perhaps it had been they and not Nicholas who had put it about that they lived abroad, my question catching Mrs Baxter temporarily off guard. All at once her husband directed towards her a curt nod of the head. She got up immediately, turned her back on us and strolled over to the French window. The signal seemed prearranged, long anticipated by Mrs Baxter who had been staring at her husband through her sunglasses, when it came devotedly obeyed. Whatever Mr Baxter had to confide was to be man-to-man stuff.

'Tell me,' he said, 'are you in Mr Spark's employ?'

'No, I'm a friend. I'm staying here for a few days.'

'Even better. My dear,' he called out to his wife, 'this is the chap who can tell us where our host hides the gin.'

I was glad of the errand. Nicholas was in the dining room. He and Joanna were in the last stages of mixing sundowners.

'Does the pink stuff go in now?'

'Yes, my angel.'

'Nicholas, why did you tell us the Baxters were colonials?'

'Are they not?'

'They're from the Isle of Wight. As you well know.'

'That's quite a long way off, dear boy.'

'Don't start snuffling again. What went wrong about the land?'

'Not a thing. They signed like lambs.'

'Yes,' Joanna said. 'I witnessed the deed. I "put my hand" to it, didn't I, Nick?'

'Indeed you did. Most elegantly too. Illegally, I might add. And falsely. "The Lion's Lair, Kidderminster," that's where she said she lived, Tom. Aren't you coming to join us?'

'Not for a bit. The going, as you'll find, is tough.'

I sat down at the dining table. A rosy lobster was laid in each place. The sundowner, like drinks in the Rum Cove, matched in taste, soon too in benefits, visual appeal. It was much needed. Up to an hour ago, the day's events had bolstered the unwisdom, once propounded by Bastable, of going on holiday with a girl. Joanna's altered appearance, the late arrival of her train, the harrassing hour or so with Nicholas before the Baxters' arrival, now the prospect of a 'difficult' evening ahead, none of these had been anticipated.

Admittedly, Bastable's strictures—even more sternly expressed in the matter of honeymoons which, he said, wrecked many a marriage before it had properly got under way—were based on the inadvisability of exploring anywhere 'new' rather than returning, as Joanna and I were, to a scene of a previous assignation. Nevertheless, basic doubts concerning re-evocation of desire on demand and upon unfamiliar territory still, to a certain extent, applied. Warming to his subject, Bastable had exampled problems about what had to be said and done while lovemaking was not in progress. Methods of whiling away those intervals—fairly lengthy ones, he had added, given the comparative infrequency of the male crisis—could prove irksome in the extreme. One's partner's conversation (if any), her enthusiasm for a long walk or a punishing excursion to neighbourhood ruins, shortcomings of accommodation, food, drink, weather conditions in the selected milieu, could all conspire to force incompatability very quickly to the surface.

Bastable's apprehensions, expressed at a time when I was still giving heed to the possibility of trying to change Joanna's mind about the holiday, had played a certain part in my thoughts, their gloomy practicalities interposing every so often between other anticipatory speculations. Now they could be dismissed. As I had watched Joanna through the drawing-room window, ideas had begun to change, to alter perspective, to redispose themselves like the slow-moving figures on the lawn before me. The pink-and-blue dress she was wearing and her still spiky hair made her look quite different, as if I had never seen her before, as if indeed she were the first girl I had ever set eyes on. In the solemn way she attended to what Mrs Baxter had to say, she breathed a new, adult confidence. Yet, when she fell behind and imitated behind his back Mr Baxter's rolling gait or spurted off to collect Nicholas's wayward documents or, all of a sudden in sheer exuberance, spun herself round in circles, she was even more of a child than I had ever perceived; and, as I was presented with each of the ever-shifting aspects of her that, like a tapestry of enormous richness, she unrolled before my eyes, as broad and as sweeping as the vista of the grounds that Nicholas's window afforded, I came to understand that what I had seen her about through the altogether meaner dimensions of another, her bedroom, window, took up only a few spare moments of her life and was far from the time-consuming addiction I had, until then, suspected. As if I had awoken from a fever, which, in a way, I had, because those watching moments enabled me to slough off the sickly desires for her that had been torturing me for so long, I felt surging through my veins a novel, more bracing exhilaration. I seemed to be watching not a lover but a newfound friend, perhaps even a sister. What I had to tell her, to listen to her telling me, now seemed limitless. We would talk around the clock, as we went for walks, as we ate, as we sat with Nicholas listening to his music and to the music of other bands, as we rode. In the confusion of our arrival, Vindictive had been forgotten. Surely Joanna would have gone in to greet him when the 'reading party' had visited the stables. I wondered if he had remembered her and given one of his whinnies of welcome. Now that the woods were rightfully Nicholas's, they could be explored in safety and at leisure. With luck, the sickly blossoms within their depths had long since withered and died.

Joanna appeared then, threw open the dining-room door and executed one of her great leaps that landed her in the chair next to my own. The Baxters were hard on her heels. The sundowners had done much to improve their demeanour. They came fairly beaming in. Perhaps a cheque had already changed hands. Now that colonial affiliations so credibly, even glibly, suited to their looks had to be discountenanced—the heated features, the dated, slightly dilapidated evening clothes, their manner of looking at the same time at home and marginally disorientated all pointing to a recent return from the bush or the veldt—origins, ties, professional skills, financial stability, way of life in all its aspects, proved elusive of reappraisal. From being landowners, householders too it was to be supposed, in this part of the world, it now had to be considered that the Baxters had suffered a decline of fortune, taken a hard knock or two that forced them now into the sale of what might have been their one remaining capital asset. On revision, they looked like, almost certainly were, habitués of public houses—one favoured public house at the 'top end' of the widely variable, socially speaking, range of those establishments, oak-beamed, log-fired, full of panting dogs—at closing time awkward to dislodge; maybe even publicans themselves, amply 'sampling' (to use Sgt Barker's expression) stock in hand after licensing hours had ended: before they had begun as well, most likely; doubtless on a smallish income; perhaps now pensioned off, or, it had to be taken into account, relieved of their licenseeship as being, as Rastus would have said, 'unsatisfactory,' that was, if publicans they ever had been; in some indefinable way, down on their luck.

Whatever their circumstances, to judge from enthusiasm on entering the room, at least in pausing in the doorway and surveying from that distance the dining table prepared for them, square meals were these days something of a luxury. Mrs Baxter gave a cry of delight as she spotted the lobsters. She plumped herself down at the end of the table and swiftly unfolded her dinner napkin. Approach to culinary fare on her husband's part was more circumspect—though no whit less keenly mobilized. Mr Baxter was not to be hurried, hungry though he was. I myself, though in excuse after drug dalliance, was soon to experience in this house the same heaven-sent prospect of eating food that Mr Baxter was savouring in full measure. From where he stood on the threshold he began for some reason to initiate a volley of sparring movements with his fists, running on the spot and pummeling the air around him as notification, perhaps, that he was in fighting trim for a substantial evening meal or, so bizarre were these preprandial athletics, as a warming-up exercise in case his lobster should all at once bound from its plate and challenge him to a few rounds in gloved claws.

'Lobster,' Mr Baxter declared. 'Ah hah.'

'Come along, Harold,' his wife called over her shoulder. 'You're blocking the entrance. Mr Spark can't get through to pour us some of this gorgeous wine. I expect he's ready for his supper, just like the rest of us.'

Mr Baxter altered footwork to allow Nicholas—impeded as Mrs Baxter observed from entering his own dining room—to follow her to the table. Then he hurried to the chair opposite me and examined his lobster from closer quarters. For the punch-bag mannerisms of a moment ago he now substituted another set of actions, in case the first lot had been imperfectly grasped, to communicate his almost ungovernable passion to begin feasting on a lavish scale the moment etiquette permitted. Staring down at the food before him, he struck his palms together and then began to rub his hands up and down from wrist to fingertip and back again, wringing them out until the knuckles cracked, as if, under running water, he were eagerly, even ghoulishly, 'scrubbing up' preparatory to the performance of major surgery. He, the rest of us, set to. I helped Joanna in extricating her shellfish's flesh from its intricate exterior casing. Mrs Baxter, not always between mouthfuls, started to expatiate on advantages in Nicholas's acquisition. She mentioned the possibility of money's being made from a judicious felling of some of the trees.

'It was once done. The path for the timber wagons begins on your side at the edge of the field.'

I felt Joanna's knee pressing against mine.

'Where does that path lead, Mrs Baxter?' she asked in a sweet voice.

'Nowhere in particular, my dear. In one end and out the other.'

'Don't forget the apple trees, Topsie,' Mr Baxter put in. ' "Baxter's Gubbins" as we always called it. Don't forget those.'

Mrs Baxter gave a sudden tinkling laugh as if, in a pantomime, she had descended upon wires and touched a princeling with a silver wand.

'Oh, Harold, such things at table,' she corrected him. 'Should they be mentioned?'

It was Mr Baxter's turn to show amusement. He went off in a long, painful burst of hacking laughter that oscillated his bow tie upwards and downwards and further suffused a complexion already overheated. It was now much the colour of the lobster shell that still occupied him despite this outburst of mirth.

'But you have just mentioned them, my dear,' he chortled, 'in the most basic possible way. "In one end and out the other." Like this food, more's the pity. There could be no better description of the necessity for a gubbins.' He shone his steaming face around the table at each of us in turn. Joanna looked puzzled. Nicholas proffered one of the broad, utterly guileless smiles he usually reserved for fans of his encountered unexpectedly and imperfectly under emotional control.

'Everybody twig now?' Mrs Baxter's laugh rippled again around the room. Realization slowly dawned. I recalled Major Giblin's vague direction, 'Gubbins at the end of the passage. Pull hard. Pause of two, three. Then pull again.' The grove's unnatural luxuriance was now explained in the most natural, as Mr Baxter had said, 'in the most basic possible way.' He leaned confidingly across the table.

'Gubbins. Good old-fashioned word for latrine. Cesspit in this case. Those pretty trees, young lady, are planted on a sewer.'

Joanna stared at him. I thought she was about to join in the merriment. What seemed to be the beginnings of a prurient grin spread over her features and caused Mr Baxter, when he saw it, to go off again into his rhythmic coughing laughter. His bow tie leaped furiously up and down. A further trill from his wife rang like a struck wineglass across the dinner table. Nicholas fell back in his seat and lifted his eyebrows at the silliness of it all. Then Joanna's face, compressed, it seemed, by a giant hand, crumpled into a terrible rictus of pain as if she could feel under its fingers her cheekbones crumble and hear in her head the breaking bones. She gave a choked, sobbing cry and clapped her hands to her mouth. She fled in tears from the room.

▪▪

'I hate them, I hate them, I hate them. They're disgusting. It's all spoiled. It was our bridal bower. It was. It was.'

'Joanna, it's not important. We'll find another nook, a dingle. I've always wanted to know exactly what a dingle looked like. We'll go riding; ride and ride until we find one.'

'No, we won't. I don't want to ride. I hate Vindictive. I hate Nick and his stupid disguises. He's mad. Get away from me. You're mad as well. Leave me alone. Leave me alone.'

She cried and cried, long into the night. I sat by the bed and stared at her as at last she slept. It is a fact of life, despite what poets have written, artists painted, sculptors worked in clay and chiseled in stone, that the human physiognomy is less pleasant by far to look upon asleep than awake; and how cruelly was this truth substantiated by Joanna's still tear-stained, tear-bloated face that, in her sleep, seemed no more tranquil than when she had been sitting up in bed crying her eyes out; as if, dreaming, she wept on and on. Search as I might its every line and contour and though I bent to kiss the slackened mouth that donated to those otherwise racked features no atom of composure but endowed them rather with a benign foolishness that bordered upon imbecility, the lovely girl in the party dress who had skipped laughing across the grass only hours before had vanished as if she had never existed.

In comparison with my own preoccupations, morbid though they had been, Joanna's fascination for the blossom-decked trees, always to me indefinably unpleasant, seemed more misbegotten by far; and whereas before the Baxters' revelation I may have believed there were endearing undercurrents, romantic ones too, attached to her notion of the grove's being a 'secret' place, I now saw that subconsciously I had found that conceit of hers as repellant as the area itself. Perhaps that was what had disturbed her too, that when she had clapped her hands to her mouth and run out of the dining room there had risen again in her nostrils the asphyxiating scent of the blossoms in which she now discerned the choking spirals of ordure and decay.

Although next morning she appeared to have recovered her spirits, as time went on she began to drop into a form of behaviour that little more than bordered upon the deliberate cultivation of the scruffiness for which she had envied me the year before when she had seen going about unwashed and in dirty clothes as part of the holiday 'fun.' It was not as if she had adopted an affectation she found dramatically to her liking. On the contrary, she seemed to have fallen prey to an infection she could not shake off, like a heavy cold or one of those ailments that, because they are not serious, are as irritating to the patient's friend as to the sufferer himself, a lethargic, almost a sleepwalking sloppiness of attitude that extended not only to her personal appearance but to her disposition towards any form of entertainment with which I sought to beguile her. Unkempt and forever in her one-piece camouflaged overalls she mooned about from room to room, watching television or fiddling with Nicholas's video equipment. She answered when spoken to but with a muffled politeness. She accompanied me riding if I asked her to go, not on Vindictive but on a sad chestnut gelding of Nicholas's who had to be urged along as if he, too, had been infected with Joanna's commixture of truculence and wretchedness. We shared the same bed but no more than that. When I touched her, I felt her flesh contract like a fingered snail in distaste and fear. Furthermore, out of boredom or as an adjunct to her contempt for the world, she began to embark upon a chapter of minor wickednesses—taking sips from people's drinks or 'hits' from the marijuana-tainted cigarettes that circulated in the house for most of the day—which I felt required admonishment as much to stop her from making herself sick as for any moral reason and for which I was then admonished in my turn for being as stuffy as her father.

All the time we were there, Carpenter's was full to bursting. Nicholas's 'Crippen' persona had been the precursor to a period of haphazard, indolent, one suspected drug-induced, behaviour when, like a dissolute monarch, he held court to a seemingly endless chain of ministers and sycophants for whom he showed his contempt by very seldom deigning to put in a personal appearance. Sometimes with, sometimes without the three other band members, he vanished into the fastness of his second-floor accommodation without bothering to let anyone know when, if ever, he would again come down. Every day, the house overflowed with those who called in, by invitation or unasked it was hard to say, to pay their homage. Much of my age for the most part, as casually dressed, carelessly shaved, longish hair, his visitors gave first impressions of aloofness, even of hostility; but as I mingled in their company and tried to make conversation, I came to revise these judgments. Music, even Celestial Praylin's heavy, imponderable, disturbing music, had engendered in these people a patience, even a gentleness that conversation, speech of any kind, seemed to threaten and despoil. They occupied, those contemporaries of mine, some other mental plateau. They moved along an alien time-scale. A quiet, flowing force, some beat they heard of the pulse of life, propelled them, almost floated them, along its choppy path. They wandered at will all over the ground floor, cooked themselves meals, played records, read books, fell asleep; and while they seemed to be taking advantage of Nicholas's prodigality, they were in fact, like so many patient dogs, awaiting their master whose loftiness postponed almost indefinitely whatever business needed to be discussed or ties of friendship renewed. After the manner of an Eastern court, the court of some potentate whose borders are peopled with strange tribes and to whom satraps are despatched over long distances, other, more exotic ambassadors came to pay their respects. A huge Jamaican with a shaved head, a crippled dwarf supported by an aluminium walking-frame, an Indian in flowing robes, Tex Ringenberg—the band's elegant manager—still retaining the air of highly placed consular connexions, mingled with the blue jeans and the sallow faces of Nicholas's musical retinue. As night fell, all those various factions who had been forgathering all day, whether Nicholas showed up or not, by the same sort of unwritten decree that forbade their climbing the stairs and, by the simple expedient of knocking on his door getting an answer to what they wanted to know, fell into a party mood. Someone would be sent down the drive to select some girls among the faithful at the gates; new arrivals rolled up in cars and in the station taxi. Soon Tex Ringenberg could be observed with a girl on his lap, the dwarf in earnest conversation with four or five of the bejeaned young men, the Jamaican adroitly rolling joint after joint that, along with Nicholas's fiery brandy, cocaine and blaring music, sustained proceedings for hour upon hour; and although cars could be heard every so often speeding off into the dawn, always when I came downstairs the next day, a residue of the intoxicated, the drugged and the stranded, those, too, who had not joined in the fun but were newly assembling for orders or for information, formed a nucleus around which, the next evening, another party would be composed. Among this shifting, noisy, chaotic household, Joanna and I wandered, eyeing each other with mutual suspicion and distaste.

I could not always be at her side; and, as the fortnight progressed and, out of boredom and frustration, I began to share more and more in the limitless supply of stimulants and soporifics, I grew careless of supervision. On our last evening came disturbing news. A rowdier party than usual was in progress. Joanna had gone upstairs to our room and was watching *Ferguson on Thursday.* For five minutes or so, I watched with her but the programme seemed just as unpleasant as when I had seen it before. Joanna had been naked then and had drawn my arms about her waist. Now she sat slumped in an armchair smoking and sucking at a can of lemonade. I had sought refuge in the dining room, bored and repelled both by Ferguson and his disaffected spectator. The door was flung open. Scotty, Praylin's drummer, entered the room. He carried a bottle of milk and a packet of cornflakes. This might be his breakfast. He poured out milk and cereal into a bowl and, plumping himself down beside me, began devouring his extempore snack at high speed. At last he raised his eyes.

'I know you,' he said. 'You did me a favour once.' His heavy face behind the drooping moustache was no less lugubrious than in the past. Ineffable sadness still floated in the small brown eyes. I could not think what he meant. The favour had been all on his side. I reminded him of his fishing Phyllidula out of the gong and dumping her in my arms.

'No, man,' he replied. 'I'm talking about Belinda. The chick you brought to our Earls Court gig and so obligingly left behind. I liked her. I really liked her.'

So it had been Scotty with whom Belinda had slept or become embroiled: whether pleasurably or to her great revulsion was still unclear. Seemingly the latter, to judge from Scotty's dourer aspects. Violence as an accompaniment to passion was not out of the question, a taste for its acceptance as much as for its administration. Neither course of conduct was hard to imagine. Scotty's gloominess proposed a self-examination, even a self-destructiveness, gratifiable by a weaker partner, physically speaking, telling him to buck his ideas up: orders enforced with cane or knout. On the other hand, his physique, rather his brute strength, adumbrated a two-way traffic could not easily be dismissed. Then there arose the question of the indulgence he had required of Phyllidula for what, when she practised it on myself, had nearly precipitated the swiftest of achievements. Belinda's repugnance for any of those three variations on amatory byplay could well explain why she had so studiously avoided seeing me again after the concert or putting in an appearance at the yoga class where she knew she would bump into me, especially if, as Scotty assumed, she thought she had been provided for his amusement. Reproach, however, would have been altogether inappropriate if—the possibility had to be considered—it induced some small masochistic *frisson* or, far more probable, generated an equally sharp reprimand for my going up to Scotty's room without his permission, Phyllidula in tow. After all, Scotty's scooping Phyllidula out of the urn was nothing more to his—to all the band's—way of thinking than a *quid pro quo* for the provision, on my part, of a girl found to his liking after a tiring concert. Besides, I very much wanted to hear what had become of Belinda.

'Ah.' Scotty pulled at his moustache. Had it been feasible for emotions to superimpose on his beleaguered countenance still profounder levels of despondency, recollections of Belinda's fate could have brought about those alterations. As it was, he was forced to make other efforts to convey his feelings, a shake of the shaggy head, a shrug of the broad shoulders, sustenance of a second plate of cornflakes. That finished, he burrowed into a shirt pocket and produced one of the Jamaican's fat cigarettes as if what he had to impart could require solace only drugs were able to induce. He lit up; and passed it across the table.

'She fell in with T. R., man.'

'T. R.?'

'Tex Ringenberg. White-haired bloke with a 'tash. Our concert manager, that's who old Tex is: very influential.' Scotty tapped his nose and closed one eye as if selflessly passing on a jealously guarded secret. 'You must have seen him around.'

'I have. I talked to him once, ages ago. The "Phyllidula" night as a matter of fact. He said he would like to kiss the seven entrances of a girl's body.'

Scotty took the joint from my hand, inhaled, held his breath, blew out the smoke through his nostrils, scratched his head, then moved his hand to his crotch as if sexual horizons had been arousingly broadened by what he had heard. He leaned back in his chair and threw up his head to watch the whorls of smoke ascend to the ceiling. I sat waiting for him to continue but he seemed to have mislaid images a moment ago providing modest excitation. He passed over the joint.

'I make it nine.'

'Nine what?'

'Nine entrances. That's my reckoning.'

'You're counting the eyes. Strictly, they're not "entrances." Or not in Mr Ringenberg's book.'

'Are they not?'

'I don't think so.'

'Oh. Well that would make it right then. Without the eyes it would be seven. Incontrovertibly. Don't Bogart that little number. The gear's getting very thin on the ground around these parts.'

'Sorry.'

'As I was saying before we got all mathematical, Belinda fell in with T. R. Three times her age he must be, going back to numbers again. You weren't around anymore as far as she could see and I was going on tour. You weren't around a couple of nights ago either. That new bird of yours, the sort of punk one . . .'

'Joanna?'

'Listen, man, T. R.'s bad news. It's not only sex, it's witchcraft, magic, the "ninety-three current," he calls it. Wants everyone to join in, chicks especially. He fucked Belinda up one way or another, maybe drugs, maybe magic, maybe just mentally shoved her over the edge. I hear that he wants to get his claws, to say nothing of his willy, into what's rightfully yours if I may judge from appearances.'

'We're going home tomorrow, fortunately.'

'Tomorrow's another day. There's still tonight. T. R.'s around somewhere, very much around.'

'I'd better go back to her then. Make sure she's all right.'

'You better had. Make sure she's all right. Off you go. And, er, you wouldn't be thinking of taking that little passport to paradise away with you, would you now? This fucking edifice is nearly clean.'

'Sorry. Here. And thanks for the warning.'

'Is all right. Is all right. You go off and look after that girl.' Scotty slid down in his chair. The cigarette smouldered in his lips. He appeared to be falling asleep. I hurried back upstairs. Joanna had switched off the television and was packing her bag. That was a relief. She intended, then, to leave tomorrow as planned. If I kept an eye on her for the rest of the evening, all would be well. Some sort of warning, though, needed issuing, a promise on her part she would not attempt to see Tex Ringenberg again; but as I began to put an ultimatum of that sort into words, I became aware that Scotty's cigarette that seemed to have contained not marijuana but some other substance untried before began to induce a semi-soporific, semi-elating calm on all my senses. It was accompanied by an ever-increasing desire for food. As words failed me and I too began desultorily to pack a few of my own belongings, the natural but at the same time supremely novel sensation of hunger set off oddly heightened perceptions, perceptions of Man, Man at his simplest and most untrammeled. All the multifarious levels of sophistication and artifice with which I cluttered my life began to be swept away on the wings of this urgent appetite. I felt amazed, humbled, cleansed by this unexpected visitation as if I had undergone a religious conversion, retrieved by the experience of this basic, animal pang the innocence of a child, rather of a baby newborn. It occurred to me this transition, rather this reversion to simplicity, this sudden cold blast of pureness, had been the corollary of Joanna's experience when the Baxters' disclosure about the 'bridal bower' fell on her ears and that the cry she had emitted on hearing it had not been one of disgust and shame but, enigmatic as Nicholas's cries on *Dreams, Waking Thoughts and Incidents,* of jubilation at innocence regained.

'I'm hungry,' I said. 'Very, very hungry.'

Joanna looked at me oddly. Perhaps I had spoken too loudly: shouted, even. That must be it. I had been yelling my head off. My appeal, like the hunger itself, springing from primeval sources, had been the cry of the male to his mate, a great keening call across rainswept plateaux.

'I'll get you food,' she replied. Then, as if she divined something of the primitiveness of my need, the raw, savage, gnawing hunger that had made me bay out my words like a howling wolf, she added, 'we'll eat it outdoors.'

No plan could have been more appealing. Joanna paused to collect from the bed what looked like a pillow or a cushion, white, satin-sheened, which perhaps she would use to sit on or place on the ground for my comfort and led the way downstairs. I followed her eagerly across the crowded hall, into the kitchen and out into the garden. It had grown dark. Ravenous though I was, I was as enchanted by the garden as by the onset of my primordial hunger. The stilted vegetation, trees, shrubs, flowers, grass, hedges, all silvered over with light from a full moon that rode steadily in the velvet sky, engaged me now entirely. I wanted the walk to last forever, to float on and on through this baroque, formal landscape; and, in response, my appetite, shifting from savagery into an exquisitely refined, artificially devised sensation as if I had set myself to savour from a distance the fumes of an exotic and expensive perfume, tortured me in its new, ostentatious voluptuousness as agonizingly as had its original instinctive demands.

In the most theatrical yet of our many playactings, we processed in mimetic solemnity across the moonlit grass. From the kitchen Joanna had procured a silver bowl which she bore on her satin cushion in slow ceremonial march before me. Master and servant, duke and page, priest and acolyte, we traversed the wide lawn and plunged into a dark, leafy aisle of trees. Joanna halted, knelt down before an opening in the thick clumps of bracken that fringed the path. Holding the bowl, which seemed to bear in it a dark, glaucous mass of delicious ripened fruits, she began to ease herself backwards through the gap and out of sight. I plunged in after her. Bracken, moss, ivy had been beaten down to form a rough sloping bed, its head the trunk of a huge gnarled oak through whose boughs moonlight, in grey shafts, descended upon us and upon the shimmering, irresistible repast. Sitting down, I stretched out a hand. Joanna slapped it away.

'Let me.' She put her fingers in the bowl and selected a fruit from her shining pyramid. I lay back to receive it but she put it between her own lips. Her strange, dye-spattered garment absorbed all light. Only her white head and hands hovered above me and bore down on my face. Our lips met. Her teeth closed on her morsel. A salt smoky spray shot onto my tongue. I rolled away in disgust.

'Don't you like olives?'

The burst of the fat oily olive when, with all the refinement of my hunger, I had been expecting sweetness, to receive into my mouth the juice of a grape or a ripe plum, had been violently repellent. It was as if Joanna had sensed my lust for fruit and capriciously filled the bowl with their choking, acrid contrarities. She gave a sharp mocking laugh of delight at the trick she had played. Her pale sleepy face hovered over mine. She began to speak softly, through soiled shining lips.

'I have a confession to make. Those things you have wished to see, I have done every day. When you were watching cricket, once when you were asleep, in the toilet our first night, here two or three times. I have been to the grove . . .'

I stared up at her. She was speaking her words liltingly in the way she had delivered the ones of the weird Masonic ritual when, the first time we met, she had anointed her father with the serving spoon, intoning them with her face upraised as if she mouthed lines memorized from some infernal rubric. The moonlight shadowed her face, etched dark bruised shadows around her eyes. She looked deathly pale, stricken, half mad.

My mind was still confused. Her singsong revelation only slowly wakened anger, a jealous, seething, frustrated rage that rolled as lazily into consciousness as the palls of smoke had risen from the drummer's tainted cigarette.

Visions of her purposely and in sordid places, which had perhaps heightened her pleasure as much as the fear of discovery or the knowledge she deceived me and racked her body into those spasms I had so longed to witness, made me clench my fist and try to smash it in her face; but even if she had not, by then, been sitting astride me and pinning me down, the drug still stupefied movements and dammed up all but the thinnest trickle of fury and of desire. I lay quite still and sampled that sneaking rivulet of love and pain as fastidiously as I had been toying with my pangs of hunger, turned it over in my mind like a thief who gloats over stolen gold. I wanted very badly to cause her pain but by some infinitely more refined method than by simply hitting her, to devise some slow torture in which my lust as much as my anger could protractedly exult. I struggled to entwine my fingers in her hair and bring her face close enough to mine to sink my teeth in her greasy lips and taste the metallic tang of her blood. She struggled wildly in my grasp and tore herself free. She got slowly to her feet. Her floating face rose higher and higher above me. Then she let fall from her body, sloughed off with infinite slowness, her disguising garment, that, as it slid from her, revealed inch by inch the nacreous whiteness of her skin. I found myself on my feet as well and imitating this almost ritual disrobing that seemed not to herald lovemaking since her moonlit presence was too ethereal, too ectoplasmic, a phantom merely of her own invocatory chanting, but some other ceremony whose nature I could not divine. Yet angered as I was, determined now not only to hurt her but, by twisting her arm or slapping her and hearing her cry of pain, to avaunt her disturbing etheriality, I all of a sudden caught the odour of her unwashed body. She smelled stale, feral, sour as the ivy that hugged the oak tree at our backs. As if to cloak me in those odours, she flung her arms around me, pressed her foul body against mine and sank her head on my shoulder. For a moment, she seemed spent, exhausted, yielding, once again the impure girl of my dreams. Then I felt her teeth bury themselves in the thin layer of flesh across my collarbone. Pain, exquisite, refined, its bright blade striking upwards into my brain as if, under my skin, she had injected still more of the drug that was altering perceptions and intensifying all my senses, enflamed desire even further and made me grab her hair and attempt to force back her head and kiss her bloodstained mouth.

Her lips were moving. She began once again her singsong chanting.

'Do not try to kiss me. Kisses are no longer a part of love. The Serpent shall no more enter the Chalice or the Blood of the Lion commingle with the Gluten of the Eagle. Behold now the true path to fulfillment.'

She leaned against me with all her weight and dragged me awkwardly to the earth. She crouched shuddering over me as if her flesh anticipated those blows I no longer had the energy to deliver. When I felt upon the puncture she had made in my skin the warm, stinging spray from her body, I took it at first for fear, until, once more, she echoed her mocking laugh and I saw slide across her eyes the vicious lateral beam of her impending pleasure. Slowly she moved, changed positions, rolled herself in my place on the dampened earth, gave signs, lay still and opened her slack enquiring mouth; and all the time, whenever our eyes met as, turn by turn, with the slow pedantry of some unholy rite, the blesser and the blessed, obeisant and abased, celebrant and supplicant, we bequeathed and accepted the offerings of our bodies, prostrate, crouching, kneeling, towering the one above the other, that gleam, the great greedy stare I had first seen in her nursery, flashed along the moonbeams that illuminated the foul altar where we worshiped; but when, at last, I staggered away from her to vomit and left her vomiting and there poured from our mouths the solids and liquids of our mingled ordures, a great darkness descended and, as in the blossomed grove, I heard the patter of raindrops. A vivid flash of lightning hovered in the thickened sky and lit with a trembling light the edges of the bank of thunderclouds above us. A fork of lightning spat and crackled down the fuse of the darkness, hung almost caressingly over the oak tree; was withdrawn. Briefly, like a guttering candle, a yellow flame flickered in a topmost branch; died down; went out. I called to Joanna. She had risen and was standing between me and the tree, gazing up into its branches. Another lightning shaft extended from the clouds. I shouted to her again, afraid that it would search her out, strike, as at the tree, the pale soiled bole of her body. She shook her head and raised her arms. There was a clap of thunder. The rain increased in volume. It fell no longer in drops but in slow, heavy curtains that sloughed off streams of filth from my skin and rendered Joanna almost invisible. Then it ceased as suddenly as it had begun, seemed up-rolled, as though the mists that now rose from the soaked earth like smoke from a dampened fire carried it upwards in their columns. The moon broke through and revealed Joanna enswathed by pearly clouds. She moved slowly towards me. The mists, more substantial around her body, swirled about her, seemed to follow her path as she approached and cocoon her nakedness. Her skin shone through their insubstantiality with a brilliant glowing whiteness. Then, with a wave of her hand, she conjured out of the air a long billowing swathe of those mists, an undulating bolt of their own luminosity, which she tore off and whirled over her head and sent leaping and curling towards me in billowing folds. I clutched at it as it buried me in soft, scented textures. Then, as senses still moved with infinite slowness, I defined the feel of silk. She had tossed over a robe, a white silken robe. She was robed herself. I let the flowing garment slide over my head, envelop my streaming body from neck to ankles. We kneeled briefly, as if in thanksgiving, before the gap in the undergrowth and crawled through. With our raiment clinging to our soaking bodies, our feet bathed in the moisture of the rain, we began to dance, to skim as if we waltzed on water, across the shining silver carpet of the lawn.

8

The men, standing one each side of a central, seated figure, gazed out over the cricket ground. Thoughts elsewhere, miles away—'Come back, come back, wherever you are,' Ma would have called out if faced across her desk with such distraction—they saw nothing of the match in progress. Their companion, the man they flanked, he was watching, though. His eyes were focused keenly, even fiercely, as if he observed, and not without partisanship, a far severer tussle than a game of cricket, a fight to the death between bloodied opponents or the sort of clash of arms that had so noisily concluded Lindo's uncle's rendition of *The Silver Palace.* One wondered what bond it was, apart from the cricket, that had brought the three men together, at the sort of affinity, family, business, school, club, regiment, that linked this contrasting, one was tempted to say motley, trio. Perhaps it had been this very disparity, the quite inexplicable juxtaposition of three so violently opposed personalities, that had inspired the artist to set up his easel and paint their communal portrait, the reason too for Nicholas's lengthy examinations of the imposing Victorian painting whenever he visited the pavilion of the ground where it hung; where, that July morning, for no especial purpose, I had chosen to linger.

Halting in front of the work and feeling upon me those three divergent pairs of eyes, I thought I recognized at once why it was engaging me: that it was because the last time I had looked at it had been just before going down to Carpenter's; that I was longing merely to be taken back in time and allowed the chance to have reversed my decision to have made that journey; but then, as it continued to fascinate me, I speculated whether its substance might convey some 'message,' could bode for good or for evil the events that would shape my immediate future.

My mind, still impaired by the drug or half-crazed from the vile ritual its effect had brought about, was assailed all the time by omens of this nature, as if my original 'belief' in the sighting of the herons in the park had been extended to include almost every unusual item impinging on the eye. Portents bedeviled me not only by day but by night. Three weeks on from my return to London, dreams, visions and nightmares still disturbed my sleep. In daylight hours I could sometimes convince myself that what had happened had been devised by Joanna (perhaps in collusion with the magician, Tex Ringenberg) to convey in the most revolting way possible just what she thought about 'love,' to desecrate the act itself after the manner that her place of love, her 'bridal bower,' the grove of flowering trees, had been revealed as a place of desecration. Yet, asleep, rather half waking since sleep now came but rarely, deeper significances were drawn that, in the daytime, trailed around constructive thought like the wreaths of mist that had arisen after the thunderstorm—of Joanna's own conjuration, it now seemed, as I remembered her uplifted arms—from the rain-soaked earth. The ceremony—it had hardly been less than that in its degrading way—had been meant perhaps as a formalistic 'shriving,' purity achieved after uncleanliness, the 'foule werke' in Thomas Norton's words, that vital stage in the transmutation of base metals into gold. Our assumption of two of her white nightdresses as they must have been, produced from the quilted bag I had taken for a cushion, that had arrayed us as we processed across the lawn afterwards, took on in those dreams the nature of a canonical robing as essential to the rite as our lustration by the hissing rain; and when, as I sometimes dreaming did, I found myself walking beside my own shape or hovering above the ground, our two robed figures became indistinguishable, hermaphroditic, physical abnegation, at last, of male and female bodies as much as of the desires that earlier had so tortured and inflamed us both. Sometimes the dreams spilled over with earlier memories, none that did not in some way connect with Joanna and our fateful meeting. Vindictive reared black against a flaming sunset; Nicholas and his band entered as fearful Tritons from a blown-up scene in *The Silver Palace,* its trite plot and aquatic set pieces endowed now with allegorical meanings I could not perfectly translate, elements of fire and water blending with the thunderstorm over Carpenter's into a heaven-sent retribution. Voices too haunted me, echoed around deserted caverns of the mind: Nicholas's banshee wailings on *Dreams, Waking Thoughts and Incidents;* the boom of the great brass gong above the clamour of his wild parties; Mrs Baxter's silvery laugh. Oftenest of all, I heard Joanna's lilting voice intoning the strange, symbolic language of her liturgy; and they, in my disordered mind, were interwoven with lines from Thomas Norton's delivered in her lazy, nasal tones or in Uncle Hamish's stentorian cockney accent and shot through with truths I could neither understand nor interpret.

I continued to stare at the painting. Members passing by on their way to and from the bar, outside which it had been suspended on giant chains, impeded for a while concentrated study. Eventually I was alone again.

All three spectators were elderly. 'Buffers,' I had heard a spectator describe them, though that suggested a comicality entirely absent from two of their number. For the one on the left, the oldest by about ten years, laughter, so much as a smile, any touch whatsoever of happiness, had not for many years been bestowed on his noble, whiskered, almost ravaged features. His was more than glumness, the disaffection with life, severe though it was, that troubled the countenance of Nicholas's drummer. Dressed entirely in grey, a grey top hat surmounting frock coat, waistcoat, cravat caught with a pearl pin, pearly grey trousers, he gazed at the match in progress behind the artist's easel with eyes so filled with despair that he seemed to be contemplating not a bereavement—at his age that was to be expected—but a terrible wrong committed in the past that he had not only witnessed but in some way himself brought about. Yet one judged that he had only been a passive agent in whatever had happened, physical strength, mental strength either, to cause suffering never part of his nature, that he had sat back and watched an altogether less merciful acquaintance—one of his two companions perhaps—bring about the catastrophe he now so dreadfully regretted.

In contradistinction every bit as drastic as the contiguity of the masks of Comedy and Tragedy, the artist had depicted on the right of his canvas a bearded, florid, broadly smiling, rotund man buttoned into a thick suit of sporting cut. He too wore a hat but of a jauntier design, brown, flat-crowned, curly brimmed. Things of the mind, so signally an occupation of his thinner, far older friend, touched this man—in his early sixties, I suppose—but rarely. If imagination were called into play, it was to dwell on the breakfast sideboard or the memory of a chorus girl in fleshings observed through opera glasses from a music-hall box. One sensed too a surfeit of these pleasures, over-indulgence at table, 'hanky panky' with two chorus girls at a time; and this exudation of unrestraint, as much as the loudness of tailoring and the hearty smile, set him apart from his friends, 'let the side down,' as it were, an expression perhaps whispered about him behind his back in the cricketing circles in which he found himself.

Tragedy and Comedy, for so I had come to think of them, flanked a central figure, the vastly superior, silk-hatted personage the artist had made the focal point of his arresting canvas. In the nobility of his presence, those latent, assuredly excusable interiorities of his companions—the weakness of will of the one, the disagreeable buffoonery of the other—stood ruthlessly exposed. For those shortcomings, if he were aware of them, he cared nothing at all. He watched the cricket with haughty, patrician eyes, the eyes of a general who observed, on a reined horse, the manoeuvres of a crack regiment under his command. Yet, sooner or later—and how imperiously he would ask for it—he would require the aid of his two unsteady companions; for he was in a bath chair. His huge frame was encased to the neck in the waterproof coverings of his vehicle. Apart from one arm, he was straitjacketed into it. The limb that was visible had been amputated at the wrist, the stump enswathed in a knitted mitten banded in red, gold and black, the colours of the club that he had founded. He had conducted that limb across his chest as if he had just smitten his heart in an oath of allegiance with a mailed fist; and similarly, he saw himself, he commanded us to see him with those proud, inflexible eyes that bade us as well dismiss from our minds anything of pity for his crippled state, not as a man in an invalid carriage, the unsightly, even ramshackle vehicle that had conveyed him to the boundary's edge, but as a conquering emperor, an emperor chariot-borne.

The picture's message remained elusive. I began to look at it through Nicholas's eyes. If I could discover why it fascinated him, I might discover why it held me also. I had never seen him imitate the characteristics of any of the three old gentlemen, the gloom of the one, the concupiscence of the other, the hauteur of the third, conspire though their aspects might to the sort of burlesque which Nicholas, once smitten, enjoyed indulging to the full. I was about to turn away. Perhaps that was the reason, the taking of a step backwards, unfocusing for a moment my eyes, then letting them rest for a last time on the canvas from slightly further off and to view it from a different angle, that its message was at last revealed. It was a study, a masterly one, of madness. Each of the three men was mad, mad as a hatter.

There could be no doubt about it. Tragedy's sagging mouth that at any moment could drop open and exude a drool of spittle, the grin that split Comedy's face and preceded only the bleating of rut, the inexorably cruel eyes of the military commander in his chair that seemed to watch not a game but a wounding, proclaimed, almost like a cry, like Nicholas's wailings on *Dreams, Waking Thoughts and Incidents,* their debility and their doom.

It was Nicholas who obsessed my thoughts as I went back into the sunlight and tried to concentrate on the cricket. Because of what had happened in his house, because too of his chaotic life-style, his inhospitality, the exhausting *va et vient* that had reigned within walls where I had hoped to find shelter and affection, I had already branded him as, after all, rather unpleasant, because of stardom altered beyond recall of friendship, long established though that had been. Whatever magic I had found in his music, not at all the magic the alabaster boy had discerned—the invocations of supernal beings—but nonetheless an undeniable enchantment, had been entirely dissipated; and whereas it had once seemed to reflect only the sort of chaos that had reigned at Carpenter's, it now represented something much more sinister. I saw now why he so often journeyed here to gaze at the disturbing canvas, to worship, it now appeared, at its shrine. It was not old age that riveted him to the spot but insanity. I recalled his expression when, one day, unconscious of my presence, he had been gazing at the portrait. It had been with the same gloating stare the photographer had caught for the poster in Joanna's bedroom. His eyes had been imbibing greedily every inch of the compelling brushwork. He had sunk his head in contemplation, raised it once more as if to bathe his face in the glow from some baleful altar light where he received his inspiration and his energy. It was no wonder that, as well as with adulation, he was showered with anger and abuse, nor that Major Giblin had punted the shrieking radio from the hand of the rat-faced schoolboy in the empty street. His frightening disguises, his wild parties, his whole mode of conduct, public and private, were revealed to me now as a crusade to instil madness in other people. His strange court, his dwarves, his jesters, the pale band of youths who dogged his heels, the prostitutes at his gates, he had infected them all. It seemed no longer a caprice that he had once arrayed himself like a plague doctor, for to spread the disease, he would need to be arrayed against its infection: the infection of madness.

That its spores had touched Joanna, I was also convinced. The excrementitious rite she had prepared with Tex Ringenberg, who must have taught her the enigmatic words she had whispered, was the working of a deranged mind. She might have been unbalanced before, her strange stares and trances and sudden rages symptomatic of the disorder that, in Nicholas's company, had overtaken her completely. When I saw her the morning after in the pink and blue dress she had worn for the Baxters' supper party, she had looked quite differently from ever before. A smugness sat upon her plump features, a saintliness even, at any rate some great inner satisfaction that rolled up her eyes and sent her smiling off on the train as if she did not care where she was headed or as if her journey was in some indefinable way 'meant.' This composure had alarmed me then, but for different reasons. At the time, I had interpreted it as amusement, a self-congratulatory contemplation of how she and her new, aging lover had conspired to disgust me and send me packing. Now, though, I saw she was seriously ill. Her stricken face in the garden, like an animal's at bay, floated up to me in my dreams; and each minute of each hour of each day that passed without Freddy's reporting that anything was amiss conspired, as I saw it, to nourish the demons within her who, sooner or later, would burst cackling from the seven entrances of her body and hound her to her death.

This anxiety haunted me all the time. I awoke with it in the forefront of my mind, only the continued presence of the herons in the park able, ornithomantically, to banish it as day succeeded day. Seven weeks later, they gave me a sign that all was over: for the first time I saw a heron in flight. As the bird rose spectacularly skywards, the elongated neck and exceptional wingspan giving illusions of a far older, extinct, even nontellurian, species, and then set a long, loping course towards a pair of willow trees overhanging a lawn at the park's farther bank, it seemed to me after all Miss Benke's, rather the Master of the Orange Robe's, interpretation of the augury had been wrong. At rest, the herons' clumped, brooding, motionless, faintly grubby shapes must symbolize evil, the grey, ovoid barnacles of thought-forms that lodge in the mind and, like tumours, distort its proper functions. I realized I had never enquired whether Miss Benke meant by 'lucky' the birds in flight or the birds grounded and sunk in churlish thought. Now I felt sure she would have insisted on the differentiation and gone on to stress that only in the flurry of release I had just observed, in the joyous uprising and swoop of the bird on the wing, were auspicious oracles assured. I saw the portent as revealing that Joanna had recovered her health: like the heron, unpinioned, her mind soared again on the broad wingspan of reason. It came to me she could herself have been drugged during the 'rite,' absorbed, when she had drunk my blood, some of the substance I had inhaled into my system; that she recalled nothing of what had happened afterwards; that perhaps none of it had ever happened at all. At her release, I felt a great release myself. I walked on to ALEMBIC.

Passing through the pinkish-beige façade, I collided with a man coming out. I assumed the figure to be a man. I could see a pair of blue trousers, wide brown shoes. His face though, all of him to his waist, was obscured by a luxuriant plant he bore by its roots in front of his body, its long, umbrageous, mobile, for a moment apparently articulated branches masking his vision and causing, as much as my own precipitous entry, a collision of some force. I put out a hand to beat off the leaves. Cold, olive green, adhesive to the touch, they threatened to wrap themselves round me, their propulsion by the unseen bearer and their inclination to attach themselves to the skin suggesting an alien life-form, one of thousands that might be roaming the streets in search of human prey. Earth from the roots rattled onto the linoleum floor. A voice spoke from within its folds.

'Watch where you're going, squire.'

I apologized. The tree was set down. A man in dungarees and thick pebble glasses stared anxiously over the top. It was Pte Potts.

I recognized him at once. He was still plagued by acne, the beret he sported, like army dress, adjusted to an unorthodox angle, rather not to an angle at all but worn flat on his head: 'like a Froggie,' Sgt Barker would comment. 'All 'e needs now is a Gow-loise cigarette and a button accordion.' Long wrists still sprouted red, beefy hands. For his part, identification took somewhat longer. Vast dredgers heaved up memories, heavy as the earth that clung to his plant, and endowed his expression with the glazed incomprehension that had prompted Sgt Barker's obscure comparison with the Goddess of Mercy.

Eventually recognition dawned. He clapped me on the shoulder and aimed a variety of playful punches around my head with his big fists. He gave himself a great shake of disbelief like a dog emerging from water.

'Well, I'll be fucked,' he said.

The meeting was indeed a surprise. In other circumstances, there would be much to be gone into: four intervening years of life to be filled in; some news perhaps of amatory progress now Sgt Barker's surveillance had been withdrawn; a postmortem on the drunken night I had tried to seduce Valerie Latham; current whereabouts of Cpl Kinnell, Major Hamilton, Sgt Barker himself. Here, though, it was distinctly awkward. I could not invite him into ALEMBIC quarters. The majestic pot plant forbade adjournment to a café. News would have to be delivered later on over a drink, two or three drinks probably. I wondered if he would care to visit the Rum Cove. Then I recalled he did not, could not drink, his abstention the reason I had got so thoroughly tight myself, circumstances leading, by a classic example of Sgt Barker's 'Titless Susans,' to my recruitment here. Potts seemed to pick up this train of thought.

'Still reading those funny old books, then?'

'No, not really. I got a bit bored with books.'

'D'you work here?'

'Yes.'

'I couldn't find a way in. I've been hammering and hammering.' Potts looked through his glasses at the bleak, ill-painted, totally empty hallway. The two fireproof doors, ALEMBIC's and the refurbishing department's, were locked. The lift's sheet-metal gates shone blankly in the grey daylight. Something had gone wrong. Ma, for whom the plant was unquestionably destined, should have been in the hall to receive delivery; have commandeered the lift for its transport to her roof garden. She was in fact flouting ALEMBIC regulations by giving an outsider our address. Probably she had not yet arrived. It was only just nine-thirty.

'There isn't a way in. You've got to have a key.'

'What sort of place is it, then?'

'Civil Service. Inland Revenue, that sort of thing. They lock us away in case we're assaulted by the overtaxed or the underprivileged.'

'Oh.' Potts nodded sagely. He picked at a spot on his chin. I wondered to which bracket he belonged. He hardly looked prosperous, yet the nursery business, a private enterprise it might be, could pay good wages. I asked exactly what he did.

' 'Aulage. They taught me to drive after you got your demob. It's not only these buggers. You should see what I've got on my lorry. Everything but the kitchen sink. It's my 'orticulture week, you might put it. I'm on my way down to Suffolk with a load of hydrangeas. Will you see to this, then, give us a signature, like?'

'Of course.'

'I could come in for a bit of a natter once I'm properly parked. We could start a brew going. Got your own office, I take it?'

'Look, David, I'm a bit pushed this morning. Let's meet after work one night.'

'I'd like that. Bear in mind, I'm still on the orange squash though. My guts, if you recall.'

'Yes, I remember. What about tomorrow?'

Potts shook his head vigorously. 'No dice there, Tom, my old mate. Tomorrow's right out. All Thursdays, come to that. It's *Ferguson on Thursday* on the telly. I'm hooked on that.'

We arranged another evening. I used my Yale key on ALEMBIC's door and began to lug the plant up the stairs. Potts seemed unchanged. I had accompanied him to his lorry. A heap of his puzzle magazines lay on the passenger seat. A transistor radio was playing, perhaps the same one to have exuded the seductive Eastern music that had so enraged Major Hamilton the day he had invaded the Orderly Room. Today it was filling the van with Nicholas's screaming voice and the thunder of Celestial Praylin guitars. Potts had climbed in and switched it off.

'Can't stand those sods,' he had shouted down. 'They're off their trollies, in my opinion.'

He had waved good-bye and driven off. In a way, I had been pleased to see him, in a way not. He represented earlier, happier days I suddenly longed for again: the peace of the Orderly Room, mugs of Sgt Barker's tea, the crunch across the barrack square of marching men; and despite the melancholy that sound always imposed, thoughts of condemnation to everlasting drudgery that even Cpl Kinnell's calendar, with its serried ranks of days deleted, could not contradict nor convey any real assurance that time was passing, there was, for all that, a kind of homeliness which, compared with working at ALEMBIC, was freedom indeed. For within the outworn hulk of ALEMBIC, which seemed to resemble from the outside the stern of some top-heavy, elaborately carved galleon and, within, the bowels of a submerged submarine—contrasts of old and new reflected as well in the antiquated texts I copied and the aseptic modernity of the laboratory where the furnace was being converted to nuclear power so that great hammer-blows could be heard resounding along the miles of air-conditioning pipes as if our craft were being pounded against an underwater reef—there lay a far grimmer prison than Sgt Barker's almost cosy working area. Potts, more than any of us, no less now than then, as I watched him drive away, his hydrangeas swaying on the bucking tailboard of his lorry, was a symbol of freedom, a man never completely, by either routine or by discipline, to be brought to heel. It was strange he should confirm my feelings about Celestial Praylin: 'off their trollies,' my opinion to the letter. Their music haunted me nowadays. It came from everywhere: pubs, the clothes shops in Oxford Street, cars, vans, lorries like Potts's. Like the rumble of gunfire in some terrible approaching battle, it spoke of danger, injury, death.

By the time I reached the third floor, much of the soil from the tree's roots had fallen off onto the stairs. It was appreciably lighter to carry. I laid it carefully on Ma's office floor. To my surprise, she had in fact turned up for work; was talking on the telephone. At least, she held the receiver. She looked more than usually prettified, her beauty spot meticulously heightened, yet somehow unready, in rather a state, as if, in one of the Restoration comedies I always imagined she had been assigned a comedy role, she had been revealed in her boudoir, a maid at her elbow giving news of a lover's unexpected arrival at the front door. She held the telephone like a hand mirror in which she might be seeking to repair facial ravages. She was also in a mood to impart rather than to elicit gossip, a 'Tell it not in Gath' day as opposed to a 'What news on the Rialto?' one.

'*Squattez-vous,*' she said. She leaned confidentially forward, muffling the receiver with a dimpled hand. 'This is the police, dear. Freddy's little girl is missing.'

So that was how the die had fallen. The news came as no especial shock to the system. In a way, it was to be welcomed, if only as confirmation that forebodings had not been symptoms of some madness with which I, like Joanna, had been infected. The insidious accumulation of seemingly occult pointers that had resisted rational hermeneutics had played its part in alerting me to a catastrophe. If catastrophe it was. Police involvement suggested as much, an accident, a loss of memory, a waylaying, as if tragedy had already struck; but I judged that a tragedy had yet to take place. The portent of the heron on the wing, that I now saw had foretold not a release but an escape, demanded a very divergent interpretation from Ma's one of vanishment. Joanna's action had been prompted by mental imbalance, of that there was no question, one of the three categories of madness, furthermore, revealed to me in the portrait at the cricket ground. Despair, lust, cruelty; one of those emotions drove her now. Despair seemed the least probable. There had been enough determination on her face in the train to have suggested she had already been contemplating not a flight but a mission whose call, when the time came, she would devotedly answer. Where then, summoned by lust or by cruelty, would she go, seek whose arms, into whose heart plunge her dagger of revenge? Nicholas's? Tex Ringenberg's? My own? And, if I had been mistaken, that it was, after all, a martyrdom that had sat upon her smiling countenance, a settling of the mind for death, where would she go to bid death welcome: in Nicholas's words, 'to tear him out her heart'? There was no doubt in my mind that she would return to the grove in Miller's Wood. There, as she had abandoned girlhood, she would now abandon life.

I telephoned to Nicholas. I was right. She had been to the house. She had left again with Tex Ringenberg in tow. Nicholas was at his most uncommunicative, protected by rough, unfamiliar voices who passed me from one to the other until he eventually came on the line. He passed me back to one of the number. Yeah, she'd looked OK. Why should she not? They had left by car. Nick had wanted them out of the house. He had ordered them to leave.

It was impossible to spend one more moment within ALEMBIC. Action needed to be taken. I had to go searching, although I had no idea where to look. It was fortunate Potts had not been able to make the evening for our drink. As I was about to dismiss him from my mind, it came to me that he, like the heron, was some sort of emissary, descended like one of Uncle Hamish's water sprites, to force on the action. If I could get in touch with him, he might have a car I could borrow. We could go searching together. He would be a calm and willing companion-in-arms. I regretted not having taken his telephone number where I could ring him before he settled to his evening of television. Then it dawned on me why I was still giving him consideration. He was going to watch *Ferguson on Thursday.* Robert Ferguson, benefactor of the unfortunate, helper of the helpless, righter of wrongs. I would ring up Robert Ferguson and ask him to appeal on the screen tonight for Joanna to come home. No, not ring him up, go and see him in person. I would go at once.

I saw this plan as one not only of icy common sense but as containing many of the elements of a crusade. We were symbols, Joanna and I, of a righteousness which Robert Ferguson seemed now to champion against evildoers. I contemplated him with admiration, even with reverence, saw again his smiling, indulgent, moneyed features as he gazed at the limping boy in the roadway. It was no wonder that Nicholas had refused an interview. The saint and the devil, that's how the scenario would have been played out, a confrontation between the forces of good and evil. By means of the television screen on which he had been too fearful to show his face, I would burst through whatever doors held Joanna captive and, like a knight in armour, cut her free from her bonds.

Even as I set out, at least before the train I took had traveled very far, my real motive for putting the plan into action began to cloud the radiance of its concept. What I was doing was cowardly in the extreme. If I were a knight in armour, that armour was corroded, pitted deeply with the rust of shame and apprehension. I was not on a crusade at all but, no less than Joanna, on a headlong flight from reality and responsibility. My gallantry was as much a travesty of knighthood as the scrofulous caricature of Nicholas on the band's T-shirts was a mockery of courtly ideals. I should be with Freddy, with the police, telling them all I knew, throwing myself on their mercy. I should be at Carpenter's, seeking a way past the electronic eye to batter my way into the house and fight off Nicholas's restraining henchmen until I forced him to tell me where Joanna and Ringenberg had gone. And, if I were not brave enough to perform either of those actions, I ought, for my own protection, to be doing precisely nothing: sitting at ALEMBIC, working on Thomas Norton as if nothing had happened, praying my secret would not be revealed. Then, as I approached my destination, it grew more and more unlikely that I would get to see Ferguson without an appointment. I saw myself before his house, its windows shuttered, the same security device as at Carpenter's set up on its gateposts. Ferguson's wealth, equal certainly to Nicholas's, their equal fame and vulnerability to spongers, idolaters, the half-fit, the semi-sane, would all conspire to wall him up against any possible intrusion.

His address was public knowledge though. The flag department's *Who's Who* yielded that at once: Grey Ladies, Windsor. They knew the house at the station, told me to take the station road as far as the bridge. I could not miss it. As I walked, I began to rehearse what I should say if I got inside.

It would be best to approach with a mixture of the desperation that was mine in full measure and of the reverence I also very much sustained: a falling, then, at Robert Ferguson's feet. Dissimulation would have a place only in the sort of story I would have to invent about myself—a distraught boyfriend (though he must not broadcast my name), a brother, a colleague of Joanna's father, a bitter critic of police inactivity. And then, if he listened to me, if he were at home to listen, there seemed after all very little chance he could make any immediate move. He would assuredly have to consider the inadvisability of publicizing what he might interpret as a kidnapping, even a murder, in case it interfered with official investigations. Again, it would be necessary to lie, to make him believe that Joanna had just run away and that, so far, the police had not been involved. If I suppressed her age and spoke merely of an undesirable elopement, he might perhaps be persuaded to appeal for her that evening.

The castle, elevated on ivy-covered slopes in enclosed parkland, rekindled ideas about my journey's constituting some form of crusade. Thomas Norton had come here, ridden out from London to offer his secret to the king. He had kneeled before him, been raised up, offered board and lodging and an opportunity for speech. Perhaps he had delivered some lines from his *Ordinall* in one of the many chambers whose fenestrations overlooked the bend of the river or had stridden the battlements with his royal host. In such determination and humility I must now approach Robert Ferguson. I must pray that, like Thomas Norton with the king, I would be courteously attended.

I had reached the bridge without seeing a single house. The river side, flat commonland, was undeveloped. The coarseness of the grass, dotted here and there by goalposts, muddied in part by autumnal flooding, contrasted violently with the rolling castle acreage. Grey Ladies must be on the far side of the bridge. There, arable vagaries were also observable. The commonland gave way to a golf course. Lushness of the royal turf was reflected in the well-tended fairways and greens. The bunkers were as assiduously raked of leaves as the gravel paths that ran through the royal park to the castle slopes. Rude ploughed acres of farmland on the righthand bank echoed proletarian aspects of the recreation area they diagonally opposed. As I traversed the bridge, I was gripped with the sort of terror I had once suffered in Nicholas's meadow. Feelings of isolation, that the bridge was no longer a connecting link with the road but a wherry marooned, river-girt, bore in upon me. It swayed beneath my feet as Nicholas's land had tipped drunkenly underfoot in the days of my illness. Movements of air, quite sharp gusts, blown from the direction of the castle, vied in my ears with the roar of the current as it sucked its way downstream. Clouds that, on my walk, had been barely perceptible above the castle now detached themselves like black, tattered banners from its dark battlements and swung across the tarnished river, spattering rain. From time to time, cars hurtled over the bridge in both directions. Low in the sky over the common, a huge silver aeroplane dragged itself on roaring jets towards me, so low I could examine the faces of the passengers who stared out through the portholes as if the machine were about to plunge them into the foaming river. I seemed to be imprisoned in the centre of this calyx of in-directed sound and movement that had set itself up in the landscape. Shifting crosscurrents of light slanted in like swords from all directions, across, beneath, above, and impaled me on grey, glistening blades. I felt I might fall unconscious. The waist-high parapet of the bridge was no longer adequate guard against being picked up by the wind and flung into the water. As in dreams, I found I could walk only with the greatest difficulty. To have retraced my steps or made it to the opposite bank would have been the work of hours; and yet the urgency to move was as overpowering as the inability to take a single step. As if I did battle in the teeth of a roaring gale, I managed to stagger across the road, arms outstretched to halt oncoming traffic, and to gain the opposite parapet. Here the water was calmer, slipped slowly, almost indolently, towards its fate. The word was apt enough. Death seemed very close: by water; in the air; on the road. I began to think about Joanna again. When first I considered she might be contemplating suicide, the vision had been of her on a bridge, staring into water. Now it was my turn. All sense of purpose had dissolved, vanished like the rush of cars and the beamed-in light. Silent now, the land lay abandoned, wasted, preserved from decay only by the silver precipitate of the day. The inevitable slipping river gliding beneath my feet prepared the mind for death. I leaned further over the rail to inspect what impediment—between the arches themselves it must be—was causing the water to pile up and burst through on the other side into the wild torrent whose roar, if it were not the pounding of my blood, still rang in my ears. I desired death but dared not jump. Some animal instinct revolted against being buffeted against the pickets of the weir or the rocks of the waterfall that might lie between the bridge's spans.

It was then that I saw the flash. A bubble of light burst across the river to my right. At first, I feared a return of the strange bombardment of light and sound and motion—traffic had already begun to speed once more up and down the road at my back—but it was far brighter, more abrupt, the explosion perhaps of a flashbulb activated by someone on the bank below. I found myself looking at the figure of a man. His appearance had its magical elements. Superimposed against the darkness of the riverbank, standing, it seemed, on the water itself, he materialized only gradually, and, even when I recognized who he was, he came into focus miasmically surrounded by the floating motes of light and darkness still retained in the retina from the image of the flashbulb he, presumably, had set off. Then I saw that those motes, breaking up into a thousand fragments the man's silhouette, were composed from the traceries of a willow tree, yellow, green, umber, that overhung the deck of a long, grey houseboat, low in the water and obscured under the overhang of the bank: completely, perhaps deliberately, hidden from view.

Casually dressed, with an eye to pleasanter weather than obtained, white shirt, lemon jacket and trousers, blue espadrilles, the man fished in his pockets for a cigarette case and a lighter. Both were of gold. The frosted glass door he had opened and which was the source of the flashed illumination as it had caught in its folds all the grey brightness of the morning, remained ajar behind him. Starry ripples of the river's reflection played upon its pleated surface. From the boat's interior, music wafted outwards. The man strolled to the rail of the boat and leaned over, gazing into the water.

As an 'entrance,' orchestration could hardly be improved upon; for although Robert Ferguson could not have divined the elements of mystery that accompanied his manifestation in the unpeopled landscape, there was, in his casualness, his aloofness, the summery neatness of his clothes and the graceful lighting of the cigarette, an inbred theatricality that transformed this stroll on the deck of his houseboat into a solo performance of sustained artistry. I seemed to be watching Robert Ferguson from the side box of some enormous theatre, the roar of the river the spectators' applause, the silvery day the effulgence of a thousand spotlights diffused on the apron of the stage he centrally held. Accompanied by an almost physical sickness, my excitement, a vast, concentrated effort to draw him nearer, to milk along the line that connected us every available essence of his image, so that I leaned still further over the bridge, was constituted from the same emotions Belinda had experienced when, at the rock concert, she had perceived Nicholas picking his way to the microphone, Belinda had craned forward in her seat to shorten the distance between them and given out her wild scream of joy and yelled out his name. I, too, could have cried for joy and for relief.

Ferguson extinguished his cigarette. He began, so I thought, to peer into the river, to lean over the boat's rail at much the same perilous angle that I was assuming on the bridge, to try to identify a submerged object—a fish, his own reflection, the swiftness of the deceptively tranquil current—but then I realized that what he was doing was imitating my own movements. Watching me out of the tail of his eye, he mimicked exactly my own pose, arms outstretched on the rail, body tilted from the waist almost parallel with the river. I moved a foot. He moved his. I slid my left hand along the parapet. His hand moved too. I took both hands from the ironwork and stood upright. He did the same.

I wondered how long he had known I was there, if from the very beginning what he had made of my actions. I could not remember very clearly what those had been, except for staggering, arms flailing, across the road over the bridge and leaning far further than safely over the parapet. Presumably he had not divined I had considered jumping off. I told myself in a moment of grim humour that a man 'in his position' would have rushed to my rescue, a suicide on his doorstep, so to speak, poor advertisement for his philanthropic image. More likely, he was taking me for one of his fans, his brief exposure theatrical indeed, propitiatory, dismissive too, in the way that Nicholas, when crowds grew heavy at his gate, would saddle Vindictive and ride down the drive to 'put his head round the door,' as he had it, in return for their patience and their piety. Robert Ferguson would soon retreat inside.

He did nothing of the kind. He turned to face me. He raised a hand in greeting. He waved, wiggling each finger several times in rotation as if playing in the air successive notes on a keyboard instrument. Then, he indicated in a great, lavish arc that took in the far end of the bridge, part of the golf course and the bank behind his back, the route I must take to join him on his vessel: over; around; down.

Now that I was about to meet him, I felt an even greater love for the man. As I made my way towards him, all crusading instincts returned in full measure and with them, for the first time, the realization that I was, after all, deeply in love with Joanna. This simple, blinding truth illuminated my real motive for coming here. I no longer desired her. She had cleansed me of desire. Yet in the certain knowledge that I nonetheless loved her dearly, a great raging jealousy of Tex Ringenberg welled up in my soul. I was convinced they were still together. To get her out of his clutches surreptitiously would not now be prize enough. She must not only be returned but be seen to have been returned. I had been imbued with all the fearlessness and the military guile of the old general in the oil painting. I was about to command some great battle between the forces of light and darkness that I wished played out in full view of all the protagonists: Joanna and her father; Ringenberg; Nicholas Spark; Robert Ferguson. In a way, I would be engineering the very confrontation between Ferguson and Nicholas that the latter so feared and shunned.

On the far side of the bridge a stile gave entry to the golf course and, on the left, a path wound between trees down to the riverbank. I crossed a companionway and ducked into the boat. I was in the middle of a long, white-walled saloon. Furnishings were white; a thick white carpet covered the deck. An elaborate brass bassinet in one corner held an array of bottles. Music came from a sleek, ivory-painted cabinet placed next to a doorway that led to other parts of the vessel. The room smelled of a bowl of white roses placed on a coffee table in front of a white, hide-upholstered couch; and of Ferguson's cigarettes. It was empty. Through the portholes circles of thick, mercurial light broke in huge pools on the fleecy carpet. The boat breathed, hummed with a tense, cool vibrancy, rocked almost imperceptibly but enough to give an impression not of floating but of being suspended high in space as if I had been transported aboard some deluxe interstellar waiting room, a paradisaical antechamber to Heaven itself. I waited, febrile and alert, senses reinvigorated by a more purified, headier air than outdoors, oxygen-supplemented and supplied uniquely to the shining craft, for Robert Ferguson to reappear.

His entrance when it came, coincident with a shift in the rhythm of the cocktail-lounge music, was not, after his almost magical embodiment on deck, all that might be wished. He had to negotiate the narrowness and lowness of the doorway by the white stereo, to bend his head and to step, almost doubled up, over a high carpeted splashboard before he could assume his full height. In common with many 'famous' people, Nicholas included, he was not as tall as expected. Nevertheless, he made up for lack of inches and for the awkward, clambering way he had had to come in by the most enormous protestations of delight that he should be able to welcome me, of all people, aboard his craft. His smooth, tanned, boyish face shone with the fun of it all, which, as he tried to express himself, allowed him only to make his way one step at a time and, at each one of them, to produce widespread, apologetic mannerisms with his arms as indications that, for the time being, excitement bereft him totally of speech. The normally cocked eyebrow and its fellow were upraised to such happy heights of disbelief they engraved long seams across his forehead and his mouth, as a rule faintly smiling, thin-lipped, hung open a-twitch with silent stutters of laughter. At last, he got that braying mouth under some sort of control, but only by coming to a halt and by cramming his arms down towards the floor and shooting them wide apart as if he were demonstrating that a quite wonderful and precious object lay in his path which we must now examine together and expatiate upon at some length. That was, when words again became available; for through lips which he had now pursed into the tiniest of rosebuds as if he were trying to signal for a cessation of the thousand delights that were shouting out at him in his teemingly excited brain and drowning, like a roomful of laughing people, the sentiments he wanted to express, he could only manage an enormously protracted 'So-o-o-o-o.'

He made the word run on for such a time and contorted the vowel with such an extravagant melisma of affectation that its preposterousness seemed to strike him as an extension of the unbridled and bewildering wealth of entertainment which my presence had so incontinently placed at his disposal; and the strange noise he had made sent him off again into paroxysms of arm-stretching and head-shaking and attempts to refresh himself by running his fingers through his golden hair until, in the middle of this performance, he managed to locate my hand and to wring it up and down for a very long time indeed without stopping.

'So-o-o-o,' he brought out again.

I muttered something about being sorry for the intrusion. He assimilated that remark, let my hand fall as if I indeed did intrude. He looked searchingly into my eyes as though I had spoken the answer to a riddle at which he had been fruitlessly cudgeling his brains to arrive and was astounded to hear from the lips of someone so 'young.' His handsome, sunburned, structured features, now he had got them back under his command, were set out in the sort of twinkling indulgence a doctor displays to a patient before informing him in words of one syllable that his illness is of trivial account, perhaps even imaginary.

'Intrude?' he said at last. 'You do not intrude at all. You happen upon me which is a vastly different circumstance.' The clipped voice with its faintly rolled *r*s differed so radically from the accent used to pronounce the affected 'so' of his greeting that it occurred to me he might have been imitating somebody, a celebrity whose languid drawl he had expected me to recognize. Abruptly, I sensed a change of mood, even of hostility. Yet, turning and making his way towards the gleaming wheelbarrow of drinks, he went quite happily on.

'I was mixing martinis like a thing possessed when I spotted you on the bridge. I must tell you, you looked positively shifty. I anticipated a r-r-r-aider in a stocking mask.'

He indicated I should sit down on the leather sofa. Behind me, he made clashing noises with bottles, glasses, ice, a cocktail shaker. He brought over a frosted, long-stemmed glass. 'People,' he said as I took it from his hand, 'can be quite unbelievably dreary about dry martinis: brands of gin, quantities of the additive, presence or absence of lemon, olives, silverskin onions, rock salt. They dr-r-r-one on for hours. Lally Bowers, I recall, talked of little else.'

I drank from the glass. Robert Ferguson observed me closely. His joy had now cooled to match the delicate flavour of the liquid he had provided. Only the turned-down mouth, which still twitched at the corners, indicated the beads of mirth that were still rising into consciousness. A disarranged curl of hair over his brow contradicted the precision of the ageless face and bridged the gap between the wonder-worker who inhabited this strange, white room, its atmosphere somehow encapsulated in the aromatic refreshment he had on offer and the poseur whose spare half-hour he found me to be enlivening.

'Are you from Eton?' he enquired. 'An Etonian out on a r-r-r-ramble?'

'I was there.'

'When?'

'Eight years ago.'

'I too. But eight times eighty years ago, or so it feels. "An Eton boy grown heavy." '

'Winthrop Mackworth Praed.'

'How devastatingly bright of you. He is little read. Did you "do" Praed at Eton?'

'No. A friend of mine is keen. Praed and Charles Kingsley.'

I wondered if Robert Ferguson knew the poem about Vindictive and Lorraine Lorrèe. I thought of reciting it to see whether it gave amusement, to ask if the willow trees that overgrew his houseboat were those of the 'pollard' variety against which the horse had dashed his rider to death. I was enough lulled in his presence to continue, for as long as he liked, the sort of chatter he was enjoying. As in the imposing doctors' houses around ALEMBIC, where pretty nurses swung open the brass-plated doors to reveal flower-filled hallways and led the visitors into surgeries as coolly aseptic, I dared think, as this and into the presence of doctors as suave, as elegant, as confidently expert as Robert Ferguson, there obtained, in his gleaming white saloon, in the 'smartness' of his cocktail and in the easeful gossip, the same promise of a curative art that, when the time was ripe, would be put into practice. The earlier ebullience that had yielded to the chuckling small talk would, in due course, give way to a calm and serious concern. As if he read my thoughts and considered that the time had indeed come to hear what I had to say, he consulted his watch, lowered himself on to the other end of the sofa and looked at me over his glass.

'An Eton boy, then?'

'Yes.'

'But not grown heavy.' His body gave a sudden convulsive twitch as if, once more, he were going to lapse into uncontrollable mirth. He drained his drink, set the glass on the table with the roses and stared vacantly into its depths. The spasm seemed to presage pain rather than mirth. Robert Ferguson looked extremely tired, aged, drawn, quite ill. His small tight mouth hung open, this time not in amusement but in exhaustion. He flung his arm along the back of the sofa and ran his eyes along the sleeve of his yellow jacket to consult for a second time the heavy gold wristwatch. I could hear its ticking. His fingertips squeaked on the taut leather upholstery. A faint tang of cologne on his hand mingled with the scent of the roses.

'Most assuredly not grown heavy,' he said; and pinched my cheek.

The tweak, more a rolling of the flesh between finger and thumb, pressure applied to fruit or the breast of a bird for the pot, do what he might to turn it into a playful 'chucking' to rouse me from an overserious mood when he found himself in an altogether larkier frame of mind, was susceptible of only one interpretation. There could be no doubt of what had to be regarded as his 'intentions.' I sat exactly where I was. I found myself unable to move. Shock, if any there had been, came from the quite unexpected turn of events, rather as if Robert Ferguson had all at once taken a header through one of the portholes or leaned forward and been sick on the white carpet. Resentment mingled with vexation at not having, from the very start, recognized him for 'what he was.' All the fragrances and whitenesses of the room, the bland music still oozing from the stereo, the crisp, clean, outdated clothes, the gusts of mirth and the brittle patter he had trailed under my nose to test compatibility, the considerable strength of the dry martini into which he had most likely dashed a good deal more gin than normal measures, had all been pointers and reasonably obvious ones that, in the newfound assurance of his goodness, I had quite failed to recognize. Now he had shown his true colours, I found myself overcome almost to the point of grief not because I disapproved in the least of homosexuals but because, by announcing himself as of that class, as being what Sgt Barker termed 'humpty-dumpty,' I found myself applying Barker's corollary that these people devote their entire lives to the seduction of young men, of men indeed, since, in their company, he considered himself at risk, considerably older; and that whatever they did for a living or pursued as a hobby was aimed at the gratification of their desires. So, just as Sgt Barker, who suspected one of the army cooks to be of that persuasion and, when he produced now and again food of some excellence in the Sergeants' Mess, reasoned that efforts had been made only to impress one of the NCO's who would then give him a word of praise leading, in time, to more intimate conversation, it now seemed to me that Ferguson's bounty and beneficence were employed only to ingratiate himself with the young men he came into contact with on his television programmes whose families he appeared to be helping along. Furthermore, Robert Ferguson's assault, because it had thrown me into a state of indecision about what on earth to do next, turned that indecision into an alarming, almost womanly passivity; and I found I was putting myself in the place of a girl seated next to a man on a sofa and realizing she is only required for the texture of her skin. From among the several excuses that could be made, an angry rebuff, an edging away, the hasty gathering up of her 'things' preparatory to storming out of the house, I too would have to come out with one of those excuses and take myself off; but the understanding that I would need to have recourse to one or other of these 'girlish' contrivances, a sort of affirmation of attractiveness coupled with a denial of favours, exacerbated those trappings of femininity in which Robert Ferguson had cloaked me and brought with it an even more disturbing, though less passive, extension of ideas. Because I had not repelled him or jumped up or looked, so far as I knew, the slightest bit put out by what had happened, my passivity, this strange female persona that seemed to exude from me like the smell of Ferguson's cologne and of the roses, could be put to considerable advantage; and without further inconvenience to myself.

The reason I had so long to think along these lines was because Robert Ferguson had become extremely ill at ease. He had got to his feet and was pacing the saloon in a melancholy way, shoulders hunched as if he carried pieces of heavy luggage. Small smiles, little laughs he tried to set up, died instant deaths. He looked yet again at his watch. At first, I conceived he might be regretting a move he saw had been injudicious: premature, at any rate. Then, as he walked behind me and looked out of a porthole, I realized there was being visited upon him, even on him with his poise and his money and his overweening pride, the scourge, and a roundly punitive one, of a 'Titless Susan.' While, to his knowledge, he held on his boat a compliant young man, one at least who had not dashed his martini into his face or offered him violence, he had now run out of time. Tightness of schedule allowed no prolongation of our tête-à-tête. Robert Ferguson now had to go out.

The cooks in the Rum Cove one night, over Tallulah Twisters, had lugubriously commenced some sort of written inventory on paper napkins of the occasions they had suffered this sort of unsportsmanlike stroke of fate. Lindo had recalled a girl who had fallen down outside ALEMBIC and broken an ankle but could not, by Rastus's decrees, be carried inside and had been whisked off by ambulance never to be seen again. Bastable spoke of a Japanese girl, lost in London, encountered while he was on an uncancelable errand of mercy to a dying aunt. Brows had been furrowed, eyes clouded over, at amassed evidence of providential implacability. 'The Lord our God is a mean old bastard,' Bastable had opined. The others bowed their heads as if they felt again his yoke.

I got up too and looked out of another porthole. Robert Ferguson's predicament was exactly revealed. Across the water, a white limousine had been parked by the roadside. A uniformed chauffeur was making a remorseless passage across the bridge. He stopped where I had stopped and looked down into the boat. Ferguson opened the door and raised an unhappy hand. Then he turned back to me and made one last effort. He drew on all his resources of charm and poise, the massed experience of a lifetime in the theatre. He could risk no mistake.

'I would dearly love to go on talking to you all day, "to tire the sun with talking and send him down the sky," as our fellow Etonian so pr-r-r-ettily had it, but I must now, alas, repair to London by Rolls-Royce. As you will know, my programme is on air tonight. There are rehearsals, lighting plots, sound checks, a myriad tedious duties to be fulfilled. But . . .' He raised his hand as if

I were already making a move to be out of his way, 'I positively will not budge an inch until I have extracted a promise from you to come here again: for a pr-r-r-oper visit.' He felt into the pocket of his jacket and extracted a thin black morocco engagement book and a gold fountain pen. 'I stand with diary erect.'

'Sunday?' I said.

'Sunday as ever is. Sunday at six.' He made a note and returned diary and pen to his pocket.

'There's something I have to ask you. Something I came especially to say. I need your help. You are the only person who can help me.'

'Is that a fact?'

'My sister has run away from home. Could you say a word about her on your programme, please?'

The anxiety I felt now that, once more, hopes of success had been revived, the tiredness that overwhelmed me, the love I felt for Joanna that seemed mocked by this scented, impure, stilted room, made the request sound as genuine and concerned as I had intended. I was trembling with fear and apprehension; close to breaking down. The words came in a tearful rush.

My distress was not lost on Ferguson. Doubtless he was weighing my unhappiness against his own expectations, its alleviation at his hands, if that could be managed, the necessary bargaining power he sought to make quite certain I would keep our Sunday tryst. He retrieved his diary. His turned-down mouth dropped vacantly open.

'Her name?'

'Joanna Palin.'

Ferguson sensed danger; indicated it by a questioning eyebrow.

'Indeed? She is then married?'

'No. She's only fifteen.'

'You announced yourself by the name of Graves. I am to take it that is a pseudonym.'

'Yes. I'm sorry. I don't want her to know I've been to see you.'

'Have you a photograph?'

I still carried around with me the snapshot I had purloined from her father's desk. It showed Joanna standing in the porchway of their house, the pose achieved, I knew, only after protracted contortions when, as I had so often seen her, she had been struck all at once by her own awkwardness, by the way she found herself entrammeled by her own limbs and unleashed great thrashings and writhings of the body as if she threw off invisible bonds. I could see her flapping her hand at the camera to indicate she was by no means ready to have her photograph taken; and, when she judged at last that she was suitably poised and turned her profile to the lens and smiled to think herself caught in such natural mood, her hips had been thrown disjointedly sideways, her right hand had slung a leather jacket over the shoulder of a violently patterned jumper and the thumb of her left hand had been stuck into her jeans pocket so, like the portrait of Nicholas in his drawing room, she was all angles and zigzags; and quite unutterably beautiful.

Ferguson gave the picture a cursory glance, then re-examined it, more closely this time. I wondered if, by some extraordinary chance, he had seen her before; but then there passed over his face a look of such appalling evil that he could have been studying a picture of her dismembered corpse. In a way, which I could only liken to Joanna's frenzied reading of her erotic novel, he was absorbing the essence of the awkward, carefree adolescent and transporting that image across time until he had secured in his imagination a vision of her here and now: wandering; imprisoned; done to death. Because he could not conceal his relish, the deep, tranquil relish of the general in the Victorian oil painting as he contemplated past and bloody warfares, there was revealed to me in that moment that Robert Ferguson was not 'in it' for the money, even for the glory, but for the fun. By some fearful alchemy, his weekly feeding on the carrion of despair was refined not into his riches alone but into his very being, his clean, limber, breezy healthfulness. He had found that for which ALEMBIC had been so long established: the elixir of life.

I wondered how he managed to disguise that greedy, narrow-eyed, meditative stare from the camera lenses when, for instance, he had been watching the agonizing progress of the boy in calipers whom I now felt sure he had very much desired. He seemed to be in no hurry to put Joanna's picture in his pocket or to return it to me nor was he in the very slightest measure aware that he had changed his radiance for the gloating mask that still covered his face. Then, when he was ready, he set his eyes once more a-twinkle and turned them back on me.

'Have you any idea where your sister might be?'

'We think she's with a man; a much older man.'

'Is he fucking her?'

'I suppose so.' The word, as intended, had struck with brutal force.

'Um.' Ferguson once more consulted his watch; then looked back at me; and, because he now really had to be on his way and needed to know that Sunday, when it came, would not be wasted, he allowed himself a piece of such gross theatricality, both to leave me in no doubt as to his nature and to ascertain my own standpoint in the matter, that I could scarcely believe he was being serious and was not once more imitating someone whose identity he would reveal or expect me, from his actions, to recognize. He gave a great, arch simper and patted the nape of his neck like a woman who puts up her hair before a glass or confides to a friend how she has always been 'sensitive.' Then through his thin lips that he had set in the pertest of little *moues* of connivance and in a quite different, high-pitched, almost petulant tone of voice, he risked the final question:

'You don't do naughty things like that with the ladies, do you, dear?'

'Oh, no, Robert,' I managed to simper back.

Epilogue

'Did you go back?'

'When?'

'On the Sunday?'

'Of course not. I've told you a thousand times.'

'I know, Tom; but you were always so polite. I like to think you did, just to say thank you and then let him crush you in his arms and drain the poppy from your scarlet lips.'

'Did I have scarlet lips?'

'You did. I fell in love with your scarlet lips. Your scarlet lips sent me all of a doo-dah.'

'Oh.'

Joanna smiles. I smile back. Ferguson has been dead long since, the statutory, lengthy biography affirming homosexual commitments. Joanna recommences my manuscript from the beginning. Because all the pages are loose, she has settled herself at the writing table in the window where we have just eaten supper. She cups her chin in her hand and begins to read. I turn back to my writing, not to the completion of the unfinished book she insists on reading and rereading but to an arid article for a genealogical quarterly on the descendants of Thomas Norton. The room is filled with the gold and green of the setting sun and with a great peace, as if a third person sat among us, a woman, elderly, herself absorbed—sewing, knitting—a nun, perhaps, or a children's nurse, someone blessed and blessing who charges the room, the two of us as well, with this almost tangible tranquillity.

After my chance encounter with Lindo four years ago, a full twenty almost to the day from what Joanna might be considering was the 'end' of things, the evening her photograph had filled the nation's television screens and, a few hours after that, she had been deposited unceremoniously on her father's doorstep, temptation arose to put it all down on paper. I had got as far as my chivalric riding-out to Robert Ferguson and then consigned the manuscript to a bottom drawer. Dissatisfaction with a book which, as it had progressed, appeared unlikely to attract even the small critical attention a catalogue of mine itemizing World War II directives issued by the Board of Trade had attracted—'of signal assistance to scholars of the period' seemed an unlikely accolade for this foray into the world of letters—had been succeeded by the inability, even given Lindo's revelations, to bring the account to any very satisfactory conclusion. Evidence, coming to light over the years and bulked out now by what Joanna has recently told me, has altered perspectives, blurred outlines, propounded different, darker, more ominous features that I see as either unduly prolonging the story or from which I subconsciously recoil. Work, at any rate, has come to a halt.

Joanna looks up. 'I can see your problem. It was all pretty dull, my rescue and everything. Unless of course you make it all up and say I had a wild affair with Tex Ringenberg and describe how he spent hours teaching me to conjure devils from the vasty deep. Remember what a fuss you used to make about that: "Old enough to be your grandfather"; if you said that once, you said it a thousand times, my darling. And,' Joanna grows serious, 'you can't tell the truth. You won't do that, Tom, will you? Tell the truth and publish it? That could be the end of us.'

'Of course not.'

'Good. I'd like to be kissed now, please. Hard and rather a lot.'

Looked at just afterwards, the outcome had indeed been humdrum enough to be excluded from any written account with pretensions—already under debate—to forcefulness, suspense, comment upon the human condition. Joanna had come home. It had been as simple as that. Only a couple of hours after her snapshot had been flashed on the Ferguson programme, the door of the hotel room where she and Tex Ringenberg had been holed up for the night preparatory to taking off for the continent had burst open and a man wearing a loud tweed jacket had manhandled her into a car and driven her home. She recalled the owllike face, the dreadful claw on his left hand with which he had pinned her to the passenger seat while steering with his right. She had thought she was being kidnapped which, following hard upon an elopement, had more in it of drama than she could have wished; and, although, during the telling, it had bothered me how Rastus could have appeared out of the blue and what words he could have said to Tex Ringenberg to have made him release Joanna without protestation—even a stand-up fight—I desired, the first time I heard the story from her own lips all those years ago, only to know whether she had felt any love for Celestial Praylin's manager. In the limited time at our disposal while her father had gone out to buy a celebratory bottle of wine, I pressed her only on that one point.

'No, no, no, nothing like that. I was mad, I suppose, just as mad as you say I looked on the train after our holiday. Tex was very kind to me and ever so grand and rich and I felt you had rejected me, so, in my muddle, I suppose I thought he would be a sort of second-best. I did it to spite everyone. We never ever did anything, I promise.'

'Rejected you?'

'Our last night. Just as I was going to prove I loved you, to reconsecrate our marriage in a new bridal bower.'

'The garden?'

'No, in bed, dickhead. But you fell asleep. Fell over, more like it. Don't you remember? You came rushing in, yelled "Food" and collapsed on the floor. I had to pick you up, undress you, put you to bed . . .'

'In one of your nightdresses?'

'Wow, you really must have been wrecked. And you grumbled at me for smoking dope. Mind you, it would have served you right if you'd woken up in girl's clothes and found me gone. It was our last night . . .'

'So we didn't go into the garden?'

'No.'

'And eat olives?'

Joanna shook her head.

'Because I dreamed that you fed me olives and then told me you had been . . .' Joanna shook her head again. She had been standing by the table that was laid for dinner. Now she gave one of her great leaps and propelled herself into her father's armchair, curled herself up into a ball and stared at me over her shoulder.

So there had been no hideous coupling, no 'foule werke,' no shriving by the thunderstorm, no hermaphroditic robing, no abnegation of our physical bodies. We were still boy and girl: could now soon be man and wife. The dream had been terrible, the worse for being drug-induced, terrible as dreams when orts are transmuted into sumptuous feasts and the girl we are holding into a bearded man or our own kith and kin, when blows sustained or delivered bleed unstemmed and pour not blood but other, more revolting fluids and where the outside world impinges only in a cramped arm that our dream interprets as being severed at the elbow or in the crack of thunder of the storm outside it distorted, that night, into one of Joanna's magical summoning.

'You're dreaming now.' Joanna was speaking, her voice, by the catlike position she had assumed, muffled in the shoulder of her woollen sweater. 'I don't want a dreamer as a lover. I want someone who . . .'

There was a pause. For a moment, I thought she was going to throw herself upon me, offer herself to be taken in her father's chair. Then, all of a sudden, she uncoiled her body and, with a great leap that raised her in the air and splayed her out so she seemed to be floating on her back, legs and arms scissored open, her small breasts pouting through her jumper, she landed upright at her father's feet.

'Hi, Dad,' she said. 'We didn't hear you come in.'

Freddy was flourishing his bottle of wine as if, garlanded at the wheel of a racing car, he were acknowledging the plaudits of his companions in the pits. He set it down on the table.

'What's the matter with you two,' he said. 'Cat got your tongue?'

I believed everything that Joanna told me, just as I then swallowed other facets of the story-book finale that had united us, as far as we could tell, for evermore. It seemed that the hotel proprietor, watching *Ferguson on Thursday,* had recognized Joanna from her snapshot and telephoned the police. That branch of officialdom, all too sensitive about ALEMBIC operations, had got in touch with Rastus rather than acting on their own initiative. Rastus, in filibustering mood, had taken it upon himself to effect the rescue rather than sending some understrapper: the alabaster boy, perhaps. There remained only the passivity of Tex Ringenberg to explain away: why he had just sat around and watched things happen; but here, because Joanna swore they had not made love and because she had set the whole enterprise up herself in a mad dash down to Carpenter's where Nicholas, in a drunken fury, had ordered Ringenberg to take her off the premises, Praylin's manager might have been quite relieved to see the back of her. No charges were pressed against him; indeed, nothing illegal had taken place.

There seemed no need for further reflexion. We walked that year, Joanna and I, as if clothed with the sun. I still own a photograph her father took of us both in the spring following the 'rescue.' Joanna is standing by my side in one of her tremendously laboriously achieved poses. I recall her panic as she saw the camera and her fevered attention to her clothes and her hair and the way she swung round to ensure we were against a suitable background; then, her taking my hand and putting on a smile of readiness. Cleaving the trees behind us is a thin shaft of blinding light that, as it reaches our touching shoulders, splinters about us as if a stream of liquid silver has poured down and showered us in a myriad sparkling droplets that enframe our bodies in their glistening aura; and, although Freddy claimed the roll of film had been defective or that he must have tilted the camera and inadvertently caught in its lens a flashing raindrop or the edge of the dipping sun behind our backs, it was to me a testimony that there had been cast about our shoulders, at that moment, an astral sheath, some distilled essence of the universe, that surrounded us and rendered us invulnerable in its supernal armour.

Perhaps Freddy, too, perceived something supernatural about the photograph and judged that we had been somehow singled out, linked by a divine decree. He was forever smiling upon us and saying, 'We'll see, we'll see' when conversation turned to marriage, as if he had already made up his mind on that score and observed us already as husband and wife. Yet, until Joanna was sixteen, he would never permit us to go off on our own for very long and the few moments we had together were when we repaired to Joanna's room to play records, not Celestial Praylin ones anymore for fear, perhaps, we should call down that baleful magic the alabaster boy supposed was celebrated in their music but fairly loud ones all the same, so that, over the noise, we could whisper our secret words. Then Joanna would extract, sometimes from her old toy box and sometimes from beneath her pillow, the tattered paperback I had at last persuaded her to admit to possessing and place it on the bed between us and select a passage for us to read together. As we read with our cheeks touching, she would point to a line of type and whisper, 'I wish it was you doing that' or 'If Jane was me and you were Jake Morgan would you say those things?' and, under cover of the music, would entreat me to repeat line upon line of text while her eyes sparkled and her knees clashed together until she urgently ordered, 'Go now, go on, go away, talk to Dad, keep him talking, give me five minutes' and banged the door tight behind me. Then, having engaged Freddy in conversation in such an agony of desire I was convinced he discerned my agitation and, after Joanna had come flushed in and precipitated herself onto the sofa, on the pretext of having forgotten my cigarettes or needing to put out a record on the hall table to remind me to take it home, I used to plunge back into the curtained room and bathe myself in its laundered sweetnesses over which, if I were quick enough, there hung a new, even more delicious aroma, sharp, acrid, like coffee freshly ground.

That we should become engaged on her sixteenth birthday and marry the year after delighted Freddy extravagantly. Perhaps, after all, he had not been resentful over my years of employment at ALEMBIC, what I had taken for envy a critical appraisal from all angles of a future son-in-law. Even if that had not been the case, his adulation of Robert Ferguson, which extended to his inviting him to the wedding although, naturally, he received no reply, and his admiration at my having persuaded him to make the appeal for Joanna's release, over which, at ALEMBIC, he and Loder ceaselessly reminisced, took me many miles along the road to being what he saw as 'suitable.'

It was at the wedding that an incident occurred to prompt a radical reinterpretation of the events that had brought the ceremony about. Not one but two discrete pictures now presented themselves, so that the tritely sensational news-story 'rescue' (which, as a matter of fact, Rastus had had some trouble to keep out of the papers who saw it not only as a Robert Ferguson article but, because they discovered I knew Nicholas, as a Celestial Praylin one) became only the central image of a triptych, the pendant angles depicting shadowy, surreal contours of the original, as it were, naive composition.

Ma, who had been looking forward to the event as much as if Joanna had been her own daughter and offering advice here and there on procedural etiquette, had predicted from the start it would turn out to be a 'gathering of the clans,' by which she meant the sort of get-together she organized, every so often, at ALEMBIC. The cooks, too, took that line, anticipating something of a 'thrash'—Bastable's word, invoking the 'swiving' aspects of Sgt Barker's weekend carouses—involving a fair amount to drink and a free hand with bridesmaids and other of the unattached female guests Joanna or I might ask to come along. Despite continued nuptial resistances, Lindo found himself as much endeared to the match, in his own way, as Ma herself. 'Let's see,' he said, 'the French recommend the wife be half the husband's age plus seven. You're what, twenty-nine? That means Joanna should be fourteen-and-a-half plus seven. Oh, no, dear boy, even given past gallantry, you cannot escape the charge of cradle-snatching. Still, it should be a good day. Me and the lads are coming by train: safer, we think, than bringing cars, assuming there'll be a reasonably steady flow of the effervescent neck oil.'

The wedding did not take place in London but in my parents' village church which, for reasons bordering more on the picturesque than the sacred aspects of the occasion, had been preferred to the undistinguished late-Victorian edifice in Freddy's suburban parish. The rectory, close at hand, of suitable proportions for quite a large gathering, would be at our disposal for the reception. For many, the journey had been a long one: despite the bright weather uncomfortably chilly. Nevertheless, as far as ALEMBIC staff was concerned, there was a full house. On processing down the aisle, I noted Rastus and his wife; Bastable, Lindo, in the same row; Ma, in a maddish hat; Loder; one or two of the filing clerks. The sun was shining as we emerged. We posed for the photographs.

It was my mother who caused me to re-enter the church, indicating, as everyone began to move off through the churchyard to the rectory, that she had left her gloves on the pew. In the normal way of things, I would have delegated the job to Goodwin, my best man, but, because the rectory was hard by and guests were going on foot to the reception, spreading out, picking their way among the gravestones where I recalled my mother had set one of the steamier chapters in *Cry, For We Are But Angels,* any sort of formal procession, bride and groom at its head, had been abandoned. Goodwin, in any case, was some way ahead of me, out of earshot, accompanying with bypasses behind the nobler of the funeral monuments the most nubile of Joanna's three bridesmaids. I started back.

Halfway up the aisle, a figure was standing. In the sudden dimness, even murkiness, of the empty church, I took the shape at first for one of the effigies, also figuring in my mother's novel, removed—or stepped down, it alarmingly crossed my mind—from a niche in the walls where, gloomily recessed, they had overlooked the service. Then, as my eyes grew accustomed to the dark, I saw that it was Loudermilk. His figure was unmistakable. He stood shrouded in the darkness that he seemed, like a mantle, to have gathered up and cast about him, grey-suited, hunched up like the herons, his eyes riveted on an incised memorial tablet beneath his feet as if he were contemplating there his own mouldering remains. It was odd I had not spotted him among the congregation. Perhaps he had been late, daylight commitments as heavy as I recalled his saying were those of his evenings, slipped in behind a pillar and caught only the tail end of the ceremony. Presumably, he intended coming to the reception. He would cause quite a stir. That may have been his intention, to bestow by his presence a laical as well as a spiritual blessing on the day and to put himself forward as a sort of extra, 'surprise' wedding gift. A younger man, Bastable for example, might have considered bounding from the wedding cake in a gorilla skin and stripping to the buff. He seemed to sense it was I and nobody else who had interrupted his train of thought. Without looking up, he said: 'Now is the fair white woman married to the ruddy man.'

To begin with, the quotation from Thomas Norton's *Ordinall of Alchemy* seemed no more than conversationally interpolated, Loudermilk's way, by quoting from my 'favourite' alchemist, of conveying he had by no means forgotten who I was and where my interests lay. He could equally well have mentioned England's cricket team or offered criticisms of my mother's books as he had done at his club the only other time we had met, topics perhaps that had crossed his mind and been discarded as on the irreverent side considering where we found ourselves. He appeared, for once, to expect some sort of reply. He raised his head and, just before he sank his chin back into his breastbone, gave me a glimpse of his careworn face. A ghost of a smile hovered round his lips.

I wondered if that smile hinted at a play on words, 'ruddy'—'wuddy,' as it had come out—conveying he had got wind of my being rather a nuisance, a tearaway, a lazybones ('unsatisfactory,' Rastus might have reported), the ceremony he had partially witnessed a step in the direction of settling down and shouldering adult responsibilities. Yet there was a nuance in the satisfied, indeed in the self-satisfied way he had spoken the line to signal that he himself had had a hand in the arrangements.

'A marriage has been arranged . . .' Later, when Joanna joined ALEMBIC, I often wondered how Loudermilk would have reacted if I had replied in those words. Methods of recruiting ALEMBIC personnel, always devious, might well have included marriage, intermarriage in this case, as a guarantee against security problems: looked on as a way of strengthening ties of loyalty forever threatening to rub thin. Perhaps, at some point, he had summoned Freddy to his ill-heated club and made those points.

In the crepuscular atmosphere of the nave, though, and because Loudermilk passed no other remark, as if to allow time for the trenchant line to sink in, his utterance had seemed shot through with the precise alchemical profundities that Norton in the *Ordinall* had intended, the 'marriage,' in his terms, a personification of the alloyage of two dissimilar metals, advancing a stage further the Great Work. Wedding Joanna proclaimed a step forward, that was for sure. I sometimes contemplated the future with misgivings. What was more disconcerting and the reason why, for what length of time I could never recall, I stood rooted to the spot, was that the words were the very ones I had heard intoned, as if oracularly delivered, in the tainted silence of the woodland grove on the afternoon, three years ago now, when the true consummation of our marriage had criminally occurred.

The coincidence was as shocking as if Loudermilk or his disembodiment, some astral shape he had assumed, suddenly pictured as of enormous size, birdlike, heronlike, suspended by broad wings above the sickly trees, had invigilated our caresses and, for private purposes, that only in his own time he would reveal, had conspired to join us this day in legal matrimony. I must have managed some sort of reply: thanked him for turning up, I suppose. I found my mother's gloves and hurriedly stumbled from the church. Goodwin and the bridesmaid still wandered among the tombstones. I talked to them for a while and managed to calm myself down. The reception proceeded. Joanna and I left for the honeymoon. There was cheering. Confetti was thrown. The day was over.

Retrospectively, I saw that I had deliberately blocked the incident out of my mind, so that when Loudermilk did not put in an appearance at the reception, I passed no comment on his absence nor did I ask any of the guests where he had been seated during the service. Nobody volunteered that he had been seen. I wondered whether I had dreamed him up, rather as I used to suspect I dreamed up the alabaster-skinned boy. Perhaps in the deserted, unlit church where the pale, multicoloured, multifaceted light filtered through stained glass and striking on the pillars, gave impressions of being submerged in some underwater grotto, pink, blue, green, like a gigantic set from Lindo's uncle's water pageant, and in the one moment in the bustling and noisy day I found myself engulfed in silence and darkness, I had seen Loudermilk only in my mind's eye and heard his words only as echoes in its so precipitantly emptied caverns. I would not have been surprised, on my return from the honeymoon, to have heard he had died, my encounter with him precisely coincident with the moment of his death. That was not the case. I felt a little disappointed. The incident, real or imaginary, was eventually forgotten.

Joanna was an adopted child. Freddy had told me that early on. She had not 'arrived on the scene,' he said, until she was six years old, by that time able to comprehend what was going on. There had been, for that reason, no question of having to conceal the fact from her, no anxiety about how she might react later on. There might have been problems there, Freddy opined. He cited the example of a neighbouring child unapprised of adoption until his teens, thereafter becoming 'difficult.' He named the children's home where she had spent her first years, in a provincial town where, a little while after Joanna had joined ALEMBIC, I one day found myself.

The idea came to go and look over the establishment. It was almost a compulsion but not one born of curiosity, the inquisitiveness that drives people—Ma, for instance, who had made the arduous expedition to the birthplace of Bartholdi—to visit houses where people were born, but arisen from deeper, even less rational motivations. Perhaps I was plagued, all at once, by the sort of alarms that, for all I knew, upset Joanna from time to time, that she was the daughter of some monstrous derelict of society, a murderer's child or a murderess's—that seemed somehow awfuller still—and that the 'orphanage,' as I now conceived it, would be revealed as a women's prison where her mother, criminally insane, had agonizingly given her birth; and those speculations, easily allayed though they were as I arrived in the leafy, broad-avenued, thoroughly 'respectable' part of the town to which I had been directed, had nonetheless left a residue of milder, still agitating enough worries of some sort of 'unsatisfactoriness' about her parentage and fears of an hereditary eruption at a later stage of our marriage or in our children, if we were to have them, which could only be appeased by examination, both inside and out, of the house where she had passed the first six years of life.

The last in a road of substantial properties, St Mary's turned out to be of some splendour. Its distinguished frontage behind raked gravel driveways and oval, richly filled flower beds belied any suggestion of being an 'institution.' Set considerably back from the road as if to afford passersby the most advantageous view of proportions, the house stared blankly out at the world. Net curtains concealed what were almost certainly adult quarters. Their immaculate folds and spotless whiteness signaled that, at any rate; and had it not been for a scarlet tricycle placed centrally at the porticoed entrance, I would have thought myself mistaken about being at the right address. I began to try to find a side entrance that would lead to nurseries, playgrounds, classrooms, the children themselves and their minders. I envisaged apple-cheeked nuns who would recall Joanna and vouchsafe to her husband the names of her real parents. The grounds were enclosed by a high brick wall that ran down the righthand side of the house and skirted a narrow unmade lane dividing the property from its neighbour. At its end, a pair of high wooden gates had been painted with the name of the place: St Mary's. These were locked. I retraced my steps and followed the wall on the other side of the frontage along the road which at once took an upward and circular ascent and debouched quite suddenly into a new, indeed unfinished, housing estate being laid out on the undulating slopes ahead of me; and the wall, which perhaps St Mary's had had constructed to afford protection from the forthcoming residents, was lost to view behind a row, the only finished one, of small, semidetached houses of which counterparts all about were still in the process of elevation. Further on, the road, like the scarred landscape, had been torn up. Earth, mud, bricks, rubble, roughly flattened by the passage of vehicles to the building site, afforded a barely passable surface to the crest of a rise that overlooked St Mary's from the rear. There, trees, growing inside a half-dilapidated wire fence, still precluded inspection.

I nearly turned back. Desire to explore had very much abated. The roundabout ascent through the building site, which had no look of expectation about it but, on the contrary, exhibited ravaged, battle-torn aspects, a village collapsed by mortar bombs, and the uneasy silence that overlaid the area as tangibly as brick dust hanging in the air and choking the foliage of the trees in a pink, floury deposit, had been infinitely depressing. The more so as Joanna and I, 'house-hunting' at the time, might well have to settle for existence on just such an estate as this. Her father had spoken of 'nice little houses' in course of erection close to where he lived. My own flat, so convenient for cricket and for ALEMBIC, where I had somehow envisaged Joanna could transport her bedroom lock, stock and barrel and where, across the hall, we could keep the sitting room much as it had been furnished in bachelor days, was proving too small, at least for Joanna who, each day, seemed to be shedding insouciance and, in its place, assuming an overadult, not to say matronly, outlook on life that motherhood, if that were to be, would irredeemably impose upon her. She, more than I, complained every so often about lack of space.

I had caught a glimpse of a structure on the face of the rise, a sort of summerhouse it looked like, which, if it could be reached, would afford a bird's-eye view of the house from the back; and climbing over the wire fence, I began to move through the dry and dying trees and down the slope until I reached, in fact put my foot upon, the slab of moss-covered stone that formed its roof. One more step would have cast me eight or so feet down onto a trampled, semicircular, railing-girt platform of earth forming the tiny forecourt to the folly that, so conspicuous from the housing estate, had been rendered invisible by the undergrowth beneath my feet.

I scrambled off the roof and made my way round to the front. Two pale, egg-shaped stones, about the height of a man, had been embedded into the hillside. They framed a narrow pitch-dark embrasure that led into a cave or a tunnel penetrating deeply into the earth of the hill itself. That was now revealed not as a natural fold of the land but as a high mound thrown up by the excavation, immediately below, of an ornamental lake sunk into the far end of St Mary's garden. Neglected, weed-ridden, brackish water was overhung with damp grey mists. On the far side of the lake, tennis courts, surrounded by wire netting, gave on to a wide lawn with children's things on it, swings, tables and chairs, pedal cars, bright toys embedded in the grass. Beyond the lawn, skirting the back of the E-shaped house, there ran a driveway as immaculately graveled over as the one that swept up to the front elevation that would disgorge, when the double gates were unlocked, into the lane leading to the road I had traveled by. Somewhere in the house, recorders were playing.

It dawned on me why this strange edifice had been so conspicuous sideways on among the trees. Its protruding rotundity had made it appear like the replica of a huge eyeball, an animal's, a goat's, the narrow entrance its dark, slitted pupil, specifically set up to watch over the house below. Close up—I was touching now one of the smooth, faintly pinkish stones—it seemed more welcoming, a shrine perhaps, or the temple of a garden god, goddess more likely, whose statue might be displayed in the interior, a place of rest and repose. There was a sense, too, of its being internally heated. A warmish and decaying, though not at all disagreeable, odour was wafted from the interior as if, at some point of the day, perhaps exactly at noon, because the folly's central positioning on the hillside seemed as much horologically as architecturally appointed, the sun had struck deeply into its recesses and had fallen upon a combination of grass-mowings and a rich pile of humus that had retained solar heat and was releasing its fragrances through the furrowed aperture.

Suddenly the recorders stopped. It could be I had been spotted. I imagined a class of children staring up at me from the house where, despite the foliage above and about the shrine, the two big stones against one of which I was silhouetted, would be plainly visible. Under their eyes, the eyes too of one of the imagined nuns who had silenced her pupils at the approach of strangers, I suddenly felt extremely guilty. I edged myself around the stone and slid into the opening of the cave. My body, all but obliterating the light from outside, was immediately muffled in warm, impenetrable darkness, swaddled as if by a sable fur hung over heated, perfumed water and then cast about me from head to toe. The densely textured, pitch-black air, no warmer probably than a hot summer night, was sensuously luxurious, recommended lying down and drowsing within its plump, cushioned folds. I edged to the side of the hollow and the daylight the repositioning of my body allowed to reenter displayed it as only a tiny atrium, three or four feet across. In front of me, stout wire netting, the netting of the tennis courts in the garden, barred my way. There seemed no reason for this barrier's being erected since I could make out dimly beyond it the back wall of the cave no more than six feet behind, but then, as my eyes grew accustomed to the darkness, I discerned it had been put up not to impede progress but to guard against descent. I was on the edge of a well. Inky black, warm, pulsating air throbbed upwards from unfathomable depths. There was no impression of water, however, except perhaps at the very deepest level, nothing of the miasmic chill that hung over the lake outside such as might be expected to be rising from a well of this depth, abandoned or not. I tore a spill from the newspaper I had in my coat pocket, ignited it with my cigarette lighter and poked it through the wire. The upward current of air extinguished it at once. I tried a larger fragment, a whole page this time, folded it, lit it, threaded it through the steel mesh. This time outlines were revealed. Hay, tightly packed and kept in place with chicken wire, insulated the perimeter of the circular shaft, some five feet across. I tried to drag the spill of newspaper back through the mesh of the wire but succeeded only in tearing off a small unburnt strip. For a moment my homemade torch floated aloft in the current of warm air, then began to drift slowly back down again. I was afraid the burning paper could float to one side or another of the shaft and set fire to the insulated walls, but it parachuted itself in an exactly central descent and, just for a moment, before it was extinguished, erupted in one last dying blaze as it touched the well bottom. Twenty feet below, thirty it might have been, a metal object, a box or canister, gleaming in the flame, had been rested on the black earth floor. Around it, cast in by the children no doubt, lay discarded objects: toys; clothes; woolly animals. The paper went out.

I had no time to light more newspaper—it would, in any case, have been far too dangerous—because another sound, musical again although of very different instrumentation, all at once arose from the house below. Celestial Praylin's 'Love's Mansion' was being blasted out at full volume from an open window. Nicholas's banshee voice howled over bleak plateaux of electrified guitar:

Death stalked my spore, a spectre
I tore him out my heart.

I peered out of the aperture. The garden gates had been flung open. A tiny green car, leaping like a frog, was being propelled through the entrance. It skidded round the graveled drive, flinging up a shower of chippings and, with a squeal of brakes that could hardly be distinguished above the shrieking feedback of the guitar, came to a halt at the rear of the house. The driver switched off his radio, wound up the window from which the music had been raging and emerged from his vehicle. It was Tex Ringenberg.

'How could it have been Tex Ringenberg?'

'That's what I'm asking you, Joanna.'

'Well, I don't know. And don't sound so sniffy and accusing. It's as much a mystery to me as it is to you. He must be looking for me, I suppose, although goodness knows how he knew I'd ever lived there.'

'Perhaps he's your real father.'

'Oh, don't be so stupid. Thank the Lord you didn't go barging in and introduce yourself to the staff, who aren't nuns at all by the way, so you're wrong again, and tell them where we were, where I'd moved to. You know how you drone on sometimes.'

'My dear girl, if Ringenberg wanted to find you, he'd only have to ask Nicholas, wouldn't he?'

'Perhaps he was enquiring about adoption.'

'The children he has in mind to adopt are a bit older than the ones in residence at St Mary's. Only a bit older, mind you.'

'Don't bring all that up again. Why do you always throw Tex Ringenberg back in my face when you're in a bad temper? I was fourteen then. Anyone can make a mistake at fourteen. Maybe he's got a child there. That girl's perhaps, the one he pinched from you after the Praylin concert.'

'Belinda. Belinda's child. That would be the most extraordinary coincidence.'

'Perhaps he was born there like me, ages ago. That would be an extraordinary coincidence too. But then coincidences don't come singly, do they? There's no such thing as a single coincidence. They come in batches like goods-trains being shunted. One bangs against another and starts another off. Life is a whole series of coincidences, bang . . . bang . . . bang . . .' Joanna trailed rather hopelessly off.

She was probably right. In fact, her aphorism about 'life' contained qualities as ponderable as any of those Sylvia had been given to putting forward: 'only beautiful people lose things' or 'a neurosis shared is a neurosis halved.'

I did not suspect Joanna of 'anything,' accusation she discerned in my voice attributable to vaguer, stranger apprehensions, as if there had been a shift in the order of things, perspectives, like blocks of bricks, demolished and reconstructed in different places, people with whom we fraternized, like cricketers in a match from which one has absented oneself for some time—batsmen now in the field, the fielding side at the wicket—redisposed, the very tenor and pace of life itself awarded readjustments. Ever since Joanna had given her word, I had accepted there had been nothing 'between' Tex Ringenberg and herself, a protestation I had urgently wrung from her just after the elopement when I had been obsessed with their having slept together and his having kissed, as he had confided to me was his way with young girls, the 'seven entrances' of her body. Of course they had only been together a very short time. Dalliance would have come later if Joanna had allowed it: not otherwise. Ringenberg's good manners—ambassadorial good manners—that extended into his politic yielding of Joanna to Rastus without a word of protest would have won Joanna over, I was sure of that, but only if she had felt mutual attraction. That too seemed likely. My own brief meeting with Ringenberg on Nicholas's staircase had been long enough to intuit he was a man of infinite charm, good looks come to that, 'old enough to be her grandfather' (words I kept petulantly exercising to get the truth out of her) no hindrance to Joanna's thinking him attractive: his riches and his grandness of manner added bonuses to a by no means disagreeable physical appearance.

As for drugs and the occult, Ringenberg's involvement in those areas seemed most improbable. I only had Scotty's word for that; and, indeed, when I considered how I had fallen victim to one of Scotty's drugs, or a mixture of several, he, rather than Ringenberg, was to be marked down as the danger man Joanna should have avoided. Yet Scotty had been perfectly straightforward when thanking me for my 'gift' of Belinda about which he would surely have held his tongue had it been he who had lured her into magical practices or had plied her with drugs. He had been good enough to have alerted me to the perils Joanna faced under Nicholas's roof, a warning he would never have issued if he had had an eye on her himself. Perhaps, after all, Ringenberg had been a menace to girls, the sort of nobody—a 'hewer of wood and drawer of water' as Ma called us all at ALEMBIC—whose frustrations at being merely the band's manager and not a musician had precipitated him into mental disarray and into the fantasy roles of lecher, drug addict, magus, to be awarded, as Scotty had advised, the widest of berths.

Either way, there remained the feeling Joanna and I were pawns in a game. I still had the very strongest impression of manipulation, of being 'used,' of our marriage's not having been the outcome of a chance meeting on horseback, coincidence as Joanna would have seen it, but of some ALEMBIC-like strategy that had manoeuvred us, like Uncle Hamish's figures in his water pageant, into stage positions useful for its own functions. The wedding seemed to have induced almost audible sighs of relief all round, Freddy's antipathy to me changed to a parental matiness, Rastus's accusations of 'unsatisfactoriness' withdrawn. Loudermilk's complacent words, 'Now is the fair white woman married to the ruddy man,' sounded like a little prayer of thanksgiving for a job well done. I wondered if Major Giblin had been apprised of the match; if, in his labyrinthine den, he had updated my index card and prepared a new entry for Joanna Palin.

I did not think of Giblin again until the night Nicholas was murdered. It was said he kept singing a full half-minute after he had been shot, that, as the silver bullet arced up towards him from the floor of the hall, he appeared to catch it in his hands and to alter its trajectory so that it exactly pierced his heart. Then, as the blood welled and, with each breath, burst out in spurts between his bony fingers, he was reported to have raised the jagged white mask of his face and, for the last time, although that was not the tune being played, to have bayed out the stricken melismata of 'Love's Mansion':

Death stalks my spore, a spectre
I tear him out my heart.

There were other myths put about, morbid elaborations on the sort of news story that had plagued him in his lifetime: that he had been 'officially' assassinated; that he had himself hired the killer whose haunted face was photographed again and again staring through police-car windows; and, of course, that he was not dead at all. Genius, martyr, saint; megalomaniac, Satanist, the devil: these names were all bandied about, prompted by the increasing isolation in which, during his last years, since, indeed, he had dismissed Joanna and Ringenberg from his presence, he had enveloped himself. Now I had sensed that the 'dangers' of Joanna's being in his house had passed, I had very much wanted to resume our friendship, to ride Vindictive, to talk as we used to talk, to pass the sort of evening that ended, the world and its ways thrashed out, in drunken oblivion. But into this increasing and ever more lordly inaccessibility from which he would ride out in his great car past new, solider gates through which his fans could no longer poke their heads and peer at him through bars now replaced with sheet metal, all means of access had been proscribed. He would neither speak to me on the telephone nor answer my letters. It was as if he had already died.

Many people, 'good men and true,' welcomed his demise. Indeed, Ma's spirited defence of Celestial Praylin, the morning she had castigated Freddy for not being 'with it,' was rare, certainly among her generation. Among all the talk of approved assassination, there emerged a shred of evidence to suggest the gun had been supplied by a fanatic among those critics, austere, rich, influential enough to have acquired for the killer the tiny and, again it was rumoured, ultrasophisticated weapon that had done the deed.

As I read about that, the vision of Major Giblin came back, his face twitching with disgust as his little polished shoe had hacked the Praylin-playing 'ghetto-blaster' out of the hand of the boy in the street. Perhaps it had been Giblin who had masterminded Nicholas's murder, found among his index cards the name of the youth with the mad eyes—the son, it might be, of someone in the service on whom he had 'tabs'—attached himself to the family and, in his gnomish, diligent way, worked the rich seam of that madness. If that were so, I had been right when, on seeing the little house where Giblin lived with his cat, I had had the distinct impression it was occupied by a criminal. I mentioned the possibility to Joanna.

'Oh, honestly, Tom, how suspicious of everyone you're getting. You see conspiracies everywhere.'

'I don't think I do. Giblin wanders the streets kicking portable radios to pieces just because they're playing Praylin stuff. Why shouldn't he commission his murder?'

'One radio. And I expect it was only because it was making a din. That doesn't brand him as an assassin.'

'No, it wasn't. Well, yes, I mean it was making a din, but he knew it was Nicholas's voice on the tape because I'd just told him. Nor do I see conspiracies "everywhere." It's just that we work in the middle of one, so it's sort of tricky not to assume there are others right around the corner.'

'I prefer to call it a "cell," ' Joanna said. 'Shall you go to the funeral?'

'No. Nicholas never really liked me very much, I've come to the conclusion, not after we left school. Just tolerated me as a friend from the old days. You two got on well, though.'

Joanna nodded. 'Yes, I liked him to begin with, when we three were alone, which God knows wasn't often. He was terribly rude to me when I went down on my mad dash after Tex. Then we never saw him again, did we?'

I made some noncommittal reply. Even six years on, I could hardly bring myself to contemplate that awful fortnight, Joanna still under age, in the drug-tainted country house: the establishment, of course, where she had nearly been lost to Praylin's manager.

Tex Ringenberg made a brief appearance on the television documentary on Celestial Praylin, aired the day after Nicholas's murder. Far from unashamedly partisan, the programme reflected viewpoints of the band's art—the word used—very much my own: awesomeness of attack to be balanced against implicitly deplorable verbal content, 'young people' on both sides of the fence invited to provide a moderately balanced, in the final account not entirely sympathetic, summary of Celestial Praylin's body of work. That was to be expected on a BBC channel. There followed some footage of the band in concert. Leaving aside some dramatic close-ups of Nicholas at the microphone very much reminiscent of, perhaps the inspiration for, the vorticist portrait hung at Carpenter's, television was unable to impart the spirit of almost revolutionary fervour those occasions invariably called forth. The past dealt with, the interviewer turned to the future. Here were problems. In loyalty to Nicholas, in pursuance too of his antipathy to the 'media'—discourtesy to Robert Ferguson in denying him an interview on *Ferguson on Thursday* remarked upon—his fellow musicians had declined to participate in this memorial. In no manner giving impressions of being merely second-best, Tex Ringenberg, photographed introductorily emerging from his little green two-seater, later ensconced in a leather armchair under studio lights, spoke a few impartial words. Soberly suited, MCC tie, dazzling white hair, looking more than ever as if he had spent a lifetime in the 'diplomatic,' Ringenberg parried a question or two about Nicholas's fortunes and their distribution. I could not help sneaking a glance at Joanna to see if any glimmerings of affection for this strikingly debonair figure disturbed a countenance blankly attentive, so far as I could judge, to what he had to say. The announcer asked: 'What will you do now?'

Ringenberg scarcely hesitated. 'Retire. I shall go and cultivate my garden.'

'Would there still not be a place for you in the Ministry of Information, Mr Ringenberg? I am right in thinking you were once in the employ of the secret service.'

Ringenberg indulgently smiled. 'This is hardly the time or place to discuss my past career, or my future plans if it comes to that. We meet tonight to commemorate an old and valued colleague.'

The announcer was suitably chastened, passed to other topics, other colleagues of Nicholas, musical and unmusical. Attached to the secret service myself, in a manner of speaking, I wondered if we might have rubbed along better together—Ringenberg perhaps desisting from trying to seduce Joanna—if he had known that I was, as Rastus always said about his cronies, 'in the same game.' Tabulating the names of people I knew who were—everyone at ALEMBIC, Loudermilk, Major Giblin, those names he had mentioned and to whom I had yet to put a face, Adams, Vanderplank, Frith-Liddiard—there suddenly came to me, flashed before my eyes as plainly as if the picture had been transmitted by the television cameras, that I already knew Ringenberg's service connexion. It was Major Giblin. Among those cars outside Giblin's front door the day I had paid my call had stood the little green car belonging to Tex Ringenberg. Everything fell into place. I could hardly wait for the programme's climax to reveal to Joanna the extraordinary details of how we had both been 'set up.'

'It's just come to me that Tex Ringenberg knows Major Giblin. That green car we've just seen was parked outside his house the day I went there and he did his radio-smashing stunt. The same car he was driving when I saw him at St Mary's.'

'Go on.'

'So I think I know why he planned to elope with you; and why he didn't kiss the seven entrances to your body.'

'Tom: don't start that again.'

'It was all part of a larger plan, you see, to discredit me with ALEMBIC because of Giblin's antipathy to Praylin. He thought I was mixing with the wrong set: a security risk, in other words. So I figure if I hadn't gone to see Robert Ferguson after your disappearance and advertised your being missing to the nation, they'd have kidnapped me as well, chucked me into the same hotel room. Then Ringenberg would have buggered off, the police would have been called and I'd have been arrested for sleeping with a minor. As it was, as soon as he'd heard you'd been appealed for by Ferguson, Rastus had to abort the operation and come and pull you out. That's the only thing that explains Ringenberg's just sitting back and letting it happen.'

'But you claim Ringenberg seduced your friend, Belinda.'

'I don't believe that anymore. I think he just warned her to have nothing more to do with me. On Giblin's orders. After all, I had been behaving rather wildly at Carpenter's. Drugs; girls. There'd been some of those. Then, when I persisted in consorting with the band and began to court—Ringenberg may have been able from observation to report a more serious involvement—a girl below the age of consent, Major Giblin devised his kidnapping strategy: one of considerable ingenuity and, if it had worked, of unequivocal denouement.'

Joanna remained unimpressed. 'If their plan was to chuck you out of ALEMBIC because you were drugging and whoring around, how come we're married with Loudermilk's blessing—or so you say. How come I've got a job at ALEMBIC? How come we're living happily ever after?'

I had worked that out while we were talking. As I saw it, there had been a change of front, a thawing of the atmosphere. I visualized a meeting—what Ma called a 'conflab'—at a pretty high level: Giblin, Ringenberg, Rastus, Loudermilk. Others may have been present, those people I had never clapped eyes on: Adams, Vanderplank, Frith-Liddiard. I envisaged its taking place at Loudermilk's club over the rhubarb pie or superintended by the slaughtered elk-heads in the Flower Court below. Joanna remained steadfastly unimpressed. In fact to defuse the seriousness—almost the passion—with which I outlined these ideas and which, in honesty, I suppose allayed at one fell swoop, now I had placed where I had first seen Ringenberg's car, those stirrings of insecurity in domestic life as well as at ALEMBIC that clouded, like my old fears of losing my sanity, what should have been a more or less idyllic existence, she commenced a running monologue involving all those 'characters' I judged to have attended this, to her, absolutely mythical conference:

' "Perhaps I can run a couple of ideas across you, Major Cleave - By all means, Vanderplank, although I should say I shall not look kindly upon any notion you may be putting forward that ALEMBIC should be turned into some kind of *Stundehotel* for runaway teenagers - Gentlemen, if I could put in a word? - Certainly, Loudermilk, fire ahead, take first pot, as it were - Thank you, Wingenberg, I only wish to urge you to wecall our own youth when we stwode the earth with fire in our bellies, fire of a young man who has wescued as the knights of old used to wescue however inaptly and to the confusion of our well-laid plans for his widdance that young maiden — Louders, we cannot allow sentiment (this is Adams who once had an orgasm watching a little boy being sick at a funfair, the only time he ever came actually unless you count the dry run earlier on in his life when he was groped by a suffragan bishop) we cannot allow sentiment to cloud an issue as sensitive, security-wise, as the organization we all hold dear. Hearts we may have but we are men of steel, as Frith-Liddiard here would be the first to agree - Pardon me for breaking a lance with you on this one, hop over to Louder's side of the jolly old fence on the point, when opinions have been put, and strongly put over, meaty ones, ones to chew hard before finally ejecting them as we must eject them onto our plates – Perhaps the moment is wipe for a show of hands" – Oh, Tom, you are mad.'

We burst out laughing and kissed each other; but my laughter was hollow and my kisses dry and cold on Joanna's warm, mocking lips because I had remembered something else—an object—that connected Tex Ringenberg, Giblin and the children's home where Joanna had been born. At ALEMBIC the next day I went into the laboratory to ensure I had not been mistaken.

The workplace still awoke disagreeable sensations, feelings of disorientation, a belief that, within its brilliantly lit interior, blows were being struck at the very core of natural things. Joanna and Bastable stood talking at the far end. They turned sharply round when I came in. I hoped they would not ask me what was the matter; for, as I had entered the room, pushed my way through the sighing, airtight doors, last night's misgivings were appallingly confirmed.

I suppose I had fallen in with Joanna's viewpoint that Ringenberg's presence at St Mary's had been a 'coincidence,' one of many, as she said, with which the passage of time is apportioned, yet it had been striking enough, given now that he was acquainted with Major Giblin, to have obfuscated another factor that could no longer be overlooked: the bizarre pit-shaft in the grounds from the atrium of which I had heard the strains of Celestial Praylin arising from Ringenberg's green runabout. Not the pit-shaft itself but the object that had lain at its foot that my sheet of burning newspaper had briefly illuminated as it had floated down. No larger than a garden urn or, metallic, glinting in the flames, one of the grander of the silver trophies displayed, along with the Victorian painting, in the cricket pavilion, it was now recognizable, because Joanna and Bastable stood awkwardly before its original, as a miniature copy of ALEMBIC's hourglass-shaped crucible.

Joanna came over then. I found myself being roughly shaken by the elbow.

'What's the matter?'

'Nothing.'

'There is.'

'No.'

'You don't think there's anything in it?'

I could only stare at her. That she had so correctly picked up my train of thought, as if she had in fact said, 'You're thinking about the well' when, for some reason, I had never told her I had discovered it, made her divination that much more astonishing. There had been, in the deep dark womb of the cave, a febrile purposefulness, the same silent coursing of forces I sensed in ALEMBIC's laboratory, stirrings of life as audible to the inner ear as the rodents' scratching among their straw-lined cages. It was not that there had been anything there: or, not yet. It was what was potentially at the base of the shaft, what, in the little hay-cosseted crucible was being fecundated by the sweet-scented air that had seemed to flutter with the regularity of a sleeper's breath or perhaps with the breath of some creature that had a waking being, an organism for which the children had passed through the wire-netting their offerings of tiny garments and rattles and little toys that would clothe and amuse in the first days of life one of their own kind: one who would soon join them in the classroom and play along with them on the recorder.

Joanna was going on pummeling me, repeating now more urgently, 'You don't? You don't?'

'That's precisely what I do think. What I know to be a fact.'

'You're wrong,' she shouted. 'Wrong, wrong, wrong. We were just talking, for God's sake.'

▪▪

It was inevitable that Joanna would leave me, fortunate that Bastable was there to give her sanctuary: for that was what it came to. A marriage such as ours, founded on desire alone, vicarious desire too, it had to be said, was bound to founder before very long. For myself, I had been quite happy. Every so often, I found myself looking at her as I had looked at her through Nicholas's French window on the lawn with the Baxters, as a newfound friend, someone in whose company enormous vistas of enjoyment would open up, along which we could walk forever hand in hand, smiling, smiling. Yet some censor, the censor maybe who, in the old days, had stalked beside me and questioned whether I were really happy, stalked now again between the two of us or hovered, like a winged demon, above our heads and threw a shadow across our path on which, the year of our engagement, I believed the sun would never set. Perhaps the shadow was ALEMBIC. Within us both, like the sound of horses' hooves, had rung the thunder of the young, but ALEMBIC muffled it in its stultifying, boring routines. I had the *Ordinall* to fall back on, Joanna nothing at all. Within ALEMBIC's crumbling façade, she grew bored to tears. To begin with, straight from school, she may have been pleased, proud even, to have had a decent job and a living wage; but, ensconced in the gleaming office of Disbursements and Documentation the alabaster boy had painted in the cold sheen of his own skin, forbidden to play the radio and with Loder's rasping voice answering her father's questions and with Freddy across the room beaming worshipfully on, her days rapidly became trivial, fruitless, tedious in the extreme.

Perhaps if she had not misinterpreted my shock about the well as anger at having found her and Bastable together, the affair might have harmlessly run its course. As it turned out, she had to look to him for protection as much as for love. Ringenberg, the children's home, the well, especially the well, obsessed me now entirely. Almost without knowing I did so, I initiated a barrage of questions about St Mary's, who the other children had been, whether their parents ever visited them, who the administrators were, if she recalled ever seeing anyone from ALEMBIC there; why the well had been cut off on the inside by the tennis-court netting, on the outside by the high brick wall. When, because she had been too young, she quite naturally had been unable to throw any light on these matters, I demanded her birth certificate on the pretext that it was needed by a building society we were using to try to get a mortgage, but of course it bore on it only Freddy's name and his wife's, who had been called Jane. It impressed me as strange I had never heard her Christian name before, why, too, there was no picture of her in her father's flat, no evidence that she had really existed at all. I urged Joanna to try to locate her real parents.

'We could go down together, look at the records. I could show you the well.'

'I don't want to know who my parents were. I couldn't care less. And I certainly don't want to see the well.'

Slowly, the idea took root that Joanna had not been born of woman. I became convinced she was a mutant, conceived, like the other children, by a mad, long-lost process ALEMBIC had stumbled on many years ago, in the darkness of the well. In the warm, sighing, mossy depths I imagined amalgams far fouler than even the most deranged of the early alchemists had conceived—ichor, gluten, marrow—bellows-induced to fruition. I saw a wizened alchemist, Vanderplank or Frith-Liddiard, berobed, wire-spectacled like Nicholas the day he had disguised himself for the Baxters, his skeletal fingers, again like Nicholas's, leafing through the sort of manuscript I daily handled, in search of instructions for nurturing the foetus he had compounded. I imagined tiny human glands, those even today incompletely understood, sapped for their secretions to the detriment of their owners' health, some of the children perhaps who wasted away because of the deprivation of their life-forces, smeared onto slides and incubated in the steamy, vegetable breezes that fluttered in the well's interior. If Joanna were not a mutant, I felt sure she had been implanted with the ripening culture of those glands, that it grew even now within her womb. That was why she could not make love in the natural way, because she had no need, because motherhood, unnaturally prolonged, was already upon her. Furthermore, the mystical words she had intoned over her father all those years ago and those others she had mouthed beneath the oak tree that seemed no longer sentences in a dream could be childish memories of ceremonies witnessed at the well-head, a consecration or a baptism of the silver crucible before its induction into the pit. I saw white-robed children, each clutching an offering, extend their hands, and, at a priest's behest, commend into the darkness those toys and teddy bears with which the ground at the foot of the well had been bestrewn.

Alerted by a passage in Thomas Norton thitherto construed as a satirical attack on a fellow chemist who incorporated all kinds of animal and vegetable substances into his experiments, blood included, 'mannys blude,' in Norton's quaint spelling, I ransacked the library for supplementary evidence of its employment in the Great Work. Not much had been amassed: put down on paper, anyway. Yet Nicolas Flamel, a French scientist flourishing some seventy years before Norton, gave assurance that the practice was by no means uncommon: 'I tryed a thousand broulleryes, yet never with bloud, for that was wicked and villainous.' In bed with Joanna, I initiated the practice of touching her flesh, pinching her, running my fingertips over her skin, to see if I could adjudge an unusual body temperature, one too high or too low for a normal human being. One evening, watching television, I fell asleep with my arm around her and awoke not to the touch of a bright sequined blouse that Ma had given her as a 'thought young' for her own use but to the silvery scales of a fish, a mer-creature, an homunculus removed, as Lindo used to say the figures of Punch and Judy were removed for performances by his uncle, from stoppered jars. I insisted she went for a blood test. She refused. I demanded this again and again, each time more frantically than the last. She remained adamant in her refusal.

I cut her then: came at her with scissors. As the blood pulsed from the wound in her neck, she rose to her feet and crossed the room with slow, deliberate strides. Reaching the door, she turned back to where I stood with arm raised to strike at her again and settled her eyes upon me with an insulted look, no more than that, the pained yet haughty, almost derisive expression of both disbelief and disdain that the mother in the park had delivered whose mongol daughter she had imagined I was taunting; and walked on, still slowly, still calmly, out of the room and out of my life.

▪▪

For a while, Goodwin came to see me. I say for a while because I do not know if it were every week or every fortnight: if his visits extended over a period of six months, a year, two years. Memory, acting faultily and permitting only apportionments of itself at any given time, so that the birds outside my window and the glimpse it afforded me of a stretch of water made me suppose I was in a house by the herons' lake and the recorders played, therapeutically, somewhere in the building, that I might instead be resident at St Mary's, evoked only a recollection of Goodwin's having resembled in ALEMBIC days the youthful Sigmund Freud. For that reason, and there again I am unable to measure the time span of this misapprehension, I assumed him to be one of the doctors.

I led him always to the vast painting that dominated the entrance hall. I sat sipping plastic cupsful of coffee he bought me from a machine in one corner of this bustling concourse as if savouring the wine the soldiers were imbibing: or had been imbibing before their carouse had been disturbed. Dimensionally as ambitious as the vorticist painting at Carpenter's although almost certainly only a copy of an 'old master,' it was in its way every bit as vigorously imposing as Nicholas's portrait: 'busy,' so Goodwin used to remark. The soldiers, eight or nine of them, gladiatorially arrayed, naked under shining bucklers, had loosened swords and removed helmets preparatory to sitting down to some feast or other in a palace, either their commander's or an enemy's believed put to rout. Drunkenness, overindulgence anyway, had ensued. Now they were proving no match for a party of bareheaded warriors who had burst in and were laying about them. Several of the militia at table were already dead, others mortally wounded, screaming and spouting blood. On the marble floor, a severed head had joined a fair quantity of food—haunches of meat and great silver fish and pewter jugs of wine—that had cascaded, in some cases were still cascading, from upturned trestle tables where they had been making their meal. The intruders, more lightly armed, clad only in neatly pressed white togas, were only four in number. Clearly, surprise had been the essence of this victorious assault. Indeed, beyond the carnage other people, civilians this time, women and children among them and some rangy dogs, were still enjoying the festivities that, in the foreground, had been so fatally interrupted. Shortly, they would either have to flee or to join forces with the invading quartet. If flight were decided upon, there lay beyond them a green, tranquil garden with plashing fountains where neat, clipped hedgerows might afford cover enough for them to make their escape. Yet the feeling was they would never make it into the peace and the sunlight for already one of the white-toga'd raiders, who bore a curious resemblance to the alabaster boy, also dimly remembered, was alerting his fellows to the junketing behind them, waving his sword in that direction and shouting at the top of his voice; and it seemed only a matter of time before the last of the soldiers was put to death and the invading foursome would set off into the middle distance and, with the same ferocity, despatch each and every member of the nonmilitary picnickers.

I used to sit staring at the picture and drinking my coffee that tasted sometimes of the dark, spilt wine and sometimes of the soldiers' blood. To woo me from macabre thoughts, Goodwin would give me news of ALEMBIC matters which I could only in part assimilate. A kind of preliminary reshuffle, where Lindo had been posted to Alternative Power Executive in Scotland, had been the precursor to more sweeping changes. Rastus had been relieved of his command and put in charge of the flag-cleaning department next door; Freddy found a job in D.O.E., Loder and Ma 'put out to grass.' Some time later, Bastable and Joanna, now married, had followed Lindo to APEX. Goodwin, gloomily predictive of a dearth of local 'goers,' anticipated his own posting at any moment. It was the first time anyone had mentioned Joanna's name to me for a long time. I turned to look into Goodwin's serious, bearded, eminently comforting face.

'I didn't mean to hurt her.'

'No, no.'

'I needed her blood.'

'You should think less about blood.'

'I think of wine.' I let my eyes drift back to the battle-torn canvas. 'Sometimes I am feasting. But it will not last for long.'

'Do you never think of yourself in that lovely garden?' Goodwin asked.

'No, it is too far away.'

'Indeed it is not.' Goodwin got suddenly to his feet. The bench next to ours was empty. At great speed, he began to propel it across the polished floor as if he were putting into motion a toboggan on a downward run. He sent the piece of furniture crashing into the wall immediately beneath the painting and tipped it up on end. Then clambering up the woodwork like a workman ascending a stepladder or perhaps as the artist had had to mount a platform in his studio to paint in, as an afterthought, the soldier's decapitated head in the lefthand corner, Goodwin straddled the arm of the bench and beckoned me to join him at the foot of his improvised and distinctly precarious scaffolding.

From a squatting position on the arm, Goodwin hauled himself upright, all the while running his forefinger along the surface of the brushwork, through the overturned wine and the dying soldiers and the murderous intruders and the table of neutral junketers—where he allowed it to linger for a moment on a wimpled girl whom, again to raise my dejected spirits, he had once declared looked like a 'goer'—until, at full stretch, feet planted on the armrest of the upturned bench, he touched upon the veridian oils of the distant, enchanted garden. By this time, a crowd had begun to gather, men in white coats with bleepers on their lapels, uniformed nurses, ambulance men, dark-suited doctors, a visitor or two, but, unsure of what Goodwin was actually doing, purloining hospital property, saving the heavy frame from crashing down onto people's heads, estimating from close quarters on the cost of the picture's renovation, or simply, as I had once done, running amok, everybody stood silently at the foot of the bench, staring up at him to see what he would do next. He inclined his studious face to look down upon us all. His spectacles glinted in the light with impassioned fire. He shouted down:

'There you are. Here it is. It is not too far away. If I can reach the garden, so can you.'

For a blinding second, one in which I felt the shackles of my illness begin at last to fall away, another story-painting was revealed. Goodwin had again transmuted himself into the young Freud, Freud on a rostrum, his admirers and detractors held spellbound at his feet at the climax of the most cataclysmic yet of the series of lectures they had attended, for there was being demonstrated before their eyes a journey, rather the arrival, into the very centre of the human psyche.

What Goodwin was conveying with his pointing finger and glinting glasses and voice that rang imperiously across the hospital waiting room was that the garden did not lie, as I had always perceived it to have lain, at the apex of the painting, way, way in the distance, to which escape from the besieged palace was impossible, but, by a trick of perspective, had its situation at the very heart of the swirling mandala of human hecklessness in progress all around it; that the human mind, like the human finger, could attain to peace; that the garden was within one's grasp, so to speak; and ever afterwards when I came to reappraise the composition, it seemed that, by Goodwin's clarification of perspectives, its time schedule had been reversed so that the garden, instead of being illusory and inaccessible, was the only 'real' part of the landscape, one that depicted after all, not order threatened by chaos but order retrieved from its ashes.

In the half-stupefied state I occupied almost all the time or in which, after my one vain dash for freedom, I had been maintained, and bolstered very much too by the misconception that Goodwin was an analyst assigned to me as being a master of his craft, I almost immediately began to get better. I found myself as easily able to transcend darkness as Goodwin's traveling forefinger had traversed the tumult and the slaughter and touched on the cool, green heart of the waiting garden. As time went on and I was discharged and given a job in Public Records Office, a dusty storehouse of documentation, genealogical for the most part, in a Cotswold town, a sort of 'putting out to grass' by ALEMBIC who, now I had a history of mental illness, was probably not too worried if I revealed their existence since they could claim my disclosure was the raving of a lunatic and produce documents to that effect, this method of rising above and then sailing across time with no commitment to emotions became rather a knack. I did my work, went for walks or to the cinema; read books; even tinkered with my edition of *The Ordinall of Alchemy;* all with a curious mixture of enquiry and nonconcern. Actualities, imbued with any kind of harshness, any kind of love for the matter of that, impinged hardly at all. If they did, it was with the apportionment of a disagreeable jolt to the system like the mild shock administered to cattle by electric fences as a prevention against their straying from designated pastures and the effect, much the same, was to send me shearing off into the tranquillity Goodwin had located for my ever steadier recovery.

It was with the application of this technique that, some ten years after coming out of hospital, I found myself 'getting through' my father's memorial service. Spun out by the performance on the organ of one of his gloomier compositions to which the congregation, already risen for the singing of a hymn and receiving no signal from the officiating clergyman to do otherwise, was attending on its feet, the service had threatened to extend boundaries of mournfulness into areas of tedium; and I had 'switched off.' In my green floating world, where apprehension and noncommitment oscillated amiably together without either's getting the upper hand, the chords of my father's piece, a 'fugue,' arguably, perhaps composed in a disconsolate frame of mind for this very occasion, seemed underpinned with the same mystical preponderances—the reason, most likely, we had remained standing up—that devotees of their music used to intuit in Celestial Praylin's, a measure of sublimity arrived at in the teeth of arbitrary, even chaotic, notation. If I thought of the old days, it was Nicholas I missed the most, Nicholas in fact who prompted such reminiscences at all since I had lost touch with everyone else from that epoch. His name still cropped up regularly in the press, reports of his being sighted in Paris by fans—a whole new generation—who would not accept his death, of a memorial concert of Praylin records accompanied by a light show of laser beams, of a medium who claimed he had 'come through,' news items of that sort. I regretted not having made my final peace with him. Even in my present state, I would have welcomed just one more of our drunken evenings. If I dwelled upon it, his murder still appalled me.

The fugue ended. We knelt in prayer. Being in church with my mother brought to mind the last occasion we had worshipped in each other's company, on my wedding day when Loudermilk had uttered his enigmatic words in the empty nave. By the time I had kissed her good-bye and put her into a taxi, I had half a mind to go and see whether ALEMBIC headquarters still stood. I had time before my train. I thought of hovering in the hallway where Potts had delivered Ma's undisciplined plant in the hope of encountering a familiar face; then, perhaps, of paying a visit to the Rum Cove. It seemed improbable the bar had survived, at any rate that its star-ship interior had not been refurbished to suit modern tastes, whatever those might be. By and large, it would be more sensible to kill time just by having a drink in a pub. There was one next door to the church, in confirmation of a maxim of Sylvia's who used to propose the juxtaposition of public houses and churches as almost an inevitability: like the siting of shoe shops next door to fishmongers, another of her unqualified coefficients. I sat down at a table and took a pull from my drink.

When Lindo came up, hovered apologetically before me, it was hardly a surprise at all, a reward, rather, for having given ALEMBIC the benefit of a certain amount of thought after so long: the keeping, so I saw it, of a pre-arranged appointment. As Ma used to do, I settled myself pleasurably for the consumption of an abundant diet of news.

I saw, though, that little of coherence was likely to be forthcoming. Lindo was in the sorriest of states. He was sodden with drink. He managed to support himself against the table where I was seated. His body swayed back and forth as he fixed me, more or less, with bloodshot eyes.

'I tender unto you my condolences,' he said in a voice deeply slurred. 'I too have been paying my respects. I did not wish to intrude into a family occasion. A brilliant man. He will be a sad loss: yes, yes. There again, I could not be sure at the church, whether you were . . . would recognize . . . had been, though of course when I saw you, I knew you must have been returned . . . to the land of the living. The bastards, the bastards . . .'

Lindo tailed off and stared about him as if those he railed against might have entered the saloon-bar behind him and been ringing him round. If ALEMBIC had not been in my mind, I doubt if I would have recognized him. Only the brown curly hair remained unaffected by the ravages of time: rather, of alcohol. He reeked of drink. Sour, rotten-apple smells exuded from his pores and from a crumpled suit down which he had precipitated a quantity of whatever he had in a nearly empty glass retained only at the unsteadiest of angles. His once handsome features—'open,' 'frank,' 'fearless,' adjectives once upon a time not at all out of place—were now battered, flushed, contused, the eyes puffy, the swollen nose of a blueish tinge. He had the appearance of having been unremittingly pummeled with fists. A rag of a tie, seized, it looked, to administer one of those many blows he had taken, did little to cover up a mostly unbuttoned shirtfront revealing small thickets of hair that seemed to have been ferociously torn out by his opponent and gummed back into place by Lindo, as much as could be recovered, onto his pallid, musty flesh. At a lower level, the colour more or less of his skin, the elastic waistband of a pair of underpants was exposed to view by an attachment to trousers sacrificed in the same fight or by concerted play against a swelling potbelly that sooner or later would burst through those infinitely shabby confines. One of the shoes he wore was black; the other brown. Both were unlaced. He slumped heavily down beside me.

The barmaid, who had been observing what she might have suspected as some sort of 'approach,' solicitation for a drink or a collaring preparatory to an autobiographical rigmarole of some length, came over and set before Lindo another glass, brimful. He must be, then, a regular, drinks carefully tallied, this one fetched to his table to avoid the accident to his suit with the previous measure or one perhaps consumed earlier on, elsewhere, to help him through the rigours of the memorial service. I wondered how on earth he had managed to remain upright during the rendition of my father's lengthy fugue. I had no idea Lindo cared for his music. As far as I recalled, his tastes in that direction had never been revealed, only those of Stephanie, the girl described by Bastable as his 'living-in poke,' who had liked jazz and had kept Lindo from his bed to watch the television programme to have included the performance of 'When Rastus Plays His Old Kazoo,' the singer's loud draped jacket reminding us all of the one Major Cleave sometimes sported at ALEMBIC headquarters. It was strange how the nickname, 'Rastus,' had stuck. Later on, I might jog his memory about that. Now it seemed polite to thank him for his condolences. When I came to think of it, he was the only person I had ever met who had expressed a liking for my father's work. I said as much.

'Then you move in philistine circles.' Lindo acknowledged the barmaid's offering with a wave of his hand. 'Perhaps when you first knew me, I did not care for music, not so much anyway. Music is the refuge of the sad: even of the tragic. These days, therefore, I listen to music a good deal. The modern variety especially appeals: Stockhausen, Penderecki, Ligeti, Reich, Glass, all are grist to my mill. But your father tops my list. He had, to my mind, a talent quite unparalleled. Genius, old boy, genius. I give you my sympathies. From the heart, from the heart.'

Lindo thundered on his more or less naked breast. The blows initiated a fit of coughing that went on a long time. When it was subdued, doused finally by a swig from his glass, it seemed best to move on to other topics; then to be gone. I found it unbearably sad to be in his company. His condition had clearly not arisen from a binge, a sort of one-off lapse into 'over-sampling,' as Sgt Barker would have put it, the tail end of which I had encountered, but a steady deterioration, over several years, of mental as well as physical health. His preliminary account of ALEMBIC's closure, to which I led him, constituted only a general raving about those who had brought him to some sort of dreadful pass. Then, despite having consumed about half his drink, he pulled himself together somewhat. I felt able to ask him for more exact details, beginning at the beginning. He launched into this saga with an eagerness that made me suppose it was a topic he had wanted to discourse on for some time, perhaps for security reasons unable to tell anyone without ALEMBIC connexions. Again, it might be because he had always owned a confiding nature. I recollected the night of the Tallulah Twisters when he had taken me on one side and vouchsafed the difficulties of living with Stephanie. Now he again reminded me of his passion for the opposite sex.

'You may recall I used to be rather fond of "the ladies," ' he said coyly. 'I confess it could have been accounted a Ruling Passion. Not like that shit, Bastable, who pinched your missus, not like that, I was never a poacher on others' preserves, but I was far from averse, after hours, to a little gentle philandering. Jesus Christ, and why not? You flog your bleeding guts out for those buggers, you deserve a little amusement on the side. I was partial to a drop of the old broth too, not too much, you understand, not so much you have nothing to offer when it comes to the showdown but sufficient to keep a sod afloat. I was shy of women, damned scared of them if the truth be told, easy to have overdone matters in the drinking stakes, found no wool in my needles when it came to the nitty-gritty. Porter's speech in *Macbeth*—mustn't quote it, unlucky—desire over performance. That could easily have come about. But in my case no, *absolument pas,* by no manner of means.'

'You were going to tell me what happened at APEX.'

'Yes, well, when we all got to bonny Scotland, we counted up to see who had survived the holocaust. Precious few, was the short answer. Bastable and your old lady; the bloke who replaced you, called himself Adams. Did you know him?'

'No. Major Giblin mentioned his name once.'

'Giblin. That's a name from the past. He never made it to the banks and braes. Couple of the filing clerks came along, Janet Sears, girl with the big charlies; Anna Bennett; one or two more. Vanderplank was CO. He took over when Rastus got the heave-ho. Peter and Gary.'

'Who were they?'

'The heavenly twins. They weren't ALEMBIC personnel. Sidekicks of Giblin, I always believed, looked about twelve years old, sent up to sniff around, keep an eye on you. One of them, couldn't tell you which, like as two peas, was mad on that rock band of yours.'

'Celestial Praylin. So they were twins. You're right about their doing Giblin's dirty work. They kept a tail on me before I was recruited. They scared me stiff. To this day, I believed there was only one of them and he could be in two places at once. Like some of the saints.'

'Saints in a bloody odd martyrology, my man,' Lindo said. He searched in his fearful suit for his cigarettes. 'They weren't brothers, you know. They were one of ALEMBIC's little games with nature, sort of . . .' Lindo broke off to effect ignition of his cigarette, an action that required of him the concentration of a partygoer competing in some vastly complicated parlour game wherein, blindfolded, he has been called on to take a bite from an apple on a string or to pin a tail on a cardboard donkey.

'Sort of what?' I prompted.

'. . . gotten,' he replied. The word sounded like 'forgotten.' That was on the cards. Lighting his cigarette had taken long enough to have disconnected strands of thought already tenuous. Yet, alarmingly, I had the feeling he had said not 'forgotten' but 'begotten.'

'And Goodwin, of course,' I went on. 'He came up, too.'

'Did he arseholes.'

'He told me he was being posted there.'

'Never reported for duty, notwithstanding. Nor hide nor hair of him. Surplus to requirements, my man, just as I turned out to be. Face of the earth department.'

'What in the world became of him, do you suppose?'

'I've just told you, I don't know. Vanished, murdered, drowned in his own beard.' Lindo banged on the table. 'I thought you wanted to hear what happened to me. It's this baby you're bloody talking to.' He pounded his chest once more and activated again a dreadful coughing fit.

'I'm sorry, Colin. Please go on.'

'Almost before we'd settled down, bought some warm undies—it was brass monkeys up there, wind like a whetted knife day in, day out—they announced various fundamental changes of direction, laboratory-wise. There was to be no more tooling around with crucibles, the good old five processes: fusibility, permanence, penetration, tincture, multiplication. That formula was right out. We were in the big time, my man, swept straight into the nuclear age up there, reactors, heavy water, zero energy, crap like that. Bastable took to it like a duck to whatsitsname, always pissing around in protective clothing, but to yours truly what we were up to was even crasser than ALEMBIC days. Adams was feeding us some bloody interesting stuff, Chinese, old as the hills, something that looked like a new system of cupellation. "You're off course," Vanderplank said to me, "lost your bearings, in the wrong ballpark." "Fuck off," I said. "So," he said, "you don't like our new methods." "I fucking don't," I said. "No projection without incineration, that's how I was brought up." '

'Thomas Norton thought the same thing.'

'Hah, good old Uncle Hamish and his manuscript. Yes, well, they wouldn't listen to me, just kept on trying to bypass the processes in the reactor until one day there was an accident. Remarkably neatly timed, I might add. I go into the lab and there's five or six blokes all in D-suits. Absolute silence. Not a word spoken. Pin-dropping job. Still can't figure out who they all were, though I swear one of them was that prize shit, Bastable. "What gives, lads?" I ask. Eventually, eventually, mark you, how many seconds later, God knows, half-a-minute at least, eventually someone says through his visor, "Oh, dear," he says, "you shouldn't have come in here, we've had a bit of a spillage." Spillage . . .'

Things had been too much. Lindo howled out the last word. To demonstrate its meaning, he retrieved his glass, upended it and leisurely poured the contents over the tabletop. He buried his battered face in his hands. Liquid seeped into the elbows of the already vastly dilapidated jacket of his suit. The barmaid came hurrying over. She surveyed the slumped figure as a nurse surveys a recalcitrant patient. She addressed me as if Lindo were out of earshot.

'It's time for his supper. You'd be welcome to join us if you liked. I try to keep him something hot in the kitchen. He wouldn't eat properly otherwise. One good meal a day. At least he gets that. Ooops-a-daisy.' She prodded Lindo by a sodden elbow. He looked up.

'Ready, my dear.' Lindo launched himself suddenly upright, rather as Joanna used to do, motivated as if by unseen hands, then clutched at the table for support. He let go for long enough to produce a brisk military salute and tried to click together the heels of his unlaced shoes. 'Ready and willing. But able, no. Able, never again, fuck them.' He allowed himself to be led off.

I pondered his story for many months. Despite the garbled half-sentences, it had the ring of truth. Whether the debilitating accident had been deliberately staged would never be known. Had there really been an accident at all? Were Lindo's problems, like my own, self-induced, womanizing in early days manifestation of a fear of impotence now made reality, rather as my fear of madness had eventually driven me clinically insane? Goodwin's disappearance, too, was a mystery. Again, there might be an explanation as simple as the alabaster boy's turning out to have had a twin brother. Yet Lindo had said they were not brothers. His use of the word *begotten,* if I had heard him rightly, was sinister in the extreme. Begotten how and where? I began to think of the dark, throbbing well in the grounds of St Mary's, then, in the way I had learned from Goodwin, to dismiss the thought as too painful and to return to ruminating on Lindo's 'accident.' That too was unpleasant. Ill at ease as I had always been in the ALEMBIC laboratory, I found myself all too readily able to reconstruct the scene he had described, the fierce lights, the new nuclear reactor, the chemical apparatus—the 'diverse instrumentis,' as Thomas Norton called them, 'both in nature, and also in shape'—and especially the eerie, visored assistants with whom Lindo had found himself confronted. In a dream I had some time afterwards, I was transported back to the laboratory, the airtight doors locked behind me and those five or six men who, in the dream, were garbed not in protective clothing—the 'D-suits' of Lindo's description—but in the plague doctors' scarlet capes with the beaked masks that Nicholas had sported that day in the street, and I awoke to hear myself crying out, as perhaps Lindo had cried out when he sensed enter into him the rays of the bombardment they unleashed from the reactor, 'Why don't you speak? Why don't you speak?'

For the first time since coming out of hospital, I experienced an inability to rise above such musings. I began to write it all down, starting with my visit to Lindo's uncle and his performance of the water pageant. Joanna has read the book three times. She likes that bit best, that and our meeting in the teeth of Miss Speechley's opposition, occurrences she calls the 'funny' bits. She does not comment on the darker speculations, the dreams, the obsessions. 'You had it bad,' she will say, 'you had it bad. Never mind, we are together now, properly, even if it's taken twenty years.' She has been here six months. When she telephoned, a wild excitement had gripped me, the same excitement with which I had anticipated her visit to Carpenter's nearly twenty years before. Her voice had been instantly recognizable.

'Stripping Nuns Kiss-o-Gram Service. We are calling to confirm your order for two Discalced Carmelites.'

'Joanna.'

'How are you, Tom?'

'OK. And you?'

'OK. I want to see you.'

'Is that a good idea?'

'Best ever. Look, I've got to be quick. I'm going to be in your neck of the woods, as Ma would have said. May I call in?'

'Of course you may. Where are you phoning from?'

'The place that may not be named.' Joanna's laugh was brittle, flawed. Perhaps someone was listening. Her child, I wondered.

'You'll have to come via London then.'

'I know. I'm coming down tomorrow. I'll get the 18.40 from Paddington. Are you sadly changed?'

'Sadly. And you?'

'Oh yes, Henry, yes. Time has served scurvily her unwilling handmaiden. The mockingbird of reality sits on the bough where once the fanciful lark took his accustomed rest.'

'Is that a fact?'

'Honest Injun. 'Bye for now.'

I met her at the station. She had hardly changed at all. The aging process, if such had been at work, had not sunken bones nor wrinkled skin nor dulled the burnished helmet of her hair, but had imposed on her a smallness as if I looked at her through the wrong end of a telescope. Perhaps she had always been small. It was, after all, a long time ago. What was new about her was an ineffable sadness. She looked as if she were going to cry then and there. I took her bag.

'I saw Loudermilk yesterday,' she said. She was staring at me as if in a trance, hypnotized to be made to say the words, Trilby under Svengali's control. This was a 'part' I could not remember. We had seldom, if ever, brought the living, though in Loudermilk's case, of course, the dead, into our melodramas. There was much to be said for starting off in such fashion. Like the old days, it would allow a natural falling into place. Perhaps, as in the past, she was covering up some shyness, an awkwardness she felt about this impulsive reunion. It could be, she had not just found herself in my 'neck of the woods' but had been obliged to make the journey to get my signature on some legal document or other or to repossess a piece of furniture, one of our wedding presents it might be, she felt had been wrongly retained. I too was ill at ease. Passengers streamed by us. I launched into the best reply I could muster.

'You have seen but the spectre of Loudermilk, weanling. It is his ghost haunts your infant steps. 'Tis said returning shades oft seek out bairns whose innocence streams like sunlight upon their darkened souls and, like a salve, can heal the wound of their damnation. But beware, chitterling, he does not hie you back to his enchanted realms.'

Joanna did not move. I took her arm and tried to lead her along the platform, but she resisted. Her eyes pierced me through and through. I had obviously got it wrong.

'Sorry. I can't remember what I'm supposed to do. "Chitterling" is wrong in any case. "Pigwidgeon" is perhaps what I'm aiming for.'

She repeated her words mechanically. 'I saw Loudermilk yesterday. He was in a car, one that came to collect Rick. I've been thinking for ages that something was up. The cars have been getting bigger and bigger, blacker and blacker. Rick had forgotten his briefcase. I ran out to give it to him. It must have been the warmest day we've ever had up there. It's so cold always, so dreadfully cold. The window was wound down. Loudermilk nearly jumped out of his skin. Then he hid. He grabbed a plastic carrier bag and put it over his head. He looked so silly. I almost laughed.' She leaned her head on my shoulder. She smelled still of moss and laundered towels.

'Oh, my God, they've found it.'

'Yes. Hold me, Tom.' I held her close. She began to cry. People still went by, hurried past as if avoiding us, as if Joanna had been taken ill. Not for one moment did I suspect she was in error. Loudermilk had always been unmistakable, his spectral stooping figure as readily identifiable as the brooding herons among the other birds on the island in the park. He would have been close to a hundred years old. He had confessed to being nearly eighty when, in his club, he had mentioned he had pensioners' rights on London buses. In my five years at ALEMBIC I never really considered seriously the possibility we might one day make a breakthrough. The elixir of life, the Stone of the Wise, the *prima materia,* these had been fancies, philosophical conceits, misconceptions of a science in its infancy. Yet there had been the feeling of striving towards a goal at once repulsive and forbidden.

'Can they make gold as well?'

'Yes. It's one and the same thing. Come, come here.' She drew me to a bench at the far end of the platform. She seemed fearful of being overheard. She talked for nearly an hour.

She had led a terrible life, excruciatingly boring, parochial in the extreme, condemned, almost without a break, to the flat, sour land on which ALEMBIC had been established. She had only been tolerated because she was married to Bastable, she said. There had been no place for her in ALEMBIC's documentation section. At first, there had been holidays, long lazy fortnights, twice a year, on foreign beaches that made, though, the cold and the damp of the Scottish coastline even more unbearable on her return. Over the years, Bastable had become more and more withdrawn: 'smugger and smugger too and more and more high-powered. He was drinking too much. Five or six years ago, I asked him to stop. "You'll kill yourself," I said. Do you know what he replied? He was drunk then or I'm sure he'd never have said it. He said, "That's most improbable, my dear. With the progress we are making, I'll go as far as to say it's virtually impossible." Drink had been Colin's downfall. They had to get rid of him. But Rick still won't see he's going to go the same way.'

'I knew about Colin. We bumped into each other three or four years ago. He looked ghastly.'

'I know. He was sweet. I missed him; despite having to fight him off every so often. He had the most accurate pinch of any man I've ever known. He must have practised his pinch like other men practise their forehand smash.'

Joanna suddenly smiled. It didn't last long. It was a wraith of a smile, the tiny, disobedient stretching of the lips she used to allow herself in photographs, one or two of our wedding ones, for instance, when she felt she was expected to be serious.

She had attempted to make friends in the university town inland, ten or so miles away, but that was discouraged. 'A hotbed of extremists and radicals,' Vanderplank had said. 'Don't want them turning up here waving banners. Better steer clear, Mrs Bastable, better steer clear.' Then she had run a crèche for APEX's staff's babies, given riding lessons to the older children, arranged occasional dances for employees. As work gathered intensity, those became more infrequent. 'Sometimes I didn't speak to anyone for weeks on end. I even used to look forward to the Leech Days as we called them.'

'Leech Days?'

'Oh, you were right about blood. We all gave blood. By the gallon. Once every three months. We didn't have to, but it was rather a "thing" of Vanderplank's. "I've got a rather rare group, Mrs Bastable." God, if he said that once, he said it a thousand times. Like you and "old enough to be your grandfather." ' Joanna squeezed my arm and snuggled against my shoulder. 'He said he felt privileged to be able to help mankind. Rick insisted on my donating blood, too. Said it would be frowned on, otherwise. Actually I quite enjoyed it. We girls used to let our hair down over the tourniquets. You could sometimes glean a bit of news there. Sometimes, someone actually laughed. I used to count the laughs, chalk them up in my mind like you used to cross off runs in your scoring book at cricket matches, see how many I could count. So far this year, I've counted eight.'

I did not dare say what I was thinking. A stanza of Thomas Norton's ran through my mind, something about his horror of the use of blood in the Great Work: a most 'selcouth thing.' I stared at her neck where once I had myself drawn blood. She had knotted a silk scarf around her throat, perhaps to hide a still livid scar or a pale indentation where the scissors had torn the flesh. She seemed to sense my thoughts.

'Am I going mad, Tom? Are they making me mad like you said they made you? I had to talk. You used to say a neurosis shared was a neurosis halved. I've tried for months to find you. Every so often when I felt desperate I'd go into the library, choose a telephone directory, copy down all the "Graves, T's," go to the bank and get a pile of coins, then ring them all up from call boxes. Book by book. County by county. Perhaps it's as well it took so long. They're ready now, you see, ready to do something, make a public announcement. The pressure's off. It'll be all right: for the moment: for our lifetimes. Except that the meaning of the word requires revision.'

'Are you quite sure?'

'Positive.' She looked round. We were alone. We sat now with our arms round each other, gazing across the tracks as if we were going to part, not, as I now knew, to be reunited. On the other side of the railway lines people gathered who, in the increasing dusk, we could not clearly see. A loudspeaker announced destinations we could not distinguish. Lights, not yet illuminated on the opposite platform, isolated us in their glare as if a curtain had been raised upon us, the black gulf of the lines between us a darkened orchestra pit from which bizarre music would at any second strike up to which we would be expected to dance, to sing, perhaps as in Uncle Hamish's water pageant, to mouth couplets of stirring verse. Joanna stood up.

'Take me home,' she said.

Joanna was right. A bulletin was forthcoming. That first evening it was not the lead story. Progress had been made, the newscaster said, with disarmament talks. A breakthrough might be on the cards. Then slowly, the news built up. Night after night on television we watch the politicians, the statesmen, the warlords, purr and preen about the thawing of international relations. We see tanks withdrawing, missile sites demolished, space stations floatingly disassembled. Our prime minister, waving treaties, moves radiantly among crowds of cheering schoolchildren, housewives, factory workers. The screen switches itself to 3-D mode. It fills with cubes of glistening gold to demonstrate holographically our newfound wealth in the wake of unilateral disarmament. Towards the end of the summer we are shown Russians, Tibetans, Iraqis, Chinese, on package holidays to Britain cavorting in funfairs or mingling with the natives on draughty seaside promenades. A cookery programme is devoted to Russian recipes. Caviare becomes cheaper. We buy it by the pound. Sometimes we eat it for breakfast before I go to work or we go off riding.

We ride a lot. We begin to laugh. In the old days, those of my trepidation that I was becoming unhinged, I would have questioned whether, for my part, it was not the laughter of desperation. I still have irrational fears, of being pursued, hunted down, separated from Joanna by force. By whom I am never sure: Bastable; an emissary from APEX; the avenging gods awakened by Joanna in the grove of blossoming trees. In gloomy moments, I speak of these forebodings but, like the dark side of the book I now know will never be finished, Joanna refuses to discuss them and says, 'It will not happen. A neurosis shared is a neurosis halved.' I do not tell her of other obsessions, Goodwin's disappearance, the crippling of Lindo, the monstrous, blood-infused fecundations in deep pit-shafts: the fact that I suspect that, like Loudermilk, Joanna will never die. Joanna's fears are more realistic. She apprehends, in the rediscovery of the alchemists' secret, the onset of fiercer wars, more widespread destruction, global anguish on a larger scale, in a way reiterating my idea that there has been a shift in the order of things: but a long way in the future. Yet, because I have never known before the efflux of love, the love, when I see a belonging of Joanna's lying about the flat, one of her 'things,' that in its beauty and its sadness makes my heart leap up so I almost cry out for joy, 'She's here, she's here,' and because I have never known its reception either which she can bestow by taking my head in her hands and turning my gaze from the scar on her neck and focusing upon me her green eyes and smiling her smile, I cannot find the aims of ALEMBIC as repulsive as I used. For is not the elixir of life what I too desire, if offered to be paid for with my last coin and drained to the dregs so that forever I may sit with her in our peaceful room: and laugh and laugh?